Westland Ltd

31

A banking and finance professional by day, an engineer and MBA by background and from a peppy part of Mumbai, by accident, Upendra is married and has a son. While he lives in Gurgaon, he remains a Mumbaikar at heart.

Upendra first bit the writing bug when he was invited by one of India's leading finance dailies *Mint* to write for them. It soon blossomed into a love affair that turned him into an avid blogger and finally encouraged him take the plunge into the unchartered waters of the Novel. Upendra now takes complex and dry ideas like loans, foreclosures, investments among other things and turns them into nail-biting thrillers which make those dull and dreary numbers come alive. But he really hasn't shifted his focus as such, for he still thinks of his books as numbers: 31, 60, 8 and so on.

31 is his first in the NUMBERS series.

You can get in touch with Upendra at upendra.namburi@gmail.com

31

Upendra Namburi

westland ltd
Venkat Towers, 165, P.H. Road, Maduravoyal, Chennai 600 095
No. 38/10 (New No.5), Raghava Nagar, New Timber Yard Layout, Bangaluru 560 026
Survey No. A - 9, II Floor, Moula Ali Industrial Area, Moula Ali, Hyderabad 500 040
23/181, Anand Nagar, Nehru Road, Santacruz East, Mumbai 400 055
4322/3, Ansari Road, Daryaganj, New Delhi 110 002

First published by westland ltd 2012

Copyright © Upendra Namburi 2012
All rights reserved

10 9 8 7 6 5 4 3 2 1

ISBN: 978-93-81626-75-7

Inside book formatting and typesetting by Ram Das Lal

Printed at Manipal Technologies Ltd., Manipal

This is a work of fiction. All names, characters, places and incidents
mentioned in the book are the product of the author's imagination.
Any resemblance to any actual persons, living or dead,
events or locations, is entirely coincidental.

This book is sold subject to the condition that it shall not by way of trade or
otherwise, be lent, resold, hired out, circulated, and no reproduction in any form,
in whole or in part (except for brief quotations in critical articles or reviews) may
be made without written permission of the publishers.

To …
Mom, who always believed in my passions.
Dad, who never let go.
Niru, who tolerated and lovingly supported my idiosyncracies and stood beside me like a rock.
Yashvardhan, who has given me a new meaning to life.
&
Those who made me understand the true meaning of friendship in this journey:
Lakshmi, Rashi, Colin, Payal, Srikanth, Sridhar, Prasanth, Oscar, Sandeep, Hemant, Matthew, Kanthi, Umesh.

March

1	2	3	4	5	6
7	8	9	10	11	12	13
14	15	16	17	18	19	20
21	22	23	24	25	26	27
28	29	30	31

'I get email ... therefore I am!'

– Dilbert

8:32 @ Home

'Savitha, hurry up, we're getting late. I have a team meeting at 9:30.'

'Chill, Mr Zonal Head! Even I need to get in early. One of those infinite project review meetings,' she turned and walked back into the bathroom again.

There was always something that required straightening, adjusting or trimming.

Savitha stepped out of the bathroom flashing a smile, 'Okay sweetheart, ready to go?'

'Sweetheart!'... Either I had forgotten something or I was being set up to do something I detested. She looked absolutely stunning!

'That was fast! By the way ... neat dress!'

'Thanks. So, why are you here? Thought you were in a hurry.' Savitha smiled again.

The BlackBerry beeped. Probably Maithili with her morning dose of humour in the 'Jokes' group on BB Messenger.

'What's common to a prostitute and an investment counsellor? You pay both of them to get screwed!'

8:44 In the Car En Route to Office

The BlackBerry kept buzzing. What was all the fuss about?

From: Khanna, Amitabh

Subject: Outstanding Performance in February

Ravi & Team, Outstanding performance in Feb! Keep up the good work. March has to be a bumper month. Am sure you'll exceed your targets ...

Couldn't this guy write a straight out congratulatory note?

The email had been marked to the senior management at the head office and other regions as well. He was getting to be a real pain in the ass.

And, this was just Monday morning!

Clicked on the Twitter icon. Had to get the daily gossip on the office from the unofficial 'Imperial Insider'. All the office chatter got tweeted on a daily basis. We didn't know who it was – but it had become a lifeline.

Imperial, my bank, had grown considerably over the last five years, expanding into new markets and business lines. The informality and camaraderie that had existed within the smaller team and organization earlier, had given way to a larger, impersonal and bureaucratic ecosystem. Decisions took longer, and personal agendas often overshadowed organizational goals, making it like just any other multinational bank in India. The need for dirt on people seemed even more crucial than the bottomline.

Imperial Insider: Jaideep Mehrotra will be swinging both ways in Bangalore today!

The Human Resources head was in Bangalore, attending a conference on human resources. That was the official version!

8:59 Outside Savitha's Office

Dropped Savitha outside Amtek, her office, but had to return when I saw her handbag still lying on the front seat. She was waiting in the lobby with a beaming smile.

The spider senses started tingling.

'You're such a sweetheart. What would I do without you? See you at dinner! Remember?'

Oh yes! It finally clicked. Her parents had invited themselves over.

'You know ...'

Savitha toggled to her stern look.

'Be home early tonight, okay?' Savitha closed the argument with a peck on the cheek.

As I winked and reciprocated with a kiss on her forehead, I

noticed her office staff staring, curious about the uncharacteristic exchange. As I walked away, I turned to grab another look at her. We hardly spent any quality moments together these days.

It had been over seven years since Savitha and I had taken those seven inebriated twirls around the flames. It had been an 'arranged' marriage. We had met at a mutual friend's party, gotten sloshed and found ourselves in each others' arms the following morning.

She had been working in an advertising agency those days, and was known as the wild one. New to Mumbai, a bright engineer MBA and three years younger than me. She came to my place after the party the following morning, freshened up and rushed out to a client meeting. A couple of months later she had moved in with me ... 'to save on rent' of course! I had been blown away.

The courtship lasted over a year. We tweaked the astrological charts, and convinced the temple priest to send our profiles to the families. Both sets of parents were hysterical. Our vitals – caste, sub-caste, sub-creed – and all matched.

We even maxed the compatibility score in one of those ludicrous tests in some random women's magazine. I still couldn't believe she had actually made us take one of those quizzes together. She had been giggling all through the quiz, as she saw her 'man' fumble on her favourite colour, food habits and passions! Surely a match made in heaven, subtly powered by Mr Bill Gates and his wonderful applications. We loved having redefined the concept of arranged. Now we were terrified how our two kids would probably redefine it further.

Srikanth, now a five-year bundle of questions and joy, seemed to have his mother's iconoclastic and revolutionary streak. But the hospital must have swapped babies when we had Revathi two years later. Her obsession with colour co-ordination and all things pink, accessories included, repulsed Savitha, whose own make-up kit comprised toothpaste and bindis!

The BlackBerry kept buzzing persistently. Scores of

congratulatory messages! Looked at the ccs again and noticed our CEO had been included. Everyone getting trigger-happy with congratulations and counter-congratulations, desperate to get noticed.

This hysteria would continue till the next flavour of the hour came across, for everyone to pile on again.

9:54 @ Office

Taking deposits and lending money used to be the bank's conventional lines of business. But now, we were selling a bouquet of investment and insurance products to all sorts of customers, who had been lured in by the premium MNC tag we flaunted.

Thus far, it had been an abysmal year for Imperial, with huge losses on the Credit Card and Personal Loan portfolios. The first three quarters had been a bloodbath, with the bank incurring huge losses right up to the third quarter, or Q3, ending in December. Money was tight. Customers were not investing in mutual funds and insurance with the stock markets in a volatile state. Most customers were taking a conservative position, considering that the market fall the previous year had resulted in huge losses on most portfolios.

We were just starting to see the upside of the 'U', at least that was the geeky jargon used by the in-house analysts. It seemed to be working with the clients though, giving them hope that the markets were heading up again. We had our fingers crossed, of course; and, no clue in which direction they were truly heading.

Global indicators remained uncertain but we had to sell, SELL, SELL mutual funds and insurance to our clients in every market condition. Our commissions depended on it.

Based in Bangalore, I oversaw the South with twelve branches across Bangalore, Hyderabad and Chennai. Not a large number compared to other banks, but Imperial always managed to make it into a big deal. I, of course, played along. I had a team of three city heads, managing the branches in each of the cities. At present, they were in town for the monthly review meeting.

We had set out to at least meet, if not cross, targets for the Q4 ending in March. That would have been an honourable way to end the year. Our heads held high, possibly ensuring that we might snag some morsels of an annual bonus as well.

'Hey, boss, congrats! Bonus will definitely be better than last year's, no?' Karan Verma, the Bangalore head was gushing. Pushing one's luck into the zone of the impossible was the prerogative of every salesperson. Karan was no exception.

Devendra, the Hyderabad head, spoke, 'So boss, the head office is trying to play smart again? They just don't get it, do they? Think business happens on Excel?'

There were two breeds in Imperial. Those in the head office or High Command and the others in the branches or the trenches. The latter always found the former an incredible waste of time.

At the head office, you couldn't even get anyone to get you a cup of coffee. It was full of Vice Presidents or VPs, Senior VPs, Joint VPs, Executive VPs, Senior Executive VPs and AVPs. It was tough to find someone who was a non-VP. Almost a privilege not being a VP these days!

The regional offices were the fiefdoms of the four regional heads, with the other three in Mumbai, Kolkata and Gurgaon respectively. The Mumbai regional head had the upper hand as he was based out of the head office, but also faced more heat than the rest of us. It was much cosier out here. We ruled! Of course, once every quarter, we would be called in by the head office for a review. The standard drill. Make exhaustive PowerPoint presentations, sneak behind colourful graphs and infinite tables populated with numbers and statistics that rarely tallied with the information given by the number crunchers in the Mumbai office. Most areas of underachievement or target shortfalls were overshadowed by intense debates on why their numbers rarely reconciled with ours. The system worked remarkably well, and we returned to our respective bastions carrying increased targets, bruised egos and a fond hope that we would get some respite for another quarter at least.

'Read the mail, guys. If the numbers drop this month ... we'll need to cross our targets. East is dropping. We need to make up for them as well. So hold on to the high fives for another 31 days. *Comprendi?*'

March is an important month to keep the momentum going. Positive perceptions help, as did the morning email.

It was finally dawning on me. It was March. I was already drained and fed up with chasing senseless targets. But I had to keep my eye on the ball. Didn't have a choice, with 31 days to go!

Raghu's phone binged. 'Raghu! No calls for the next one hour!'

'Sorry, boss. My wife, you see ...' Raghu looked nervous. 'Yes, aha ... Yes ... ahem Yes, darling, it's done. I'm in a meeting. Call you back ...'

I noticed strange words and numbers on my notebook.

'What's this?'

Karan was rocking in his chair and clapping his hands. 'Boss, Rag's wife controls his bank accounts and the pennies in his wallet!'

At Imperial, Raghu was seen as the classical tormented husband. He was rumoured to have a standby sleeping bag in his office. Right now, he had been instructed by his spouse to transfer funds from his account into hers, as the salary had been credited.

The only catch was that his wife changed his Internet banking passwords every month and monitored each and every transaction in his bank account. And as she was out shopping and suddenly realized she was short of funds, instantly called up her husband and ordered a transfer. Raghu, of course, had to jot down the passwords, before he could service the request!

11:28
SMS from Jaideep Mehrotra, the HR head. 'Meet at 7 @ Leela?'
 Yes! A drink with the HR head in March! That's really good!
The BB buzzed.
Imperial Insider: Tsunami in Brazil! Watch out!
Brazil! What was happening in Brazil? Who would know? Maithili?
Sent her an SMS: 'Brazil?'
Received a response almost instantaneously 'No idea! Doesn't sound good! Wanna go for the carnival?'

11:42
The mobile rang.
 'Hi, Ravi, finished reading all those messages?'
 'Actually, just finished the team meeting, boss. Thanks for your email. A good boost for them.'
 'Good ... good ... Am sending you the revised March targets. Let me know what you think?' Read *'Don't argue with me if you fancy keeping your job.'*
 'Sure. But, boss, we hadn't discussed the targets? We're already tight on current goals. This is slightly awkward ...'
 'Awkward? By the way, great show, keep it up!' Amitabh was deflecting. A predictable tactic when he wanted to just shove the numbers down our throats and wash his hands off the whole affair. If the team delivered, it was his brilliant leadership. If it failed, our incentives and increments were on the line.
 'But, boss, how can I take these numbers up now?' Polite resistance was important. Not much. Just a little bit.
 'Your region needs to chip in, Ravi. You know the East. It's out of their control. The fire in the main branch wiped out their infrastructure.'
 That branch had been making losses for at least a decade and should have been shut down ages back! The fire was a blessing.
 'But, I haven't seen the other regions raising their targets?' I persisted.

'They can't do anything. You know that. Maithili is already behind, but then you would know!'

Maithili and I had got into a relationship, when I had joined the bank. The relationship had been brief. She cherished her single status, but the office was still hung over with our brief fling and this continued to haunt and amuse both of us. It didn't help that with her being the head for the North Region, our interactions in forums, both real and virtual, were quite frequent.

'Okay boss, if that's the way it is.'

Bastard! Always got a buzz kicking our MBA asses, like we *'had it easy'* unlike the old crop who had worked up the ranks. He restricted our exposure to the senior management always taking the credit! Manic control freak!

13:34

'Had lunch?' Savitha always called around this time each day. Making sure I had digested some morsels. Checking up on me. Being wifely!

'Yes, as we speak.'

The BlackBerry was buzzing with another round of congratulatory messages. The Insurance team had crossed some milestone and the CEO also got into the good show email act. Now, I had to find some gig to get my region back in the limelight.

'How 'bout you?' I asked absentmindedly. Brazil was bugging me.

'Eating at my desk. They've just moved our project deadline ahead by three weeks to third week March. Bloody slave drivers! The jokers in the UK office want us to be around when its closing time for them. Can't they ever figure out we're bloody five hours ahead of them. Think they still rule us!'

Savitha was lusciously desirable when agitated, if only I could be beside her now. She had joined Amtek, an IT firm, as a project manager when we had moved to Bangalore two years earlier, switching from advertising to IT, convinced that she

9

needed to flex her intellect more than her smile. She had been swiftly disillusioned.

'Have a great day sweetheart. And, go easy on the desserts,' she disconnected.

19:24 @ The Library Bar, The Leela

'Hey, Ravi! Hope I didn't keep you waiting too long?' Jaideep walked in, looking short of breath.

'Hi, Jaideep, no problems. What can I get you?'

'Single malt. On the rocks. What's your poison?' Jaideep awaited my choice. It was important to transmit the right *'senior management vibes'*. The words 'Old Monk' would have relegated me to the murky corners of the administration.

I decided to play the game.

'The same. You've got great taste.' I usually wasn't up for ass-licking, but this was not an occasion to cater to personal preferences!

'You okay with single malt?' It was about class. He was pushing. For people like Jaideep, it was in their genes. For us lesser mortals, it was cultivated. He wore a Wharton pin on his jacket and I was just praying he wouldn't meander into his discourses on the importance of an Ivy League education! Often made me reflect on my decision not to scamper abroad for higher studies.

'How was your conference, Jaideep?'

'Went well. You know how these things are. But, tell me, how have things been with you? You're on a roll. What next?' He paused as he sniggered and sent an SMS from his phone.

'Not thinking too far ahead. Just taking it by the day.' Not bad. The HR head asking 'what next?' Must be doing something right. Or, he could be playing me.

'I'm pooped. So you won't mind if we wrap up early today, right?' Of course he was pooped! Thanks to 'Imperial Insider', we knew why! Jaideep's libido was now folklore at Imperial, with several tweets exposing his 'casual threesomes' and his 'bisexual tendencies' during his pan-India excursions.

Renowned for his lavish parties, wicked humour, sharp sartorial style, passion for all things single, including malts, he was a player in every sense. One needed to be in his 'team' and in his good books to make any headway at the bank these days.

'Of course not, Jaideep, I am sure those early morning flights can really be tiring.' I pressed on.

'What's the news at head office?' It was time to dig out some juicy gossip.

22:34 @ The Library Bar, The Leela

The mobile was vibrating incessantly. Savitha must be freaking out, but Jaideep was in full flow and we were five Scotches down.

'How are the bonuses looking this year?' I had finally ventured into juicy territory.

'Of all the people to ask me that! Just keep at it this month. Vikram has his eyes on you. Good plans. Thinks you could come into the head office next year. Be good for you!' He smiled, but looked distracted.

This was good ... possibly, very good. I was beginning to relish single malt, but his restlessness was making me edgy.

'The number crunching?' I was high, and dinner didn't appear to be on the itinerary. This sophistication crap was getting on my nerves. Couldn't they serve peanuts with single malt?

'Guys in Singapore, you know how they can be? Nitpicking every number. They have no work there, so they pile on to anything that comes to table. Can be a real pain!'

'I can imagine.'

'Another one?'

'Sure!'

'How's Maithili?' He smiled, as he glanced at a message that had arrived in his mailbox. His expression hardened.

Jaideep wasn't one to be ruffled easily, but what he read seemed to have shaken him.

'Everything okay, Jaideep?'

'Hmmm ... something's brewing,' he abruptly stopped, then looked up as he realized he had spoken out loud.

'I beg your pardon?'

'You mind if we wind up? Need to get an early start tomorrow. Cheers and thanks!' Jaideep stood up and disappeared. The vibrating started all over again. Savitha! I was going to be crucified!

It was actually a Tweet.

Imperial Insider: Is Pink the new colour at Imperial?

23:43 @ Home ... Well, the Main Door

'You jerk! What the hell do you think of yourself? They waited till 11:30 pm to meet you. You know they're going to Singapore tomorrow and won't be back for at least three months...'

'Wow! Saved in the nick of time!' I thought.

It had been a strange evening. Jaideep had started off well, but the spate of tweets had been unsettling.

I handed over the box of pastries to my wife, clinging onto the front door for support. Needed to take a leak desperately, but that would have to wait I guess. The bladder was about to explode, but I was comforted by the thought of not having to see the in-laws any time soon. The discomfort was a small price to pay!

'You think you can butter me up with pastries? That it'll all be okay?'

I offered a benign smile, aware that I needed significantly greater firepower to penetrate the armour of outrage she wore right now.

'Fine! Come in then and it had better be the Dutch Truffle!'

Hadn't she disliked them the last time around? Could I never get this right? Another lost cause.

23:47 @ Home ... The Bedroom

From the bathroom, I shouted, 'Where do you want to go for a vacation this year?'

Maybe this would melt the ice, get some action? Proposing something good for the kids usually did the trick. Savitha all angry and ruffled up was such fun. Was positively drooling at the thought.

'Why? Getting your bonus early?' Aha! Seemed to have snagged her attention. She popped into the bathroom 'What's up? Something you want to tell me?'

'Nothing really. Got an email from the boss today. He appeared to be happy with my performance in February, in his own weird way, of course. But these emails in early March are usually a good sign! I was thinking maybe Disneyland?'

I was fishing for a good kiss, to begin with.

'How many times do I have to tell you they're too young for Disneyland? You're just too stubborn. I know you. We'll end up going there. My opinion has no meaning whatsoever.' Savitha was back to playing tragedy queen. Come to think of it, she had been like this since last week.

We usually discussed office at home, only after a good Merlot was uncorked and shared. That basically meant no conjugal privileges tonight for sure, and going by her tone and mood, not in the near future either. Sigh!

02.00 @ **Home, Awake**

Imperial Insider: Brazil going down and taking rest of Imperial with it!

'Damn!'

March

1	**2**	3	4	5	6
7	8	9	10	11	12	13
14	15	16	17	18	19	20
21	22	23	24	25	26	27
28	29	30	31

You can bank on us ... but not with us!

05:02 Sleeping @ Home

The phone was creating a ruckus on the side table. The clock displayed 5 am something. I scrounged around for my glasses and picked up the phone. What a time to call? This maniac needed to get a life.

'Boss, everything okay?'

What I actually wanted to say was *'Shit! Has something happened in Brazil?'*

'Why?'

'Coz *in most civilized societies you don't call up people at 5 am!*'

'What can I do for you, Amitabh?'

'Thought I'd let you know Internal Audit (IA) will be contacting you.'

'What for?' A holiday with the in-laws was suddenly more appearing idyllic. And, what about Brazil?

'What's happening in Brazil, boss?'

'Have to board my flight now. How's the family? Bye.' He hung up.

Why did the bastard call? Couldn't he have just messaged? Did he get sadistic pleasure out of waking me up and hanging me out to dry?

What did the audit snoops want with me? There had been no mention of this earlier or in the January meeting at the head office. Internal Audit spelt trouble in every sense and consumed a painstaking amount of time. These were not good times to be seen with that team, especially as the end of the current fiscal year was coming up.

And still no heads up on Brazil! He must know something for sure. There was hesitation in his voice. I knew Amitabh quite

15

well. He was either up to something or had information that he would keep to himself, on both Brazil and Internal Audit. And that tone of voice? He wasn't one to normally ask about the family. Where was he going with this?

'Is it the milkman?' Savitha muttered in her sleep.

'Not yet, Sav, go back to sleep ...'

'Who was it? Are you having an affair again?' I looked at her shocked, but she was giggling.

Again? I had told her about Maithili in one of those damn *'let's be honest with each other'* sessions. She had never really let it go. Now I would have to rake something up from her past and take her trip – had to even the score!

09:47 @ My Cabin, The Office

Congratulatory emails interspersed with those from employees across the South, enquiring about Brazil and what that meant?

I have always maintained an informal and accessible operating style. But on occasions like this, I question the approach. I assured some of them that they shouldn't be worried about Brazil and focus on their jobs! I felt like a load of crap after a while. I saved the others in a newly created 'Brazil' folder.

Murmurs and hushed huddles had already commenced with those who were early in office. Had even received an SMS from a colleague in the head office implying that the damage was greater than had been reported and it would unfold over the next few days.

I looked out the window and noticed the four new management trainees scampering up the stairs. Must have joined the organization with aspirations of a global career with the bank. Were they in for a rude shock?

I smiled. 'Poor buggers. Will be one hell of an orientation.'

As I walked towards the coffee machine, I noticed Vinesh Menon, the regional HR head in an animated conversation on his cell. Vinesh reported to Jaideep Mehrotra. A management graduate in HR from Symbiosis, Vinesh had a distinctive unsophisticated and pompous approach to people, possibly the reserve of all HR guys!

He had a strange equation with his boss but they made a lethal combination. Jaideep would be elusive to most office personnel, Vinesh would be accessible but uncouth in his interactions, often making most conversations futile.

As I opted for a cappuccino, Vinesh concluded his call and came across.

'Hi, Ravi, what's up?'

'Good. You?'

'*Aaal izz* well!' he sniggered as he used the mantra from the Bollywood blockbuster *3 Idiots*. 'By the way, some of your boys in Hyderabad want to leave. Thought I'd keep you in the loop.' Vinesh quickly assumed a serious tone.

'I know!' I was the one that had brought it to his attention to begin with.

Oriental, a rival MNC bank, had started making moves on our Relationship Managers (RMs) across India.

'No sweat. Nothing you haven't seen before. I've got a back-up anyway. On top of it.' He waved, about to leave.

He got my curiosity going. 'What was that about a back-up plan?'

'Discussed this with you before. We've good talent in the Credit Cards sales team. So, I don't think you should worry too much!'

'Shouldn't we try and retain my existing team?'

'Of course,' he smiled.

We had stopped sourcing new credit cards for over a year now, as the losses had assumed titanic proportions. More than half the sales team had been let go. The ones with godfathers and angels remained in the system, loitering around, waiting like hyenas, pouncing onto any open positions, or better still ... creating new positions, which in most cases added little value.

17

Amitabh had been against recruiting them. They were from a different camp. We didn't dare cross that *Lakshman rekha* now that he had drawn it.

'What's happening in Brazil, Vinesh?'

'Not official yet, but the bank seems to have taken a big hit there. It's sending ripples across the bank. Don't know too much, but will keep you posted, mate!'

'And, what's this about pink slips?'

'Ravi, let's take it as it comes.'

The signature abrupt and elusive end note by Vinesh — he answered little, but always opened up a larger can of worms!

15:34

'Hi, Sav, had lunch?'

'Good you called, you'll need to pick the kids up today. The maid can't make it. The project's in a bad shape and I need to sit and fix this tonight.'

Savitha in one of her moods, again. Something must have ticked her off.

'But, Savi, you know I can't. Got a team meeting, need to make sure new targets are rolled out and some other stuff. It's critical. You remember the morning call, right?'

'Damn you, Ravi. Always about you!'

I pressed on, 'I've also got an important meeting with a client!'

'You've also got a BlackBerry, a secretary and an army working for you. What's your problem? Use them!'

'Fine. Will pick up the kids.' I hung up.

'Radhika! Emergency!'

Radhika, my able-bodied personal assistant and Man Friday, walked in with the new targets and the case files of the fraud cases being investigated by Internal Audit.

'Called for your driver. The traffic should be okay. You can make it to Whitefield in under 30 minutes right now. And eat. You don't want to get lynched again!'

'Should have married you, Radhika!'

'And don't forget to buy some chocolates on your way. Will patch you in for the audit call at 4:30.'

'What call?'

'It's on your BlackBerry.'

'Shit!'

'Can't you shake them off?'

'Let me try, but I need my salary, and so do you!'

16:24 @ The School

'Srikanth, Revathi, be quiet! Papa's phone is ringing. So no noise, okay.'

'Yes, Papa, yes, Papa ...' screamed Srikanth.

Amitabh!

'Good evening, boss!'

'What's going on in Hyderabad? Heard Kaushal is picking up seven of your top Relationship Managers.'

'HR has been roped in. Will keep you posted, boss.'

'Posted? The only thing you need to keep me posted on is your numbers. Need the forecast for this month!' He was ballistic today. Had his wife left him? Again?

'Forecast, boss? But you just sent me the new targets!'

'We're already two days down in March, Ravi. How's it looking?'

'We're doing okay, but the stock market's not looking good. It's going to be tough pushing Mutual Funds this month, boss.'

'It's tax planning month. Why do you forget that? Even your trainees know that! I need to see your annual business plan by 10 tomorrow. Need to send it to the region.' He never mentioned the CEO. It was always 'The Region' à la the Singapore office.

'You'll get it, boss.' Needed to keep him happy. This was bonus deciding month.

'And how's the hangover?' Son of a gun! Possibly even knew what I had had for dessert.

'No hangover, boss. Just business,' I laughed politely, trying to diffuse the situation.

He hung up with an ominous click.

19:34 @ Home

The Internal Audit call had been mysteriously cancelled. No explanation offered. Even their team couldn't be contacted. It almost felt like they had been told to stay away and had been pulled back by someone!

'How's the session going with the clients?'

'The market is tanking, boss. Everyone wants to either sell or hold. The buzz on the Union Budget seems to be disappointing.'

'Karan, get the business. That's it! Damn the markets. Sell them India Shining for all I care!'

Karan, the Bangalore head, was my star performer. He had bailed out the region last month. Got some High Net-worth Individuals (HNIs) to move from Oriental last month. Didn't like taking that tone with him. My frustration was showing.

'Yes, boss!'

'Call me when you're done. Need to set up a con-call with the heads later in the night. It's about the annual business plans.'

'Tonight?'

'Yes!' I hung up.

Now I was acting like Amitabh. This was infectious.

23: 27 @ Home

The annual business plan Excel sheets had drained me out. The numbers didn't seem to make much sense, or I must have been just too tired!

The annual business plan exercise was undertaken to finalize sales projections, revenue and cost estimations for the coming fiscal year.

One of those organizational ironies. They make you slog the entire year and then set you up for the next year before they declare your bonus. The wheel never stops turning!

'Hi, Sav! You asleep?'

'A splitting headache. Can you get me something?' Savitha was rubbing her forehead.

'You? Taking medicines? Must be really bad!' She was holding back on something. Needed to get her to spit it out.

'Just get the damn pills. They're in the medicine cabinet in the dining room. And get me hot milk as well.'

'Sure.'

Buzz! SMS from Mayur *'TV... now!'*

I turned on the gas and set a pan with toned milk on it. Walked to the drawing room and switched on the television.

'Recap of today's breaking news. Imperial Bank's Brazil division has suffered huge losses, reported to be over $14 billion. Unofficial reports indicate the number could rise as the full picture emerges over the next few days. Our sources indicate that huge trading losses have been building up for several months now and word has it that a rogue trader has played havoc.

Yet another bank frivolously betting with people's hard-earned money and losing it. Where is the regulator? Coming up in the next segment: Should regulators play a more stringent role in regulating banks?'

The Imperial bashing had started. This was going to be trouble!

'Shit! Sav, come here. Quickly!'

'What happened, can't you even get a glass of milk?'

'Sav, this is serious...'

23:36

'Mayur?'

I was calling Mayur Singh, the IT head. A smart young genius. Got along fabulously with the Americans and the British. Imperial had started shifting some key global IT systems into India and Mayur suddenly found himself on the global stage. He was on a roll.

'Hi Ravi, I'm in Dubai. Did you see the bloodbath? Not at the Leela today?' Mayur laughed.

'What's with the Leela? Never had a drink with Jaideep before?' The drink with the HR head seemed to have sufficiently stimulated the grapevine. Couldn't make up my mind whether that was good.

He seemed uncomfortably calm about the Brazil news that was definitely going to shake up Imperial. But that was Mayur. He would be the one playing the cello and regaling the crowds even in a sinking *Titanic*. He was also the one who would surely have a lifeboat reserved exclusively for himself under any circumstance.

'Not in Bangalore, Ravi. He must really like you. Your bonus is done for this year! Where are you taking the family this summer?' Mayur couldn't stop chuckling.

'I was thinking of the carnival at Rio. Want to join me, Mayur? Now, out with it. What's going on in Brazil?'

'We figured something big was going down in January. But didn't know it was this bad.'

'You knew in Jan?'

'It was too fuzzy. My guy in Los Angeles spilled the beans. Forwarded an email to me by mistake.'

'So what now?' I was getting anxious. Lehman and a dozen others had already gone down earlier. We had survived that somehow. Now the rest of the world was rising from the ashes and we were getting butchered.

'Early days yet. Let's see if this is going to be genocide or mass annihilation? One thing's for sure – not too many guys are going to be on the golf course tomorrow. Their stock options are going to get plundered. Poor chaps, will have to let go of their Maseratis. What trauma?' Mayur was laughing again.

'You on dope, Mayur?' I was fuming. He didn't have to make my mortgage payments. The jerk!

'Why get serious, *yaar*? Some wet-behind-the-ears trading punk, halfway across the world decides to play strip poker and we get stripped. I find that incredibly funny. True globalization!' Mayur's laughter was raucous to my ears.

'So, what's your guess? How's this going to affect us?'

'Too early to say, but there's bound to be a bloodbath in the US and South America. Heads going to roll big time. Just got off a call with my counterpart in New York. He has started clearing his office. Poor chap was a key member monitoring the Brazilian operations. Doesn't even want to wait for the letter. It's going to be tough for him to get a recommendation!' he quipped. 'But, closer home ... I think this is going to trigger off something nasty. The losses on our Credit Card and Personal Loans portfolios are still mounting. India is under pressure to cut costs and find ways back to profitability. We've got hundreds of staff sitting idle. So, let's see?'

'What do you suspect, Mayur?'

Mayur had views on every subject under the sun except IT, which according to him was great for the gossip mill and fuelled the wide array of conspiracy theories that cemented an organization.

'My gut feel: the India office will be forced to offload. There have been talk of layoffs for several months. This just might be the trigger.'

An uncomfortable pause. It began dawning upon both of us. This wasn't looking good.

Mayur continued, 'The *firang* brass must be on the first flights to Singapore and Hong Kong.'

'Why?' There must be an angle on this one. Mayur was full of them!

'*Yaar*, the foreigners need jobs too. Not that they had much to do there anyway. South America is a goner. The US has been stuttering. Europe is like a ghost town. Now they'll push and park themselves in Asia!'

A change in management at Singapore wouldn't bode well for the Indian arm. One thing was definite. The sales target was going to be the least of my worries this month.

23

'What does that mean for India?'

'I suppose the top management here is going to be rejigged. Heads will roll. And knowing the way this bank operates, some jokers sitting in Singapore or even the US are going to be deciding who stays and who goes? Let's see tomorrow!'

'Tomorrow? What's tomorrow?'

'Ravi ... really have to rush. Will connect later!'

Mayur's casual tone unnerved me. He seemed to have it all figured out. He also seemed to be more adept at handling the implications.

I stepped out into the balcony and lit a cigarette. The nicotine was soothing after the long torturous day. Everything seemed to be caving in around me. I was feeling very unsettled. Was I reading too much into the situation? Or was there a real threat to the Indian operations? After all, we were a speck in the ocean for Imperial.

March

It's all about DICK!

06:43 @ Home

'Do you still have an office to go to, or can you look after the kids today?'

Savitha! Getting a high on my misery.

'Sav! This is seriously not funny!'

'Chill, Ravi! I've known you for so many years. Some shit keeps happening to you all the time. I'm used to this. Nothing will happen. Papa has seen your astrology chart. You're going to be rocking this year!' Savitha handed over a mug of warm water with a dash of lime and salt. Wished she had dropped some brandy in it as well. Would have soothed the nerves…

'Did your sweet Papa also know that some freak Brazilian trader was going to yank the chain and blow a few billion dollars as well?'

She could really get on my nerves sometimes.

'Don't say anything about Papa!'

Of course not. That would be sacrilege! The mobile rang, saving me from the trauma of continuing on this intergalactic twist with my astrological chart.

'Hi, Mayur, guess you didn't sleep last night?' He must have some good gossip, else he wouldn't have called back so soon.

'Monster and Naukri overflowing with Imperial CVs all night! Think Vikram has finally got an account on Monster now,' he chuckled.

Vikramaditya Rathore, our suave CEO, had been on slippery ground for some time now. He had two direct reports, including my boss, gunning for his slot. We both laughed.

Savitha, shaking her head as she knew this boy talk could go on for a while, got up from the bed and locked herself in the bathroom. She resented the intrusion on what she saw as her private time with me. Though a fat lot of good it did, as all we seemed to be doing was arguing these days. And the barbs were only getting sharper.

'Figuratively speaking, right?'

'I'm serious, Ravi. Thought you would have heard this already. They've been trying to pack him off to Moscow for several months now to set up the Russia office. He's been cornered from all sides. He's either on a flight to vodka land in April or a service apartment with some management trainee in New York!' Mayur couldn't hold back the chuckles, but quickly contained himself.

'So, who's replacing Vikram?'

'The word on the street is that your boss Amitabh has been flying into Singapore quite frequently of late!'

'Shit!' I don't know why that came out loud.

'I know the feeling. Listen, will catch you later in the day. Haven't spoken with my wife since I landed. Need to tell her I'm going straight to office. That should really cheer her up!' Mayur disconnected.

Hell! I had forgotten to ask him about what was going down today.

08:54 In the Car En Route to Office

SMS from Vinesh Menon *'Imperial's new HR mantra – 'DICK' Dump, Impale, Cut, Kick!'* It didn't sound quite that funny today.

Clicked on the Twitter icon.

Imperial Insider: 10,000 on their way out! The beginning of the end?

10:02 @ Office

'Ravi, don't forget to pick up the cake on your way home today. Spoke with the bakery, they'll keep everything ready at 5. Don't forget to leave before the traffic peaks!' Savitha had taken the day off to organize Srikanth's birthday party. But knowing her, she would be working on the laptop at home.

27

'Sure! Anything else?'

'Yup, turn up with the cake. On time!' She hung up.

Sure! The way things looked, I would have to take up cake delivery as an alternate profession soon!

10:03

Email from Amitabh. He had raised the target by over 20 per cent over my already inflated numbers for the next year's Business Plan. I was cupping my forehead in my hands. What in God's name did he want from me? The whole frigging organization was reeling from layoffs and downsizing, and he was taking up my numbers to suicidal proportions!

And, he wanted the reworked plan in 15 minutes!

Radhika walked in nervously.

'What happened?'

'There's something you should know?' Radhika closed the door, only ever done for fumigation, blasting sessions from the boss and rumour updates.

'What more can there be?' This was getting frustrating.

'Jaideep Mehrotra got an email, direct from New York yesterday, asking for a 20 per cent headcount reduction plan from India!'

The secretaries' grapevine had been notoriously accurate for several years now. It was gospel truth.

'Who told you this?'

The genocide had started quicker than I imagined. Didn't even have an updated CV. I was getting panicky. Is this what Mayur was referring to?

'The secretaries' grapevine, sir...'

'Twenty per cent! Are you sure?' I just realized the anxiety was showing in my voice. I needed to rein in myself, but the secretarial grapevine... It was a compelling source of the juiciest information in our gossip-hungry institution.

'There's more. They will be sending an email by the month-end with the list.'

The shocking levels of information asymmetry dislodged me from my senior VP status quickly. 'What email ... what list?'

'For the layoffs!' Radhika appeared surprisingly composed considering the events were unfolding so rapidly. Did she even understand the implications of the words that she was uttering?

'There's more, sir!'

I hated it when she used the term 'sir'. It didn't bode too well.

'Spill it out, Radhika.' I smiled. A pained smile though.

'They're looking at a re-organization as well ...'

'What kind of a re-organization?'

'At the regional level. They're planning to merge the four regions into two zones.'

Was she my personal assistant or the CEO of this bank?

This was a tsunami of bad news. My gut was rarely wrong, but I kept my fingers crossed, hoping that it was this time around. Where in frigging hell was my God-fearing father-in-law and his blessed solemn predictions?

10:18

The phone rang in 15 minutes like clockwork. Boss! I hadn't sent across the annual business plan yet.

'Ravi?' He appeared to be in a hurry.

'Good morning, boss.'

'You didn't send me the numbers. We need to send this off to Singapore now. They have a review meeting in the evening.' He was piling on the pressure.

'What's the news from Brazil, boss?' After all, he was my boss. He needed to give me some information too, even if it was bullshit. At least, I could then quote him and peddle it within my region.

'You know as much as I do. It's on the news, Ravi. Now, why haven't you sent me your revised numbers?'

The *Titanic* was going down and the jerk was getting dressed for dinner. Was he on dope or had he genuinely lost it?

'I needed to discuss them with you, boss.'

'Discuss what, Ravi? I don't have time for these childish discussions!'

Childish? The son of a gun was running me off a cliff. When rationale doesn't work, use abuse and brute force.

'You've taken up my numbers like crazy, boss. How're we going to do these kind of numbers? It's nearly a 40 per cent hike over the current year!'

'Are you saying you can't, Ravi?'

The gloves were on!

'Boss, you know I didn't say that, but I need resources for that as well. When do we discuss that?'

'That's always been your problem, Ravi. You've always relied on more manpower and headcounts. How many times have I told you that you need to think out of the box and increase your productivity. You're setting yourself low!'

Low! How could the slimeball even say that after what I had pulled off over the last two months. I was bailing him out big time.

'But boss ...'

'Now don't just keep saying boss. Seriously, Ravi, you need to multi-task and get this over with. Do you want me to sit down and revise your Excel sheets as well?'

This was brutal. The last nail in the coffin. Damned if I did, damned if I didn't!

'I need to meet Vikram with the final version. Send the numbers across, and write down a summary in the email.' He hung up.

What was he up to? Trying to corner me? He was setting me up. Radhika probably was right. Something big was going down, and I seemed to be right on course

10:42

'Boss, you called?'

'Yes, Karan, come in and close the door behind you.'

He was looking restless. Closing the door usually didn't augur well for my team.

'Boss, there's a bad buzz outside!'

'Why, what's new on Twitter, Karan?' Clearly, the only reliable source of information these days apart from the secretaries' grapevine.

'Not on Twitter boss, but everywhere!'

'Spill it out, Karan!'

'Is there a list coming out this month?'

This news had travelled faster than expected. Needed to deflect.

'Listen, I called you for something else. We can catch up on the gossip later. Need to rework the numbers.' I shouldn't have started off on that Twitter discussion. Should have seen that coming.

I passed across the even further revised targets and for a moment I seemed to sound like my boss.

'Is this a joke, boss?' Karan wasn't amused. He knew he had to do more than 40 per cent of those targets.

'Do I look like I'm joking, Karan?' I said deciding to take a stern tone.

'You need to fight back, boss. They're screwing us!'

'What the hell? Karan, just finish it in the next 10 minutes.'

He was right. Even my team wouldn't take me seriously with those numbers. We were walking into a minefield.

11:44

'Radhika, no calls or meetings for the next one hour. Is that clear?'

'Okay, sir!'

'Has Karan sent across the numbers to the head office?'

'Yes, sir!'

'Did he check everything?'

'Must have, sir!' I hung up.

I had taken the call. I had taken on increased sales targets but had also asked for more people, which would increase the cost budget. The head office would shoot down the request for additional manpower. But I was buying time. This possibly meant the end of the road. Took the targets for the moment. It was a bad call. But had asked for a rider seeking for additional manpower next year. Needed to crack this. At least they couldn't fire me for not taking on aggressive targets in the coming year.

I shut down the laptop and BlackBerry. Then I dimmed the lights in the room and drew the curtains. I settled on the couch on the far end of the room, took off my shoes, placed my feet on the sofa and rested my head on the cushion.

I closed my eyes, but my mind wouldn't settle down. I tossed around for a few minutes and finally got up and walked to the window. Peering though the curtain, I noticed the Relationship Managers outside in intense debate. Rumours of layoffs and pink slips seemed to have consumed everyone in the office today. Even clients had begun calling in to check if their money was safe.

I needed to address the troops. Act fast. I owed it to them.

'Radhika, call for a townhall. Next 30 minutes!' We used to call these townhalls, when I addressed those in my team or updated them on key items, achievements or just for a quick interaction. We hadn't had a meeting for quite some time. There hadn't been too much good news worth sharing. It wasn't any different today. But I had to do the whole motivation thing.

'Now?'

'What do you understand by the next 30 minutes?' Why was I snapping at her? I needed to cool down.

'But many of them are on the field.'

'Then call them in,' I snapped again.

'Okay, sir!'

She was being sarcastic.

'And get Jaideep Mehrotra. Track him down. Need to speak with him.'

Radhika rushed into the room. 'Sir, I spoke to Jaideep's secretary. She doesn't know where he is! He is not picking up his mobile either.'

'Radhika, where's our local HR head. What's his name?'

'Vinesh Menon, sir?' She knew I was terrible with names.

'Yes, that's him. Need him in my room in the next five minutes.'

12:30 pm

The team had assembled on the floor.

'Good afternoon!'

'Good afternoon, sir!' The room resonated

'Thank you for coming to the townhall on such short notice. As you may have heard, February has been a good month. All this is due to your efforts. Give yourselves a good hand.' I started applauding and the whole team joined in. Good. They looked charged up, but not very convinced.

'Now, let's not forget. We have one more month to go. March is crucial. So let's keep up the good work.'

My audience started looking restless. Most of them started clicking on their mobile phones and a buzz swept the floor.

I cleared my throat. The heads looked up at me briefly, but then descended back towards the mobile phones.

I continued for another three to four minutes, responding to a clearly muted and reluctant set of questions. I had been expecting a fairly involved and volatile session but noticed hesitation and even hints of sarcasm and cynicism in their tone. This was very unusual behaviour. Not too many questions about Brazil or the possible layoffs. What was holding them back?

Radhika followed me into the cabin. 'You may want to check out your BlackBerry, sir!'

Twitter!

'Imperial Insider: Is Ravi Shastry on the firing line?'

'Shit!'

Wanted to take a double barrel gun and shoot this Twitter freak!

14:53

'Ravi?' It was Maithili on the line.

'Hi, Maithili. How's it going?' I was banking on her for some reliable information.

'Where are you off to, Ravi? You didn't tell me!' She had obviously read the Tweet.

'Buzz off, Maithili! Now tell me ... I'm not getting through to anyone in the head office. What are the freaks doing there? Radhika has been trying to chase the top brass since the morning. How 'bout you?'

'Blank. Bloody blank!' Maithili sounded grim. She was also a tough nut to crack. Her proximity to the top brass in Mumbai and Singapore was common knowledge. She had been trying to secure a senior slot in Mumbai for over a year, to get away from the intrusive family circle in Delhi, and had almost displaced the marketing head a couple of months earlier. She had played hard ball with the regional HR head in Singapore, and had been asked to cool her heels in Delhi by Jaideep for a while. Her frustration had been reflected in her sales performance, but Maithili would somehow get away with it!

'Tell me about it. Six meetings since the morning ... with the lobby staff, two groups of RMs, the operations chaps, the collections team and even the damn watchman walked in!'

I had developed a migraine and had popped two painkillers already. All I had been doing was doling out bullshit to all and sundry on how the bank was stable and they should not fall victim to baseless rumours.

Maithili burst into laughter. 'How are you holding up there?'

'Not sure, Maithili.' I really wasn't any more.

Maithili finally opened up. 'I've heard the list is coming out on the 31st!'

'Reliable source?'

'My HR guy... Cornered him! He finally spilt the beans. They've been told this verbally. No emails exchanged. All hush-hush! They've been asked to prepare their lists and hand it over by the end of the week. But, the decisions are going to be taken in Singapore. Not even the India head office. Can you believe that?'

Maithili was renowned for her conspiracy theories – fact and fiction would intermingle effortlessly. But I needed to hear her out. Should I believe her? She could be exaggerating because she liked dramatizing matters.

'But why India? We're doing fine, right? Or is there some trading freak here as well?'

'Not that I know of the Ravi, but that's the diktat from Asia head office. Our blessed Asia head Shinzo Kawasaki is steering this. It's happening across Asia. No questions asked. It's worse in the US and Europe. Bloody illogical. No one's got the balls to stand up to New York and ask them why in India? Soon they'll be cutting down on paper cups on this cost-cutting drive. Idiotic!'

'But why? Can they do it legally? This is insane,' I was venting my frustration.

'They'll find a way. They've got global experts for this kind of stuff. Can you imagine, they pay experts to define a headcount reduction strategy! It's warped. Have you seen that George Clooney movie ... *Up in the Air*? If you have, you'll understand what I'm saying.'

I hadn't watched a movie in a multiplex for ages. Somehow, with two kids and our tight schedules, Savitha and I just didn't get around to it. I briefly recollected how I had kissed Savitha while watching a movie at Sterling. It was the late night show at 10:30 and the hall was thinly interspersed with inebriated couples and frustrated bachelors watching a Kevin Spacey movie. The empty seats beside us and in the rear had stimulated some frenetic activity. Those were different times...

'But, you will be okay! You're in Amitabh's good books!' Maithili had a way of working with all types.

'Not sure. Haven't slept with him yet! But will find out on Twitter soon, I'm sure!' She burst into laughter.

I looked at my watch and saw the time. 'Gotta rush, need to pick up my son's birthday cake.'

'Hey, sure. Have fun and my love to Srikanth.' She disconnected.

17:02

Email from Amitabh.
Subject : Re. Business Plan
Ravi,
What's with the 20 per cent headcount increase? Your numbers are all wrong. So is the format. Why are the Personal Loan and Credit Card numbers so low? And bring down the headcount. Need this before you leave office.

I was exasperated and shocked. What in frigging hell was he up to? Personal Loans and Credit Card numbers low? He must be senile!

I wanted to kick him in his balls, but with my current popularity and the uncertainty in the air, I couldn't take any risks! Needed to be careful ... this Twitter freak could possibly be reading my mind!?

17:05

'Radhika, ask the driver to pick up the cake and drop it home. I need to finish these numbers again.'

'Sure?'

'Yeah! And call in Karan and tell the team to patch in on a conference call. It's going to be a long night.' I sighed.

'Yes, sir!'

19:18

'Ravi?'

'Yes? Who's this?'

'Shekhar, from New York. How're you doing?' Shekhar! Savitha's older brother also worked with Imperial, heading the Internet banking business globally. A big shot with a fancy apartment overlooking Central Park.

'Yes, Shekhar, thanks? All well with you I hope?'

'A trick question. They'll fire me if I say yes to that!' Shekhar laughed.

I had hoped he'd call 'How's it going for you guys there?'

'Bloodbath! We've got guys waiting to jump off the windows. It's crazy. It's like 9/11. This was supposed to be the 'U' in the recession. Barely scraped through Hiroshima. Now we've got Nagasaki! Don't think we'll make it through this one.'

'But the Fed (US Federal Bank) would step in right?'

'Looks tough. The trading freaks had bet big time on some currencies, petroleum and a whole bunch of other options. The market turned and they were left in a lurch. Everything tanked. The Feds may not bail us out this time. We missed the bus for the begging bowl!'

'So, what next?'

'They'll start with layoffs in the US and Europe. South America is as good as shut down. They'll prune the headcount in Asia as well. It was expected even without this. Now it just gives everyone an excuse to do the obvious. Too much deadwood. Might even pawn off the business in Asia. It's anyone's guess right now!'

'How much time, Shekhar?'

'You've got some at least. Out here it's a matter of days if not hours.' Shekhar sighed.

'How much time?'

'At least a couple of weeks. Think India's managed to get time till the month-end.'

'But we don't have that much deadwood here?'

'Seen the number of VPs you guys have? It's like a zoo. Even New York doesn't have so many VPs. Your designations are your bane, not the pay packet. The HR analysts keep seeing fancy designations and say chop chop chop! They're loving it!'

Shekhar attempted a feeble laugh but then withdrew into silence.

'How're you holding up, Shekhar?'

'Will know soon. But, Ravi, I read the Tweet, what's the situation there?'

'Should be okay, Shekhar.' I was lying through my teeth. Wanted to go down on my knees and beg him to pull some strings.

'You sure? Let me dig and see if there's anything I can do for my kid sister's husband. Take care and be in touch.'

19:43

The mobile buzzed again. 'Papa, what time are you coming? Want to cut the cake. My friends are leaving.'

'Srikanth, listen baba, am going to come soon. But why don't you cut the cake and leave some for me, okay?'

'But I want you here, Papa ...'

Shit! Damn these Business Plan numbers. Damn my boss. Damn this bloody bank. May they all burn in hell!

It then dawned on me. My wishes might just come true after all!

21:32

Been avoiding her calls. Five calls in the last two hours!

'You really have been a prick today. You know that, right?'

'Sav, I couldn't do anything, love. Had to get these numbers off to head office ...'

She tore into me. 'Try telling that to your son. You know he hasn't even eaten. It didn't help that some of his friends came with their fathers.'

An SMS from Amitabh as Savitha continued, *'Call once you send the email!'*

'Sav, I don't like what happened today. But trust me I had no choice!' I disconnected.

I rarely disconnected calls while speaking with Savitha. But this was one of those days.

23:28 @ Home, Finally

'Got any cake?' I thought humour, though forced, might ease the situation.

'Don't!' Savitha wasn't pleased. It was Fort Knox!

She paused and then decided to rescue her miserable husband, for a few minutes at least . 'What's happening at work?'

Shekhar may have spoken with her. 'It's all very fuzzy right now!'

'Believe you've hit the popularity charts on Twitter!'

'How the hell did you know that?'

'I'm not some village bimbo, Ravi! I am familiar with that sophisticated thing called Twitter!' Great. I had managed to upset her, yet again. Must have set a record today!

She collapsed on my shoulder and started crying. 'Major shit at work, Ravi. Can't take this any longer!'

Damn! What was all that about?

March

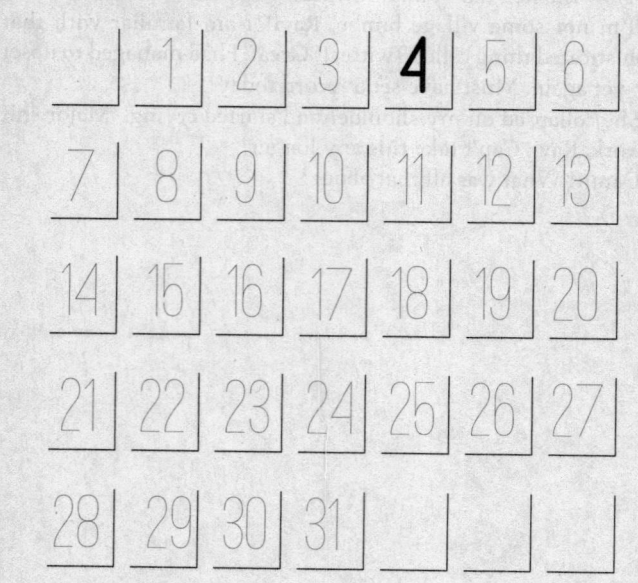

	1	2	3	**4**	5	6
7	8	9	10	11	12	13
14	15	16	17	18	19	20
21	22	23	24	25	26	27
28	29	30	31			

Bheja Fry

00:14 @ Home

It had taken us over half an hour to settle down Revathi, who had woken up crying. We were on the floor beside her bed, with Savitha stroking Revathi's hair. Srikanth too had woken up during the commotion and his imitations of Donald Duck had eased the situation.

The laptop, placed on a bean bag, was playing Revathi's favourite nursery rhymes.

Savitha was glowing with a resplendent smile.

'Feeling better?'

'Not sure, Ravi. But it feels good to be here with the kids. They make more sense than all this office bullshit…'

Revathi was finally asleep. Srikanth was holding his newly acquired Star Wars laser gun across his chest. Savitha let go of Revathi's hand and tucked her under the blanket.

'Am I overreacting, Ravi?'

I paused. She looked calm, but I still wasn't sure if she was in the mood for a full-fledged conversation.

'I'm sure it's crazy, Sav. But you just stay calm and focused…'

Savitha and I had divergent work philosophies. And we more often than not disagreed on our approaches to work situations. I still wasn't sure of the exact details of her challenge at work, but knew it must be something that was really ticking her off. She wasn't the one to react the way she was. I would have to give her space and the latitude to share the details at her own pace.

'They've been cornering me. I can feel it. Some crazy shit is happening …' She paused midway and then rose quickly.

That was a signal. She wasn't ready for the chat as yet. I followed her, switching off the lights in the children's bedroom and closed the door behind me. She was waiting in the corridor outside. I reached out and held her hand.

'Don't worry, kiddo! Hang in there.'

She smiled. The tension and anxiety was back on her face.

06:10 @ Home

Sneaked out of the bedroom to switch on the TV in the drawing room.

'... in other news. Officials at Imperial have approached the US Fed for raising additional capital, but sources indicate the meeting did not go favourably. It is rumoured that Imperial will be laying off several thousand people and even selling their Asia business to reduce costs and raise capital ...'

Great! Already moved from breaking news to other news. Jesus, a multi-billion dollar hole, and we're the other news on day 2!

'Ravi! Where are you?' It was Savitha. Didn't sound too good.

'Coming, Sav.'

She was sweating and restless.

'Sav, what's going on?'

'Nothing. Think it's just the BP. Need to start taking those pills and should be fine.' Savitha continued tossing on the bed.

I held her hand, 'Out with it, Sav! You didn't say anything last night either.'

'Some mess in the office. There's talk of shifting the Indian operations to a new centre in Shanghai. Will probably converge all Asian operations out there.'

'That would take time, right?' This didn't sound good.

'That's what we thought. Remember the major issues on the current project and how they preponed the project timeline?'

'Yes ...'

'They want to wind down our team and shift to Shanghai in April. Guess what? We're the first ones ...'

'You're kidding, right?'

'Very comforting, Ravi!'

'What? What did I say? Have you spoken with your boss?'
'That bitch!'
'Excuse me, Sav...'
'Ravi, have you ever reported to a lady boss?'

Savitha at it again. It was incredibly amusing and arousing, listening to women bitching about each other.

'Afraid not, Sav. Why?'

'They can be such moody temperamental hags. It's unbelievable. She's paranoid and bloody insecure. She'll hack me to bits if she even gets a feeling that I'm vulnerable. And top that up with their mood swings. It's a living nightmare. They are especially bitchy with women. It's bloody frightening.'

She was hysterical again. This was going downhill. I got off the bed.

'Where are you off to now? Don't tell me you're getting upset like some sissy girl!' Sav's voice rose another few decibels.

I pushed her down. 'Hang on. Will be right back.'

I returned with two glasses and a bottle of fine Mexican tequila.

'Is that what I think that is, Ravi?'
'Yes?'
'And what are you proposing to do with that?'
'It's not what I propose to do with it. More like what we both would be doing with this fine liquid!'

I opened the bottle, poured it into the shot glasses and handed one to Savitha.

'You off your rockers, Ravi?'
'Cheers, my dear!'
'What are we drinking to at 7 am on a weekday morning?'
'To the most screwed up couple in this neighbourhood, possibly even this city! Cheers?' Metaphorically, only. We hadn't done it in quite some time now.

'Sure! Only one condition!'
'And, what might that be?'

'I'll kick you between your legs if we stop anywhere before we down three shots each.' Savitha smiled.

07:26
Srikanth on my lap, playing with my T-shirt collar. Clicked the Twitter icon.

Imperial Insider: US layoffs to begin Friday. India confirmed for month-end! All the best guys ...

Nothing about me ... or my boss ... or the CEO ... and even worse ... nothing about my peers!

'Papa, you know Arjun in my class? He is going to Disneyland.'

Damn his parents. Sure, son! May need to get employment there in a Mickey Mouse costume if the shit really hits the ceiling, I thought to myself.

Three days down in March. If everything got really screwed, both of us would be jobless by the end of the month! I looked towards Srikanth and could visualize his dream of seeing Disneyland vanishing. Maybe, it would be best to buy him the comics instead!

09:48 On the Way to a Meeting
'Radhika, you in?'

'Yes, Ravi.'

'Got off to a rocky start. Savitha down with high BP. Dropped the kids off. The driver got into an accident and my BlackBerry is busted. It fell during the collision and won't restart. And I'm running late for the client meeting which Karan had set up ...'

'Why are you calling me then? Hope you're not hurt, by the way?'

'Thanks for asking. I'm using the driver's phone. But please get through to Karan and tell him I'm running late and tell him to check if there are any more emails on the Operating Plan numbers ... and ...'

'Hey boss ... take it easy ...'

'And, send me the address of the Jaiswals. I have a 10 am

meeting with them. And please speak with the admin guys. Need a replacement BlackBerry. I'll die without it …'

'You're almost there!' She hung up.

A sense of helplessness was sinking in. My inability to access emails or receive calls made me nervous. These were crucial times. I needed to be wired at all times. The uncertainty was getting me worked up. This was not who I was, normally!

13:22 @ Office

'Sir, your boss on Line 1,' Radhika was amused.

'Great! Put him through. Make my day!'

'Ravi!' Uh! Oh!

'Yes, sir, how are you?'

'How can you be late for a meeting with the Jaiswals? Are you out of your mind? Don't you know who they are? I just got off the phone with him, eating humble pie, apologizing for your tardy behaviour.'

I put down the receiver, turned on the speaker and resumed clearing my emails. The monologue lasted precisely 134 seconds.

'So, what do you have to say for yourself?'

'Sir, Savitha is unwell and my car met with an accident. That's why I was delayed.'

'Don't make excuses and check your email, you're getting sloppy …'

I decided to cut in. 'Boss, I need five minutes. It's very urgent.'

'Not now. Just reply to the email first. Bye!' Wow, he actually said bye today.

I pressed the 'from' tab on Outlook and searched for the devil's name. What was he throwing at me now?

The expected. He had revised the workings on my plan numbers again! I was surprised at myself for being surprised again!

14:44

The chaos continued. Calls had been pouring in from across the region. I needed to speak with someone, get my sanity back.

'Hi, Maithili!'

'Hey, champ, how're you holding up?' She seemed chirpy.

'On top of the world. What news on your side of the trenches?'

'Update: The watchman actually did ask me today if his job was under threat!'

We both laughed. It felt so good. I really needed that.

'Any more stuff on this supposed list? It's haunting the living daylights out of everyone here. I am playing the role of a priest, hearing confessions, dreams, loan details, divorce stories and one case of sexual harassment as a child. This doesn't include the outstanding achievements of everyone working here, which if logically added together, would have wiped out the debt burden of Thailand! The poor kids actually think you and I have a role to play in this. We are such big dickless suckers, I tell you!'

Maithili cleared her throat. 'I can relate to that!'

Oops! I winced as I realized my faux pas. 'Sorry about that. Not that there's anything wrong with not having one. You do know that, right?'

'You sexist pig! I think I'll report you to the brass in Mumbai!'

I shot back, 'But you're the one who keeps talking of sleeping with the senior management.'

'Hmmm! Forgot about that,' Maithili responded.

'Okay, we're square and screwed. Listen, what's with your budget numbers?' I pushed again.

'Boss just sent out an email with some more changes. It's ridiculous. The firing list is coming out at the end of this month and we're targeting higher revenues with more people! What the shit is happening, Ravi? There's talk of the regions getting merged. They're talking two zones instead of four regions. You know, like the South and East into one zone.' Maithili was getting uptight. At last! She had cracked!

'Where did this come from?'

'Don't ask me that, but it's reliable. At least as reliable as it can get under the circumstances.' She was now speaking in a hushed tone.

'What does that mean for us?'

'We're done for, sweetheart ...' Maithili paused. It appeared as if she wanted to say something.

She thought about it and continued. 'It's obvious, isn't it? Boss hates your guts, 'coz the CEO has the hots for you. I'm supposed to be your close ally, in more ways than one, which clearly alienates me from the equation. Our colleagues in West and East have a PhD in ass-licking. And we just don't have those connections in Mumbai!'

'Maithili, do you do anything at work or just make up these stories the whole day?'

'Usually, I entertain questions from watchmen on their careers at the Imperial!' She hung up.

15:23 In the Conference Room – Bangalore Team Review Meeting

A team review meeting felt awkward under these circumstances. Questions could emerge. The team of 15 insurance specialists seated in the room were already stressed with the targets for the month. The talk of layoffs had severely dampened their spirits and enthusiasm.

Had been trying to get through to Jaideep but he had been avoiding my SMSs, calls and emails. He had gone cold. The camaraderie at the Leela meant nothing today.

Even the boss remained unsurprisingly evasive.

'Karan, how's the month looking?' Felt like a jerk asking prisoners on death row about their targets.

'Sir, the market has plateaued, but analysts have no clue where it's heading. Can't tell my clients to move in large positions at this stage. We're pushing the tax saving plans to corporate clients, so we should be able to meet our volume numbers there. Insurance is looking flat. I'm not sticking my neck out on personal loans ... blah ... blah ... blah ...'

Karan kept talking. I couldn't focus. Then I noticed his lips had stopped moving. He must have finished his piece.

My mind was elsewhere. Hadn't spoken with Savitha since the morning. I was getting worried. She was strong and determined, but something else was happening, something she was holding back.

I fidgeted with my phone and stepped out of the conference room.

I paused for a couple of moments outside the room, thinking about Savitha — Was worried about her health — was thinking of telling her to quit and take a break for a few months. But, I needed to figure out where I stood amidst all this shelling. I needed to keep up my end...

In the end, I simply sent her an SMS ...

15:36 @ Office

'Hey, Sav... how're you feeling?'

'Finally found the time to call?'

'No excuses, Sav, but I have been messaging you!'

'You're a shrewd one, darling!' She wasn't letting go.

'How're you feeling? Took your meds?'

'Yup ...'

'Taking some rest?'

'What do you think?'

She must have been slamming the keys on the keyboard of her laptop.

'You could have taken it easy today at least ...'

'You could have stayed at home today?'

Touche! Pistols drawn. It was time to retreat.

'Will try and be home by 7 today ...'

An eerie pause again.

'Sure, that would be UK time or Brazil?'

Game, set and match to the missus.

'Stepping into a meeting — will have to call you back ...' I disconnected. The tequila seemed to have worn off for sure!

18:33 @ Office
Imperial Insider: 6,000 losing their jobs in the US tomorrow! More heads to roll for sure!

19:15 In My Cabin
Mithilesh Kumar, the regional Credit Card sales head and recent chairman's award winner at the door.

'Mr Big Man, may I come in?'

I would have preferred whacking him on his backside and throwing him out.

'Come in, Mithilesh. In late today?' I smiled, hinting at the total lack of work at his end.

The Credit Card sales team had been loitering around idle for over six months now, usually a situation of sympathy. But with Mithilesh, it was different. Officially, the regional head for Credit Cards and Personal Loans, he also had an attitude and a titanic ego that was sure to be his downfall. Had the inordinate ability of pissing off people. But more troublesome was his complete lack of regret on any of his actions. He could eat you alive and not even bat an eyelid.

'Catching up with some things. How about you? What's keeping you awake?'

'The usual ...'

A strained silence. Mithilesh and I had history ... and it wasn't particularly pleasant.

'I'm in Hyderabad tomorrow. Anything I can do for you?'

What was he up to? 'No, but thanks for asking.'

Mithilesh started fidgeting. 'Listen, Ravi. Feel like a drink today? It's been ages!'

Ages? We had never gone out for a drink. Was this a hint? Was it a truce offering? I couldn't place my finger on it. My gut suggested that I take him up on it, but I needed to get home to Savitha. Tough call ...

'Not today, Mithilesh. Lots of work to catch up on. Closing the plan numbers for next year.'

'Okay! Some other day, perhaps.' He got up to leave and walked out of the room. But stepped right back in again.

'Ravi, just thought I'd mention this. Spoke with HR. They're looking at giving my team some training on investments and insurance. Would be great if you could pop in and drop in a few pearls of wisdom. And the head office asked me to run through some of your forecasts for next year.' He left without waiting for my reaction.

What the hell did he want with my Operating Plan numbers? The slimeball was making his move. He had something up his sleeve. Damn! Should have had that drink with him. Could have slit his throat if I didn't like what I heard. But this wasn't good.

Imperial Insider: India Firing List coming out on 31st!

19:45 Outside the Office, Waiting for the Car

Vinesh Menon walked up to me as his car entered the driveway.

'Mr Shastry, end of day's play?'

'Depends on what you're throwing at me, Vinesh!'

'Depends on which game you're playing, Ravi. You really like taking pangas, don't you?'

Must have spoken with Mithilesh.

'So, what's the news?'

'Another hat in the ring for zonal head. It's formal now.'

'You're kidding me, right? You're actually considering that sham?'

'It's a matter of perception, Ravi. And one is referring to the chairman's award winner! So you may want to see how you would like to play your cards.'

'Thanks for the heads up, Vinesh.'

'Any time. So how's the job market?'

Shit! The slime ball!

23:51 @ Home, With a Bottle of Old Monk and Kishore Kumar!

'You planning to sleep with the bottle or your wife?' Savitha stepped out into the balcony where I was seated in the dark. I was totally sapped. The Monday morning congratulatory email seemed like such a distant memory.

Even the idea of Mithilesh joining the fray for the Zonal Sales Manager (ZSM) position was sickening. The pack was getting crowded. Four Regional Sales Managers (RSMs) and now Mithilesh ... for two positions!

'You mind if I sleep with both of you?'

The BB buzzed again. An email from Shekhar ...

'Have got some info ... will call you soon! You need to watch out for your friends!'

March

	1	2	3	4	**5**	6
7	8	9	10	11	12	13
14	15	16	17	18	19	20
21	22	23	24	25	26	27
28	29	30	31			

Of Chaos and Choices

04:12

I had been tossing in my bed since 2 am. The clock read '4:12' now and of course, the sun was still fast asleep.

I found myself wandering into the children's bedroom. I kissed them gently on their foreheads, so as not to disturb them. Actually wanted to wake them up and hug them tight. Savitha was in deep slumber.

I was alone.

I noticed the BlackBerry. In my hand. Inseparable. Clicked on the Twitter icon, dreading further tweets. There were none since last night. I slumped along the wall in the passage outside the bedrooms, not wanting to go into the drawing room, knowing I would be tempted to switch on the TV and sink even deeper in my misery. I couldn't take my mind away from thinking about the thousands of tables and bars in the US and Brazil filled with Imperial employees waiting to see what the lottery had in store for them the next day.

That feeling of helplessness hurt the most! The ignominy of being fired was a stigma that was always difficult to shake off. One could never do that easily. One pretended that one had overcome the fear, but the shadows were always there.

I couldn't resist the temptation and flopped on the couch in front of the TV. I turned on the news, dreading what I would hear. It took about 12 minutes, but it was bang on.

'Misery for employees at Imperial continues. As rumours abound of the proposed layoffs of 6,000 employees in the US, news has also emerged that the Canadian employees too would be in the firing line on Friday. The Brazilian operations have been formally closed and legal proceedings have been initiated against the traders who brought down Imperial. The stock has

plummeted by over 80 per cent in the last three trading sessions and the NYSE is considering cessation of trading in the stock.

'Closer home, the India CEO appears to be under fire for the bank's under-performance and may be on his way to an international assignment. Rumours suggest several more heads might roll in India as well and hundreds of layoffs are in the pipeline ...'

The migraine set in again. Felt like a few swigs to calm my nerves.

It finally sunk in that I needed to think of options outside Imperial. Having spent over eight years at Imperial, I hadn't been in the market. I was out of touch. Didn't really know any consultants that mattered. Would need to start from scratch! Shit!

Did I still have it in me? Or was Imperial running in my blood?

There were two points of view. The first suggested that working too long in an organization made one less flexible. The other indicated a higher level of dedication and commitment. I would be banking on the latter.

04:23

Savitha had suggested that I connect with her brother again.

'Hi, Shekhar. What's the scene?'

'Did some digging with people here about India and particularly you!'

My heart started racing. 'And?'

'Your senior management is a bunch of loons. Here's the gig. Kawasaki, the Asia head, was under pressure to reduce costs and the headcount was the first and obvious victim.

'He didn't think India needed to get rid of 20 per cent, because in the larger scheme of things, the size of the operations out there are too small anyway. His team messed up on the Excel sheet that got sent out to NY. Some joker did a copy paste and ended up showing 20 per cent reduction in India as well!'

'What? So why not change it?' This was the most ridiculous thing I had ever heard in my life.

'Ego! He was in a video conference with the top brass here, when he realized his mistake. The top brass even asked him about it. He didn't want to be seen as having made a mistake. He's on a weak wicket as it is, and didn't want to screw himself up further with the board by saying that he'd sent in a wrong Excel file! He wants to retain his golfing privileges and retirement benefits even if he gets fired. Just playing safe, I guess!'

'Bastard!'

'So, India's losing all those people 'coz some freak didn't use Microsoft Excel correctly! It gets even better or maybe worse for you. Your HR head?'

'Jaideep Mehrotra?'

'Yes, Jaideep. He's gunning for the Asia HR head position. The current Asia HR head is too close to Kawasaki and most likely on his way out. He wants to show what a mean ass he can be. He is pushing for the restructuring in the Indian operations.'

'Really?'

'Yup. Jaideep and your boss, Amitabh. Both have their agendas. Amitabh wants to get rid of your CEO, which is a well-known fact, and is working with Jaideep on this restructuring plan. They're both trying to take credit for this, so they're okay with the Excel error. Works brilliantly for them. It's making their plans easier.'

I felt like screaming, but decided to leave it till after the call. The nails were being driven in, albeit faster than I had ever expected.

'And, you said you had some info about me?'

'Okay, hold your breath. You're on the top talent global radar. Your CEO had given two names from India. You were one of them. Jaideep knows about this, but your boss, I think, is not too happy with it. That makes you a threat, 'coz you'd then be a New York boy in India and in the spotlight. And he wants his boys with him! So, I'm guessing they've possibly got another angle on you.'

'What?' The mystery deepened.

'No clue, Ravi. You'll have to crack that one. Will let you know the moment I hear something.'

'And when you said Amitabh's people. Whom did you mean?'

'How well do you know this lady, Maithili?'

'Why, Shekhar?'

'Weird story man. She's got some sexual harassment thing going on against Amitabh! It's been all hush, hush.'

'What?' Why didn't Maithili ever share things like this with me?

'The best part is yet to come. She withdrew it on Wednesday.'

'How do you know all this?'

'The compliance guy here is also an Indian. We go home together. I think he's Maithili's uncle or something!'

'How much of this is reliable?'

'About Kawasaki, confirmed. Jaideep, not confirmed, but I think I'm on the right track. On Maithili, quite certain. India is too far away for the folks here to bluff around. Plus we've got different challenges of our own out here, as you can imagine!'

It was getting murkier, much quicker than I had imagined. Should have slept it out instead. I was unprepared for this. Things were unfolding too quickly for my comfort and further fuelling my helplessness.

Needed to put up a strong front for Savitha. But I wasn't able to keep my sanity together.

08:48 @ Home

Savitha was looking stronger and more composed, but I was sure she was going through a fair bit of trauma herself.

'You sure, you want to go into office today? It's Friday. If you take today off then you'll get the weekend to get some more rest.'

'No, I'll be fine. Need to figure out how long I've got my job, plus I have the project deadline. Totally ridiculous. Working on completing a project that'll be the end of my team! It doesn't make any sense!' She had tears in her eyes, as she walked away.

11:18 @ Office

'Hi, Sriram, returning your call.'

'I'd popped in a couple of painkillers. Sriram Iyengar, the Business Head, Assets, had been on leave for a week, attending a cousin's wedding and had returned to a less than jovial office of a week earlier. Must have been calling in from his *'trading room'*. His stock portfolio was rumoured to run into tens of crores. He spent most of his time surveying the tickers, rather than reducing the losses on the loan portfolios.

'Good to hear from you, Ravi. Needed to catch up with you on the Plan.' This was increasingly getting more idiotic with each passing moment.

'Which version?' Shit! Shouldn't have said that. Needed to play this without upsetting my boss, a near impossible task under normal circumstances.

'The one you had sent out day before, I think. You have to take up the Personal Loan targets, Ravi. Why are you hesitating? In fact, as I keep telling you, you should consider taking some of the great guys we have in the Credit Card sales team. They can really help you pick up your numbers.' Sriram was pushing his team's case, again!

It then struck me that I was speaking with a potential CEO in the running, if rumours about the current CEO were to be believed. Needed to be gentle yet affirmative, and exercise self-restraint. Shit! Suicide either way.

'Sriram, we are still facing huge losses with the earlier Personal Loans portfolio. The team would love to get back to the good old days, but there are just too many variables. Let's go with what we have right now and review it later in the year, perhaps ...'

I was pushing back politely, but knew he could pull rank if he chose.

'You haven't left too much for me to say, have you?' He seemed offended and obviously under pressure to deliver. Battle-lines had been drawn! And I was now on the wrong side.

The year had been a forgettable one for him and the whole industry. He had fought hard to get the management to buy into Personal Loans and Credit Cards again. The recent turmoil would have only further blunted the risk appetite.

The bank used to earlier have different Profit and Loss statements (P&L) for the asset products and for the other business lines. Now, as a regional head, the P&L for the asset products (excluding Credit Cards) also came within my purview. This meant the clean revenues we were bringing in by selling Investment and Insurance products were getting wiped out with losses in Personal Loans.

'Think we'll have to speak again on this subject. You're not listening to reason,' he was rolling out the artillery.

'Sriram, please don't mind. I'm already taking very high targets on the other product lines. I'm really stretched.'

Amitabh and Sriram were not on speaking terms. They both had CEO aspirations. There was no room in the head office that could accommodate both their egos at the same time. It used to be hell seeing them both in the same room. The Operating Plan negotiations were being conducted directly by Sriram with the regional heads. He was pulling his weight on us.

Didn't know how this would play out in the new scheme of things. It didn't augur well for me, for sure!

13:43

I was about to step out for lunch when the BlackBerry rang. It was Sameer Prabhu, the Internal Audit (IA) head, from Mumbai.

'Hi, Sameer. Long time!'

'Hi, Ravi. How's the family?' Enquiring about the family seemed to be in the rule book.

'Great, thanks. Yours?'

'Good, thanks. I am through with the divorce finally. Got some peace of mind.' Shit! I'd forgotten about the divorce. Not too good a start to this chapter. It really wasn't my day!

'Ravi, I am in Bangalore on Monday. Will need time with you. So, can we block 11 to 1?' It didn't sound like a request.

'Can I get back to you, Sameer?'

'Ravi, I didn't need to make this call. You know that, right?'

I had already figured that out. 'Great, see you on Monday. Should I arrange a car for you?'

'No. My office is arranging that. Thanks.'

16:27

Received an SMS: *'Hi Ravi, free for a drink @7 pm? Akash Saldanha, M.B. Ayers'*

I could have kissed him on both cheeks. Akash, an acquaintance from booze sessions back in college, now with one of the world's senior management recruitment firms, M.B. Ayers.

Was he looking for a reference, or was he evaluating my candidature on an assignment he was working on?

17:04

'Ravi, you were looking for me?' Vinesh was at the door.

'Ha! The guru of HR. Please come in, sire!'

'You're in a good mood.'

'What's happening in Hyderabad with the RMs? How're we doing on retaining them? You do know that if we lose them, numbers in Hyderabad will plummet. It'll also set off a ripple effect with everything else going on here!'

'Don't like your tone, Ravi.' That was the HR way of saying we haven't done anything yet, so we will throw attitude.

I wasn't going to duck on this one. 'We'll discuss my tone later, but what's going on? How do you plan to keep them back? We are in this together, you know.' Threw the team angle smoothly, I thought. The SMS from Akash had charged me up.

Vinesh looked nervous. He hadn't seen me like this before.

'We can't match the offer from Oriental, but if they stick

around we can see what we can do for their increments and bonuses. But they have to deliver this month. Plus, I don't think they would want to leave without collecting their quarterly incentives.'

'Vinesh, in the current market and with the shape of things at Imperial, they just might. They are a bright bunch you know. The ball is in our court.'

'But Ravi, if we do manage to pull off something for them, what do we do for the others in Hyderabad, your entire region and across India? Oriental will be swooping in across India soon. Hyderabad is just a start.'

'I agree. All the more reason to take your thumb out of your ass and get something going. I can't manage this without you.'

He finally cracked. 'Ravi, I know where you're coming from. But off the record?'

I nodded.

'Haven't been able to get through to Jaideep since Wednesday. He's just too caught up! Plus Sriram is also on my case on this one. I can't shake him off. You know how it is?' Vinesh was busy drafting the list of team members to be laid off by the end of the month. The Hyderabad thing wasn't anywhere on his agenda. But I needed to get Hyderabad back on his agenda, or at least protect my team. I had to pull out all stops.

'You do have time to discuss the list though, right? We are off the record, Vinesh!'

'Don't do this, Ravi!'

'I haven't even started yet, my dear friend.'

'Off the record, Ravi ... we really may not mind losing people right now. That would be fewer heads to chop in the coming weeks! Think about that!'

I had to have a clear case to keep the team back since HR wasn't going to back me on this! In the larger picture, my team leaving was good for them. It would reduce their pink slip count, and made it easier to get rid of me!

I rather liked going on an offensive with Vinesh.

'Why don't you look at the guys in the Credit Cards team? We have even given them training in Investments and Insurance. They'll be up the curve very soon.'

Too much uncertainty. The vultures would come swooping in the moment they saw cracks. Needed to wrap this up. Or I would be handing it over to Mithilesh and his scoundrels on a platter.

19:00

Savitha and I had a doctor's appointment, but I missed it. Had sent the car and driver to pick her up instead. My decision sickened me, but I just had to meet Akash. Just had to!

My priorities were getting hammered.

Akash was already there waiting and rose from the sofa as he saw me enter. He hadn't changed since the last time we had met at a mutual friend's place five years back. Seemed to be in an Armani. The Rolex could be seen from a mile. I obviously needed to upgrade my wardrobe. I could see the Mercedes key chain dangling conspicuously from his pocket. This was the big league.

'Hi, Ravi. Good to see you. Thanks for seeing me on such short notice.' The Californian twang was also distinct. He was struggling to Indianize it and doing a terrible job.

'Good to see you too. It's been quite a while. You're as fit as ever. Been working out?' The guy looked liked a professional triathlon athlete. Must have been working out three to four hours daily. Where the heck did they get the time for all this? My eyes wandered towards my slight paunch and I decided to get seated quickly.

'Thanks, Ravi, but you're looking stressed! Everything okay?'

19:24

The chatter had meandered across sports, friends, the stock market, sex lives, broken marriages and ... I was getting restless. I wanted to go home. *Is there anything in it for me or not, you freak?*

He had ordered the second round, so I guess he was paying.

Didn't mind, didn't want to put this on the company tab. My damn middle class moralities. Really needed to work on that!

And then he dropped it. 'Singapore Development Bank?'

'Yes, they've been looking at entering India for quite some time now.' This sounded good.

'We've been retained by them and are looking for someone to set up their India office. It would be small, of course, initially. More like a rep office for the first two–three years. But they're looking for someone who could eventually graduate to the CEO's role once the formal approvals and branch licences come through. We wouldn't normally engage at this level, but this is part of a long-term strategy.'

'They've really taken their time. They have been prospecting India for several years now.'

He looked at his watch. 'Extremely sorry to do this to you, Ravi, but just realized I had promised to take my wife out for dinner. So let's work it out like this. I'm scheduled to be out of town next week, getting the Mumbai office up. You think about it and let's connect week after next. Okay?'

What a bitch? How could he build up the drama and expectation and then leave me out to hang like this?

We could connect in the next 10 seconds if you really wanted to! Hadn't he heard of email, mobile telephony, video-conferencing? Why wait a week? And, you're rushing to take your wife out to dinner? And I'm sitting here knowing pretty well that I'm going to get castrated when I reach home!

'Sounds good. Let's connect then.'

A ray of hope in what was turning out to be a very long dark tunnel. I was feeling good. Wanted to hold onto the moment. My fingers reached out to the Twitter icon. There were two tweets.

Imperial Insider: Is Amitabh on his way out too?

Imperial Insider: The India firing list may come out sooner than the 31st!

Misery is better shared! This was getting farcical. Was no one going to be spared. I should have played it differently with Sriram. Had I screwed this up for myself?

March

1	2	3	4	5	6
7	8	9	10	11	12	13
14	15	16	17	18	19	20
21	22	23	24	25	26	27
28	29	30	31

If wishes were horses ...

04:15 @ Home
Had dreams of getting a good night's sleep on Friday night, but found myself restless, thinking about the Imperial employees serving their last day today. Some of them had probably spent their entire working lives with the bank. Their lives had now been brought to a rude halt by an impersonal email telling them their services were not required any further. I probably even knew some of them.

I had heard of layoffs, seen enough footage on the news and even knew a few people in India and abroad, who had gone through the trauma. Most had recovered and found decent jobs, but some were still wandering in the corporate jungle. This time it felt closer home. Especially because, with the events that had transpired over the previous week, the probability of my name appearing on a similar India list seemed distinctly within the realms of possibility.

I switched on the BlackBerry, which had been switched off after the expected and predictable argument with Savitha the previous night and compulsively clicked on the Twitter icon.

Imperial Insider: Over 6,000 employees received their pink slips across offices in the US today. More to come.

Imperial Insider: Over 800 employees received their pink slips in Canada today. More to come.

Imperial Insider: Pink slips in Europe to be rolled out on Monday.

Should have kept it switched off!

06:20
Resolutions of getting up late on Saturday had been forgotten. One tossing body on a double bed can be traumatic for the other.

Two tossing bodies, just terrible. We were both wide awake, with the pillows and our heads resting on the bedrest. Too tired to continue with the hostilities, a silent truce prevailed.

'You look miserable, Ravi. Didn't you get any sleep?' Savitha looked liked like a mess herself.

'Yes, of course, about 20 minutes, I think.' Both of us smiled, too tired to laugh.

'Is all this worth it?'

'Nope!'

Savitha looked out the bedroom window, smiled when the sun's rays caressed her face. 'So why do we keep pulling ourselves down? I am sure there is a silver lining out there, if we just step back and take a fresh look. '

I got bugged. 'What don't you understand, Savitha? My boss hates my guts, my CEO, the one champ I had, is being shunted to Siberia, the organization has a diktat to lay off 20 per cent of its staff, a merger of regions into zones is on the cards, I've been given suicidal numbers for the next year. So even if they don't fire me now, they'll have every chance to fire me in June – that's if my team doesn't take a contract out on my head when they see their final targets even before that ...'

It felt good to vent my frustration. But the objective outburst depressed me even further. The bullet points started appearing on the slide much more clearly. In perspective. A big black cloud minus the lining. Would have made for a fascinating presentation!

'Don't be a jerk!!'

'I hate it when you use that word, Sav.' It was okay when she used that word before marriage. I used to get turned on. But now it sounded offensive.

'Good. Purpose served! Now listen. You've been a good performer this year. Remember those congratulatory emails floating around at the beginning of the week ...'

'How'd you know about that?'

'I read your emails, honey. But ...'

'What do you mean, you read my emails! You can't do that!'

'I just did, so shut up and listen. You've made your numbers in the last two months. You've been a star performer for the last five years, got three promotions, you know your work, your team respects you ... and business comes in from the business guys. They're going to think twice about laying off performing guys. They do need the revenue clocking in. Logic demands they go after deadwood at head office and the support staff who can't easily justify their costs or contribution.'

Bravo, Savitha, bravo! If only she were my frigging CEO! It did make me feel good though. 'But Sav, if everything were so logical, it would have been very different. You know that.'

'Ravi, listen. I do need you to act or at least pretend to be positive when your wife is suffering from high blood pressure and is equally afraid of losing her job for even more irrational reasons than yours. Get it?'

'Yes, darling ...' I planted a kiss on the her cheek. Hmmm, maybe there will be some action finally.

Ding dong! Damn, the door bell.

I realized I should have been spending more time with her on her office situation. But I was so messed up. I just couldn't muster up the courage to have a sensible chat with her about it.

07:22

'Sav, are the kids up?'

'No. Told them they could sleep some more if they liked. Wish I could give them some tranquillizers or something. I just like it quiet like this.' Savitha seemed more jovial now.

'You're kidding, right?'

'No, Mr Banker! I mean it. God, you acting like a child, Ravi!'

Savitha inched closer and rested her head on my shoulder. She was still restless.

'Chill, Sav. We need to cool down, weigh our options.' Though I was trying to comfort her, I was hoping somewhere inside that the words would have an equal effect on me.

'I worry about the kids, Ravi. What's going to happen if ...' she shook her head vigorously.

'Don't worry, Sav.' I desperately needed to work on my motivational capabilities. I was sounding like a prisoner on death row. 'What are your options?'

'Good, you asked me about that. I listed them out yesterday in my diary. Just hang on,' she grabbed her purse from the bedside table, thrust her hand into the right pocket and pulled out an old brown leather diary. A gift from her father, of course.

'So, you reading it out loud?'

'Hang on, here goes. And not a word from you, okay?'

'Yes, ma'am!'

'One, sack out at home and eat your brains; two, painting and pottery making; three, fishing ...'

'But, you're a vegetarian.'

'You're too logical. That's your problem. Learn to think laterally! Four, teaching; five, sleeping 16 hours a day; six, go to the best spas in India and pamper myself and seven, join an NGO. What do you think?'

'Impressive. Think I should write one too?'

'Yes, it's very therapeutic.' She handed me her diary, a first ...

'Okay, here goes ... One, write a book; two, take out a contract on my boss; three, hire a cottage in the hills and take up teaching school kids in some quaint government school; four, trek across the Himalayas; five, go bungee jumping; six ... can't think any more ...'

'Do you see something? Neither of us actually wrote anything about working in some fancy corporate again. So, either we're genuinely screwed and incapable, or not really interested in this kind of life. Have you considered that?'

'Listen, Sav, these discussions always come up when things are tight. When mortgage payment dates come, we'll want to go scampering back to those same filthy jobs.'

'But, my dear husband, you still don't get it. Start thinking from scratch and see if it takes you to another path!'

67

Bucket lists may be fun. But the current situation needed focus and objectivity. Escapism was the easy route. But, if it helped her ...

'Listen, let's work it this way. I'll be the practical one and try and see how I can get the food on the table ... the same boring corporate salaried conventional way... why don't you go off the beaten path?'

'Buzz off, Ravi. You jerk!'

I was turned on again.

10:42

'What are you doing?' Savitha walked in with two cups of coffee.

'Looking at our investment statements!'

'And...'

'It doesn't look like the investment statement of a family with two senior professionals working in leading multinationals!'

'So, what's new? We're both impulsive. You're the quaintest of bankers, who guides everyone in town about their savings, but is almost suicidal about his own. So don't be so surprised, and out with it. This is my second cup of coffee, I can take it.'

'After the house purchase and renovation, the two international holidays of the last two years, our adventure with equities in some hot tip stocks ... you would be better off if I were to die today. I do have money on that stock tip given by Mayur. It's a matter of weeks. It's already up by over 23 per cent. It's a matter of a few more weeks and then we can exit. The mortgage is covered by an insurance policy, the term plan cover should see you comfortably through your spa treatments and a couple of affairs with men in the neighbourhood ...'

'Oh yummy! Which ones did you have in mind? Always wanted to do it with really older men. Less complicated,' she bit back, sipping coffee. I had a feeling she would have preferred pouring it in my lap right then.

'That also on your bucket list, Sav? Or are you waiting for me to kick the bucket?'

'You think I can wait that long? Na! I think I'll just get it over with this weekend.'

I wasn't sure whether she meant it and not liking the way this conversation was headed, I decided to deflect.

'Okay Sav, I'll line up all the retired men for you in the evening. But can we get back to the subject?'

'Yes, *Mr-I-Have-To-Be-Serious-On-A-Saturday-Morning-Banker*. How long can we make it if we're both fired on the 31st?'

We hadn't said it aloud till then. The thought made us sick.

'A few months easily …'

'I told you to keep buying me jewellery!'

'But, Sav, I am your jewel, sweetheart.'

'But I get bored of you very quickly too, darling! Plus I can't really polish you, can I?' Her smile was saccharine sweet.

11:38

'Boss!' Devendra was sounding frantic on the crackling connection on the cell.

'What's happened, Devendra?'

'Minor crisis in the Somajiguda branch at Hyderabad.'

'What happened?'

'Skirmish in the branch, boss. Two customers came in wanting to withdraw about ₹ 40 lakh. They wanted it in ₹ 1,000 notes!'

This didn't sound good. We didn't need a scandal … definitely not in my region, not any time soon!

'The customers started raising their voices, the situation started getting unruly. And then, Mithilesh landed up there, took the situation into his hands. Pushed our branch manager aside, throwing his seniority around.'

'But why did the branch manager allow this?'

'Boss, you know Mithilesh…'

'That has nothing to do with this. Why was Mithilesh in Hyderabad?'

'Don't know, boss.'

'So, what happened finally?'

'Mithilesh took the customers into a meeting room, apparently talked them out of it, defused the situation.'

'Anything else?'

'No, boss, that is it.'

'Devendra, visit each and every branch in Hyderabad in person! Got that! Every branch and report back. And I don't want silly rumours about Imperial running out of cash! You got that?'

'Yes, boss.'

I disconnected. What the hell was Mithilesh doing in Hyderabad?

The BlackBerry started vibrating furiously again. I scanned the emails and saw one from Amitabh. He had forwarded an email from Sriram that had been sent across to the entire senior management. Hyderabad had been thrown to the hyenas.

Soon, as expected, Amitabh was on the line.

'Ravi?'

'Sir?'

'What's all this nonsense about Hyderabad? Can't you manage even one simple situation? Can't your RM manage even one city?'

'Amitabh, please let me ex ...'

'No! You listen to me. If you need Mithilesh and his team to manage your region, tell me so. I'm very disappointed.' He hung up.

I read the emails again. Mithilesh had shot off an email to his boss Sriram, taking credit for quelling a potential volatile situation in Hyderabad that could have brought down the bank to its knees. Lord Mithilesh, the saviour! *Bastard!*

This was war. And the vultures were moving in.

22:18

The phone rang. I placed my glass on the floor and went to pick the phone up from the dining table.

Dad! Hadn't spoken with him for over two weeks.

'Dad! How are you?'

My father was an ex-army man and had been reluctantly supportive of my decision to move into corporate life. Not that I had given him too much of a choice.

'Good. How're the children, Savitha?'

'Fine!'

'Your mother and I are coming to Bangalore tomorrow. We're taking the afternoon flight. Pick us up at the airport, okay?'

I was being informed. Great! Battle on another front as well. 'Sure, Dad, would be great to have you over!'

I had barely 12 hours left to drink. Better top up quickly.

Received an SMS from the CEO: 'Will call around lunch tomorrow.'

What the hell? Was this a pink slip in advance? Was I being fired? But then, Amitabh or HR would have called me? But then again, these were strange times. Should I reach out to Amitabh? What did the CEO want? This would drive me mad. Another sleepless night loomed.

I couldn't speak with Vinesh, not this time. All these years in the bank and I didn't have a soul to reach out to. Why was everything caving in and around me?

That sinking feeling of helplessness had set in again. It was like quicksand, it just sucked you in, deeper, deeper and even deeper! I desperately needed something to clutch on to. Was there a rewind button somewhere?

March

	1	2	3	4	5	6
7	8	9	10	11	12	13
14	15	16	17	18	19	20
21	22	23	24	25	26	27
28	29	30	31			

To be a successful manager, you must learn to be insensitive to the needs of your employees.

– Dilbert

11:44 @ Home

'Sir, good to hear from you. How are you?' The CEO rarely called. I realized I was terrified and decided to calm myself. I needed to be positive. Think of good memories, happy things, smiling faces, bright colours and all that other psycho babble!

'Saw your email. Good to see your team so charged up. Will see you in Bangalore next week.'

'The team is looking forward to seeing you too, sir.'

Come out with it, you jerk. If it's bad news, don't give it to me the hard way. Maybe he genuinely wanted to speak with me about the restructuring. Or were they planning to send the security team over to my house and pick up my laptop? No need to even go into the office tomorrow. They would probably seize my car as well! They might as well have lined me up against the wall and sprayed me with bullets. That would have been a chivalrous way to leave this planet! Not over some frigging phone call!

'Ravi, how many times have I said, call me Vikram? Did I mention I have nominated you as the top talent with the HR leadership in NY?'

He knew he hadn't told me. We hadn't spoken for months, courtesy Amitabh, of course.

'Thank you, sir!'

'They're trying to come up with something for you in Hong Kong.'

Great! The bullshit session had started. He must need something bad. Hong Kong was the holiday home for dignitaries passing through Asia.

'But I thought we were in the midst of layoffs? Would this be a good time, sir?'

'That's in wholesale banking. Retail should be fine. How's your family?' He was really stretching this one. Had I missed something somewhere?

'Fine, Vikram. The kids are growing so fast, barely recognize them any more.'

'Good to hear that. I was just thinking, how's your relationship moving with the Milsons Group?'

Milsons was an old and diversified conglomerate based out of Bangalore. They had recently taken a stake in a south Indian bank and had also launched a Finance Company, though it really hadn't picked up steam. We managed their corporate accounts, but not for too long, considering their recent banking acquisition.

'We manage their corporate accounts, sir. We are one of three banks ...'

'Think you can fix up a meeting for me with their chairman when I'm in Bangalore?'

The son of a gun was asking me to line up his interview! Must have been really desperate to call. Something big must be going down. Discretion was being bartered for the good word that he had put in with the HR team. Shit, no gossip value in this one. Had to let this one go.

The nerves finally calmed. I would retain my car and cabin tomorrow morning. I had survived. The panic attack receded.

'Will get back to you by day after, sir!'

'Thanks, Ravi. And have a great day.'

Imperial Insider: Vikram has started packing his bags!

For a change, I was ahead of this blasted Twitter! I smiled to myself.

15:48

Picked up my parents from the airport. It felt good to have them over. My job status, professional progress, work–life balance, nicotine addiction, obvious slurs in the evening conversations and a host of other subjects were discussed at some length.

Once a discussion started on post-graduate academic options for my children, I threw in the towel and retired, leaving Savitha to address these world-shaping events with my parents. A Sunday siesta beckoned.

17:48
Sunday siesta brutally interrupted ...

'Ravi? Ravi, get up! Why are you sleeping? We'll be late for the 6:45 movie.' It usually took Savitha a couple of days to settle down when my parents were in town. She got along fabulously with them. But it took her time to find the balance between the traditional Indian daughter-in-law and the corporate professional.

'Why don't you go with them? The driver is there. So they won't miss me either? I hate that Shah Rukh fellow anyway. Reminds me of my boss!'

'I'm the one with the high BP and I spent the whole morning in that hot kitchen making hot food for your parents, Ravi!'

'Got the message, Sav. You win ...'

20:36 @ The Multiplex, in Pain
I walked out of the movie and sat in the common area at a safe distance from the food stalls. The kids were bored enough to sleep off and even Savitha appeared to sympathize with me as I walked away.

'Sir?'

I looked up and saw Karan with his wife. Quite a stunner. I suddenly realized that, from my vantage point, I had been staring at her bosom longer than would be considered decent. But they were truly blossoming and seemed eager to break free from their shackles.

Shit! Now I was getting orgasms over my junior's wife's bosom. Really had to to get some action, de-stress ... Or, given the way the bases were loading up, I would end up with a harassment charge too.

I forced my head back towards Karan, though the my eyes continued to wander in the direction of the dual wonders.

'Hi, Karan. Which movie?'

'Came to watch Shah Rukh Khan, but decided to catch a few drinks midway! Couldn't take it any longer!'

The bosom excused itself to go to the washroom and Karan sat down beside me. The situation within the trousers eased. But the mind continued to wander in smoky bedrooms. How the hell did Karan manage to work till so late at the office?

'Boss, I've been meaning to speak with you. Can I take a few minutes?'

'Shoot, Karan?'

'Should I be looking out? Not that there's anything out there. The market is quite dead.'

'What's on your mind, Karan. Speak freely.'

'Raghu was on a long call with Amitabh yesterday!'

What the heck was my Chennai head doing on a call with my boss?

'Must have been a routine chat. Who told you this?' I was simmering inside.

'I was trying to reach him to get some details on one of my clients who had moved in from Chennai. Couldn't get through. So I spoke with his team. Their meeting got postponed twice because of the call!'

His wife emerged soon after, looking just as ravishing as earlier.

'Thanks, boss. Let's catch up in office.'

Not that I had a choice. But I was intrigued with this new twist and ended up tormenting myself even further that night.

Force of habit prompted me to click on the Twitter icon as I walked back to Mr Khan's magnum opus.

Imperial Insider: Shakeout @ Imperial India. Top brass heads to roll this week!

Imperial Insider: Frauds being investigated in Bangalore @ Imperial. Heads to roll!

At least they didn't take my name. Not that it mattered. I was the boss in Bangalore. If there was a screw up, I would be held responsible. And the whole frigging world would know about it.

I was exhausted. Seriously wasn't ready for Monday, and SRK wasn't helping!

March

	1	2	3	4	5	6
7	**8**	9	10	11	12	13
14	15	16	17	18	19	20
21	22	23	24	25	26	27
28	29	30	31			

'Mondays are not part of the productive work week ...'

06:36

An SMS from the Risk Head.

'*Check your gmail ... urgent. Amit*'

Why the hell didn't I put my BB on silent? The damn wi-fi connection took forever to boot. I moved to the balcony and lit a cigarette. As I opened Amit's email, the doorbell rang.

'Savitha, please get the door!'

'Don't lose your head so early in the morning. You can be such an asshole,' she snapped, then realized my parents were in audible distance, slapped her forehead and muttered as she got off the bed.

I had finally managed to open the email attachments, as Savitha came into the balcony with a cup of hot coffee.

'Savitha, I need to rush into office ...'

'What's going on, Ravi. You're scaring me! At least have breakfast with your parents. You just can't run off like this. You also promised to take the kids out shopping with their grandparents today! Remember?'

As if on cue, the kids came running into the room and the ritualistic pillow fight commenced. Their shopping list soon emerged. Why in God's name hadn't I got their shopping done yesterday! Why in God's name did Barbie emerge with a new avatar every week and why did Ben10 need to produce T-shirts, now that their cartoons had ruined the family fabric as we knew it!

I hugged them tightly till Srikanth said I was choking him. The email flashed into memory again.

'Not now, Sav ... please not now ...'

07:22

I called up Karan. 'Get ready. I'm picking you up in 20 minutes!'

'What? What happened, boss?'

'Get ready!'

I hung up.

As I approached the main door, my mom walked towards me; a silver platter laden with a lit lamp, a *prasadam* of yoghurt and sugar and a host of other holy stuff.

'Amma ... I'm in a hurry.'

Her reply was succinct. 'Shut up!'

Possibly not the most holy of utterances, but had the desired impact. I bowed in silent obeisance. She swung the plate with the lamp around my face and applied a speck of vermillion to my forehead, to get rid of evil spirits haunting my life. A similar ritual was performed in medieval times when warriors went out to battle or when lambs were put to slaughter! She was on the right course, in either case, but I had yet to decide which one I was.

07:59 @ Office

I picked up Karan as I sped into office. The traffic hadn't picked up yet and so I managed to make it in record time. I parked at an awkward angle in my rush, blocking two slots and raced up the stairs, not even waiting for the lift, with an alarmed Karan following on my heels.

'Karan, log into the Core Banking System (CBS) and extract these account details!' I handed a piece of paper with details of three accounts.

The CBS was Imperial's main database in which all customer banking records and transaction details were stored. I opened my room and booted my laptop. As I waited for the screen to light up, I searched for my cupboard keys in the desk drawer but couldn't find them. *Damn!* I was getting too dependent on Radhika!

'Karan ...' I shouted.

He came running.

'Get the cupboard opened ASAP!'

The Internal Audit team would be in by 10, I needed to rush.

Karan ran out and returned quickly, dropping the piece of paper I had handed over to him earlier on my table. He had scribbled the names of the account holders against the numbers. I read them aloud.

1043576548 : Mayur Agarwal
1043576952 : Srinath Ramnathan
1043578557 : Natwar Kamal

Karan returned with a member of the admin staff and the cupboard was opened. I handed the paper to Karan and asked him to log in from my laptop and show me the details.

I shut the door and searched for the compliance file in my cupboard. It was on the second shelf from the top in the front. I opened the file and found the documents I was looking for. The KYC (Know Your Customer) deviation requests for the three accounts. They all had my signature on them! *Shit!*

The KYC deviation requests were taken in exceptional cases where a VIP customer was unable to furnish all the KYC norms, with the express understanding that they would be completed within 24 hours of account opening. Checks and balances were put in place to ensure the account could not be used till the formalities were completed. But somehow these accounts seemed to have slipped through.

'Karan, what's the transaction activity on these accounts?'

'Fishy, sir, very fishy. All accounts were opened on 25 February. Seventy thousand dollars transferred into the first account in February and one more for $20,000 came in on Monday. But these have been transferred into ... guess?'

' ...the other two?'

'Yup, and all three accounts are now cleaned out. Got just a few rupees in them now. Minimum balance, right?'

'What's in the file, sir?'

'The KYC deviation requests ...'

'Sir, I remember these cases. They came from Chennai, with

a note indicating they were some important business clients moving to Bangalore and needed the accounts opened urgently!'

'Who is the bank officer in Bangalore?'

'The system is showing opening dates, but I am not able to track the officer's name here. Will need to check the actual application form to figure that one. Let me call up someone in Operations.'

'No, Karan, hang on. Any other way to crack this one?'

'Can call up Mumbai. I know the Operations Manager. He's family. He should be able to retrieve the scanned copy.'

'Get to it!'

I settled on the chair. The clock read 08:07. I picked up the bottle of water and gulped down over half its contents. I still felt parched. The heartbeat was gaining speed.

Karan returned at 08:14.

'This is crazy. No bank officer names on the application forms. Only your signature! No clue how the accounts got opened? They just passed through all the checks. You do know what this means, right?'

'I think they call it money laundering, Karan ... and KYC breach!'

'This is bad, sir!'

'I know, Karan. Damn it, I know!'

So far, I had an untarnished career. No scandals or reconciliation issues. No whiff of underhand dealings. This was alien territory. It wasn't a good place to be, especially not now.

08:38

We had both run out of clues to figure out who got these accounts opened. We had gone for a smoke and ended up finishing two each instead. Needed a guy who knew the processes inside out.

'Sridhar!' I had called from my landline.

'Yes, Ravi, good morning, you in office already?'

'Yup! How long will you take to get in?'

'Another 22 seconds!' he laughed.

'Great. Make that 15 seconds. In my office.' I hung up.

That should shake him up. But could I trust him? It was a chance I would have to take. Right now, I needed his experience and more importantly, I trusted his judgement.

'What's your take on Sridhar?' I asked Karan.

'We don't have too many options right now, sir. We need him. He understands branch operations like no one else. He's the man!'

Sridhar walked in to see us both awaiting his arrival anxiously.

'Good morning. What's up with you two?' Sridhar placed his bag on the chair, folded his hands together in a namaste and looked at me. *Is he praying for me?*

Karan took him through all the accounts on the system.

'A major breach, Ravi!'

'Crack this one, Sridhar. You've got about an hour!'

Sridhar looked at me. It was one of those *'you owe me'* looks.

'Karan, come with me. Gimme a couple of minutes, Ravi. Will get back. Oh, and cross your fingers.'

I thought Sridhar sounded sincere enough.

09:07

'Ravi, what was the rush? I needed to speak with you about something important!'

We had the whole damn weekend and she had to choose this Monday of all days!

'What is it?!'

'I'm thinking of putting in my papers. I hope you understand. I can't take this any more. It's affecting our lives. It's affecting our marriage.'

Now was not the time. I just wasn't prepared for this. But how was I to say to her that her husband might be going to jail, so it may be a good idea to cling on to whatever she had for as many days as she was getting paid for!

'Savitha, I am with you, no matter what. But I really need to rush!' I felt like banging the phone down and my head as well.

'You sure you understand?' Savitha persisted.

'Sav, trust me. It's cool. It's okay, honey.' This time I did disconnect.

Damn! Why couldn't she manage these situations? Didn't she understand that I was in too deep? I turned down the temperature setting on the AC, but the sweating continued. I was soaking wet in a freezing cold air-conditioned room. I was nervous. Not a good nervous. But one of those *'you're going down'* nervous! Was I having a frigging stroke? It wasn't uncommon for males in their 30s to get cardiac attacks and collapse. That would be better than this shit!

What the hell was happening to me? Why in God's name was I getting so pessimistic? I just needed to stay positive. It was a damn job. I could get tons if I focused. I had managed a multi-crore business, after all. I could surely get another job!

10:28

Karan and Sridhar walked in.

'Where the hell have you guys been?'

'Boss, some things you should know and some you shouldn't. But you have to trust us on this!' Karan was still catching his breath.

I paused to process his words. My career and reputation were on the line. Didn't really know whom to trust any more, but decided to follow my gut!

'I'm with you guys. What's happening?'

'We've got the KYC documents, should do the trick for now at least!' Sridhar had a mischievous smile.

'Should I ask how?'

'Let's just say I know someone. He can arrange this kind of stuff. In this case we needed only photocopies, so it became simpler.' Sridhar was thrilled. Possibly more exciting than his usual mundane existence in the back office.

'You do know what you're asking me to be a party to? What if they find these documents to be false?'

'They can't hold you on that! It's a savings account. Not a loan, so that should be okay!'

'That takes care of the KYC violation. What about the money laundering?'

Sridhar stepped in, 'That's for the Fraud team. They might rap us on our knuckles at most, but I can take the heat. Will get the Fraud guy into the loop, but you have something else to worry about?'

'What's that?' This was turning into a farcical case of mishaps.

'There are no bank officers' names on the application form other than yours?'

'*Great!* Now what? I get the feeling you're on top of that too!'

'Afraid not. But need to know where those applications did come in from? Chennai? And, who opened the accounts?'

'We've got 30 minutes at most to crack this.'

'Sir, can I log in from your laptop?' Karan was smiling again. Wanted to knock him down for smiling.

'Please be my guest, Karan,' I rose from my chair and invited him to the laptop.

'Sir, I have checked the account holders. These names don't exist. These customers don't have any other relationship with the bank!'

'What does that mean?'

'Quite clearly you've been set up. That's confirmed! The only lead we have is my recollection of these papers coming in from the Chennai office, but I can't recollect who sent them. I do have a hunch though. Should I go for it?' Karan had a twinkle in his eye.

'Go, Karan!'

Karan called up a number from his mobile. 'Raghu?'

He placed it on speaker mode. 'Hi, Karan, how're you doing?'

'Good Raghu, good. Listen, you remember you had sent three accounts to be opened in Bangalore last month? Well, you see we have their cheque books, but the courier is unable to get them delivered. Would you have the contact details in Chennai for

Mayur Agarwal, Srinath Ramnathan and Natwar Kamal? It's urgent. The system here is indicating they had placed an urgent request and I wanted to make sure your clients don't get upset.' Karan shot off the words at lightning speed, ensuring Raghu didn't get a chance to interrupt.

A long pause. 'I'll have to get back to you on that one, Karan.'

'Shall I send an email, Raghu?'

'Don't bother. I'll get back to you!'

We were silent for two minutes.

Sridhar looked at the clock. 'Your call, boss?'

'What do you mean, my call, Sridhar? How are we going to prove it?'

'You don't want to know, boss.'

Sridhar was suggesting we forge Raghu's signatures on the account opening forms.

11:07

'Hi Sameer! Good to see you. It's been a long time.'

Sameer was puzzled. Employees generally didn't miss people in his department. He also didn't seem comfortable with the effusive greeting, especially with his senior from Singapore present.

'Hi, Ravi. Allow me to introduce Mr Lee. He's from Singapore.' Lee, a short petite chap, did not present a very sociable disposition.

'Mr Shastry, sorry for not reaching on time. We do have quite a few matters to discuss and I would suggest that we get started immediately. May we sit down?'

'Please. Can I offer you some coffee?'

'No thanks, Ravi. Bottled water will be fine,' Sameer continued to maintain his morose tone. Must have been in his training manual.

'Radhika, some water for the gentlemen, please.'

They had already settled down at my table, logged onto their laptops and extracted several folders from their large black cases.

As I stepped towards my chair, Lee started, 'Ravi, the purpose of our visit is two-fold. This is a routine audit discussion. We will be engaging some of your team members along with some other department staff. Let's get started, shall we?'

I paused. The incidents earlier in the morning flashed by. I needed to mentally recuperate or at least get a breather before I dived into this discussion ... I was saved by an SMS. The phone buzzed.

'Please give me a moment. Need to take this, will be back with you shortly ...'

I stepped out of the room and clicked on the SMS from Maithili.

'I'm jealous ... you're having an affair with Sameer! Call when free ...'

Damn! Everyone seemed to know everything that was happening in my life!

Hadn't spoken with her since I had heard about the sexual harassment case. She was a friend. My confidante. We had risen together in the organization. Did our friendship finally clash with our career aspirations? It seemed so clichéd. Didn't seem right. Wasn't in the mood for such inane chatter from Maithili on the Interal Audit matter. Didn't want to give too many details either. I was just confused about her and where I stood with her in the spate of recent events.

The mobile rang. It was the boss! 'Yes, sir ...'

'What's happening in Hyderabad? Have the RMs been retained? Haven't received any update ...' He went on about some other random subjects. I didn't particularly care. Needed to address matters one at a time. Amitabh was getting on my nerves! He needed to get laid ... get a life. Something! Anything!

I entered the cabin and noticed both Lee and Sameer checking their emails and whispering some numbers.

'Sorry about that. Needed to attend to those calls. Shall we get started?'

Lee started again, 'Ravi, we've come across some high levels of fraud on some Credit Card customers referred by you.'

87

Whoa! Where did this come from? Had no clue about this. Had I been going down the wrong frigging alley for the last couple of hours?

'I've not been informed about these?'

'Well, you've referred four customers in the last three months. Each had been issued a ₹ 5 lakh credit limit on your recommendation. All of them have almost maxed out their credit and are refusing to pay the bills.' Lee's voice was getting graver.

I vaguely recollected the customer names. Again, passed to me by Raghu Nair from Chennai. Raghu had mentioned that he had forgotten to sign on the referral forms and had confirmed that he would do so later. The slime ball! What had he gotten me into now?

As a regional head, I was allowed to refer, or recommend, some customers for credit cards and suggest limits. These were typically done in cases where we wanted to make sure that some important clients got decent credit limits and were not harassed by the verification team. In any case of the customer failing to pay up, I didn't have a legal obligation to pay the dues, but a moral responsibility in aiding the collection effort from the customer.

'But if it's on their cards, how can they refute?'

'Well …' Lee handed over the statements, 'You will notice many high-value international transactions on their cards.'

I scanned quickly through the statements and noticed some fancy brands, mostly in Canada and North America. The cards had been used for extravagant purchases, including luxury watches and fancy restaurants.

'So, why didn't these customers receive calls from the fraud team when they noticed so many high-value international transactions. Isn't that the standard procedure?'

'We are checking on that as well, but that's a different matter,' Lee seemed to have the case details covered. He had come in for the kill.

'So, why aren't they paying up?'

'They've shown the collections team their passports. They haven't left the country since last October!' Lee looked blankly into my eyes, waiting for my response.

'What's the total amount due?' I was dreading the response, too afraid to total the outstanding amounts myself.

'₹ 16.78 lakh and that's only the principal. Late fees and charges are climbing even as we speak,' Lee continued to hammer in the details. He was obviously relishing this.

'Have you matched the signatures on the charge slips?'

'We have received some ... The signatures match!'

'So, that makes them responsible, right?'

'Possibly, but they have their passports to defend them!'

'So, these are cases of fraudulent cards?'

'All four, Ravi? Too much of a coincidence, don't you think?'

Sameer's mobile started vibrating. I looked up. It was an SMS from Amitabh. They were exchanging notes?

12:43

I tried reaching Raghu, but he wasn't taking my calls or replying to my messages. Radhika finally tracked him down from another line and patched him in.

'Hi boss! You trying to reach me?'

The prick!

'Yes, Raghu, you've been busy?'

'No, boss, some problem on my cell phone!' He sounded tense, or was I reading too much into this?

'How's business, Raghu? Your numbers are not looking too good in the first week!' Needed to play him.

'No, boss, we are on track.'

'You're behind by 18 per cent, Raghu. How can you be on track?'

'But we had an off on Friday, boss. You know how that impacts business? If we had that day, we would have been in line.'

'Don't bullshit!'

Muted silence on the other end. Raghu wasn't going to counter. He had decided to lie low.

89

'... And, Raghu, audit is examining some of the Credit Card customers referred by you!'

'What query, boss?' he shot back. He had been prepared for this one.

'Four customers who are taking the bank to the cleaners, Raghu! They are committing fraud ... and ...'

'What customers, boss? Please send me the details.'

This was going to be an uphill climb.

'Radhika will be sending the details. Have a look and call me back.'

'Yes, boss ...' He disconnected.

He was in on it. My gut just told me. No, actually, it was screaming at me that he was the culprit. But what the hell was he up to? A smart banker wouldn't risk his career on some small-time card fraud! Didn't make sense. What did he have against me? Who else was in on this? Raghu couldn't possibly be in on this alone. Quite unlikely!

15:18

'Sav, how're you doing?' I had been meaning to call her since morning, but wanted to make sure that at least I would be able to talk rationally.

'As good as can be. How 'bout you?' She wasn't sounding too good.

'Listen, why don't you leave early? The folks are also there. You'll be able to get your mind off things.'

'Don't want my mind off things. I need to address them. Been drifting around for days now. I'm better than this and want to take down some of these suckers before they touch me. I've served this company for eons. They can't behave so heartlessly.'

'Chill, Sav, it'll work out.'

'Don't "chill Sav" me, okay? I know you're fighting back yourself. Need to start my battles here as well. It's just that ...' She paused, restraining herself.

'Sav ...'

'I don't know if I want to fight any longer. Not this fight, at least. Is it really worth it? Not sure if this is what I want? Am I making sense? This is all muddled up, Ravi ... think we can step out for a few margaritas today? Really need to sack out. Like we used to ... God, that seems like another age!'

Radhika stepped into the room. 'Sir, the auditors are asking for you.'

Damn!

'Sav, we'll have to catch up later. Let me see if I can step out early. Hang in there.'

'Right!' Savitha hung up. She would have possibly hung me as well if she had the chance.

'Radhika, can you get me out of the office by 5 today? I'll owe you a million bucks!'

'You don't have a million bucks! But let me see what I can do.'

16:24

Sameer and Lee had moved on to investigating some other cases of mis-selling insurance and investments. I walked into the conference room and saw Sameer and Lee interrogating my team, flashing documents, photocopies of cheques and client investment summaries. The team was looking flustered. This was a new experience for them. The bar near the office would be doing brisk business today for sure.

'Sameer, how's it going? I have an engagement at 5:30 and was wondering if we could summarize for the day.'

The team heaved a sigh of relief. Karan whispered, 'Thanks.'

'We will be staying back tonight, Ravi. We are scheduled for a flight tomorrow. So let's connect in the morning tomorrow. I think your team can leave as well.'

'Thanks, Sameer. Karan, you and your team can leave for now. Is there anything else I can do for you?'

Sameer waited for the team to leave.

'In fact, Ravi, remember those three accounts I had asked you about in the morning? There appears to be some suspicious transactions on those accounts. We are investigating those. We were under the impression that the KYC documents were not complete, but they are. So that one appears to be fine for now.'

He appeared frustrated as he said it. That would have demolished his ratings for sure.

I wanted to press on when the going was good.

'Okay! And on these client complaints?'

'We'll file our report next week, but these appear to be cases of clients changing their minds after giving their consent. Nothing out of the ordinary. The paperwork seems to be in order. But will let you know tomorrow. We've got a conference call with Singapore in the next half hour, so we will continue using this room. Is that okay with you?'

'Sounds good. Do let Radhika know if you require anything else?' I shook their hands and walked out. My hands had been perspiring.

Had I crossed the line? My conscience was killing me.

18:36 @ Koshys, Two Down ... Several More to Go

I was two beers down and was halfway down the third. The world felt tons lighter. Savitha had stuck to her fresh lime soda, avoiding the margaritas!

We had avoided discussing office and went down the memory lane of favourite songs, bands, family screw ups and all the other good old stuff. The simpler times when we had both started out and were terribly broke. Partying heavily, maxing out our card limits and even borrowing from home on occasion.

'Sav, you're looking distracted.'

'Maybe because I've got something else on my mind!' she paused again. I hated it when she paused. What bombshell was she about to drop now? I just couldn't take any more missiles today. My defence mechanisms had been obliterated. Needed time to recoup!

'Are the kids okay? Has Srikanth got fever again?'

'No, Ravi. Srikanth is fine ... at least, he was in the morning.'

'Then it must be Revathi? What did she do now?'

'It's not Revathi, Ravi.'

'Let this be something good. Or, I'll need a pacemaker very soon!'

'You'll need to find names for another baby!'

'You're kidding, right?'

'I had come prepared for any and every possible reaction. And trust me I understand. My head's been screwed up since morning too.'

'A baby!' I released a smile, though it did take some time.

Then, Savitha surprised me. 'Ravi, do we really want this baby now?'

I was taken aback by her objectivity. *Was this a trap? Was she testing me?* Shit, the beer wasn't helping. If only she would say what she was actually thinking? If only I wasn't so many beers down! If only ...

'Sav, what do you have in mind?'

'I'm thinking of dropping the baby. Think I should have an abortion. I don't think we're ready for this right now. And it's not as if we had planned for this anyway. We hardly get enough time with the two we have. What do you think?'

This was good, but was it? Didn't I have an opinion or role to play in this decision? How could she have just made up her mind? I agreed with her, but she could have at least pretended to wait for my viewpoint. The beer was soon losing its kick.

'I'll support you in whichever decision you take, Sav!'

'Don't be a prick, Ravi. This has to be a joint decision.'

This meant I needed to figure out her choice and back it. She wouldn't tell me clearly. That would have been too simple. I needed to get her sloshed ... and quickly, but on lime soda?

'I think I agree with you on this one. There's too much happening right now for both of us.'

I crossed my fingers below the table. Did I just screw up my marriage? I hated having to take critical decisions with Kingfisher. What a waste of good draught!

March

9

Shades of Grey

06:24 @ Home

My parents hadn't taken too well to the unannounced and joint return home of an inebriated son and a beaming daughter-in-law the previous night. We had planned to be back by 8 pm, but the potent mix of Koshys, Kingfisher and nostalgia had kept us going till well past 10.

Both Savitha and I woke early to make amends. Savitha couldn't stop giggling, watching me change into a pristine white kurta and pyjama. Felt like a kid again. Dad was seated in the balcony adjoining the drawing room and Mom was preparing coffee, as we stepped out of the bedroom scrubbed clean. The kids were mercifully asleep, allowing us quiet time with them.

'Good morning, Dad! Slept well?'

He had the newspaper folded as he poured over the written word. It was on his favourite – the edit page. He glanced up at me and then decided to get back to the education system.

I sat next to Dad. Fortunately, Mom arrived shortly after with piping hot coffee in steel tumblers. A quaint but delightful ritual that reminded me of my childhood every time.

Savitha and I had decided to share with them the recent incidents at our respective offices as well as the potential risks that we faced on our salary slips. It would help clear the air.

'Dad, we have something to share,' I started tentatively.

'Let me guess, you're both ashamed of your irresponsible behaviour. And also that both of you might be losing your jobs. Right?'

I was perplexed. Savitha and I had made every effort to keep our current professional issues out of our conversations with the folks, but they had obviously figured it out.

'What have you heard, Dad?'

'Savitha's parents called last night from Singapore. Can you imagine? We hear this from your in-laws, Ravi! Don't you trust us enough to share these important matters with us? Don't you think we read newspapers?'

Great! My frigging father-in-law! Couldn't he do something else with his life rather than sabotaging mine?

'But, Dad, we didn't want to trouble you with such small issues. These things are common in corporate life, you should know that,' Savitha stepped in, hoping to appease the hurt.

She looked at me and then continued, 'Dad, Mom, we actually have something else we would like to share with you. Something more important!'

'What? That you both have been fired, already?' Dad could be biting when riled.

'I'm expecting again, Dad.'

What?! What in frigging hell just happened here? There were hugs and kisses all around. Savitha appeared obviously thrilled. *Bloody illogical!* My mother bounded towards the guest bedroom searching for the Hindu calendar! *Jesus!* The whole family had gone insane!

06:48

Received an SMS: *'In town. Let's meet for lunch? Rgds Kaushal'*

Though Kaushal, the ex-sales head, had moved from Imperial under unpleasant circumstances, the move to Oriental had been a positive one for him. Oriental was nearly four times larger than Imperial and had much wider interests. They had been quite strong in the North and West and were looking to expand their presence in the South. With Kaushal moving in, the South territory had possibly started gaining momentum.

I had been wondering why he hadn't contacted me yet. I had a fairly good equation with him and had even taken him out for dinner with Savitha when he was in Bangalore towards the end of his stint. So, there was the family connect as well.

Checked the calendar on the BlackBerry. It was a packed day

with several meetings clashing. My early departure yesterday would have further screwed up today's schedule with the added bonus of the Internal Audit team pissing around in the office.

But I had to keep him warm and decided to be warm, yet noncommittal. *'Will get back to you by 10. Would need to reschedule some engagements. Rgds Ravi.'*

I had yet to recuperate from Savitha's morning announcement. Everything around me seemed to be in a haze. Nothing was making sense. Memories of swollen ankles, late night warm milk preparations, diaper-shopping, outrageous mood swings, astronomical medical bills – all started coming back to me. The glory of seeing one's progeny, the wonders of seeing the head pop out of the womb were soon overshadowed by the prospect of borrowing money to buy the morning milk for the newborn.

Mine was increasingly getting to be an amazingly pissed-on life.

08:43 En Route to Office

Had volunteered to drop Savitha off to work. The talk at Koshys had put things in a clearer perspective. I was livid about her decision to keep the baby. Why couldn't things just be simple?

'Sav, what happened this morning?'

'Why? What happened?'

What happened? You freak, you just turned my world upside down. We had made a decision. We shook hands on something. We had a rational discussion, for a change. I endorsed your decision. We reviewed our financial and professional positions and the rapidly changing dynamics in the world order and our miserable lives.

'What do you mean, what happened? Why did you change your mind about the baby?'

'I didn't change my mind, Ravi. You said you would support my decision. I don't understand you, sometimes …'

The prospect of jumping out of the moving car was terribly appealing. I felt like banging her head and mine right then.

Murky clippings from *Psycho* and *Nightmare on Elm Street* played rapidly in my mind. Suicide seemed an appropriate reaction, but I wasn't particularly sure if my insurance would cover self-inflicted death.

There was only one logical explanation. Savitha had adopted senility as the chosen path. Decided that further confrontation would be a lost cause.

'So what have you planned at work? What's your next move?'

She seemed surprised with the deft change in subject, but appeared to welcome it. This was neutral territory.

'Couple of options. I can take a gun and shoot some of those Americans hanging around in the office leading this integration programme ...'

I smiled. ' Sav, I really don't want our child to be born in jail ...'

'That would be the least of my worries. I'm also looking at positions in other departments. The problem is that with 12 years' work experience, I would be treading on some senior shoes outside my department. Would need to either pray for someone to leave or literally displace some other poor sod. A major reorganization is being undertaken across other departments as well. The shit is spreading. Everyone is in a turf war, clinging on to whatever they've got. The inter-departmental meetings are beginning to look like cockfights. It's pathetic. You know what's even sicker?'

'That, you are losing sleep over that bunch of assholes,' I said.

'Yes, that too. But that I'm becoming like them. Even I've started picking up small issues and blowing them out of proportion. It's a bloody email war out there. Ridiculous!' Savitha was clenching her fists.

We remained silent for a few minutes.

'Any further news on the list? How's it going to work?' Savitha asked.

'Possibly two to three months, advance pay and bye-bye! I've been doing the math. If the shit does hit the ceiling, we can stay afloat for a few months. I'm sure I'll get something decent.

The market has opened up now. I have a decent track record. It's just a matter of time and sticking around, I guess.'

'You believe what you've just said?'

Savitha was as sharp as ever. I hated her guts, right now. But I knew I had made the bullshit speech of the century. Even I didn't believe a word of it!

'The prospect of sitting at home is scaring the living daylights out of me. It's driving me crazy. Don't know what's gotten into me! I've become a nervous wreck. My confidence has taken a beating in the last one week. This is unfamiliar territory, and now with the baby coming …'

But there was a lot I did not say. There was a lot more. The prospect of seeing Maithili and Dheeraj rising up the corporate ladder, with me out of a job was tearing me apart. It had been haunting my every living moment for the last couple of days.

10:08 @ Office

I was heading towards the coffee machine, when the BlackBerry vibrated. An email from Fiona, the CEO's secretary. A super-efficient perfectionist, she had come in from the hospitality industry and had been around for five years. She was the CEO's eyes, ears and Man Friday. Ran a very tight ship. You didn't want to get on her wrong side.

'*Subject : Mr Rathore's visit to Bangalore*

Ravi, please call. Need to finalize boss' schedule in Bangalore. Believe you are fixing some meetings for him there. Please ASAP.'

Got the coffee and bumped into Sameer who had just walked in.

'Good morning, Sameer. Slept well?'

'Yes, thanks Ravi.'

'And, where's Lee? Coming later?'

'He's down with a stomach infection. Was up most of the night. The hotel doctor advised him bed rest and put him on some medication.'

'Poor chap! So, how's it going?'
'Not well. But Amitabh called last night. Gave him a download.'
'How about one for me?'
'Ravi, I have worked in a branch you know. I know what happens and what can happen? I didn't want to say this with Lee around, but off the record, you did something which you shouldn't have. You do know that, right?' He was staring at me.

I maintained eye contact and responded calmly, 'I have no clue what you're talking about, Sameer.'

'Those documents are fake. You know that!' Sameer was testing me.

The pauses were emphatic. He had an agenda, and he had been thwarted. He wasn't going to let go so easily.

'No clue, Sameer. And what's the issue with those accounts anyway?'

'They appear to have some underworld connections. You don't want to be anywhere near them!'

'Thanks for the heads up. Will await your memo.' I smiled.

Sameer smiled back. 'See you in Mumbai some time.'

He had maintained his silence on the Credit Card matter. I wasn't interested enough in pursuing the discussion either. Raghu hadn't reverted yet.

12:58

I hadn't yet cracked the key to Milsons. Karan had backed out of this one. His connections only took him up to the middle management. I needed to claw my way up, quickly. And alone!

Clicked on LinkedIn and searched for people working with Milsons. The query displayed over a few hundred results. These guys were really active on LinkedIn. They either believed in the power of networking or were desperately looking for jobs!

As I scrolled down, I noticed a familiar name. My classmate from business school. We hadn't been in touch for quite some time.

'Radhika!'

She stepped in, this time grumpy looking. 'Ravi, please don't keep screaming my name. There is an intercom, you know?'

'Can you get hold of Ravindra Kodapally at Milsons? Track him down through the board number.'

I looked up Ravindra's profile. He was heading risk at their Non-Banking Financial Company (NBFC) arm. Must have got a sweet packet to switch from an MNC.

13:06

I called up Raghu. He still hadn't replied to the email.

'I was waiting for your reply on the cards matter we discussed yesterday?'

The customary pause and then he replied, 'But, sir, I don't remember these applications. They may have been sent by one of my team members.'

'Who, Raghu? You should know, right?'

'May have been my sales manager Chaturvedi ...'

'Have you spoken with him?'

'Can't trace him, he quit last month. But have asked the team to trace him.'

He had played me. This was going nowhere.

13:24 @ The Taj Residency Lobby

I was waiting for Kaushal. There were too many familiar faces floating around and I was contemplating requesting a change in venue, when the mobile rang.

'Ravi? How're you doing? Come to room no. 358, please. Thanks!' Kaushal disconnected.

This was better.

As I rang his door bell, I ran my fingers through my hair and adjusted my tie, hoping to quell the nervousness. I was feeling like a greenhorn on my first interview.

'Thanks for meeting me on such short notice, Ravi. Do come in.'

Kaushal seemed to have lost weight. The last six months at Imperial had been torturous for him. He had looked extremely stressed. Looked fresher now. Invigorated. Rested. An alumnus of IIM-Ahmedabad, he had worked in banking for pretty much his entire 20 years of corporate life. Extremely well read and articulate, at times intellectual, he had the unique ability of inspiring his team. A very good mentor as well.

We shook hands and I seated myself at the chair beside the large window overlooking MG Road.

'Good to see you, sir. You haven't changed much. Been working out?'

'Nothing much. Around 5 km a day, a light run and weights three to four times a week. But all this travel is ruining my schedule. How 'bout you?'

'I think the walk from the bedroom to the bath keeps me together!'

Kaushal laughed. 'Look, I'm not going to beat around the bush. I would like you to join Oriental. I think you'll be able to build a good career here.'

Much more direct than I had expected. No pleasantries about lunch, family, well-being, sex life … nothing. He had gone straight for the kill. I could have kissed him, but controlled myself by gripping my knees. Had wanted to dance around the room and scream, 'Finally, the angel from heaven! My hopeless father-in-law must have been right somewhere with his damn astrological charts!'

A peck on his cheek was an option, but I decided to hold back for now. I needed to underplay the excitement till I got what was up on offer.

'It will be good, Ravi. Very challenging and fulfilling. Oriental could do with talented and hard-working professionals like you. We have a great team in place already, but I am going to build a larger and bigger one now. We are going to be expanding rapidly and need people who can perform under pressure.'

I looked around the room, trying to avoid eye contact.

'... and you're one of them, Ravi. I hear you're doing well in Bangalore?'

'Yes, Kaushal, it's been a relatively good year, but let's close March first ...'

'Modest as ever! I like that.'

'But, Kaushal, what's the role you had in mind?'

'Good question. Should have covered that. I want you to manage south India. You know the region, have connections and won't have to move base.' It sounded good, but not exceptional. Larger bank, wider area, more products to manage, many more branches and possibly twice the size of the current team I was managing now.

I should have latched on to this, but options fuel greed. The head went spinning in different directions. Should have just closed the damn deal first.

'But, sir, you already have a team. Is a reorganization underway?'

'Let me explain. Oriental is setting up an NBFC, so we are shifting some personnel from the bank to that division. India is a focus market for Oriental. Not some McKinsey jargon or BRIC (Brazil, Russia, India, China) strategy you would have heard of at Imperial. We are committed to the Indian operations and we are in for the long haul.' Kaushal had always been a good orator. You immediately felt like following him to the ends of the earth. Maybe this was fate, my break! But ... was it exciting? What I was looking for?

'Haven't you considered people within Oriental?' Was I digging my own grave? Why the hell should I care? I should be happy. Should be grabbing this and kissing him on both cheeks.

'We do have people, but I am also looking for some fresh blood. Need to blend in some old with the new. It's a good team you'll be managing,' Kaushal had put his case forward and pushed his chair back to stretch his legs. This was about turf and control. He wanted his people.

I had a job offer. So what was all the fuss and reluctance about?

I began to heave a sigh of relief. I could make a clean getaway. But what about my team? Mithilesh would eat them alive. Karan and Devendra would be the first in the firing line. I needed to back them. The Relationship Managers across my three states – I owed it to them. I wouldn't have been able to pull through this the year without them.

'Kaushal, if I may, there are some things I would like to discuss with you,' I was hesitating as I spoke. I had a feeling I was going to regret this.

'Yes, of course. What's on your mind?' Kaushal looked sharp.

'I would like to bring some of my team on board too.'

'Whom did you have in mind?' Kaushal didn't seem surprised. He was already poaching my team across the board. If I was going to switch, might as well bring them on board.

'I have some senior team members and some good Relationship Managers in mind. Would need to discuss this with them, of course.'

'Sounds interesting. Why don't you get back to me with the profiles of those you have in mind? And I'll consider it.' Kaushal sat back and smiled.

'Sir, you're thinking about something?'

'I'm thinking about what you said.' But his look seemed to say, you son-of-a-bitch!

'I would need to understand your current team set up first, Kaushal.'

'It's similar to the one you have in Imperial, Ravi.'

'Can you share the structure and numbers?'

'Let me email something across. In fact, let me see if I've got something with me in the bag.' He walked across to the bed.

As I looked around the room, I noticed a visiting card with a familiar name. Manish Malhotra, Triton Computers. I couldn't place the name immediately though. I noticed Kaushal still shuffling papers in his bag. I made a note of Manish's mobile number on the BlackBerry, but wasn't sure why!

Kaushal walked back. 'Not carrying them with me I am afraid, but I'll email them to you.'

'Sir, one more thing? You've been going after some of my team in Hyderabad and Bangalore. Let me bring them in.' I looked at him, wondering how he would take this?

Kaushal was beginning to show his frustration. This wasn't going as he had expected. 'I'll take that into consideration.'

'Thanks, sir.'

'I know I called you for lunch, but my wife has given me some errands to run. I've got a jam-packed schedule in the second half, so would you mind if we caught up for lunch another day?' Had I just managed to piss him off? Would I have to kiss my job offer goodbye?

'Sure, no problem. It was great to meet you.' I rose from my chair when he cut in again.

'Aren't you interested in understanding the softer aspects?'

'I'll have to think this through carefully, sir ...'

'Good. I've got big plans for you! We'll be in touch. Thanks for coming once again. And Ravi, we'll need to make the move this month ... that's the only condition. Need to get started in April!' He extended his hand, flashing his new Rolex.

For that Rolex, I would switch right now, my friend.

As I opened the door, Kaushal walked towards me and whispered, 'Ravi, we have very high standards of ethics and compliance. You need to make sure you don't have any baggage. You understand?'

Shit! The fraud investigation was now out in the open.

15:32

The mobile rang. An unknown number.

'Ravi here ...'

'Hey dopey, how're you doing?'

This had to be Ravindra. I had been caught trying hash in college so the name stuck!

'Hi, handsome, How've you been?' Ravindra was vain, as vain as they came, spending hours in front of the mirror.

'You made my day, *yaar*. You should tell my wife ... that reminds me ... how's Savitha? Has she left you yet? What are you now? A VP ... a Senior VP, sleeping VP or a frigging joint-executive masturbating VP. You've got such dopey designations at Imperial! You guys possibly keep looking at your fancy designations and shagging in the office!'

'Don't be such a prick! We need to catch up, Mr Head of Risk at Milsons!'

'Would love to, but very tight right now. Year-end and we're running with our tails on fire ... but hang on ...' I heard him turning some pages and he came back on.

'Listen. We're sponsoring a golf tournament this Saturday. The who's who of Bangalore is going to be there. Would you like to join me? Have a luncheon meeting with the chairman and some of the senior brass. He's planning to take our pants off as he sips beer at the golf course. Could do with a drink after that I'm sure ... or even some dope eh?'

Your college days always came back to haunt you. But, I had a thought.

'Listen, is your chairman going to be playing at the tournament?'

'Sure, it's his gig.'

'You need to do me a favour!'

'Shoot.'

'My CEO is in town on Saturday. Need to keep him engaged. One of his meetings cancelled on him. Was thinking if he could tee off with your chairman?' I was praying for a positive response.

'This is short notice, but let me see. Give me till tomorrow. That okay?'

'Buddy, need you to do this now!'

'Don't be such an asshole, Ravi. You can't fix things like this in minutes!'

'I'll owe you, man. Will even get you some of that dope!'

'Gimme an hour. Will SMS you in case I'm in a meeting. Have fun and don't call back!' He broke into laughter and hung up.

He must have thought me to be a major ass-licking son of a gun. I didn't really care right now.

17:04

The BlackBerry beeped. An email from Jaideep marked to all.
Subject: Cost Optimization
Dear All,
Business is going through a difficult phase. It is important that we manage our resources well. Look forward to your support in driving down costs in your daily work. We will be placing suggestion boxes in each branch and regional office, inviting ideas and suggestions for cutting costs. Blah ... blah ... blah ...

The way things were, now they would charge us for using the damn washroom. Did they expect us to pee in our coffee cups and then wash them at home?

Jaideep must have written in from his business class seat, sipping champagne and hitting on the air hostess at 36,000 feet, as the limo awaited his arrival at the airport. I hated these head office suckers.

18:34

Hadn't done any work today. Nothing strange there. Everything was screwed up. Maithili had been quiet too. What was she up to? Wished I could sit across a table and have a chat with her. I was sure we knew each other well enough not to bullshit one another. We had our moments – but did I still have a soft spot for her?

It's not like I wasn't happy in my marriage with Savitha. It's just that Maithili had been different. Brutally honest and playful.

I got up from the chair and walked in circles within the room. A sense of guilt began to engulf me.

18:58

I wrapped up for the day and asked Radhika to call for the driver.

As I stepped out, Radhika came to get me to sign on a few papers. In the normal course, I would have quickly browsed through the documents and signed. But with the recent spate of developments, I had decided to take a more cautious approach.

'In the morning, Radhika.'

She gave me one of those *'that's not like you!'* looks.

Had I become suspicious of everything around me?

19:01

As I waited for the car at the entrance, I could overhear a conversation between my Relationship Managers, who hadn't spotted me as yet.

'Speak with Spectra Consultants. They're the ones hiring for Oriental. I'm not waiting around for that damned list. Been working my ass off for this bank … and for all you know, they'll send some damn email and fire me! Bloody hell! I don't get these American banks, man. What the hell am I supposed to do on March 31st? Go home and show my three-year-old son an email from some HR number cruncher telling me how his daddy doesn't need to go to office the next day? Jerks! We have been reduced to a bloody number on their Excel sheet, man. We're just numbers …'

19:42

I was wondering how Savitha was holding up. Hadn't spoken with her through the day. Neither had she called. I also needed to spend some time with my parents, but there was so much going on.

I needed to prioritize! The Internal Audit menace was turning into a bigger roadblock than I had imagined. It was getting out of hand. Needed to get a view from an outsider.

I scrolled through the contacts list. The Collections Head of Imperial had an unceremonious exit in January with charges of fraud. He had been asked to leave and was given less than an hour to pack his bags. I hadn't really connected with him after that.

I dialled the number. 'Kumar?'

'Ravi? What a pleasant surprise? Good to hear from you.'

I hadn't even bothered to enquire how he had been. He had been sacking out at home, looking for a job. But Imperial had screwed his reputation. He had become a corporate untouchable.

'Thanks, Kumar. How're you doing?'

'Can complain, but will leave that for later. Anything on your mind?'

'Actually ... yes. Needed your view on something quite important.'

'Why don't you come home? I could do with some company.'

20:14 @ Kumar's Residence

The house was sparsely furnished. The stench of rotting food, liquor bottles and strewn cigarette stubs was overpowering. He seemed to be alone and seemed to have been that way for a while.

He had managed to gulp down half a bottle as he heard me recount my tale of woes.

'Sorry to hear this, but someone's really buggering you up. I think you've got pulled into the Canadian racket. I'm surprised they've surfaced again!'

'And what pray is this Canadian racket?'

'There was this scam several years back. A couple of guys would get credit cards issued in Canada, and then either courier them off or hand them over to relatives travelling to India. The local contact would fly across India, buying jewellery and stuff on the card and send them back to Canada. The guys in Canada would show the banks their passports and be in the clear.'

'Interesting! Should try it out myself some time.'

'Even I've been tempted. But I can't seem to get myself to doing the fun stuff! I could do with the funds though,' he grimaced.

'What do you suggest, Kumar? I really need to clear this!'

'I can understand, Ravi. Especially with those firing lists coming out on the 31st. This is the last monkey anyone would want on their backs.'

'Yup, you could say that!' It was a despondent response, but the best I could muster under the circumstances.

'Let me make some calls and I'll get back to you tomorrow. Can't promise anything, but I may have a way.'

'Way?'

'There are ways to resolve these situations, Ravi, and you are in a hurry. But the question is – will you take those steps?'

'Let me know, Kumar. And thanks for this one.'

'Don't thank me just yet. You still owe me for the KYCs!'

'What?'

'Who do you think your kid called when Sameer was making minced meat with your balls?'

The joint was obviously taking its desired effect. He had started opening out.

'You?'

He winked. 'Yup. I can take the credit for that.'

I paused, not knowing how to react. How many others knew about it? This wasn't good news. I had already exposed myself to Karan and Sridhar. This was one more. One too many?

'Well ... thanks. How're you holding up?'

'Great, man. Absolutely delightfully painfully great!'

The guilt began gnawing me again. I had been swamped in my business turnaround and glory of the last two months. I hadn't even called or sent him a text message, to see how he had been.

'I'm sorry I didn't call earlier, Kumar.'

'No probs, Ravi. At least you called me when you needed help. Most other jerks don't even call me when they're in trouble. Everyone thinks of me as some white collar crook who embezzled millions!'

I looked at him blankly. *Was this a confession or a self-exoneration?*

'You're such a jerk! You are in my home, taking my help and sit there judging me? You're more selfish than I thought, Ravi. And, don't give me those *"I'm sorry for you"* looks.'

He was right. He was guilty, as far as I was concerned. I hadn't even bothered to figure out what really happened.

'Cool it, Kumar. Seriously chill, man.'

'Chill? Don't ask me to chill, you bastard. You're as bloody guilty as I am. You got that?'

'Yes, man. Yes.'

'Do you know my wife and kids left me? Do you know Imperial called in my mortgage? Do you know my so-called friends won't take my calls? Do you know ...' he broke down.

He got up from the sofa and poured himself another large amount of cheap brandy and then slumped back.

'What happened, Kumar?'

'I haven't told anyone, man. I don't know why, but I guess no one wanted to hear either. I was running an operation for Sriram and Mithilesh. Essentially cutting deals with customers on their personal loan recoveries.' He took a large swig and then resumed. 'If a customer had a total outstanding of ₹ 100, we would ask him to pay of ₹ 20 to the bank and the bank would write off the balance ₹ 80. We would in turn make a cut on the side, as much as ₹ 20 to 30 on the deal. We had a company that offered credit counselling services to these customers. A freaking legit business. We even gave bills to the customers!'

This was too much to digest. Sriram had an impeccable record. The freak even headed the Business Ethics cell at Imperial.

'This can't be, Kumar. It's too farfetched.'

'I know. It was ingenious. But then Mithilesh decided I was making too much.'

'And, you got cornered?'

'Yup! Overnight. You know Mithilesh. He has Sriram eating out of his hands ...'

'Who owns this counselling company?'

'Sriram's cousin and Maithili's uncle!'

He rolled up another joint. This time I joined him. It didn't help too much though.

I couldn't help but feel sorry for Kumar. But he hadn't been totally clean either. This was all messed up. Morals, ethics and integrity were getting bastardized. It wasn't making any sense. But I could not afford to search for a moral compass now. There was too much at stake. But Maithili was beginning to amaze me. Did I even know her? Why did she have to do this kind of stuff? What was driving her?

21:57 @ Home

Mom had laid out a great spread. The meal was a great rejuvenator even though the meeting with Kumar had been quite depressing. Having the parents at home gave Savitha and me much needed moral support.

As I rose from the table, my father called out, 'Ravi, if you have a few minutes, I want to speak with you?'

'Yes, Dad, will just wash my hands and come back.'

I had wanted to get to the bedroom and crash. I was exhausted! And Dad's chats took time and were mentally taxing.

As I walked back to the dining room, I noticed Dad heading towards the door.

'Dad, you heading out?'

'Let's go for a walk. Will do you good. You spend too much time sitting!'

I slipped on my sneakers and followed.

'Ravi, what's going on? You don't look good. Your health okay?'

'Yes, Dad, the usual year-end pressures. Will last till the month-end and then it will be back to normal.'

Normal as in unemployed normal, disgraced normal, imprisoned normal or all three of the above normal. Shit normal surely.

'I do read the news paper you know. I've worked for over 35 years of my life. The armed forces is not just about polo and whisky. I've seen my fair dose of ups and downs. Not that I've shared much with you. But there's one luxury you have that we never had.'

'What's that, Dad?'

'There was no looking back or looking out. The army was our life. There were no options. No placement consultants or fancy websites to switch jobs. My working life started with the army and I was always clear it would end with the army, no matter what.'

'Any regrets?' I shouldn't have asked. Didn't seem right, raking up old wounds.

'To be honest, yes, a few. If I had played it smarter I could have possibly notched up a few more promotions. Could have got a few breaks serving with the United Nations Peace Keeping Forces, which would have helped us monetarily. A few things that could have run differently ... if only ...'

'What happened?'

'There was a point when a senior officer got after me. He made my life miserable, absolute living hell. I even contemplated suicide. I'm not exaggerating, Ravi.'

I had always pictured my father as the Rock of Gibraltar. Nothing ever affected him ... at least it didn't show.

'Suicide?' This was news. This was scary. But, did I want to hear this?

'Yes! Sounds silly, right? Hearing this from your father. But think about this coming from just another man. It will give you a different take ...'

'Okay ...'

'Then your mother sat with me one day and helped me think it through. I had always thought this officer was after me, for no clear reason. On introspection I figured I had done some things that would have upset me if I were in his position. So, it wasn't totally his fault after all.'

I stuck to monosyllables.

'So ...?'

'Well ... two perspectives. There's always a way out of a tight spot, you just need to look hard enough and be brutally honest with yourself. And, the easiest way is the way out. True champions stick it out. You'll come out stronger. You may not agree with me, not with the kind of salary hikes you kids get these days. But there is still merit in the argument. Else you'll always keep adding ghosts to your closet. And that'll be the end of good sleep for you. Which ... trust me, is not worth it. But, that's my view. Feel like some ice cream?'

'Dad!'

'Just thought I'd give it a shot.'

23:44 @ Home

Savitha was looking drained after the elaborate dinner and was tossing around on the bed, unable to sleep.

Revathi had decided to sleep with us and Srikanth had sneaked in with his grandparents. We both looked at Revathi and smiled at each other. It was apparent that we were both trying to support and give strength to each other, but we also needed to confide in each other and discuss our situation. The events that had unfolded over the last nine days could radically impact the family's future.

I was regretting having met Kumar earlier in the evening. There was already so much going on, and now to know that the murky scam had Maithili linked to it unsettled me. It was disgusting. Were my emotions interfering with my objectivity? Why was I so surprised, outraged, cheated? I was well acquainted with Maithili's business acumen, but hadn't thought she could work on a scam like this.

'Where were you this evening?'

I wasn't sure if I wanted to talk about my meeting with Kumar. I wasn't sure if I wanted to get her even more involved with all these murky details.

'Catching up with an old friend ...'

'Anyone I know?'

'No, *yaar* ... an ex- colleague ...'

'You sure?'

I noticed tears rolling down her cheeks. Revathi was now cuddling up against me and had her right hand resting on my chest. I gently lifted her head and placed it on the pillow and shifted her body to the right. I wanted to walk around the bed and hug Savitha, but wasn't sure if she would receive the overture well.

'What's happening, Sav?'

She turned her head away from me and murmured.

'I saw Maithili in my office complex today ...'

'But Sav ...'

'I don't want to talk about it Ravi ... good night!'

Maithili in Bangalore? Why didn't she call me? Did Savitha actually think I was involved with her? Damn ...

Pregnancy ... possible layoffs ... parents in town ... possible penury ... this was getting out of hand!

March

	1	2	3	4	5	6
7	8	9	**10**	11	12	13
14	15	16	17	18	19	20
21	22	23	24	25	26	27
28	29	30	31			

Another Brick in the Wall!

06:42 @ Home

An SMS from Manoj Kohli: *'Hi Ravi. Call when free. Cheers.'*

Manoj Kohli, Business Head for Credit Cards and Personal Loans, reported to Sriram Iyengar. Manoj was my peer, with around 13 years work experience – he had started his career with the Imperial and assumed his current responsibility less than a year ago. An IIT, IIM blue blood alumnus. Rich! In fact, filthy rich! Hailed from a business family that always considered his time at Imperial as being of very poor economic value. He was probably trying to reach me on the Credit Card fraud matter. But why so early?

Savitha was still asleep. I pulled myself out of bed, brushed my teeth and stepped into the balcony. I noticed Dad was already awake, sipping his coffee and devouring the newspaper. I just hoped there was no further news about Imperial.

I dialled Manoj on his mobile after checking the emails on the BlackBerry.

'Hi Manoj, saw your SMS. Returning your call.'

'Good morning, Ravi. How've you been?'

'Let's say I've been occupied …'

Manoj laughed, 'Guess Lee has been bowling yorkers at you? He can be quite a pain. Don't know how you could tolerate him!'

There was something in his voice. He had something on his mind. It certainly didn't seem to be my well-being or good health.

'I've had my hands full, Manoj. What's happening at the head office?'

'The usual. Lots of meetings and Excel sheets! This Operating Plan is really taking up a lot of time. Can't wait for it to end. Listen, can I take a few minutes of yours?' That meant this was serious business.

'Have to get ready for office, but sure. What's on your mind?'

'Just wanted to bounce something off you. You know, Sriram and I are both concerned with the way in which you've been treated on this Credit Card fraud matter. It's very unfortunate. Amitabh should have backed you on this. Should have put in a word, taken off some heat. But it was too late by the time Sriram and I found out. Do let me know if I can help in any manner.'

Where was he heading? Was he also in on the racket with Mithilesh and Sriram?

'You could still ask Lee to politely forget about this matter!' I laughed.

'Maybe there is something I could do on that. I'll get back to you.'

'That would be great, Manoj.' He definitely had something up his sleeve.

'You know Vikram is moving on? It's sad to see him go. He's done wonders for the bank in India. We need a good leader like him to see us through these challenging times. What do you think?'

Vikram's leaving had not been formalized yet. What was he hinting at? Ah! The litmus test. I had to display my unconditional allegiance to his boss?

'I know, he's done a great job. I'm sure he'll do well wherever he goes.' Played it safe, I think.

'And do you think Amitabh has it in him?' This guy was ruthless. He could play me either way irrespective of my response.

'He has his qualities. He's risen through the ranks,' I would have lynched Amitabh if I could, but that was between us. This prick had no play in that equation … or did he?

'And where do you think you fall in the new equation? With the zones getting formed and regional roles being dismantled. You need to make sure you don't get short-changed. You need someone to back you in the head office. These are unusual times …'

Was this a threat?

'Focusing on my numbers right now. Let's see what happens.'

Manoj took a deep breath, 'But is that smart? Amitabh is banking on you to do your numbers. You do well, so does he. If, God forbid, you're unable to do your numbers, that'll put him in a tight spot. You hold the key, Ravi. Don't ever forget. He needs you more than you can imagine. But, the question is, will he back you? Honestly!'

He continued, 'Now, I know you and Maithili are close, but she's taking your pants off. She's playing you inside out. You have no clue. She fancies herself as the new Head of Sales, but Sriram doesn't think she's ready right now. Hell, I don't think she can even manage her own region, let alone a zone! That's ridiculous. And Shashank in Kolkata? Well, what can I say? Dheeraj, however, is a guy who's got his head on his shoulders. That's where Amitabh has his shortcomings. He's a great guy, but a CEO needs to understand his people, their true potential. Don't think Amitabh is ready for that. Sriram is well respected within the senior management team. He has been around and even worked with Patrick in the UK.'

So, this wasn't a one-man race after all. Sriram was vying for the CEO spot, and Mr Slimy Kohli was gunning for the National Sales Head.

'So what does Sriram have in mind?'

'He thinks you'll make a great zonal head, possibly even the National Head of Sales ... soon. But, it's in your hands. And don't worry too much about the card fraud. There are ways out. You just need to be clear. Okay?'

And what was I supposed say? Any response had its implications.

'Ravi, have you heard of that unfortunate incident with Amitabh and Maithili. Very sad ...'

'Those were rumours, right?' I asked.

'You could say that, Ravi. But, very sad. I mean for such a senior and respected resource. You have worked with Amitabh for some time now. It's our duty to report these kinds of incidents to the management. It's not good for the bank. What do you think?'

'I couldn't agree more with you, Manoj.'

'Good. Do let me know when you would like to chat. I am there for you ... you know that, right?'

'Sure! Thanks for calling, Manoj. Let's connect soon.'

The bastard was asking me to pull down Amitabh with whatever it took. He wanted me to show my allegiance to the Sriram camp, and I needed to pay a dowry – in this case, Amitabh's head.

08:36

Savitha and I decided to eat breakfast in the bedroom as we got ready. She hadn't felt like going to office and had been cajoling me to take the day off. With the morning call, it didn't appear to be an option. Needed to be in on the action. And with the CEO coming into town, I had to set things straight at work. There was, surprisingly, no mention of Maithili after last night's conversation. It was sure to emerge at a later date.

'Sav, sorry about today. There's too much happening. Have to go in.'

'I know, wouldn't want to hold you back but I'm really not up to it today either,' she said, sounding low.

I needed to charge her up. This wasn't her.

'Sav, I'm cool if you leave your job. But it has to be on your terms, not theirs. You're better than this.'

As I was saying that to her, it struck me – was I being selfish? Maybe I wanted her to work to cover my back in case I got laid off myself. I should have told her to take it easy, look after her health, but the words always seemed to come out all wrong!

'I know, Ravi. But I just don't know what to do. Feeling helpless. Just want to hang up my boots. Got any ideas?'

'Listen. You either play it clean or you play it.'

'Yes, genius. But can you be more specific?'

'The clean stuff? Firstly, figure out which new projects are coming into the other departments and see if you've got a play? If you do, go for the kill. Second, are your bosses affected?'

Savitha thought through that and responded, 'Funny you should say that, but no! They've all clung onto something or the other. Some of them have taken on lesser responsibilities and even downgraded their work scope, but they're clinging on. They're all roaming around the office like a bunch of hyenas, looking for scraps to hold on to. It's like watching a cockfight. Funny isn't it? They are after all a bunch of cocks ... except my boss, of course. But I hear she is heading for a transplant!' she burst into wild laughter.

'Felt good saying it out aloud. But, that's good advice. Need to shed my ego and go around with a begging bowl. Welcome to MNC life. We're all professional white-collared beggars! And double damn the great work I've done all these years. All those shitty projects I've delivered on time. All those white asses I've listened to like a dumb bimbo. It's all come down to whose ass I can lick? I'm setting a great example for our kids, Ravi!'

'Don't be so idealistic. You're teaching them to survive. And there's nothing wrong with that. Fight for your rights, Sav. No one's going to hand it over to you. Go grab them by the ...'

'Got the message. Need to rethink. How I wish I could have a tequila!' she smiled.

'Sure. Will ask Mom and Dad to join us as we down a few shots!' I winked.

'Wouldn't that be so cool, Ravi!'

'You are losing it, you know?'

'My job?' Savitha winked.

'Have you considered looking outside?'

'Need to, I guess. Let me see ...'

12:14

Radhika walked in. 'Can I ask you something?'

'Sure, what's up?'

'You leaving?'

It was brutally direct, with eye contact. 'Why do you ask?'

'One of the Relationship Managers saw you at the Taj. Believe Kaushal is staying there.'

'Nothing to it, Radhika. Just rumours!'

She left, obviously unconvinced. I needed to watch my every step from now on.

12:39

Karan walked in.

'Boss, on that Credit Card matter, I'm working on something. Had a word with some of the executives in collections. I'm trying to see if they can chip in with something.'

'So, what did the local collections guys say?'

'Off the record ... they've been asked to pull back. It's too hot!'

'And, what's that supposed to mean?'

'They've been told to stay clear by the head office ... in as many words.' Karan looked outside the window, avoiding eye contact.

'Thanks, Karan.'

14:36

Wrapped a sales review call with the team and headed back towards my cabin. I kept checking the phone for messages from Maithili, but there weren't any. Her hush-hush Bangalore visit had made me curious about what she was up to.

I couldn't call her office. Neither did I want to message her. But I had to know what she was doing! I knew she didn't have family here, so it must have been work-related.

I SMSed Kumar: *'Is Maithili in Bangalore?'*

'Yup... cleaning up...'

'How do you know?'

He replied *'J'*

I messaged Maithili: *'Up for a drink?'*

In the office, I reviewed the sales performance tracker till March 9th. The numbers were better and the pipeline seemed healthy enough. The sales teams seemed reasonably charged up, despite everything going on around them.

The call from Manoj Kohli had intrigued me. He had asked me to slowdown my sales numbers. The momentum was just picking up and I had been pushing the teams hard. But the larger question remained – should I be backing Sriram?

Radhika walked in. 'You need to work on the annual team appraisals. Vinesh has been hounding me on that one.'

'But that's not due for another two weeks!'

'Didn't you read yesterday's email?'

'Which email?'

'They've pushed the date ahead ...'

What was going on?

'You manage Vinesh. Tell him I'm working on them!'

'Of course, sir!'

17:54

I couldn't hold back any longer – I had done so the whole day. I called Kumar.

'I've got something, but you may not like the approach.' He was all business right away.

I had already crossed the line on the KYCs fiasco. Was another line emerging? Ideally, I didn't want make those calls, but then ...

I got up and closed the door. 'All ears, Kumar. All ears.'

'These are professionals, Ravi. They run different rackets, but this is a new and lucrative area for them. They operate in murky waters, if you know what I mean?'

'Think I get the drift!'

'I'm guessing they're colluding with someone on the inside!' I hadn't mentioned the role of my Chennai manager. Didn't think it necessary. Maybe it was.

'Why do you say so?'

'Under normal circumstances, no bank in its sane mind would have ever issued them a Credit Card. They're a shady lot and even if you do go legal against them, it'll take ages. Still be very difficult to prove.'

'And I don't have that kind of time, Kumar.' I was getting that sinking feeling again. This was new and uncharted territory for me, ideally one I would have never wanted to traverse.

'The only way out, Ravi, is for them to confess to what they've done?'

'And, how's that going to happen?'

'You'll need professional help. I mean real professional! Well, either the cops or some others …'

For the cops to step in, my local collections team would have to initiate proceedings. Which from what Karan had just mentioned, was not an option.

'Let me think about it, Kumar, and thanks once again.'

'We'll work this out together, Ravi. Don't worry. Let me know.'

I was about to disconnect when I remembered I had to ask him about Maithili's visit to Bangalore.

'Hey … almost forgot … what's Maithili doing in Bangalore? You didn't tell me earlier.'

Kumar sniggered. 'Was wondering when you would get to that. She was here to meet Mithilesh.'

'But why travel all the way? What's happening?'

'I think their consultancy services scam may have been picked up by the Internal Audit guys during their Bangalore visit. She may be trying to cool down operations and clean up the act.'

'So, she's withdrawing?'

'Too early to say. But the heat is on for sure!'

'And how do you know this?'

'Coz … she came to meet me!'

'What?'

'Some old stuff that needed to be cleared, Ravi. Don't worry!'

18:16

'Ravi? Akash here, Akash Saldanha.'

'Hi Akash. Good to hear from you. Still in Mumbai?'

'Yes, in fact. But something has come up. Is this a good time?'
'Sure.'
'Remember that opportunity I had spoken about with you last week?'

I couldn't forget even if he had asked me to. 'Yes, Akash. Quite well.'

'Well, their Asia Head is on a whirlwind visit through India. He was in Mumbai today and I met him for breakfast. Things appear to be progressing well. They're expecting things to move faster than originally expected. Which means ... he's in a hurry to get someone on board quickly in India.'

I was crossing my fingers. 'Okay ...'

'I know this is short notice, but he is going to be in Chennai on Friday and Saturday, attending a conference. He was keen on meeting you there on Saturday early morning ...'

'But, Akash, my CEO is in town on Friday.'

'Come on, Ravi. Don't bullshit yourself, man. He's on his way out and everyone knows that. I've got his CV! You need to get your priorities right. Thirty-first March is not too far away. Take your call. I've blocked Saturday breakfast for you. Let me know by evening today.'

'Will do, Akash, will do.'

'... And Ravi, one more thing ... are you sure you're okay there?'

Was he alluding to something?

'Why, Akash?'

'... saw the tweets on Imperial Insider.'

'Just office chatter, Akash.'

Shit! Hated the damn Internet right now!

I would need to leave on Friday evening to be in time for the breakfast meeting on Saturday. Bloody impossible! How the hell was I going to pull this off?

22:34 @ Home

My parents had left earlier in the evening to spend a day with one of my father's army colleagues in Mysore. We managed to get the kids into bed early and uncorked a Merlot that I had picked up on the way home.

I placed the cane chairs in the bedroom balcony. Billy Joel crooned on the music player as I turned down the lights, leaving only the bedside lamp on.

Savitha sat on one of the chairs and rested her feet against the railing. She sipped her wine hesitantly, knowing she shouldn't be indulging herself. But the first sip tasted so good as it rolled on her tongue. It calmed her nerves instantly. I heaved a sigh of relief.

'That feels good!'

I sat beside her and started fiddling with the BB.

'Shut that damn thing, Ravi!'

I dutifully placed the BB on the floor between our chairs.

'And, now you'll ask me about my health ... and my office or some crap I did with your parents?'

Ouch! There was no exchange of words for several minutes thereafter. Billy Joel's *Piano Man* finally seemed to soften her.

'You remember the first time we heard this together?'

I didn't, but hazarded, 'You've always loved this number!'

She smiled. 'Not really... but I know you like it!'

She wasn't drinking her wine, but her hands were caressing the stem glass.

'Let's take off this weekend? Just you and I? The kids can be with the parents.'

'You think your folks would be okay with that?'

'We owe this to ourselves ...'

'That would be awesome, Ravi ... just you and I ...'

I got up and pecked her on her forehead.

'I'll get a refill ... you going slow?'

'Yup ... I'm fine, darling ...'

I poured some wine and returned to the balcony. The last few minutes had been the first few moments of quiet and peace that Savitha and I had had in the last several days.

As I sat down, she handed over my BB. 'Sorry ... thought it was my BlackBerry ...'

I noticed an open SMS message. It was from Maithili.

'Sorry ... couldn't make it for drinks today!'

March

	1	2	3	4	5	6
7	8	9	10	**11**	12	13
14	15	16	17	18	19	20
21	22	23	24	25	26	27
28	29	30	31			

Humpty Dumpty had a great fall ...

06:43 @ Home

The kids had converted our bed into their pillow fight battleground! Savitha had decided to take it easy and allow them a few minutes of mischief.

The message from Maithili had triggered a cold war. We weren't exchanging any words and were even avoiding each other's gaze. I didn't want to pull her into Maithili's scheming ways and the larger scam but knew I would pay a price for this silence.

I was concerned about Savitha's health and wasn't sure how she was coping with her blood pressure so I decided to break the ice.

'You taking your medicines regularly?'

Savitha was laughing as she played with the kids. She nodded.

I turned on the TV and surfed the news. Imperial had disappeared from the news over the last few days. Twitter remained the only source of any new information.

The maid came in and rushed the children off for their baths.

'I have a doctor's appointment in the evening today. Will let you know how it goes.'

'Join you?'

'Don't pretend, Ravi. Just go enjoy your cocktails!'

'It's not what you think, Sav!'

'Of course it isn't, Ravi. It never really is, isn't it?'

'That's not fair, Sav!'

Oops! Possibly not the best choice of words.

'How dare you? Fair! Don't talk fair to me, Ravi! You have the time to meet her for cocktails when your job is on the line, my job is on the line, your parents are in town, I'm expecting

… and you say I'm not being fair? Goddamn it! Get your priorities straight!'

10:34 @ Office

The sales numbers were looking even better. We seemed to be on track even for the stretched targets for the month. The conversation with Manoj suggesting that I slow down on my numbers was still haunting me. I noticed Maithili's numbers were also looking up, though West and East remained sluggish. It was clear Maithili wasn't slowing down!

Amitabh hadn't even called yesterday, again unusual. Had he been busy fighting his own battles at the head office?

Karan walked in.

'Boss, you've seen the North numbers? They are rocking! They're likely to beat us at this rate! What's happening there?'

'Focus on our numbers, Karan… and while you're at it, why don't you make a few calls to your friends in Delhi and see what's going on?'

Karan winked and left.

The BB rang. *Maithili!* This was going to be tricky.

'Hey! Maithili, how've you been?'

'Good!'

An extended silence. She must be curious about how I knew about her Bangalore visit, considering that she had kept it from me.

'You back in Delhi?'

'Yes, came back yesterday itself.'

'Good trip?'

'Yup.'

A silent gap again. It was becoming quite clear over the last few days that I possibly had more of an adversary in Maithili than I had dared imagine earlier. But I also knew she was a rich source of information, I couldn't ignore. Had Kumar tipped her off?

'Savitha saw you in her office complex the other day.'

Maithili appeared to heave a sigh of relief. 'Oh ... I didn't see her!'

'So what brought you to my city?'

'Just some stuff. How've you been, Ravi?'

She wasn't going to give in easily. But I was sure she knew I was on to her. Just a gut feeling. Could make out from her tone.

'Pulling along ... what's the news from the head office?'

'Nothing much. Sriram was enquiring about you the other day!'

'About?'

'Generally... How did your Internal Audit meeting go?'

'You know how these go?'

'Clear it up, Ravi. Let me know if there's something I can do?'

'Sure, Maithili. See ya!'

Did Maithili have something to do with the card scam as well? Was she setting me up? It seemed to me that Maithili was placing her bets on Sriram for the CEO slot.

11:22

Vinesh walked in and sat down on a chair. 'What's up?'

'Everything other than what should be!'

Vinesh laughed, 'I always enjoy your sense of humour, Ravi! That's one great quality that you have!'

'Thanks!'

'I'm just going to take a minute of yours, Ravi. I know you'll be busy with Vikram's visit for tomorrow.'

'Sure, Vinesh. Tell me, is this about the Relationship Managers quitting in Hyderabad?'

'That also ... but we can talk about that later ...'

'Then?'

'This is off the record, Ravi. Are we clear?'

'Sure!'

'Have you noticed? Amitabh has been very quiet the last couple of days?'

I wasn't sure how I should respond.

'Why do you ask?'

Vinesh paused, leaned towards me and spoke in a hushed tone, 'He's been asked to see if you should be put under forced leave or suspension for a few days till this Internal Audit matter blows over …'

'And … where did you hear this?'

'You know better than to ask me that, Ravi!'

He rose and walked away.

13:02

I called Amitabh. I needed to check on Vikram's itinerary and to see if he was coming in too. I had wanted to meet and speak with him in person after my conversation with Vinesh earlier, and a Bangalore visit would have given me the right opportunity.

'Sir, which flight are you taking tomorrow?'

'Won't be coming in, Ravi.'

Whoa! This was big. Amitabh leaving me alone with the CEO? This was surreal. Vikram was surely out of the game. Or was he keeping a safe distance from me?

'I had told the team you would be coming, boss!'

'Next time, Ravi. How're the numbers shaping?'

Amitabh appeared relaxed but not his usual self. No questions about the CEO visit. Almost as if he didn't care.

'Looking okay, but it's still early days.'

Where the hell was he heading with this?

'Boss, I hear you're merging four regions into two zones?'

A pause.

'Yes. There is talk about that. I am resisting though. Singapore believes that's the way to go. A similar approach worked for the bank in Italy and they want to try it here.'

Italy? Italy! Even Bangalore did more business than the whole frigging bank in Italy. We were a joke in Italy. It was always considered an exile posting. It was the damn Siberia at Imperial. Holy crap! Had all these guys gone insane?

'I see. And by when would this be rolled out?'

'Should be soon. Will keep you posted.' *Sure!* I'd receive one of those emails marked to everyone in Imperial.

'How will the new structure pan out?'

'We're still working things out. It's too early to comment,' Amitabh was sounding pensive. This was a dead end, but he continued. 'Ravi, just thought I'd let you know. This is not something I favour, this merging regions into zones. But Singapore believes this would be best. It does pose a challenge for us in aligning resources.'

'What did you have in mind, Amitabh?'

'Jaideep is working on it. Let's see what HR comes up with.' Great, when in doubt or cornered, pass the buck!

Was he hinting that I contact Jaideep directly? Was Amitabh losing ground to Sriram? Something was cooking …

15:56 @ Office

Mayur called.

'Ravi, you seen the markets?'

'No, I've been kind of preoccupied. Why?'

'The Sensex just crashed. They've closed trading for the day!'

'Why? What happened?'

'You remember Silverwire Technologies?'

'Of course. You had a hot tip. Put in a lot of money there.'

'Well, their directors are being investigated for cooking the books!'

'What?'

'News came out just after the market opened today. The scrip has tanked. It's going down and the fall is not stopping. It's already hit the circuit-breakers and is taking the whole damn market with it …'

'How bad, Mayur?'

'Very. I think we got burnt on this. I'm stepping into a meeting. Will catch you later.'

I had invested over ₹ 40 lakh on that stock. Mayur had news that they would be announcing a bumper dividend and possibly even a bonus share issuance. It was supposed to have been a surefire short-term investment. No downside. A once in a lifetime opportunity! That frigging prick!

I logged onto my investments account. The ticker looked ominous as the stocks sped across in red. Silverwire was screwed. So was I – I had been banking on this money. And, it had disappeared in a matter of seconds. There went the little liquidity that I had.

16:38

'Ravi, you got a minute?'

Savitha! Had the ice broken?

'Sure, what's up?'

'It's confirmed Ravi. I'm on the firing line ...'

'Why, what happened?'

'Just had lunch with my HR manager. She is someone I can talk to ...'

'And?'

'My boss has given me a very poor rating this year and she's also managed to get some crazy feedback from my clients on my work!'

'You sure of this?'

'Quite ...'

'Take care, Sav. Just...'

'Listen, Ravi. I've just got too much on my mind! ... sorry 'bout earlier ...'

'Chill, Sav. It's okay. Chill!'

17:00

My newly found status, swamped in penury and desperation, forced me to dial Jaideep's number.

'Good evening, Ravi. How're you?'

How am I? The swine had been avoiding my calls and emails all week.

'Good, Jaideep. How's the situation in the head office?'

'Ravi, let's just say I would prefer Bangalore right now,' he burst into laughter.

'I can imagine, Jaideep. I just wanted to connect with you and touch upon our discussion of last week in Bangalore.'

'What did you have in mind, Ravi?'

'You had mentioned there could be some assignments in the head office. I was wondering if you had any further thoughts along those lines?'

He cleared his throat. 'That's strange, Ravi, but I think we may have had a communication gap or we just misunderstood each other. That's what fine Scotch can do to hale and hearty men like us!'

The Casanova had just lied through his teeth ...

'... and how's the family?' The evergreen method of terminating the conversation and telling me to bugger off!

'Good, Jaideep!'

They just want to kick you on your balls. But, they're rocking!

19:47 @ Home

'Savitha ...'

'What's wrong, Ravi? You call me that only when you've screwed!'

'I was speaking with Amitabh today.'

'For the CEO visit tomorrow?' She appeared quite connected with the events at my office. I couldn't say that was mutual though. I hadn't been able to empathize with her predicament. There was too much going on with me.

'Nope.'

'So, what happened?'

'To cut a long story short, he said I was on my own.'

She didn't seem surprised. Was possibly convinced she had married a jinxed loser.

'You're sure or are you reading too much into what he says? You've always taken him too seriously, you know.'

'No, I've thought it through. He was quite clear.'

135

I was beginning to get agitated with the perpetual quagmire that I appeared to be in.

'Great. So now you're quite clear what you need to do?'

'And what's that?'

'Take out a "supari" on your boss, you dummy!' she laughed.

It was exhilarating to see her laugh. But I was now going to dampen it. I had been hoping for some sympathy from the Amitabh discussion to act as a shock absorber for the calamity in the stock market.

'Sav ...'

'You've changed that tone deliberately. Out with it, Ravi!'

'Remember we had invested in that IT stock ...'

'You invested in, Ravi. Not we! What happened?' She glared at me and then decided to spell it out for me. 'Let me guess, it bombed today?'

'Yes!'

'We need to get some *puja* done, Ravi. Will speak with Papa,' Savitha appeared very cool, considering it was a good portion of ₹ 40 lakh down the drain.

I was guessing she had forgotten the amount we had invested. Or, forgotten one of the zeros! Either way, she was definitely getting old. Before marriage we would have exchanged high fives and downed a few pegs, now she was dropping the P-word at the drop of a hat. She had possibly given up hope. No crossfire, bursts of anger. She was keeping it all in. It surely couldn't be good for her or the baby.

'I may need to go to Chennai tomorrow.'

'But isn't your CEO in town?'

I didn't want to tell her about the interview and raise hopes. 'Yes, but something urgent has come up. May leave by the evening flight ...'

'When will you be back?'

'Should be back on Saturday. Will let you know.'

23:12

Couldn't sleep. Was planning my strategy with Vikram. The morning ride to office would be crucial to get relevant information on the head office. Needed to get the conversation off to a flying start. Vikram was a tough nut to crack, and in the present circumstances, he wouldn't give in too easily.

Imperial Insider: Sriram moving in for the kill!
Shit!

March

12

Sucking Up!

08:45 En Route to the Airport

Had asked for the Merc to pick me up at home. I was heading to the airport to receive the CEO. It wasn't mandatory, but I thought I could get some quality time with Vikram on the long drive back to office.

I still hadn't finalized the trip to Chennai for the interview with the Singapore Development Bank the following morning. The timing was extremely inconvenient. I had wanted to pack an overnighter, just in case I could get away, but forgot at the last moment. In any case, I wouldn't have been able to carry it in the Merc anyway, and it would have raised some doubts with Vikram in case he noticed it.

Went through the checklist for Vikram's visit again. Everything seemed to be in order.

09:20 @ Bangalore Airport

Summer appeared to be setting in early. Bangalore was unusually warm for this time of year. Beads of perspiration were trickling down my forehead. A suit in this weather was suicidal. Other banks had moved to smart casuals as attire but we had stuck with the suit and tie format. *A bloody nuisance!*

Was looking forward to meeting Vikram. He could surely give me insights into the murky proceedings at the head office. Desperately needed the Insider story.

I noticed Vikram stepping out of the restricted area in a sharp dark grey suit, blue shirt, flashy red tie and a Harvard tiepin. A track athlete in his younger days, his walk and demeanor still reflected that. A smart overnighter trailed him. His face, however, appeared to be weathering some storms. The greying hair and bags under his eyes marred his otherwise impressive six-foot figure.

'Good morning, sir. Welcome to Bangalore.'

'Good morning, Ravi. Good to see you too. Hope I didn't keep you waiting too long?'

'Not in the least. Trust you had a good flight?'

'The ladies in red can really look after you well,' he joked, flashing his sophisticated smile.

His sense of humour obviously hadn't been affected by the Imperial upheaval.

'Shall we? Can I help you with your bag, sir?'

'I'm not that old, young man. Think I can pull this off, but thanks for asking,' he smiled. He had been a stellar performer but then had taken a break to complete his MBA at Harvard, followed by stints in North America and Europe, only to return as CEO at the Indian arm in Imperial.

As I turned to escort him to the car, he tapped me on the shoulder. 'Ravi, have you arranged for a car?'

'Yes, sir. Of course.' A black S-class Mercedes was the protocol. It had been tough to pull off, with the vendor offering a BMW at the last moment. Finally, I had called the local Mercedes dealership, a customer with Imperial and managed to pull a few strings.

'Good. I met a client on the flight and thought we could ride into the city together. Would be good for the business.'

'Sure, sir.'

Did I really have a choice? It also meant I had only a few moments with him and needed to plunge in fast.

'Sir, the team is very anxious about the recent developments. I was wondering if you could kind of calm them down. There's been too much one is hearing on the informal channels.'

'That Twitter thing?' Vikram smiled.

'Yes, and the usual rumours …'

'Sure, let me allay their fears. We are strong in India. We have nothing to worry about.' The client walked in just then, resulting in the exchange of inane pleasantries. Some hotshot CEO in some engineering company. *Damn him!*

We walked towards the car, exchanging notes on the engineering industry.

As we approached the car, Vikram came up to me and whispered, 'This could have been avoided. We need to focus on costs, Ravi.'

He didn't approve of the black Mercedes that had been specially arranged for him. *Bloody great start to the morning!*

12:45 @ Office, In the Boardroom

The teams had completed their presentation on the performance in Bangalore. But Vikram had looked distracted throughout. He kept attending to his BlackBerry as though awaiting a call.

As the team hit the 'Thank you' slide, he looked up.

'Good show!' he said and went blank. The BlackBerry buzzed and he excused himself from the room.

Karan walked across and whispered in my ear, 'Is he going to be around long?'

Vikram walked in. 'Ravi? Lunch?'

Music to my ears. At last a few moments alone with him.

'Yes, sir. Any cuisine preference?'

'Thanks, Ravi, but it's been taken care of,' he started playing with his BlackBerry again. What the heck was he doing?

Taken care of? By whom?

Vikram walked out and was greeted by a loud, 'Hi, Vikram. Good to see you in Bangalore!'

Hell! I stepped out and noticed Mithilesh in a warm and animated discussion with Vikram. He was possibly the only guy in the South region who had the guts to address the CEO by his name and get away with it. What did this unemployable prick have that made him so unbearably adorable to the senior management? Was he a super pimp or did he give blowjobs to them all?

'Hi, Ravi, so how was your review?' Mithilesh at his miserable best.

I decided to draw out the swords. 'At least I had something

to review. Thanks for dropping in.' I then looked towards Vikram. 'Sir, shall we?'

Vikram appeared amused with our little duel, but didn't express displeasure. 'Yes, Ravi, could do with good lunch. Come, Mithilesh.'

Mithilesh smiled and walked away with Vikram. There went my cosy romantic lunch. My nemesis had struck again.

As I caught up, Vikram said, 'Ravi, I have an engagement in the second half. We may have to drop our dinner plans too. I hope that's okay with you?'

I didn't have a choice. 'Yes, sir.'

We walked out of the branch and sat in the Merc. I sent an SMS to Akash. *Will be there for the morning appointment in Chennai.*

The lunch turned out to be a lavish seven-course meal. Vikram was in no hurry to return to the branch and the urge for cost reduction had been relinquished in favour of oysters and Chardonnay.

What a frigging waste of a day! No information or gossip!

20:20 @ Kamaraj Terminal, Chennai Airport

The flight landed 20 minutes late, acceptable by Indian standards. I was looking forward to a good night's sleep. The breakfast meeting simply had to go well. Needed something, anything to go in my favour.

Disembarked and boarded the waiting bus on the tarmac. Switched on the BlackBerry, hoping to catch up with the last couple of hours.

The other passengers were restless to get off the bus and most probably eager to reach home. I must have been the only freak flying in on work to a strange city on a Friday evening. The bus ground to a halt. As the doors opened, the crowd literally shoved each other to get off the bus. Decided to let them scuttle, I checked my emails as I waited for the bus to empty. Noticed another bus coming in behind us with what appeared to be an equally restless bunch of travellers. As I got off the bus, I heard a voice from behind.

'Hey, good-looking!'

Guessed it wasn't me, but curiosity made me turn my neck towards the familiar voice. Noticed a lady in a black suit getting off the bus with an overnighter.

As she looked up, I blurted, 'Shit!'

She came across and extended her hand in an inviting handshake. 'My sentiments, exactly.'

This was bloody awkward. Maithili in Chennai?

A whole lot of emotions engulfed me. Hate, anger, intrigue ... We were good friends ... weren't we? Was she really trying to destroy me? Should I be cordial with her? But she had me in a spot.

'Hi, Maithili? What are you doing here?'

'I could ask you the same?' she continued beaming.

'Guess you could!' I couldn't force a smile through, not yet anyway. She was as calm and composed as ever. She always had been.

We walked into the terminal, not exchanging any words and excused each other as we went to the washrooms. We both needed some space to figure this out. I emerged, bearing a more pleasant demeanour. She was already waiting.

'Ravi, we can either bullshit each other ... Or ... let's not get into why both of us are here ... we have known each other too long for that, what say?'

Seemed a good enough understanding under the circumstances!

'Let's go along with that.'

I would kill Akash if he had set up Maithili for the same discussion. Hope the freak hadn't arranged for a breakfast meeting together! Would definitely slice his balls. The prick!

Sent Akash an SMS: *Is Maithili there for the interview tomorrow?*

He promptly replied: *:)*

21:50 @ The Chipstead (Bar), Taj Coromandel

We were both staying at the Taj. Trust Akash to have worked that one out. This was going to be excruciating fun.

I decided to go for single malt on the rocks, just to rip off Akash and his fancy expense account. Maithili decided to follow suit and topped it with a wide variety of starters.

'So good to see you. It feels like ages!' Maithili had showered and slipped into a tee and jeans. I retained my travel suit, but had stripped off the tie. I had been delayed at the branch with an accounting reconciliation issue as it is and had barely managed to make it for the flight.

'Same here.' I still felt like throttling her, but couldn't get myself to believe that she would intentionally seek to harm me. It wasn't her. I couldn't have been such a poor judge of character, could I? It would be scary if I were.

There were a few positives though. A new city, a new bar, someone else to speak with. It was actually rejuvenating.

'How's Savitha?'

'Good.'

'Do you think you'll move beyond monosyllables or do you still need to be drunk to speak with women?' she giggled.

'Long day, Maithili.'

'Sure, and my name is Margaret Thatcher! Lighten up, Ravi. It's just you, me and the single malt. Nothing else, absolutely nothing else!'

Nothing else?! She was teasing me with her wet hair, Bvlgari perfume and red lipstick. I hated her guts. I hated my excited dick as well. This was frigging ridiculous.

'Why, what else could there be, Maithili?'

'There is lots of talk. Both of us know that, but we do trust each other? Now that is the question.'

'And, what's the chatter Maithili?'

She paused and smiled, 'Even I've had a long day, so no shop talk for the evening, Ravi. Deal?'

March

	1	2	3	4	5	6
7	8	9	10	11	12	**13**
14	15	16	17	18	19	20
21	22	23	24	25	26	27
28	29	30	31			

Verptitude is a female quality that makes you want to jump her without knowing exactly why ...

05:40 @ Taj Coromandel, Room 202

The BlackBerry was vibrating relentlessly. I finally gave in and clicked on the messages. One email was from Akash.

> 'From: Akash Saldanha
>
> Subject: Breakfast Meeting
>
> Hi Ravi, Your meeting pushed ahead by an hour. Now @ 7:30 am.
>
> All the best,
> A.S.'

It had been sent from his Gmail ID to mine.

Fatigue and single malt proved to be a deadly combination. My eyes simply refused to open. The headache was intense. I drank a glass of water and realized I would need several more to be in any shape for the meeting.

I went to the bathroom and then realized that I had slept in my only set of work clothes. Now I had less than two hours to get the shirt and trouser cleaned up. Wow, what an awful start to the day! I really needed to get some *puja* done, perhaps that would shake off my demons.

I returned to the bed in the dark hoping to get the light switch. En route, I stumbled on a pair of shoes and somehow managed to retain my balance after flailing wildly and then clinging on to the table beside the bed. I switched on the lamp and collapsed on the floor.

'Guess ... good morning would be a poor choice of words right now?' said a familiar voice.

She was sitting on the bed. The quilt pooling around her in delectable disarray, her bare torso painting a distracting picture.

Her right leg was peeping out of the quilt in an invitation that I knew I should not have accepted to begin with, her undergarments strewn on the floor near my feet. There was no hope for it. She looked like she belonged there. Picture perfect. It wasn't a casual sleep over, that was for sure.

'Yes ...' I whispered.

'What in hell did we get ourselves into?'

'I don't even want to think about it. This is screwed up, totally bloody screwed up ...'

Maithili slipped on her tee and disappeared into the bathroom and she remained there.

The previous night was a blur. The tequila shots had come at about 10:30 and then ... I couldn't remember anything after that. I was disgusted with myself. I actually wanted to slap and throw her out of the room but realized I was an accomplice. I shouldn't do this to Savitha ... but I still had cheated on her. It hadn't even crossed my mind even once as I easily got into bed with Maithili.

I was engulfed with a deep sense of disgust and despair. I wished I could have pressed a rewind button, but that wasn't possible. I would have to live through this nightmare with my burden of guilt. Savitha didn't deserve this. We had our differences and even intense arguments. But ... what I had done was inexcusable.

What if Savitha were to find out? Or ... should I be brutally honest and just tell her? Would she understand that it meant nothing? Of course she wouldn't. She would scream her guts out and chop me to pieces! Savitha would divorce me! And what would the children do?

My head was throbbing with pain and guilt. I wanted to jump out of the window and drop rapidly onto the hard concrete road outside, hoping it would take me out of my misery. Could I justify this by saying that all the shit in the office taken its toll on me? Was there any justification for my night of sin?

05:48 @ Room 202
Maithili stepped out of the bathroom. 'Listen, we need to pull ourselves together. You have a breakfast meeting, right?'

I nodded.

'And you don't have a change of clothes?'

I nodded again.

'What time is your meeting, Ravi?'

I was pissed off. I felt like I had been raped. I felt like reporting her for harassment! I gave up and didn't try to rationalize it any further.

7:30
'Go have a bath and sort yourself out. My meeting is at 10, so I've still got some time!'

'I think I'll do this one on my own. I need some time to myself, Maithili.'

'Don't be a fool. You've got something to nail at 7:30, and it's not me,' she smiled and I could feel something stir. '… I've got till 10. Now, let me help you get sorted out. I know the manager here. We went to school together. Will throw some weight. They'll get your laundry done in sixty minutes. So, you okay if I stick around and lick you into shape?'

I wanted to slap her. But realized that it was misplaced anger. I should actually have been directing it at myself. Taking it out on her was like cutting my nose to spite my face, right now.

07:28 @ Room 202, Taj Coromandel
She insisted on ironing the trousers herself, didn't trust the hotel staff to get it in time or get it done correctly. She had already finished with the shirt.

I stepped into the bathroom, pulled up the trouser's, tucked in the shirt, adjusted the tie, slipped on the jacket and stepped out to pick up my shoes. She had left by then. No goodbye, no good luck!

I felt a strange emptiness.

I had to rush as well. Was totally unprepared for this meeting and was going to get screwed, possibly twice in the same morning.

07:32 @ The Coffee Shop, Taj Coromandel

Guilt and hangovers make for a heady morning concoction. I asked the waiter for a cup of black coffee, as I seated myself at a table in the corner.

Savitha sent an SMS. *'Good morning, hubby. Have a good day. Hope you washed your undies?'*

No, I hadn't washed my undies. I had slightly bigger things pissing me off!

As the waiter approached with a cup and pot, I noticed Chang walking towards my table. Had left a message with the *maître d'*. If only he could have stepped in after I had taken a few sips.

Had seen Chang's picture on LinkedIn, which in itself was a progressive sign. In all likelihood not a staid banker with a stiff upper lip! He appeared taller than what one would have assumed from his picture. Slim, immaculately dressed in an extremely well-tailored navy blue suit and shining black shoes. In my shabby state, I decided not to reach out to him and remained standing behind the table. My shoes looked like they had been through a cross-country trek.

'Mr Chang?'

'Yes. Mr Shastry?'

I waited for him to take a seat before I followed suit.

'A pleasure to meet you, Mr Chang. Your first trip to Chennai?' I enquired. I needed to gather my thoughts quickly.

'No ... I have been here a couple of times before. It is extremely warm here,' he was studying my attire and body language carefully. I started fidgeting with my hands and nervously shoved them under the table, out of his sight.

We exchanged notes on the weather in Singapore, the global economy, commodity prices, the unfortunate position of Imperial, but not once was there a hint about getting up and heading for the breakfast buffet. My head was still reeling.

His mobile rang, appeared to be a woman, possibly his wife, going by the intimate greetings exchanged. He excused himself from the table to finish his call, allowing me to gulp down some coffee and do a quick Google search on the Singapore Development Bank. Had actually wanted to research them the previous night. Maithili had screwed it all up. Literally!

The signal was extremely weak and the mobile couldn't download the pages. This was going to go downhill. Chang returned and mercifully suggested we check out the buffet. I topped up the plate with a heap of fresh fruits, picked up two glasses of watermelon juice and turned around. Chang approached me from the left and whispered, 'I don't know about you … but water works better for me,' and walked back towards the table.

Damn! Had he seen me guzzling Scotch the previous night? Even worse, had he seen me heading off with Maithili? He must think me to be one promiscuous, alcoholic son of a gun CEO-in-the-making?

08:44 @ Room 202

I could still smell Maithili's perfume. I pulled apart the curtains and watched the traffic below. Appeared quite heavy for a Saturday morning.

The interview had gone fairly well except for the fact that he appeared to be smiling rather frequently. My analysis of the Indian economy and regulatory banking framework must have stimulated his sense of humour. Or he may have had an equally screwed up night like me, and was delighted to meet someone in greater agony.

Savitha sent another SMS: *'Come back soon.'*

I hadn't booked my return ticket to Bangalore. Had no clue about flight timings. I wasn't even sure if I wanted to go home, at least immediately anyway.

I flung my jacket on the chair and collapsed onto the bed, shoving my head under the pillow. I screamed a couple of times, ensuring that the pillow muffled the sounds. It didn't help. The guilt was still overwhelming.

11:23 @ Room 202
Beeping noises from the BlackBerry woke me. The battery was running low. Surprising, it had even lasted that long. Was totally disoriented. Took a few minutes to regain my composure.

Called the hotel travel desk and enquired about the flight timings. There was a flight at 13:25 – I would have to purchase the ticket at the airport itself! Needed to rush, again!

Splashed some water onto my face and rushed out. As I waited for the lift, I decided to SMS Savitha before the battery conked out.

'To: Maithili
All the best'.

Shit! I just gave up. I was getting everything wrong, all messed up.

11: 27 @ The Reception, Taj Coromandel
The hotel staff looked at me suspiciously as I checked out, my jacket hanging on my shoulder. No bags, no overnighter, not even a plastic bag. As I asked for the bill, the hotel staff informed me my room number was in fact 402 and not 202 as I had stated. I hid the keys within my jacket pocket, not wanting to further complicate the situation. *Great!* I had stayed over at Maithili's room overnight. This was getting worse, not sure how, but just felt even worse.

They provided a drop to the airport and the duty manager lent me his BlackBerry charger along with the car adaptor. I felt as if I had just got my lifeline back.

12:52 @ Kamaraj Airport, Chennai
Cajoled the airline staff into issuing me a ticket. Even the damn guards at the entrance insisted on questioning my 'bagless' existence. The interrogation lasted over six minutes as they

cross-checked my identification and questioned the nature of work for which I had come to Chennai.

The airline staff finally expedited me through the security check and got me onto a bus. I was the sole passenger on the vehicle. Great ... must have kept the whole damn aircraft waiting for me.

As I caught my breath, the heat and humidity began to take its toll. The BlackBerry had been beeping for quite some time.

Five messages!

'From: Akash Saldanha

Subject: Re: Breakfast Meeting

Ravi, Call urgently ... need to chat ... what have you been upto? :) AS

'From: Kumar

Subject: Our discussions

Ravi, Call urgently ... got to talk ... have lead on your Credit Card matter

'From: Savitha Shastry

Subject: Can't reach you? Call ... worried! SS

'From: Sameer Prabhu

Subject: Internal Audit, Request Telecon

Hi Ravi, Needed some details. Call me when you read this. Regards, Sameer Prabhu

'From: Ravindra K, Milsons

Subject: Of Golf & Interviews

Hi Dopey, Call when free. Got some juicy khabar for you. Missed you at the golf tournament. You should have been there.

Cheers, RK

The bus halted for an aircraft moving towards the runway. Needed to get my head corked on straight again. I clicked on the Twitter icon.

Imperial Insider: The India firing list coming out on 22nd. More than 20 per cent on the firing line!

Twenty-second? Preponed?

13:14 On Board the Plane

Got stuck in the middle seat, worse it was non-reclining, and had an overweight old man on the aisle seat and a gadget geek student at the window.

'Hi Savitha. How're you?'

'Where have you been? Couldn't get through to you on your mobile. Couldn't reach you in the hotel! Some lady picked up the phone and said she was housekeeping. Are you all right?'

'Yes, Savitha. I've just boarded the 1.25 flight. Can you send the car to pick me? I have to disconnect now!'

'Was planning to go out with the children and parents to the mall.'

'Ok, carry on ... Will go straight home.' Why couldn't anything ever go smoothly?

'But you don't have the keys. Why not meet us at the mall?'

'Sure.'

15:25 En Route to Forum Mall, Bangalore

'Kumar?'

'Hi Ravi, what were you doing in Chennai?'

'How did you know I was there?'

'The mobile unreachable message was in Tamil! Something wrong?'

'Something' was a gross underestimation of the amount of shit I was in. Wonder who else had tried to reach me when I was unreachable?

'No, nothing. Tell me ... you were trying to get me?'

'I have set up a meeting for you today on the Credit Card matter. Meet me outside Koramangala police station at 4 pm?'

'Police station? Why police station?'

'Just get there and I'll explain. And, don't worry.'

'Fine. See you there.'

I called Savitha and explained that I'd be a little late. She didn't sound too pleased. Hardly surprising!

16:04 Tea Stall outside Koramangala Police Station

Kumar introduced me to Sub-Inspector Ashok Reddy, a stocky 5'6' man in khaki, sporting a stunning paunch and a thick handlebar moustache. Did they mass-produce these guys in a factory? Most of them seemed to have the same specs.

'I was explaining your situation to the inspector, Ravi.'

'Situation?'

'Okay …' I wasn't sure how to react in this 'situation'. The lines had blurred again.

'I have shared the names of the people who have been troubling you on this. He just wanted to meet you,' Kumar said in Kannada.

'Okay.' I decided to speak in monosyllables. Lesser chances of screwing up further if I restricted my words.

The sub-inspector remained silent throughout, then abruptly pulled Kumar aside and left.

'What in frigging hell was all that about?'

Why had I been pulled in? To show my face? I could have emailed my photograph, would have saved all three the sweat.

'Calm down, Ravi. You don't understand how this works. They need to see the party.'

'Kumar, what are you up to, man?'

'Here's how it goes, Ravi! The guys who screwed you on the card fraud are too hot for any collection agency in town to touch. You don't want to go near the mafia!'

'What the hell are you talking about?'

'You don't have time, Ravi. I saw the Twitter update.

You need to get your name cleared, ASAP. The only way that's possible is if these guys pay up. Unless you have any other bright ideas?'

'I'm not agreeing to anything, but where are you going with this?'

'I understand, but here's how it works. The cops will go across and convince them to pay up.'

'Great. So what do I do? Lodge a complaint?'

'Sure! Then you will be serving tea here for the rest of your life,' Kumar bit back. 'Anyway, cutting a long story short, the cops will keep a 30 per cent cut of the proceeds.'

'Thirty per cent? Do you know how much that is?'

'It is the only quick option I've got, unless you …?'

'Kumar, this is getting too murky. How long, if I agree?'

Kumar picked up the two glasses of tea and handed one to me 'Twenty-four to 48 hours max. That's all, Ravi. The ball is in your court.'

31

16:44 Forum Mall, Bangalore

'You look horrible! Are you okay?' Savitha hugged me supportively.

Eye contact was tough. I had let her down, in every way possible. Infidelity never even figured in my thoughts, not even for an instant. The night with Maithili had been a mistake, but I couldn't figure out why I had done it? My marriage meant a lot to me. It didn't make any sense to jeopardize that. It must be the pressure getting to me? *What a load of crap!* I was making up excuses for being unfaithful?

The pain was excruciating. I wanted to get down on my knees, hold her tightly and seek forgiveness. She was bearing my third child. She had supported me through thick and thin. She tolerated my idiosyncrasies. She had been my lifeline. And yet, Maithili … she …

I had messed this up again, big time! And this time, Savitha might not be so accommodating as in the past!

'It's good to see you. Where are the kids?' I managed to mumble.

'Your parents took them to the supermarket. Buying them chocolates. What happened to you? You didn't call last night, nor the morning?' she ruffled my hair with her right hand while she held my right hand with her left.

'Nothing much. Long story. So how long do you want to hang around out here?' I wanted to leave immediately. If only I could run up to the terrace area and jump off!

'We've just come in half an hour ago. The kids dozed off after lunch. They've been asking for you since yesterday. You have to make some time for them, you know. It's been ages.'

'I know, nothing else lined up today.'

I just couldn't look her in the eye … The BlackBerry buzzed again. It was Ravindra from Milsons. I wasn't going to get a break.

'Hi Ravindra. Thanks for everything!'

'No problem, dopey. Got a minute?' he seemed excited.

'With the family. Can it wait?'

Savitha heard that and then left to fetch the kids.

'Just a minute, *yaar*. It's hot! I think your CEO is pitching to join us.'

'What gave you that impression?'

'Dude, the news is all round office. He had dinner with the chairman last night and was at the golf gig you had arranged for in the morning.'

'Multi-crore salary packages don't get settled overnight, Ravindra, you know that.'

'I would have agreed with you. But the fact is that our chairman is looking to score some brownie points with the Reserve Bank of India (RBI), so this works for both of them.'

Lucky frigging bastard! And to think that I set him up!

'I still think this is speculative.' But I was hoping it wasn't. Surely matchmakers would be looked after as well? They were, in every profession! I could surely look to Vikram for a job if I needed to.

This cheered me up considerably.

'Think what you like, Ravi. But I know the team is drafting his offer letter as we speak. Speculating that he may sign the papers by mid next week if the numbers are finalized!'

Great!

'Listen, my kids are calling me, but thanks a million. I'll call you back.'

'Sure, dopey. Have a great weekend. I know your CEO is!'

The weekend was finally starting to look better. I allowed myself the luxury of a smile. There was a silver lining after all …

March

	1	2	3	4	5	6
7	8	9	10	11	12	13
14	15	16	17	18	19	20
21	22	23	24	25	26	27
28	29	30	31			

I'm not a Thinker or a Doer ... I'm just a Beer!

12:17 @ TGIF – Two Mugs Down ...

Billy Joel was crooning *'We didn't start the fire ...'*

Who the hell did, man? Then, who the hell did?

Akash had asked me out for lunch. I jumped at it. Needed an excuse to avoid Savitha ... any excuse!

Still couldn't shake off Chennai. I was sinking into a cesspool of shame. Needed to drink it off! It always worked and undoubtedly would again today!

I gestured for a second pitcher. Akash was thrilled with my commitment to the afternoon's programme and soon lightened up. At least, I thought he did!

'So, Ravi, how did you find Chennai?'

'Hardly any time to see any of it, but you tell me. How were your discussions with Chang?'

Akash was trying to hold back a mischievous snigger, but failing miserably. 'I can imagine why you didn't get time to see Chennai!'

He kept smiling, one of those *'I've got you by your balls'* smiles.

'Listen, Akash ...'

'*Arre*, that's why I wanted to speak with you. Chang was shitting bricks!'

'Why?'

'You must have been smashed. He had company when you and Maithili were at the bar at the Taj. You get the drift?'

'What?'

'Yup! The interviewer and the interviewees were all in action last night. I seem to be the only guy not getting any! Man! I really need to find an alternate profession!' Akash laughed.

'And Chang saw us ... uh ... me ... at the bar?'

'Saw you? I think you hugged him!'

'What!' This guy was yanking my chain.

'Well, that is Chang's version. He was with some smart chick. You bumped into their table and their glasses toppled. You apparently insisted on apologizing to both of them for several minutes.'

What the hell? Was it a Freaky Free for All Friday Night? Didn't anyone keep their pants on in Chennai that night?

'Shit!'

'So when Chang saw you the next morning, he was shitting bricks. He is happily married, you know?'

Ouch! 'Sure man ... happily married ...'

Happy marriages had just got redefined! Of course, if he was bonking chicks half his age, his marriage would be more than happy!

Akash emptied his glass and started again. 'So, you, Maithili? What's the gig? Serious?'

'Akash, Maithili and I have known each other for several years. We are also colleagues, which you know, of course. This is one of those things which never should have happened.' It felt good saying it aloud, didn't soften the guilt, but at least reaffirmed my commitment to my marriage.

'Good to hear. Trust you too will be be discreet about Chang.' I would if I bloody well even remembered the incident with Chang.

Akash's tone had changed. He was more serious now. This had been the reason for the meeting? No clues about the interview per se? Another dead end. Damn!

15:14 Outside TGIF – Many, Many Beers Later ...

'Hi Ravi, hope I'm not interrupting your Sunday siesta?' It was Kumar. It was Sunday!

I was barely coherent, 'No worries, Kumar. What's up?'

'Just called to see if you had decided how you wanted to take up that matter we discussed with the cops yesterday?'

'Been really caught up. Don't know how I can arrange that kind of money? Isn't there any other way?'

'Not that I can think of, Ravi. This is the best I can do.'

'Gimme a couple of days, Kumar. But you're assuring me there will be no complications if I do take this call, right?'

'Have done this once before. But that was years ago, Ravi. Should be okay, I guess ... but it is your call.'

'Thanks for everything. You're really going out of your way, Kumar.' I could have gone on, but realized I might say something I would possibly regret later.

'No problems, Ravi ... anytime ... If you have a minute...'

'Sure.'

'My niece is passing out of her engineering course from Mysore. She is looking for a job in Bangalore. Do you think Savitha might know of a vacancy in her office?'

'I'll check, Kumar. Gimme a couple of days. Why don't you send me her papers and I'll see if she comes across something.'

Sure she can join Savitha's organization. Does she speak Mandarin?

'Thanks, Ravi, and take care. It'll all come together!'

15:28 Still Outside TGIF ...

'Hi Savitha ...'

'Ravi? Where the hell are you? You said you'd be back by 11 and then 2. Your parents are freaking out. Tell me you're not drinking?'

'Well ... not exactly ...'

'That means you're sloshed ... Don't think Dad should see you like this. Can you chill somewhere for a while and come back when you're cleaned up?'

'You're a sweetheart. Did I tell you how much I love you?'

'Only when you're smashed, Ravi. But drive carefully. I'll cook up some alibi. Make it work-related ... okay?'

15:46 Still Outside TGIF …

I had never imagined sitting on the floor outside a bar could be so rejuvenating. The afternoon sun and heat were getting to me. Needed some cooler climes.

As I stood up, I noticed Amitabh was calling me. Great, what the hell had I done now?

This was going to be a tough one, with my brain still reeling. 'Good afternoon, Amitabh …'

'Hi. Hope I'm not catching you at a bad time?' Was he also high? He was actually being cordial. This was a Kodak moment. Hang on, was he also leaving Imperial? Or was he going to ask me to leave?

It sounded like one of those death-knell moments, when the boss is about to hand across the pink slip. Had seen it in the movies. It starts off with how's the family? … how're the kids? … you've been doing some great work … you're a good team player … you've really licked your boss well … maybe not all the time … but we should have put you in for a training programme on that one … but you know how it is? The organization's plans have changed. Now we need to restructure and realign our resources to deliver results, so you and your ass can buzz off now? We'll call you back if we need someone to clean our toilets!

'Ravi? You there?'

'Yes, boss.'

'How's business? Haven't really had time to go through the numbers in detail?' This meant he had found at least six hundred gaps and wanted to fill them up with my guts; or, his wife was refusing him action over the weekend. The freak needed to get a life! The numbers would surely look higher, if he were getting blow-jobs!

'Doing okay. It's going to be tough …'

'I'm banking on you, Ravi. I'm trying to work something out for you, but let's see … There are too many factors at play …'

Which meant if I still had my job at the end of the month, I should be grovelling at his feet, and if I didn't, he had tried his best! But, why tell me now? Was he feeling bad? Or had he heard of Manoj Kohli calling me? Manoj must have been calling everyone, mustering support for Sriram. Amitabh could do with a champion himself. He needed several in this race.

But Attila the Hun never felt bad, so how could this prick? There must be something more to it. Or, did he also want me to fix a meeting for him … with Milsons?

'What's happening on the layoffs, boss? The team is getting worried …'

'Listen, there will be some cutbacks. But I'm fighting tooth and nail for my team. Would never want to see any one of you go. But you should still brace yourself.'

'I'm sure I'll be consulted if it's affecting my team, boss?' It was less a question, more like pleading. *Shit!* I really shouldn't talk business after guzzling alcohol.

'That's why the appraisals were pushed up. We're doing the appraisal ratings tomorrow. Team members with poor ratings may be under pressure.'

'But when are we going to have that discussion, boss? You and I haven't discussed the ratings …'

'It's going to be slightly different this year. We will do that towards the end of March, or early next month. But that's like every year, Ravi.'

But 20 per cent of the workforce would not be there next month!

'Yes, but you said you're discussing the list tomorrow?'

'That's a preliminary exercise. The final ratings will be different!'

The bastard was lying through his teeth. People would get fired on some preliminary analysis of an employee's performance. Totally random and how bloody scientific! They'd probably throw darts to figure out whom to fire!

He was talking crap. Essentially this was a hit list for anyone the departmental heads didn't like, didn't care for or better still, didn't know, or for those who hadn't sucked up to them. This was corporate apartheid.

'By when will we know about the new structure? This week?'

'Let's see, there are many things happening, but, focus on your numbers.'

Amitabh was hedging. But why the hell had he called? He must have had some agenda. Had I pushed him against the wall?

'We are on top of that, boss!' *I'm actually mounting just about anything I see these days, boss!*

'Great to hear that. So, how was the golf tournament?'

High fives all around! The bastard wanted me to set up a meeting with Milsons. I was now THE certified consultant pimp in Bangalore.

Screw him!

16:17 Walking Outside TGIF ...

SMS from Kaushal: *'Ravi, what have you decided?'*

I was still beer-buzzed. Add to that Akash had chipped in with two tequila shots to round off. Hope he banged his Merc on his way back home!

I was running out of time. I lit a cigarette. Then it struck me I didn't want to go home. I couldn't face Savitha, not after Chennai and even the alcohol hadn't helped take off the edge of guilt!

On the work front, I needed to start taking calls, sides, executing. I was running low on time. Needed to look out for my team and look after Raghu Nair, my damn nemesis in Chennai. He had stooped to really low levels. But what or who was motivating him remained a mystery?

The only firm offer, hypothetically speaking, was from Kaushal. Seemed logical to give it a shot. The telecon with Amitabh was anything but reassuring. It was as open-ended as it could get.

Dad had said 'clear your name.'

Sent an SMS to Karan: *'TGIF. Quick!'*

17:05 Inside TGIF Again ...

The effects of the beer were slowly waning and I was tempted to ask for a pitcher again – but I ordered snacks and chilled water instead.

Karan had come around 4:45 pm.

'What's up, boss?'

'Wanted to check on you and the team. How's the mood in the ranks?'

'I would be lying if I said they're not looking out. I mean no one's going to get a job overnight, but no one wants to be on the firing list either.'

'What have you thought about Oriental?'

'I don't know, boss. They've gone slow over the last week, but I have been checking around. My cousin works with them in Mumbai. He's been there for five years and knows his way around ... doing quite well with them.'

'And ...?'

'His take is a bit different. Kaushal sir is well respected, but he had taken on some aggressive growth targets when he joined them. He's also more assertive when you compare him with their CEO. Heard that there have been sparks.'

'But at those levels, Karan, there will be. Growth doesn't come if everyone's kissing cheeks.'

'I know what you're saying, boss, but I've checked with a few others in the Bangalore team as well. There's a major divide between hardcore Oriental personnel and those who've come in from outside. Kaushal sir had picked up over 80 people from Standard Bank last year. It's literally trench warfare out there. The politics in that place is affecting business. Plus now they're making that Non-Banking Financial Company, so it's getting worse. I'm not sure if that's the place to be right now?'

'Since you're bringing it up, don't you think there is politics here too?'

'Every place has politics, boss. Guess we've been around here long enough to be in the driving seat to a certain extent. In a place like Oriental, we would be at the bottom of the pile again. That's a tough place to be if you don't have a godfather. These banks can be real bitches!'

Karan had a point. Oriental was not going to be an easy decision. 'Starting from scratch!' I shuddered.

'Karan, I wanted your opinion about something.'

'Yes, boss …' Karan sounded tense. He was possibly having one of those pink slip thought moments. Poor chap.

'Would you consider moving to Oriental?'

'Is this a trick question?'

'No, Karan, just straight talk …'

Karan got excited. 'Are you in touch with them?'

'They've contacted me. And I am evaluating options for you and the team.'

The questions began coming in rapidly. 'Sounds good, but how's the money?'

'Don't think you'll need to worry about that?' I hadn't touched upon the subject with Kaushal, but knew that would not be too much of a constraint for them.

'How about designations? What would I be managing?'

'I know you have a lot of questions, but why don't you think it through and get back to me? I'll steer the discussions with Kaushal. I need you to coordinate with the team here.'

'In Bangalore or other cities as well?' He was sharp, as expected. That is why I relied on him.

'Start with Bangalore and then let's connect.' That's when it struck me that I had made the first definitive move.

'And boss, what's your role going to be?'

'Karan, for now, just be assured the team will be looked after. I want you to speak only with the ones that can be trusted. This can get tricky.'

It was going to get murky for sure. I still wasn't too comfortable with the decision. Maybe I should have waited for the beer to wear off!

March

	1	2	3	4	5	6
7	8	9	10	11	12	13
14	**15**	16	17	18	19	20
21	22	23	24	25	26	27
28	29	30	31			

Gawd is Great!

05:05 @ Home
'Hi, Shekhar ...' *An unusual time for Savitha's brother to be calling.*

'Hi Ravi, sorry to call so early. But I'm leaving Tokyo and going to Singapore in the next hour.'

'You were trying to reach me? I was out!'

'I know. I left a message with Savitha. How're you holding up?'

'Great ... under the circumstances ... I guess.'

'Great?' I must be mad to use that word.

'Good, hang in there, BiL. Just wanted to tell you Patrick is going to be in India this week.'

Patrick was the European head at Imperial and it was rumoured that he would be the new Asia CEO, replacing Shinzo. There had been no formal announcements, but it had been somehow implied. All the processes went for a toss when it was the seniors at play!

'I heard. But what's his agenda?'

'I think it's about deciding the new CEO. He's doing his own pulse check. He'll want to make sure it'll be his people in the key positions. He has a few favourites as always.'

'So which way is the wind going to blow?'

'It currently appears to be in favour of Sriram. He seems to be playing his cards well.'

Shit! Wasn't sure if that was good or bad, an even worse position to be in. 'And why are you saying that?'

'I think your boss Amitabh may have gone slightly overboard, giving everyone the impression that he had bagged the CEO's position. That's upset Patrick. Sriram, however, played it cool, getting close to Patrick's confidantes in the UK.

He keeps feeding them cute presentations on the Indian stock market and even sharing stock tips, in a personal capacity! Apparently, Patrick made a killing on some hot commodity tips from Sriram.'

'So?'

'Well, the latest is that Patrick is questioning Amitabh's performance and pushing him big time on the next year's targets. Both Shinzo and your CEO are out of the picture. Shinzo is up most nights attending late night conference calls from Patrick's cronies.'

'Where did you hear all this?'

'One of my batchmates is in Patrick's executive team. In fact, I'm working with him on some Internet initiative.'

'So the sands are shifting?' Another twist to cope with. Sriram in the reckoning for the CEO's spot! Double damn!

'Actually this is more like quicksand,' Shekhar laughed. 'Now want to hear the real bitch in the story?'

'It is already sounding like a bloody soap opera.'

It wasn't going to be a pleasant Monday at work for sure.

Shekhar laughed ... 'Much worse, dude, the word on the street is that even your boss's position is under threat, not as the future CEO, but his current position as the Head of Sales!'

'What!'

'Yup, one of Patrick's executive team members is Indian. Some guy called Patel. Young, just hit his 30s. Fast-tracker! He would love to become the CEO, but Patrick is not in such a rush. So he may just make the guy the sales head.'

'What's that guy's name again?' The name sounded familiar.

'Hang on ... can't seem to place it ... Yes! Got it ... Keshav, Keshav Patel. You know him?'

'Nope, but have heard of him. He was three or four years my junior in college. Has done pretty well for himself. So Amitabh is under fire on both fronts?'

That explained yesterday's call. Even if I did survive this restructuring, I would be reporting into some juvenile college junior. I must have committed some unpardonable sins in my previous life that were coming back to haunt me.

'And, your HR head has thrown a googly. He's backing both Amitabh and Sriram for the CEO position. So he comes out on top in either case. Both are supporting his plans for headcount reduction and reorganization. He's getting his ass licked by both of them, big time. He is apparently in Patrick's good books, though I don't know how or why? I think he is close to the global HR head, but not sure.'

'Any other candidates or twists?'

'I think that is about it. That should suffice for today. So when are you going to Mumbai?'

'Mumbai? Why? Nothing is planned as of now.'

'I might be in Mumbai on the 19th, Friday. One of those morning–evening trips, en route to Dubai. Trying to see if I can catch up with Patrick as well.'

'You're flying around quite a bit. What's up?'

'Nothing, man. Everyone wants to get onto the Internet bandwagon and cut costs. The new panacea for cost-cutting. Hang on! You may want to check this out? I'm checking my calendar right now. I have two meetings in Mumbai, both tentative of course, and two of your colleagues are in those meetings.'

'Who?'

'Maithili, isn't that the sexual harassment babe? And Dheeraj Kapoor ... heads the west, right?'

'Yes! What's this about?'

'One of those "senior management meeting with the top talent of the country" kind of gigs. Shouldn't you be there?'

I chose to ignore that. 'One last thing, Shekhar ...'

'Sure.'

'Have you heard about my being asked to go on forced leave or something?'

Shekhar paused. 'Ravi ... these rumours usually come up

when Internal Audit is investigating someone. Don't think you should dwell too much on it ... but let me check and get back.'

'Thanks, Shekhar!'

06:43 @ Home, In the Balcony

I couldn't wait for it to be office hours. Was too restless. Needed to find out about this meeting.

I scrolled down the contacts list. Mayur Singh, the IT Head, was always on top of the news and could be relied upon. At least I thought so.

I sent him an SMS. He called back instantly.

'Where the heck have you been, Ravi?' Mayur appeared wide awake and alert.

'Here. Why? Where the heck do you think I've been?'

'Dude, you need to be more visible. Especially in these trying times. There's too much happening.'

'What's with you, Mayur? All well?'

'Sorry about that, Ravi. But I have been up all night making some nutty presentation on using IT to cut costs. Everyone is up making presentations for his highness, Patrick. Just got off a call with my bosses in Singapore. Even they've been up since 4 in the morning. This Bill Gates should be put against a wall and shot, man! Why the hell did he create PowerPoint? Bloody waste of time. It's more about the fonts and colours than actual facts.'

'Sounds excruciating ...'

'You're telling me? A bloody waste of time. What's with you?'

'I'm a foot soldier in the trenches, Mayur. What's happening with the generals?'

'Crazy times can make you do crazy things. It's getting chaotic.'

Great, I was going to get some more variables to deal with.

'Both Amitabh and Sriram are fighting tooth and nail on everything. A meeting with both in the same room is like a volcanic eruption. The rest of us get decimated. But you would know that right?'

Now even he was testing me. 'That bad?'

'Yup! You coming for the meeting on Friday?'

'What's the agenda?' I steered clear of a direct response. Didn't want him to know I wasn't one of the invitees. Was that a hint for me?

'Patrick wants to meet the senior management and some of their juniors. He wants to show his inclusive leadership style. But knowing him, the real story is that he wants to see whom he should back and who should be in the pipeline in case he wants to knock some of the senior management staff out!'

'But why would such a senior guy get into this?'

'His genetic code. His middle name is *'Annihilator'*. Destroys anyone who comes in his path. It's about protecting his ass. He's in the people's game at that level. Business results and strategy follow … all that jazz.'

'Who's organized the meeting?' I needed to get there, whatever it took? It could possibly be my key to survival at Imperial, and survival now meant career growth. There was no going down or lateral. It was either up or out!

'I think it is being led by HR. They're pretty much calling the shots. Jaideep should be personally managing it, but they are speaking with the department heads on this one.'

'Cool! What else, Mayur?'

'You tell me, Ravi. How's the Internal Audit mess? Any luck on getting it cleared?'

'Working on it, but let's see.'

'A real bummer, man, a real bummer. Even those guys are making a presentation to Patrick when he's here. They all want their two minutes of fame and visibility,' Mayur started laughing.

'And, what's the update on the list?'

'Don't know much. Might come out early next week. HR is working on some new revenue per employee and profit per employee calculations. It was discussed last week. The chaps in Singapore are bringing in some scientific methods of screwing us all up. I asked them, how the hell were support functions like IT and Operations going to be measured on that? The whole world was getting screwed last year and we came out on tops. No credit for that from anyone, but everyone is on some witch hunt. Brazil was in a soup and our goose is being cooked. It's insane!'

One more dimension to fight. Earlier, you were given a revenue target and a profit target. That was it. You were given a free hand. You did your numbers, you did well. You didn't get your numbers, you got screwed. Fair and square. Now all these bloody value measures and metrics. Meetings these days seemed more about management lingo classes than hardcore business practices. Things were really changing, or maybe, I was getting too old!

'What is this revenue per resource funda?'

'They see how much revenue is generated in a region, a city, at a bank branch as well, and then divide by the number of people working in each. The big question is how are they are going to calculate revenue generated for the head office? The HR and Finance is having a blast. Patrick wants to see this when he's in town. Everyone is shitting bricks!'

'I can imagine …'

'All the skeletons are coming out of the closet. All the costs at head office level are going to get distributed to the regions and branches. So the challenge is how are those costs going to get distributed?'

'I'm sure some Einstein will have a magical formula!'

'Unfortunately, we have several Einsteins here, Ravi. So the formula for now, the more business you do, the more head office costs hit you!'

'What! Are they out of their minds?'

'You still have doubts about us head office folks? But the best part is that the profit per employee ratio is the lowest in your region. In another approach, the West was turning out to be the worst off. But now that they have tweaked it, you're at the bottom of the pile. So now it's North, followed by West, then East and then you …'

The dagger dug deeper. 'And when was this to be shared with us?'

'Well, Maithili got hold of it last week. I know 'coz she called me for some clarification, and Dheeraj in Mumbai obviously has access to it. I was going to call you. In fact, I'll email this to you. Let me know if you need any inputs. Okay?'

The strange thing about IT folks is that they had their fingers in everything other than IT. They almost always had views on sales strategies, marketing techniques, employee incentive programmes – the lot. They were also the only team that was always in demand with every department. We had become so dependent on IT chaps these days, and so they held us by our balls.

'Thanks again, Mayur. You're a gem.'

'Ravi, don't mind me saying something but you really need to clear that Internal Audit mess quickly. It's not looking good for you. Seriously!'

'I know Mayur. I know.'

10:22 @ Office

'Radhika, see if Karan is around? And please come in.'

Radhika walked in with her diary. 'Good morning, boss. How was your weekend?'

Weekend? An interesting concept. Wonder where that goes?

'Hectic, but it's going to get worse this week.'

'Why's that? Is the list coming out sooner?' Radhika was beginning to look restless. She was in an administrative role. If my position was under risk, so was hers. Anxiety had been showing on her as well.

'Nothing formally announced about that yet. Let's see. What's my schedule looking like today?' I could have checked my calendar, but preferred speaking with her – needed to settle her nerves. She was looking edgy.

'Surprisingly, okay. But I think there is a call with Internal Audit scheduled tomorrow.'

Shit! I'd forgotten to call up Sameer at Internal Audit.

'Can you get Sameer for me. Urgent! Thanks.'

10:38

'Hi, Sameer. Sorry, I completely forgot …'

'No problems, Ravi. Just thought I'd share something.'

'Good news, I hope?'

'You could say. We were looking at three subjects in your region, and especially where you were concerned. The first were those cases was mis-selling by your team, the second was the Credit Card fraud and the third the issue on documentation for those bank accounts.'

'Yes, Sameer. I remember.'

'Well. We're giving you a clean chit on the first one, but the other two are still pending.'

Why was he doing a U-turn on the KYC (Know Your Customer) matter for the three customers' bank accounts? Thought that had been closed. He didn't need to tell me about this, so was there was some point to all this?

'Thanks, Sameer. Good to hear.'

'I'll keep you posted on developments on the other ones as well,' Sameer hung up.

A strange call, but at least there was some good news. I was mulling over the morning's developments when Karan walked in.

'Morning, boss.'

'Morning. Close the door and sit.'

'What's on your mind, boss?'

I was going to play dirty, not sure why, but I just needed some leverage with Karan. 'I'm pushing Internal Audit to clear you. Just got off the line with Sameer.'

'Thanks, boss. But just curious… we didn't do anything wrong. And, even they know that. So, what's the fuss? I don't see why I need to take the heat for something I didn't do!'

'I know, Karan. But, you know how these things work. It's best if we close this at the earliest and move on.'

'But ... Thanks, boss.'

'Karan ... our discussion about Oriental last night. Have you given it some thought?'

'I'm having a team review meeting today, sir. I was going to speak with you about that,' Karan smiled.

I handed him a listing of the members I thought might make sense. Only Bangalore team members that is.

'Got it?'

'Yes, got it, boss.'

14:44 @ Office, Near the Coffee Vending Machine

'Hi, Vinesh, haven't seen you around for some time.'

Vinesh appeared to have become invisible. I had been trying to follow up with him on retaining the Hyderabad team, but with little luck.

'Hi, Ravi. How're the Monday blues?' Vinesh smiled. I felt like breaking his teeth.

'Dark blue, Vinesh, dark blue,' I smiled back. I still felt like smashing his face.

'I know the feeling. What else?'

He was drafting the death list for the region and asking me what else!

'Listen, there's been no official communication whatsoever. Gossip is neither good for morale nor business. Why don't you guys go out and talk to them? Or at least give me something official I can share with them.'

'Be practical, Ravi, what do you think we can state formally? Twenty per cent of you are going to lose your jobs, but we don't know which 20 per cent. That it might actually be higher, because 20 per cent is across India, so it can vary from region to region. So please get back to work and contribute to an organization that might ask you to get lost!'

Vinesh was venting, quite obviously. I wondered if his job was at stake here as well?

'Not bad, Vinesh. You do have feelings. Not bad. I'm shocked.'

'Don't be sarcastic, Ravi. You think I like firing people? I'm just doing my job, as are you!'

'So, why don't we work together on this one? Since genocide is inevitable, let me try and save the good guys. I have worked for this bank for quite some time. I'll wish it well irrespective of what happens in the next fortnight. On what basis are you going to decide who goes? You think their damn rating means everything? How are you going to read between the lines?'

'Ravi, you're bullshitting yourself. When you get fired, trust me, you'll hate the place. You'll want to torch this building. And, that's reality. But you do make sense. I could do with your inputs. But, this will be off the record, or it's my ass on the line.'

'No prob.' Not bad. Rational arguments did work, even in these times.

16:07 In Karan's Cabin

'So, how was your meeting?' I settled on the chair opposite Karan.

'Good, boss ... They're sounding positive. Confused, nervous, but they trust you. That's quite rare. You should spend some time with them. It'll lift their spirits.'

'Any questions?' I was curious about the team's reactions.

'Quite a few, but told them it'll get sorted out. We just needed them to raise their hands and say okay for now.'

'What's your gut feeling?'

'I think they'll bite. It's finally going to be your call.'

'Okay. Spend some time with them in the evening and let me know. What about the work front? You're on track?' It felt strange pushing him about a job outside and also over-achieving his targets here.

'I'm pushing, boss. May hit a rough patch, but will let you know. I just hope the boys don't leak this conversation. Can't have the rest of the office adding this to their rumour mills. There's enough already.'

'We can't have that, Karan. That would not be good! You heard anything?'

'Vinesh was chatting with me this morning. Trying to see if I was looking at options outside. He has been talking to my team. It's making them edgy.'

What was Vinesh up to? He really wasn't the inclusive kind of guy. Did he have an inkling that I was exploring options with Oriental? If so, he would lynch me overnight. Had I moved too fast? Maybe I should have closed my position with Oriental first. Maybe I was risking too much on this one.

Karan was shaking his head.

'What happened, Karan?'

'I just realized. Vinesh has set up a meeting with my team tomorrow. They are one-on-one meetings. I just hope they don't crack!'

19:05 @ Home

'Have you thought through this pregnancy?'

I was taken aback by my father's candour. He had Revathi on his lap as we watched Srikanth playing with his friends in the playground.

'Why do you ask, Dad?'

'Well … with everything that's going on with both of you …'

A long silence. He had sensed my discomfort about the pregnancy and the tension between Savitha and me.

Savitha walked into the balcony and shouted, 'Sri … come back home!'

Srikanth pretended not to hear and Savitha had to shout another three times before he acknowledged her and waved back. 'Five minutes, Mama!'

She turned and sat down in a cane chair beside me.

My father got up, 'I'll go and get Srikanth …'

'What's happening at work, Sav? We didn't speak today …'

'The usual. The BS continues …'

'How's Revathi's cold?'

'Better ... I've been having second thoughts about the pregnancy, Ravi ...'

I turned my head towards her, wondering what had happened? Had she overheard the conversation between my father and I?

'Why?'

'So much happening with both of us ... I knew it wasn't the right time ... but I have never really endorsed abortions ... I know it's the practical thing to do ... but ...

I placed my right hand around her shoulder and stroked her hair ... 'Take it easy, Sav. I'll support you.'

The BB beeped. Savitha picked up the mobile to hand it over, gazed at the screen as she did and froze. A message from Maithili.

She handed over the phone and walked away.

'Have you heard from Akash?'

I didn't want to tell her about my Sunday meeting, and then the steamy Saturday night flashed in front of my eyes. The SMS shook me up again. I had barely been able to take that night out of my mind during the day, and then the message just brought it all back.

31

March

	1	2	3	4	5	6
7	8	9	10	11	12	13
14	15	**16**	17	18	19	20
21	22	23	24	25	26	27
28	29	30	31			

Peaking is Good!

10:52 @ Office, In my Cabin

One of the best things that can happen in life is when a placement consultant calls you. The challenge is when they use those dreaded words, *'We'll be in touch'*. Which one was it going to be?

'Hello, Akash!'

'Morning, Ravi, good time?'

'Just give me a minute. About to finish something. Just hang on a sec ...'

'Oh ... okay!'

It was also important to show some attitude with consultants. Not too much, just enough. Even more important to show that you were busy, not desperate. Else they could lynch you! I kept him on hold for about a minute. I timed it on the watch and got back on line.

'Yes, Akash! Sorry to have kept you on hold.'

'Just thought I'd update you. Had a long discussion with the team in Singapore. Chang seems positively inclined. They thought you were quite young for the role, but believed you had the maturity that was critical for this role.'

Of course, I had maturity! Enough to get smashed and sleep with a colleague on a night before an interview. And better yet, for good measure, I even made sure that I created a scene with the chap taking my interview. This bank or rather this Chang character must be on dope. *What insight!*

'Ravi, you there?'

'Yes, Akash ... with you.'

'Good. They would like to do some reference checks, however. Standard procedure.'

'That would appear to be a positive result then?' I couldn't contain my delight. And I couldn't continue to hold a subtle conversation any longer!

'Yes, it is. He met some other candidates as well, but he appears to be in your favour.'

'So, what next?' I could kiss him on both cheeks. God damn it, if this worked out, I would even sleep with him! I just needed something positive to happen.

'You'll need to send your compensation details, and I'll get the number crunchers there to come back with something soon.'

'Thanks, Akash. Thanks a ton.' I still thought he was a pompous rat, but I was grateful to him. I felt so much lighter. And then the richer and deeper source of delight gradually emerged. I had beaten Maithili on this one. This was mine! Now I just needed to know how quickly this could get wrapped up? By when could I have the offer letter in my hand?

'Ravi, you'll need to also start thinking of forming a small team. If the clearances from the RBI do come in, the set-up process will be much faster. Chang may speak with you later, but just curious, do you know any good HR guys?'

'For this company?' This was more positive than I had imagined.

'Yes, an HR guy on board could help you form your team faster.'

'Let me get back to you. I may have someone in mind. Akash, one more thing ... How long would this take?'

'This is what I would define as still early stages. You follow, Ravi? Do not discuss this with anyone else till it's closed. I'll keep you posted. Cheers.' As they say, it's not closed till it's closed!

After Akash disconnected, I rose and walked around the room. The joy had been short-lived. The caveat was not encouraging. That sinking feeling returned. Why the hell did he need to chip in with that last sentence? If only he had given me a couple of hours with that happy feeling. It would have given my morale a big boost.

11:47 In Karan's Cabin

I was feeling claustrophobic after Akash's call. Needed to get out of my cabin and decided to spend some time with Karan.

'Hi, Karan, got a minute?'

Karan stood up. 'Yes, boss!'

'Any update?'

'A green signal from the lot. Lots of questions though, but said those would be looked after well.'

'Good show. Let me get back to you. I'll speak with Devendra too.'

'How're you going to manage Chennai, boss, if I may ask?'

I had no frigging clue.

'Karan, let me know how the meetings with Vinesh go?'

Karan looked pensive. He, too, must have been unsure of the mass exodus he was attempting to pull off. This could cost him his job and much more if it didn't go according to his plan.

13:44 In my Cabin

Ravindra from Milsons on the line.

'Hi, Ravindra. Good to hear from you. What's up?'

'What's up? Everything! Your CEO is signing on the dotted line today!'

'What?!'

'You heard me right. Your CEO has received the offer letter from Milsons. He's going for it!'

'But they just met. That's impossible!'

'You're telling me? This is a case of two desperate guys hitting it off. This is going to be one screwed combination man. A Marwari chairman with a polished blue-blooded multinational corporate czar. It is painfully funny, man. But what the hell? Your CEO is getting off with a huge jump and our chairman must be delighted with the bragging rights that come with taking the CEO of Imperial.'

'Unreal. How did this happen?' I was happy for Vikram, but ...

'Well, Vikram's lawyers met up with the Milsons team on

Sunday in Mumbai. They've been at it for over 36 hours. Your CEO is meeting our company secretary at The Taj in Mumbai today afternoon. In fact, they're scheduling it to be signed by 1 pm, if all goes well,' Even Ravindra seemed stunned.

'What's the package?' Curiosity got the better of me.

'From what I hear, it's quite complex. But he's easily getting over ₹ 5 crore, a joining bonus in excess of another ₹ 5 crore plus a truckload of stock options. There even is an early termination bonus in case things don't work out. It's like signing a bloody pre-nup. He's going to be laughing all the way to the bank in every scenario. Have no clue how we will afford him. This is unreal!'

'Great for Vikram!' I was happy for him. He had been my mentor and I did have a role to play in his assignment. Maybe I could cash in on this?

'You know, Ravi, one thing I don't get. When people like you and me are desperate for a job, they're all out to squeeze us and keep haggling between a 15 per cent to 20 per cent hike. When these top honchos come in, the bidding is in multiples of 50 lakh. I mean, Vikram would have come on board for free. He was in no man's land. He was out in the cold, and still that guy pulls this off. Awesome. Bloody awesome!'

'Ravindra, why are you getting so cheesed off?'

'Cheesed off? Just finished our appraisals in December. The jokers gave me a 4 per cent increment, citing poor market conditions and weak company performance. And your boss comes in like a king on an elephant and farts at us with his gigantic package. Life sucks man ... life sucks!'

God had been kind. At least there was a clear Plan B that was emerging. I finally had someone to bank on!

'Chill, Ravindra.'

'Before I forget, your current boss was also in town on Sunday.'

'Amitabh?'

'Yup! Trying to get in on the action at Milsons. Met the

chairman, but things didn't work out. Poor blighter, left with egg on his face!'

'Amitabh was in Bangalore?'

'Yup, why? Didn't you know?'

That son of a gun must have called to see if I knew about his Milsons interaction. *Shit!* Hope he didn't find out I had set up Vikram's meeting. That would have been disastrous.

15:52 @ Office

'Hi, Shekhar, pleasant surprise … all well?'

'Hey bro, all well. Thanks.'

'Where are you?'

'Some airport … taking one more flight in an hour …'

'Jetlagged?'

'Tell me about it!'

'What else?'

'Was asking about your suspension rumours.'

'And?'

'Seems to be something to it!'

'As in?'

'After the Brazil crisis, the Internal Audit guys have been asked to pick up the ante on any suspicious activity, and not to hesitate in taking any action!'

'So? I've got a clean track record!'

'So did the rascals who brought down Brazil! Anyway, I believe Sriram may be flexing his muscles on this. He heads some ethics panel or something and possibly wants to set an example …'

'And I'm the lucky one!'

'Yup!'

'And how far has this gone?'

'Well, of the little that I hear, Vikram wants a clean slate on his turf for the next few weeks. At least till he leaves. Even Amitabh doesn't want anything on his team … too much at stake!'

'So … why Sriram? What's his angle?'

'I'm guessing he may be grinding some axe with you on

something between both of you ... and he may be trying to score some brownie points with the Singapore guys ...'

This didn't make sense. Manoj Kohli had been urging me to back Sriram. And now I was learning that Sriram himself was trying to corner me? And Maithili was offering to clear up the Credit Card mess ... or was this a larger conspiracy by the Sriram faction? Why go through all this trouble to get rid of me?

'Thanks, Shekhar. The kids were remembering their uncle yesterday!'

'Give my love to them, bro! Will be sending some CDs for Srikanth next week. Ciao!'

17:16

'Hey Ravi! Long time?'

'Hey, Maithili, working very hard these days?'

'Have to for my daily wage,' she laughed.

'Your numbers have really picked up! Who's the golden goose?'

'No golden goose ... some things are just coming together. I never question the good things in life, Ravi!'

'Such as?'

'What happened between you and me in Chennai!'

We hadn't spoken about Chennai. I wasn't sure what to make of her words. Was it just the stress and liquor that had gotten to the both of us or was there more to it?

'Hmmm ...'

'Is that all you can say?' Maithili raised her voice. She didn't seem to be in office.

'Maithili ... it's complicated ... which you know as well ... It can't happen again!'

'You should have thought of that before, Ravi!'

'What do you mean?'

Maithili paused and then seemed to take a few deep breaths to calm herself. 'Did you ever get over me, Ravi?'

I wasn't ready for this conversation. There was too much

happening around me. Maithili was also being quite emotional and I needed to manage her, knowing full well that she could severely influence my career and the next few days at Imperial. She had me cornered. Or, had she set me up?

'I don't think this is the time or the place, Maithili!'

'Then ... when?'

'I don't think either of us have that answer right now ... Let's just think through this calmly and then talk about it?'

'Calmly! Ravi do you have any clue about what I have been going through the last few days ... And then you went silent on me! I didn't think you could be this selfish.'

She was right. I had been evading her. I just couldn't handle this.

'Ravi? You there?'

'Yes ... Maithili ...'

She started laughing loudly!

'You okay, M?'

'Just wanted to get you worked up, Ravi,' she continued laughing.

'What?'

'Forget Chennai, Ravi. It was just one of those things! Chill!'

What game was she playing now?

'We will speak about this some time, M!'

'No problem, Ravi ... and ... you haven't told me if you need my help on the Credit Card fraud?'

I wanted to see where she was going with this. 'What is it that you can do?'

'I don't know... but I may know some people who can get you out!'

'And how would you know these people?'

'I'm a Delhi girl, Ravi! We know all kinds of people!' she laughed and disconnected.

18:23 @ Office

'Hi, Sav, where are you?'

'Just leaving office.'

She seemed distant. We had barely spoken in the morning. Our usual lunch time calls had also not been happening for the last few days.

'Something on your mind, Sav?'

'Yes ...'

'You want to talk about it?'

'Not sure ...'

'Something about work?'

She remained silent. Had a feeling she was about to breakdown ...

'No.'

'Sav ... what is it?'

'I found a ladies' hankie in your suit pocket ...'

This would have been Maithili's for sure ... or her way of getting back at me! *Shit!*

19:34

'Hi, boss!'

'Hi, Ravi....'

Amitabh was sounding pensive. It was going to be one of those broken, staccato conversations. I was guessing this would be a call on the numbers, and for a change, I wouldn't have to be on the defensive.

'Did Vikram have anything to say about the Bangalore visit?'

'Didn't really get a chance to connect with him.'

The long pause continued.

'The numbers are looking good, boss,' I tried again.

He ignored that and asked, 'How's that Credit Card fraud matter looking, Ravi?'

I had to be careful. This was a sensitive matter.

'Nothing much has changed in the last couple of days. Would you have any update from there?'

'That's unfortunate, Ravi. See what you can do about it!' He disconnected.

There had been no discussion on the sales performance or operating plans or anything else. What was up with him?

19:53

I wasn't sure how to face Savitha on the subject of the hankie. There was already so much brewing at home. This would be the tipping point for sure. I had tried to call her several times, but she kept disconnecting. I was worried for her, and relieved to know that she had reached home when I called my father to check about his medicines.

The call from Amitabh perturbed me equally. I wished I could get a break, that things would just rewind to a few weeks earlier, when everything around me just seemed more stable, logical. There was just too much happening and it was frustrating to know that I couldn't directly influence or control several factors.

I felt like a drink, but knew it would only worsen the situation at home. I had wanted to burn Maithili at the stake, but realized that it wasn't all her fault. I was an equal party and I had to take responsibility for my actions. I wanted to go home and tell Savitha about it, but knew that with my parents at home, the situation was an irreversible firecracker. There were too many things at stake.

I packed up for the day, exited the office building and was waiting for the car. I lit a cigarette and inhaled the cool Bangalore air. It helped just stepping out of the stifling office and seeing the hustle bustle on the city roads. People laughing, smiling, talking, rushing, running ... there was life out here.

I took another deep pull on the cigarette. The car arrived and the driver stepped out to take my bag and coat. As I stubbed the cigarette, a voice hailed me from the rear.

'Hey! Ravi! Got a minute?'

I turned and saw a panting Vinesh dashing towards me.

'Sure, Vinesh. What happened?'

He held my shoulders as he caught his breath. 'It's good I caught up with you. Radhika told me you had just left!'

'You could have called me. What happened?'

'Sriram has called for some business ethics review meeting tomorrow morning at the head office. Internal Audit is also going to be a part of it. They're gunning for you, Ravi! He's going to hang you out to dry!'

'What business ethics meeting? Never heard of it before? Sounds juvenile!'

'It's some new thing Sriram is floating. He's doing anything that can get him in the good books with the chaps at Singapore! But one thing's for sure ... he's after you!'

'Who else is attending?'

'I just got off the phone with Jaideep; apparently Vikram, Amitabh, Sameer, Jaideep and a few others ... and yes ... some chap from Singapore as well on a video conference ... Not very clear ...'

'How is this going to work?'

'Considering that this is going to be some kind of committee, there may be something like a vote. Since Amitabh is already in troubled waters with his alleged escapade with Maithili, his vote or word may not count for much!'

The hyenas were closing in much faster than I had anticipated. I needed someone to bat for me there and I didn't have any time.

March

17

The Ethics of Convenience

04:15 @ Home

We hadn't spoken the previous night, and she had gone to bed by the time I reached home. I had put the kids to sleep and even my parents had retired early. All this on a day when I needed my family around me the most.

I was feeling helpless, low. If the ethics committee did take action, it would be the end of the road for me. Forced leave or even suspension wasn't an easy situation to emerge from unscathed, assuming one actually did emerge from it. Kumar's dismissal flashed across my eyes. I just couldn't handle the thought of a similar fate.

I had been tossing in bed and seemed to be disturbing Savitha as well. I stepped out into the balcony with my cigarettes and a heavy conscience. It had been too late to reach out to Vikram after my discussion with Vinesh. Jaideep would have definitely been inaccessible, and Amitabh seemed to be in a corner himself.

It scared me that my fate was going to be discussed and I would have no say in it or even the ability to influence it. It hurt. I walked up and down the balcony at a furious pace – the limited space it offered was frustrating. I wanted to scream, get it all out of my system but the setting didn't allow me that option either. I wanted to wake Savitha up and confess all about Maithili and that one-night stand.

I needed to unload, lighten the burden. Then it struck me that I was possibly overreacting. Maybe things weren't all that bad. The Internal Audit still hadn't implicated me, but neither were they clear about whether I had anything to do in the matter.

The cigarettes were burning fast and I realized that I would need to slow down the burn rate, if I was to make them last me till morning.

I sat on the cane chair and closed my eyes, rather unsuccessfully. I couldn't leave this all to chance. I needed to do something. I messaged Shekhar, hoping he was in a time zone from where he could speak. He called back instantly.

'All well, Ravi? I got worried!'

'Sorry, but there's some business ethics committee meeting tomorrow and I have been told they may be discussing suspending me!'

'You sure?'

'That's the information I have!'

'Who's in this meeting?'

'The top brass ... and some chap from Singapore ... dunno who.'

I could hear Shekhar tapping away furiously on his keyboard. 'Think I may know who this animal is. Gimme some time, let me see if I can do something!'

Finally a ray of hope. But I wasn't sure what he would be able to do.

07:24 @ In the Bedroom

I broke my self-imposed silence with Savitha. She seemed calm and disinclined to discuss the subject of the hankie or the affair she suspected I was having. I guess even she thought there would be a time and place for this discussion, or possibly hoped there was possibly a more innocent explanation. Well ... that's what I wished!

'What's up at work?'

'Thought you'd never ask. Do you have any idea what I've been going through, Ravi?' she felt let down and was possibly taking out her anger on the other subject with this one.

'I know, Sav. I know.'

'I've been speaking with some consultants over the last week. The same response everywhere. It's March. Let's speak in April. The other one is even better. You're too expensive. Why do you want to leave? Will you be willing to take a salary cut?' Savitha laughed.

'It can be tough, Savitha, but you'll need to hang in there.'

'But Ravi, do you think we could manage if I quit? Now that I know I'm pregnant, I would need to take off in a few months anyway. Plus, I may not even get a job if they know I'm expecting. That's going to make it tougher.'

She had a very valid point. There was only one option open to her, stay on and fight within her organization.

'Sav, you need to look within Amtek. Focus your energies there. Don't look outside.'

'Sure, Ravi.'

Then it struck me! The perfect out for her!

'Hang on! You're pregnant, right?'

She knocked me on my head, 'Ravi, have you lost it? Of course, yes! But why?'

'The best thing that could have happened to you in years!'

'What? Why's that?'

'They can't fire you if you're pregnant! Just report to HR. They can't touch you! It's the immunity pill. You're safe!'

Savitha flung herself at me. 'Why didn't I think of this earlier?'

10:34 @ Office

I hadn't heard from Shekhar and was curious to know what was happening with the business ethics meeting. So I walked straight into Vinesh's office, hoping to butter him into coughing some dope on it.

'Got a few minutes?'

Vinesh smiled. 'Morning, Ravi, sure. What's up?'

He damn well knew what's up. 'Let's take a walk?' I thought the outdoors may soften him up.

'New fitness regime, eh?'

'You could say that. Come on, lazy bones!'

He had this odd habit of taking off his shoes and folding one leg onto his chair whenever he was seated. But Vinesh also hated being caged behind a desk. He pulled on his shoes and jumped off his chair.

We walked down the stairs, lit up and stood below a tree on the main road. I had an unwritten pact with Vinesh. Any discussions under the tree were 'off the record'. Not to be quoted or referred to at work. We didn't need to say it to one another. The challenge, however, was in getting him out of the office as often as I liked.

'What's happening, Vinesh?'

'Don't know what you did or it is your good luck! But the meeting got pushed to the second half today!'

I was struggling to contain my jubilation, but realized he was in a *'sharing'* mode!

'Oh ... by the way ... is the Patrick meeting still on for the 19th?'

'Yes. No changes yet, at least none that I'm aware of.'

Vinesh was a master CYA (Cover Your Arse). He had riders and sub-conditions on everything. He had a huge ego, but that seemed to be the case with most HR resources at Imperial.

'So, who's in it?'

'The usual – senior management and a few others.'

'Who?'

'I don't have the exact list of attendees, Ravi. But, let me see how I can pull it out!'

He had it. He just wouldn't let go of it!

'I need to be there. Both Maithili and Dheeraj are there.'

'You know why you're not, Ravi. So let's not go through that. And, you didn't mention your colleague from the East?'

'He's attending too?' Great start to the morning. Even the non-performer from Kolkata was going to be there!

'Yup, that's the last I knew. He managed to pull a few strings and get on board! He is quite the inventive manager,' Vinesh smiled. That was his way of saying Shashank is a slime ball.

'What will it take for me to be there? Is it only that damn Credit Card fraud matter or anything else?' I knew the answer but wanted to hear the HR perspective.

'Ravi, the problem with allegations is that even if they prove to be wrong, suspicion still lingers. It'll be your unfriendly shadow. You've had the misfortune of having three investigations hitting you at the same time. That's one too many for any senior management person and with this ethics committee meeting …' Vinesh broke off to enjoy a few puffs.

'What's the way out?' I knew the answer but needed him to say it.

'Clear the charges and keep walking. You know, like that Johnny Walker guy, keep walking,' Vinesh laughed. Corny, but I laughed too.

'What's your life story? You sticking around to draft firing lists or planning to do something else with your life?'

'Hey, don't take your frustration out on me. But, yes, the last couple of weeks haven't really turned out the way I had expected. Makes one wonder. My dad has a good trading business in Trivandrum, mostly in spices and cashews. I often think I should go there and settle down with my family. You know one thing about being in business …'

'What's that?'

'If you screw up, it's your responsibility. You can have others deciding what happens to your life, but it ultimately lies in your hands.'

Not a chance in hell that Vinesh would sit in some backwater trading in nuts. Not when he had our nuts to play with! This was obvious, knowing him – he enjoyed the ego trip one got by sitting in HR.

'So, would you like to start from scratch?'

'Sure, why not? And if it pays a filthy amount of money, might even stick around to see it grow,' Vinesh stubbed his cigarette and extracted another.

'I hear there's some action at the Singapore Development Bank,' I wanted to see his reaction. Getting Vinesh to show a genuine emotion was an achievement in itself.

Vinesh burst out laughing, 'That bag of crap? They've been doing the rounds for years, Ravi. Where have you been? They keep coming in every six months, size up the talent, big talk about how the RBI is going to give them permission to set up an office in India and then disappear. Their Asia head keeps changing every 12 months. Don't tell me they've got you talking?'

A dead duck apparently … or was it?

'So you wouldn't be interested in chatting with them, right?'

Vinesh's face changed instantly. 'One must always meet people and keep in touch … what say? So, who's the consultant this time?'

'I'll let you know, don't remember off-hand.'

'Let me know, but you may be right. I had heard some rumbles in those jungles!'

'Think about it. I believe they may be setting up shop as early as next month. But you might be right. You're better connected on these things.'

He had planted that seed of doubt. This Singapore assignment was slowly looking bleaker, but I was going to play the card.

'No, Ravi, I'm okay to explore. What's your scene?' Vinesh's tone had changed. The gates were opening.

'Nothing much. What's the story with Amitabh? Why's he yanking my chain?' I had been probing Vinesh for over two weeks. He had to crack at some point. I had given him the Singapore bait. But would he bite?

'You know Amitabh, Ravi. He has no favourites. He's one of the better guys I've known in this organization.'

Was he sucking up to the future CEO or playing it safe?

'So, what's your take?' I was fishing.

'Take on what, Ravi?'

'What's the gig with Amitabh?' I persisted.

'I thought you'd know better, Ravi, but let me spell it out. Amitabh is under a lot of stress. He's gunning for the CEO slot, which is still open, but they've said some Indian expat from the UK called Patel is going to be coming in as the Head of Sales. This is confirmed. The housing agents have already been briefed about finding a penthouse for him in south Bombay,' Vinesh was confirming what Shekhar had said earlier.

'So what happens to Amitabh, if the CEO slot doesn't work out?'

'No clue. They'll give him some corner office, or knowing how crazy this place is right now, even his name could be there on the firing list. Nothing surprises me any longer.'

'But you still haven't told me why he's on my case?'

'Is he?' Was he quizzing me or stating a fact? If only the bastard could speak straight.

'Come on, Vinesh, spit it out.'

But he remained silent. I decided to press further.

'Out with it, Vinesh! And what's this talk of a sexual harassment case on Amitabh?'

'How did you hear about that?' Vinesh seemed surprised. 'You've got hot sources, Ravi. Hats off!' Vinesh broke into a light applause.

'Cut it out. What gives?'

'This is very hush-hush. Don't know how you heard. Maithili had formally filed a charge against Amitabh on the 3rd with the Compliance Team. They got together and then Maithili and Amitabh sat in a room for over three hours.'

'When did Amitabh go to Delhi?'

'He didn't. Maithili was flown to Mumbai on the 4th. That's when it all happened.'

'Was there any truth to it?'

'Even I don't know, but the word is some deal has been worked out. She had wanted the national sales head position, but that didn't work. So she's most likely getting a zonal head position ...'

'But how could they allow this kind of blackmailing?'

'The official position – it's a business call!'

'And this, according to you, is not flawed? That Maithili becomes zonal head for North and East because she wrongly accuses someone?'

'Who said North and East? She's gunning for West and South!'

'What? And, you didn't think it necessary to tell me this?'

'Would have loved to, but Jaideep specifically told me not to leak it. And there's nothing final about it!'

'But I met Jaideep on the first. He didn't mention anything.'

'This happened after that, Ravi.'

'But why West and South?'

'Don't know, but I imagine Dheeraj is equally upset. I do know for a fact that Maithili insisted on coming into Mumbai. In fact, that was a flashpoint with Amitabh. But he had to cave in. He had bigger fish to fry.'

Sure, me! 'So, who's going to be heading North and East?'

'Shashank appears to be out of the race. Could be Dheeraj or you?'

'Am I even in the race?'

'Theoretically, yes. But Dheeraj has strong support. And don't mind my saying, a clean chit!'

11:17

I had messaged Shekhar, asking him to call.

'Hey bro, what's happening there?'

I was hoping he would have some news. 'Anything, Shekhar?'

'Oh ... sure ... I managed to get the Singapore guy on that committee into some other meeting. Did that help?' Shekhar was sniggering.

I had been hoping for more, but didn't know why?

'They've pushed the meeting to the afternoon ... but that's about it!'

'Hey ... sorry bro ... I thought they might just cancel altogether!'

'No such luck.'

'That's all I could do from here ... but let me see if I can come up with something else ... Take care!'

'Thanks, Shekhar.'

Lack of sleep and uncertainty were taking their toll. Savitha had been caught up in a meeting since morning and I couldn't even reach out to her and discuss it. I just felt I must share this with her. I didn't want any other outcome to catch her by surprise.

I paced around the room. Radhika fortunately cancelled my 11:30 meeting with a client. I was evaluating all the possible options. Vikram seemed to be the best bet for now.

I walked across to Radhika's desk. 'Can you check where Vikram is? I need to have a word with him ...'

'Sure.' She seemed curious.

'... And ... keep it informal?'

She nodded.

It was a short wait. Radhika walked in. 'Think you can call him on his mobile now.'

'Thanks ...'

She left the room, closing the door behind her.

I dialled Vikram's number, but it was engaged. *Damn!*

12:24

Life had come to a standstill. I continued pacing around the room.

The mobile finally rang. It was Vikram. It had been an excruciating wait.

'Hi, Ravi, you called?'

'Yes, sir. Is this a good time?'

'I have a couple of minutes before I get into a video conference with Singapore.'

'Sir ...' I had rehearsed the words, but they evaded me.

'Yes ... Ravi ...'

I had wanted to tell him I was calling for a favour ... but didn't know how to phrase it in a politically correct manner. He did owe me after all.

'I believe there is a business ethics committee meeting later today ...'

I paused, hoping to get a cue. Was he uncomfortable discussing the subject? Had I crossed the line? No sound from the other end. I let the pause linger, knowing quite well that I could possibly upset him. But he did owe me ...

'I'll look into it, Ravi. Will have to speak to you later!'

He disconnected.

Did he get the hint? Or had he just ignored me? Did he even have any power in this matter?

Suspense was becoming an integral part of my life and I didn't like it one bit.

14:39

I had asked Radhika to call off all meetings for the afternoon.

'This will be a good time to complete the annual appraisals for your team?'

'What's the hurry, Radhika?'

'That guy has been making my life miserable. He can really get on my nerves!'

I smiled as I noticed Vinesh standing at the door.

'Come in, Vinesh ...'

Radhika blushed and left the room, avoiding eye contact with Vinesh.

'Ravi ... congratulations!'

Vinesh couldn't ever speak in a direct manner.

'What happened?'

'Haven't you heard?'

'What?'

'They've called off this business ethics committee meeting!'

It was still sinking in, but I was curious and excited about the details.

'And?'

'Even I don't know why!'

Vinesh seemed disgusted with himself. His surveillance and intelligence-gathering abilities seemed to have shortcomings. He got up and left, shaking his head, disgusted.

I was feeling numb. Wasn't sure whether to break into a jig, when Vinesh walked back in ... 'Hey, did I tell you?'

'What?'

He was giggling, 'Heard even Sriram is being investigated ...'

'For what?'

'You know, all that stock trading that he does from his office!'

'So?'

'Well ... there may be some conflict issue!' he smiled and left.

Were the sands shifting again? Had I just got my first major break?

16:24

'How're the numbers, Ravi?'

I smiled. Amitabh was back on track. 'Looking up, boss!'

'Make sure you don't take your eyes off the ball. Hyderabad is slipping, but Chennai and Bangalore seem to be moving well ...'

'Getting some good traction ...'

'Good!' he disconnected.

The heat was back on. He possibly realized he needed me as much as I needed him for achieving the targets this month. I needed to pull off something big!

16:52

After several days, I finally had the time and inclination to analyse the sales performance numbers. Concluded a conference call with my three city heads and even threw some tantrums to keep the heat on. I was feeling charged up again, but realized I needed something that would be noticed by the head office. And it would have to be significant!

18:30

I had called Manish Malhotra from Triton Computers across to the office. Had seen his visiting card with Kaushal and had a gut feeling that there was something big enough for Kaushal to meet Manish in person. I needed a big ticket high-visibility deal. I was fishing on this.

'Hi, Manish, please come in. I'm Ravi Shastry.'

'Hi, Ravi, good to meet you. You may recollect we had met several years back.'

'Please have a seat.'

'Thanks for meeting me. Your timing was excellent. I had been trying to reach one of your colleagues, Mithilesh, but he appears to be busy.'

But he didn't even manage Personal Loans. He should have connected me with Manish earlier. Couldn't understand why that still surprised me, even worse why it upset me?

'So tell me, Manish, how can I help you?'

'Been with Triton for over nine years now. Second job after campus. Boringly stable, right?'

I just smiled and still couldn't figure out where we had met earlier.

'There is a large corporate that we are tying up with, and they want to give loans to their employees for purchasing laptops. It's a large deal and we are trying to push it through this month, before the year-end. We've been at it with Oriental for months, but can't seem to get them moving. Their risk policies are too stringent.'

'Where are you stuck?' I had a feeling I was filching business from Kaushal, but consoled myself. I was just snooping around. Should I look at this deal for my current employer or for my future potential employer? These were strange times, indeed!

'Well, you see, they want all their employees to be able to access the offer. The problem with loans is that some employees may not get approved due to the risk policies. Now that makes it sticky for the employer and us.'

'So, what are you looking for?' This was getting interesting. I hadn't really applied my brains to a business challenge for quite some time. I missed the action and the deal making.

'Simple. Hundred per cent approval of all loans!'

'What numbers are we talking here?'

'Here's the thing, Ravi. We've got a huge stock of laptops that are going to be phased out soon. The new versions will be coming in next month. I need to liquidate quickly. I've got this large corporate willing to support me on this. I just need the financing arrangement in place.'

'Sounds good, but what's the scale of financing you're looking for?'

'If my projections are accurate, we should be able to push over 2,000 units this month at ₹ 25,000 a piece. I need to get this going.'

'That's around ₹ 5 crore, Manish!'

This was huge. Oriental was not big on Personal Loans. Could I get a piece of the action? Should I get a piece of the action? But how would this help me?

'Yes, around that figure.'

'Why such large numbers?'

'We're discounting heavily. Almost by 30 per cent. Don't want to do this in the open market as that would upset the trade. So building some goodwill with the corporate and liquidating as well.'

'But approving loans for all customers? That's not possible. I can understand why Oriental is stuck.'

'I was given the impression the deal would be through and had already shared this with my senior management. I don't want to be put in a tight spot. Would make my situation ...' Manish was looking nervous. It was March after all. Ratings were on the line everywhere.

'Let me look into this. I may have something I could work on. I'll get back to you ... and soon,' I smiled. This was going to be a long shot.

I had to meet Kaushal and was fine with a brief meeting. I was obviously eating into his action, but I did work for Imperial.

This was all messed up.

19:24 @ Taj Bangalore, Room No. 234

Kaushal had suggested we meet in the room to ensure privacy. He updated himself on the situation at Imperial, though he appeared to be clearly abreast of all the gossip.

I played it out till he got impatient. 'So, Ravi, have you given it any thought?'

He seemed more mellow today.

'Sir, it is an interesting opportunity. But, I needed some clarifications.'

'Have you discussed this with your team?' He was as sharp as ever, trying to get the pulse of the situation.

'I have mentioned it to a few.'

'Good. What do you have in mind?'

'We would need to ensure they are looked after as far as their designations, grades, responsibilities and salaries are concerned.'

'Point taken. As a ballpark I was looking at an 18 per cent increment over their existing salaries, considering the situation.'

Kaushal was looking at a hardball negotiation. I had come prepared for this. He wasn't going to treat us like chicken shit.

'I don't think I can get them to move for that, Kaushal. The guys that we are looking at shifting are the good ones,' I paused, wanting to sense his reaction.

'But 18 per cent is good, under the circumstances, don't you think?'

'These are some of the best regional managers in Imperial, if not THE best. Would there be any promotions?'

'Not at this stage, Ravi. Let them come on board, and then we can see what we can do for them in the next appraisal cycle?' I was surprised, he played that one on me. One of the oldest tricks in the recruitment book. Come on board, and we'll look after you, but not now! Go take a walk!

'Sir, I know they will not come for that number. And, we do want them to bring their clients and business contacts with them as well. They know that's as good as buying the Imperial business, without actually paying for it!' We both knew the discussion was relevant to my position as well in this transaction.

'They need to be realistic. They also need to understand that they would be joining Oriental. A much larger bank and many more opportunities for growth. This is a very good opportunity.'

Time to change gear. 'I'm not doubting that Kaushal, but I know it will not work at 18 per cent. Don't think it's worth going to them with that?'

'Okay, let's park that aside for right now. What else?'

'I know you've already got an existing set of branch managers and city heads, like I do. So, how's this going to work? Who replaces whom?'

'I've got to work out the finer details, but ideally wanted you to come on board and manage that. As I mentioned quite a few would move to the Non-Banking Financial Company that we are setting up.'

This was going to be dirty and very sticky.

20:47 @ Taj Bangalore, Still in Room No. 234

Kaushal had been trying every game in the book to wear me out. I stood my ground.

'You need to more flexible, Ravi. You must understand I need to take the board's approval for this. I can't cross some limits.'

'I understand, Kaushal, but I believe we should move forward with something only when we both have conviction. I'm sure we need to up the ante to make it smooth.'

'Okay, Ravi, I told you 26 per cent was the maximum I can offer. I really can't go beyond that. This needs to make business sense as well.'

'I agree, Kaushal, but the team was looking for 40 per cent and a joining bonus of two months' salary!'

Thought I'd play it high. The stakes were higher! He had already offered an over 22 per cent hike to the team on his own in Hyderabad. He would have known that. He was testing me. The salaries at Imperial were lower. Plus there would have been a premium payable for a mass recruitment.

'That's way too steep. I also need to make sure I don't upset the salary structure with the existing team.'

'Okay, Kaushal, then let's work it this way. I'll push 26 per cent with a fixed 10 per cent increment within three months of joining.

That will ensure they too will get increments along with the rest of the team at Orient. I'm sure the increments at Orient would be much more that 10 per cent.'

'Yes, of course, for the performers, it could be more as well. But Ravi, all this on one condition that I get the full team you mentioned. I'm taking this to the board, so you can't let me down on this.' He had started the roller again.

'That would be tough, Kaushal, but let me see what I can do.'

'Good, you will have to get back soon. I've got a board meeting in the last week of March.'

'I will get back, Kaushal as soon as I can.'

'And Ravi, clear those Internal Audit matters soon. Wouldn't reflect well on me,' Kaushal rose to shake hands, signalling an end to the meeting.

Damn!

22:12 @ Home

'Sav, did you speak with HR?'

She was beaming. 'Yes! Yes! Yes!'

She hugged me again. I had already received a fair amount of hugs, kisses and more earlier in the morning.

'What did they say?'

'I'm untouchable. I am God! I am hot! Ouch! I'm sizzling!' She hugged me yet again. That is because we were in the bedroom. She would never have dared otherwise what with the folks and the kids.

'I don't think you were this happy even when I proposed to you?'

'Of course, I was. Only, I didn't think the hangover would last this long!' she smiled and planted a wet kiss on my cheek.

Some action at last!

March

18

Of Conscience and Decisions

07:12 @ **Home**

SMS from Maithili: 'You're being distant again.'

Read the message twice ... wondering how to respond as Savitha walked in with coffee.

'What're the folks doing?'

'They're in their room. Dad is resting.'

'They okay?'

Savitha placed my cup on the bedside table and rested herself on the bean bag with her cup.

'Dad seems to be feeling low. He's quite stressed about everything going on here ... with us ...'

'Did he say anything...?'

She took a few sips of coffee and looked at me. 'They both seemed concerned about us ... you know ... our jobs ... the pregnancy ... everything ...'

Heavy silence.

I had a feeling the euphoria of the previous night was dissipating. I didn't want to start the day with a volatile conversation. She was possibly steering me towards a talk on the hankie and my alleged affair. I just wasn't up to it, besides I also had Maithili to deal with.

'How's Srikanth? He had a mild fever last night?' I deflected.

She didn't respond. Camaraderie broken. Tension was back in the air.

09:37 **En Route to Office**

'Morning, Devendra, how're the numbers looking?' I was speaking with the Hyderabad head.

'Boss, we are still slogging it out. I'm really whipping the team. The branch teams are also out in the field making sales pitches, getting business. They're all working towards that number. They're kind of fighting for their lives now. I would really hate to see any of them get fired. It's not fair, sir!'

Devendra was getting quite theatrical, getting to be quite the showman, possibly overdoing it.

'I understand, Devendra. Let me know if there is anything else I can do for you.'

'Boss, do anything, but I can't see any of them jobless. You should come here and see the kind of work they're doing. We are going to break all records, boss. Then let me see who'll have the guts to fire anyone in my region!' Devendra was sounding anxious.

'Devendra ... calm down.'

'Okay, boss!'

'I've been thinking about something ...'

'What, boss?'

'Off the record ...'

'Sure ...'

'Oriental may be keen on hiring you and some of your team?'

Devendra cracked up. 'I'll go raving mad, if you ask me to even consider that option! I've spent the last two weeks pushing my Relationship Managers not to move over. And now you're suggesting that I push them over again? They'll think I've gone crazy!'

'Just think about it ...'

A long pause, then:

'Would you be moving as well? Wouldn't consider it otherwise ...' When he wanted, Devendra could roll out the butter by the truckloads.

'Think through it and get back to me. And Devendra, don't talk too much about this.'

The conversation with Devendra made me restless. Would this distract the team from its targets? *Shit!* What the hell did I want? I had no frigging clue. I was just going all guns blazing on every front. Didn't want to calm down and think. It was too frightening. Even worse, Devendra might squeal – he was sounding edgy!

10:26 @ Office
I should have been positive after the meeting with Kaushal. A 26 per cent hike for the team would have implied a much better hike for me. If I could sew this up in the next couple of days, my back-up plan might actually salvage my situation.

Maithili seemed to have Sriram and Amitabh in her pocket. Dheeraj was well connected in the head office and possibly Singapore as well. I clearly had one in Vikram, but his position and clout would surely be diluted by now.

I was going insane sitting in my cabin and being in the office the whole day. I needed to get out. The chance meeting with Manish Malhotra of Triton had got my mind working on overdrive. Imperial had been trying to pick up speed on Personal Loans for some time. A deal of this nature would give us a huge revenue upside and also bring me into the spotlight again.

I had spoken with Manish earlier in the morning and had asked him to fix up a meeting with the corporate with whom he was trying to do the tie up. It turned out to be Axis Infomatics, one of Bangalore's largest IT companies. We had been trying to start a relationship with them forever. If this worked, this would have been a double whammy.

'Karan … Karan!' I screamed. Could never seem to get rid of that nasty habit of shouting for him.

Karan came running. 'Yes, boss!'

I briefed him. 'Karan, you really need this deal!'

Karan smiled. 'Game for doing my target any time.'

12:47
Karan walked in after the meeting with Axis Infomatics. 'Boss, large deal, but no hope in hell!'

'What happened?'

'Axis wants our assurance that none of their employees will

be rejected if they apply for a personal loan! That means all customers need to be approved for the loan.'

Karan seated himself on the chair, and shook his head ruefully. 'Waste of time, boss.'

This could have been a game-changer. One of those much needed headline-grabbing emails.

'What if they guarantee the loans instead?'

Karan moved closer. 'How would that work, boss?'

'Simple. The employees sign a declaration to Imperial stating that in case they default, we can recover the amount from their salaries.'

'Have we ever done that before?'

'There is a first time for everything, Karan! Check it out with them. Figure out the paperwork with Risk and Legal. Got that?'

'Yes, boss. One more thing, you're pushing for business here and also asking us to switch to Oriental. I'm confused!'

'Karan, let me make this extremely clear. Oriental is a back-up option if things don't work in our favour over the next few weeks. And, when you speak with the team, don't mention my name. I'm trying to get them the offers from Oriental, independent of whether I move or not. Is that clear?'

Karan looked perplexed. 'Quite a risk you're taking, boss. Not you, but we.'

'I know, Karan!'

Maybe this decision on Oriental was too risky. I had exposed myself to too many people. I trusted my team, but one slip and I would be finished. I was relying on Kaushal's word.

'Boss, Vinesh has met with five of my team members.'

I looked up, 'And ...'

'I get the feeling they may have spilled the beans!'

'You're kidding, Karan?'

'Nope! Vinesh was playing hardball. He may be on to us!'

13:42
Maithili had called twice since the morning. I had disconnected each time. There were no further SMSs after the one in the morning. I finally decided to return the call.

'Hey, M!'

'Hi, Ravi …'

I was hoping she wouldn't discuss Chennai. There was too much happening in the office as it is, without the added distraction.

'The usual!'

'Have you heard from Akash on the Singapore Development Bank?'

It just struck me we seemed to have a potential competitive conflict situation on most dimensions in our lives right now, be it the restructuring, sales number achievements, the Singapore job and now even our personal lives. There was, of course, a distinct possibility that she was also involved in framing me on the fraud matters. This relationship was getting weirder by the day.

'How about you?'

She laughed, realizing a clear response wasn't coming her way. 'Do you think about Chennai?'

I didn't respond.

'Ravi … you there?'

'Here in Bangalore, M!'

These were mind games. She was trying to distract me and I couldn't afford to take my eyes off the ball. There was too much happening. This conversation would have to wait, even if it hurt her.

'Aren't you comfortable talking about it?'

'This is not the time, Maithili.'

She paused, then laughed again. 'What else is happening? Heard you're working on some large deal?'

How the hell did she know about Triton? Was Karan leaking information? Even if she knew, she wouldn't have been that obvious! Must have been someone else.

'I wish ... You still haven't told me the secret behind your recent spurt!'

'Wish I knew. Sometimes, it just comes together ...'

'I know!'

'And ... Ravi ...'

'Yup!'

'Any luck with the Credit Card fraud? Do let me know if I can do something? Even Sriram is quite concerned. He does have a soft corner for you ... you know that, right?'

What?! The damn jerk was trying to run me off a cliff till yesterday. This conversation was getting to be one full of strange contradictions!

'I'm sure ...'

'*Chal* ... Ravi ... Gotta go ... Catch you later?'

I disconnected.

15: 28

Vinesh had continued interrogating my team, and had apparently made a few calls to Chennai as well. I needed to understand if he indeed did have a clue about the mass exodus I was planning.

'Hi, Vinesh, got a minute?'

He looked at me as if he had been expecting me to drop in. I could see it in his eyes. He was on to something.

'Hey, Ravi ... sure ... come in ...'

'So, how's the bonus looking this year?'

Vinesh burst into laughter. He got up, walked around the table and sat on the chair beside me.

'Your sense of humour is unmatched in this organization!'

'Thank you, Vinesh!'

There was a long pause. He seemed to have something that he had wanted to ask me ... but was holding back. I had a hunch that he was onto me, but needed to get a better sense of it.

'You know Ravi ... these are interesting times. At one end we are looking at getting rid of people and then at the other end, you have banks willing to hire ...'

'It's a funny little world …'

'Strange things happen … and I've seen my own share of funny stuff. In these times, rumours can jeopardize one's career. I needn't tell you about that, only you know what you're going through. No one should get into something that they will find extremely difficult to get out of – even if one is only exploring …'

'Are you talking about your cashew business, Vinesh?'

Vinesh smiled. 'How I wish, Ravi …'

There was silence for a few seconds again. He seemed to be heading for the kill, but he didn't seem very sure. He wasn't a person to hold back if he were on to something. I decided to take him on.

'You should spend some time with the team you know, address some of their queries and doubts. There's so much uncertainty …'

'Will do, Ravi … I do keep in touch with them, you know?'

'I've heard … and what are they saying?'

'Oh … the usual … they're restless …'

'About?'

'Life and the options it throws at you …'

The conversation was meandering, but I was convinced he was onto something about Oriental and my role in it.

'That's your forte! Anyway… I need to head for a meeting … catch you later …'

'Sure, Ravi. Say hi to Kaushal for me!'

Shit! He was definitely on to me.

31

18:31

The Credit Card fraud situation needed to be addressed quickly. I needed over ₹5 lakh to pay the cops for their 'recovery' assistance. Kumar had been following up with me on a daily basis to keep the heat on, but I was hesitating to make the move. My back was against a wall. I needed to clear this mess up. But I wasn't sure whether I wanted to play dirty. And then there was that matter with Raghu that was niggling me.

I logged into my Internet bank account to check my balance.

If I withdrew ₹ 5 lakh, it would wipe out the free funds in the account. The recent crash in my stock portfolio hadn't helped matters. My reputation was tarnished. Nothing made any sense. It was a matter of pride and principle, but was this the right place for either? Wasn't it time I became more practical?

I logged into the core banking system and looked up Raghu Nair's Customer Relationship Number. Before my conscience woke up, I decided to dive in further. I scanned his account details. He had over ₹ 2 lakh in his account, but he also had over ₹ 7 lakh in fixed deposits and around ₹ 10 lakh worth of mutual funds in his investment account. I logged out of the core banking system and opened the Internet banking screen.

One needed a login password to access the account and a transaction password to make any transaction via Internet Banking.

I closed my eyes and tried to clear my mind. What was I up to?

Then, a shot of energy sped through me. I pulled out my notebook from the bag and moved to 1st March.

It was sitting right there. Looking beautiful, in his own handwriting. The bugger had jotted down his passwords when he was in office that day for the review meeting. Fantastic!

I called up Kumar. 'Good time to talk?'

'Yes. How have you been?'

'Listen, this has been a tough call. Let's do it. How long will it take?'

'You sure?'

'No! But I don't have any options.'

'Fine then, Ravi, I'll set the wheels in motion. Let me get back to you once it's done.'

'How long?' I was perspiring.

'I'll push them to make payments into the Credit Card account tomorrow itself. The funds should start appearing as credited into the account on Monday. That work for you?'

'Can't ask for anything more, if only they can ensure the payments are cleared by Monday.' Patrick's meeting was scheduled for Tuesday. I needed to make it for that. This was too close for comfort.

'What about the balance money payable, Ravi?'

'Got a pen and paper?'

'Gimme a sec ...'

He seemed to be at home. He scrambled around looking for a pen and paper. While he was scrounging, my mind went into overdrive. Why hadn't I thought of this earlier?

'Ravi ... I'm back. Shoot ...'

'The plan is still on, Kumar. But we are going to do this slightly differently.'

'How's that?'

'Tell the cops they can keep 40 per cent instead of the earlier 30!'

'Have you gone mad?'

'Take these down,' I read out Raghu's login id, login password and transaction password.

'Whose Internet banking details are these?'

'Raghu Nair!'

'And what do you want to do with them?'

'My suggestion is that the crooks pay 60 per cent from their accounts and the balance from the account I've just given you.'

'So, you want them to hack into his account?'

'They'll get an additional 10 per cent for it. The cops and the gang can decide how to split the additional amount. Their call. And Kumar, they're not hacking. It's an additional 10 minutes work for them. And, they'll be earning over ₹ 1.5 lakh for it!'

'Wicked, Ravi!'

'I just found myself.' I hated myself for what I was doing.

'What if they go tell Raghu about this? This is already quite messy ...'

'Hadn't thought of that? Any suggestions?'

'We could get someone else to do it. Then it remains clean, and neither the cops nor the gang know about this.'

'You have someone in mind?'

'I think the additional 10 per cent solves that dilemma.

There is this guy I know. A consummate hacker. Could do with the funds. He'll also be able to make sure they are unable to trace the IP address in case there is an investigation later. He'll be able to pull it off!'

'Great! I think we've got this sewn up! And, Kumar, in case I forget, ask him to login today and deactivate the SMS and email alerts on the account or to give some other details for the alerts. They need to make sure the account-holder doesn't receive alerts when the transaction finally takes place. That could create complications!'

'You're slimier than I thought possible, Ravi,' I could hear the admiration in Kumar's voice.

'And, one last thing ... The payment from the account I've given you should be done on Saturday. Got that? Saturday. It's important!'

I disconnected. I was feeling good. Now I needed to get Raghu out of Chennai, to be on the safe side.

19:45 En Route Home

Anxiety had set in again. Wished this could have been done instantly. Would have to wait till Monday to see this through.

Kumar called, 'Ravi, who do you think triggered this? Was it really Raghu or someone else?'

'Not sure, but I do know it involves Raghu for sure.'

'What's motivating him? You must have really pissed him off. What did you do?'

'No idea. Nothing out of the ordinary I am sure. It has been puzzling me for quite some time.'

'Gut feel, Ravi, he's not in this alone. There is a larger set of jokers chasing your ass. This may not end here!'

21:24 @ Home

Vinesh messaged: *'Let's chat tomorrow morning.'*

Had my team cracked? Was Oriental going to be a ghost that would haunt me?

March

	1	2	3	4	5	6
7	8	9	10	11	12	13
14	15	16	17	18	**19**	20
21	22	23	24	25	26	27
28	29	30	31			

Ringa ringa roses ...

06:44 @ Home

Imperial Insider: Imperial India CEO Vikram Rathore quit Imperial today. Is he taking his senior management team with him? Imperial Insider: Amitabh on his way out?

The morning Tweets had the BlackBerry buzzing with emails and text messages. I called Mayur, the IT head. I needed my dose of gossip alongwith the south Indian coffee that I was sipping.

'Morning, Mayur, I was sure you'd be up!'

'Hi, Ravi, guess you read the Insider?'

'Yup! Now it is your turn to tell me that you knew this was coming …'

Mayur laughed, 'On this one, at least, let me assure you even I didn't have a clue till last night. I knew Patrick had changed his India plans because of some issues. He didn't want to meet Vikram. I don't know what's the deal between them but the official version is that there were some other meetings he had to attend. This came in only last night. This guy on Twitter is really up to date, man. I'm impressed!'

'So, what about Amitabh? Especially with that chap Patel coming in!'

'Amitabh is in very troubled waters right now. I wouldn't want to be in his position. That could be another reason he's not been calling you too much. He's out of the Sales Head role, for sure. He's fighting for survival now. If he doesn't make it as CEO …'

'Tell me … who's calling the shots on the firing list?' I should have actually asked him earlier.

'The million-dollar question! HR is leading this one. They're looking at employee ratings over the last two years. Then they're also evaluating the impact on reorganization. Some stuff happening in Operations as well. Even my team will be affected.'

'But, they must be consulting the department heads?'

'Kind of ... They are running them through the lists, but the fact is that the heads have a limited say, considering that there might be some reshuffling and restructuring in the head office as well.'

'What kind or reorganization?'

'They are looking at merging IT and Operations under one head and Sriram is pushing for Investments to be merged with Assets. Even Legal and Compliance may be merged. Everyone is in a mess right now. Finance is the only one untouched. No one understands what they do and more importantly, how they do what they do.'

There went my chances of trying to get a role in the head office!

'I'm sorry to hear that, Mayur. But you're sounding quite cool?'

'Have no choice but to be bloody cool. Gawd is great!' Mayur laughed, but the anxiety was evident.

I had tons of questions for him, but figured he would be stewing in his own misery right now.

'Thanks, Mayur, and hang in there. They need you. Don't worry.'

'Thanks, man. I have been meaning to chat with you about something. But it's personal. Hope you don't mind?'

'No, feel free.'

'I've been thinking about your situation and have looked at it objectively. You are facing quite a few challenges right now and I'm not just referring to the Internal Audit matter. You there?'

'Yes, Mayur ...'

'You're a great sales guy. But there are many great sales guys here. You're a good leader. I have interacted with your team. They look up to you, and genuinely; but there are many other great leaders as well. You know your business, but like that as well. You know what your challenge is ...?'

'All ears ...'

'You need to make yourself indispensable. You've been doing great, but why should they stick around with you and not anyone else who has similar qualities? No one's got anything significantly negative to say about you. You've got decent visibility in the head office. Could be better, of course. And, don't get me wrong, I'm saying this to myself as I speak with you. We all need to face up to it. None of us are safe!'

'What do you suggest, Mayur?'

'You need to think that through. Work on your perception. You need people here to back you and fight for you. That's what we all need. I wish had an answer for you …'

'Thanks, Mayur, and look after yourself.'

I had a CEO who would have backed me, but he was on his way out. My boss, in all likelihood, was on a path of no return to destruction or stardom. Could swing either way. My peers were better connected or sleeping with their bosses. My subordinates were trying to screw me to hell and back.

I didn't need to work on my perception. I needed a godfather!

10:34 @ Office, In Vinesh's Cabin

I was catching up with Vinesh Menon on the morning's developments. I was curious to see what he had on his mind.

Got a call from Mayur, as I sat opposite Vinesh.

'Hi, Mayur!' I was surprised.

'Got a minute?'

'Sure. What's up?'

'He's put in his papers. It's official. He called in the senior management and formally shared it with all of us. Quite brief. He didn't look sad or happy. Just pensive. Couldn't figure it out. Sad to see him go!'

'I know, Mayur. Any news on the incoming CEO?'

'No. He spent barely 15 minutes with us. Light conversation. Was very formal. Almost cold.'

'You're sounding disturbed.'

'Yes, I am!'

'Why?'

'He spoke with Shinzo earlier, and they said he could leave before the 31st if he liked, that he didn't need to wait for the new CEO or handover to anyone. They treated him like some domestic help.'

'He told you this?'

'No, he just said he'd be leaving later this month. I know how this works. It just seemed wrong.'

'Is Shinzo coming in to see him off?'

'Nope! He said bye on the phone. There will be an email from Shinzo or Patrick, not quite sure yet, informing the India team that Vikram is moving on. If they feel like it, they might say thanks, but knowing the mood, that seems unlikely.'

'It hurts.'

'It sucks, Ravi ... it sucks.' He disconnected.

'Big boss put in his papers?' Vinesh asked politely. He was reading his SMSs. Must have got the news from the head office.

'Yes.'

'Hmm ...'

'What does that mean?'

'Well, we were expecting this to happen when Patrick came to India.'

'So, how does this change anything?'

'Well, there's no one designated to formally act as the CEO. So who's going to approve the list of people to be terminated?!'

I laughed. 'You're a funny man, Vinesh, you know that?'

He chuckled and continued, 'Your team is looking nervous, Ravi!'

'How would you feel in their position?'

'But they seem to be up to something. You may be having another Hyderabad happening here as well. Just a gut feeling, but I may be wrong!' Vinesh was directly in my eyes, trying to size up my reaction and body language.

I remained calm, 'What gave you that feeling?'

He paused for a few seconds and looking towards me,

continued, 'Let me just say that they weren't as anxious as I thought they might be …!'

He was on to me for sure!

15:25 In My Cabin

'Hi, boss.'

'Hi, Devendra. What's the news from Hyderabad?'

'Is this a good time, boss?'

'Go ahead, Devendra.'

'Spoken with the team. Getting mixed reactions. This is quite crazy … I spent the first half of the month keeping some of them back, and now I'm asking them to move on. I'll follow you, boss. I will work with you. But all this is not making sense.'

'Devendra …'

'Please allow me to finish. You've seen the way they've let the CEO go. It's disgusting. And that's for a CEO! So, what are we? And where do we fall in the larger picture?'

Didn't he understand that he was on the scanner too and would be struck off, the moment I left the bank?

'Devendra …'

'I'll convince them, boss. They'll go for the money and I know that. But, I'm not sure about myself. I'm not sure if this is the way I want to leave.'

'What do you mean, Devendra?'

'I've yet to make my mark on Hyderabad. There's lots more work to be done. I've groomed this team and now they've finally started delivering. I can't just switch off. I've delivered on every assignment given to me. Do you remember what you told me when you brought me into Hyderabad, boss?'

'Yes, I do, Devendra.'

'You asked me to double the business. You explained to me how I could do it with the same number of people. You told me which products to focus on. You came on sales calls with me. I've built relationships with my clients. They look up to me and my team. I can't just switch off … It's like walking out from the ring midway.'

'I know what you're feeling. But first calm down.'

'Please don't ask me to calm down. Not on this issue. You probably think me foolish. But I choose this battle. I want someone to tell me why they want to fire me. And then justify it. I'll take them to court. I will walk out when I know I've succeeded with what you'd asked me to do here, or I'll put in my papers the day I feel I will fail. Please excuse me if I'm being rude, but I have thought this through. If you want to take my team, fine. I'll even help you. I'll rebuild from scratch again if required. But, I'll stick around.'

Was he getting senile? Or did he see an upside if I left with the team? He and Raghu would be the senior members with an understanding of the market in the South. He would show his solidarity with the new management. He was smart. Or was I over analysing?

'Devendra, do you know what a pink slip is?'

'I know what it is. It can be hell.'

'I respect your opinion and respect you for standing up for what you believe in. So give me some time. I'll come back to you.'

What was he up to? Was this another front opening up? I just couldn't take on one more pitched battle right now!

This was not going according to plan. Was I playing it all wrong? Was I dragging my team into my battle? Maybe I had a vendetta issue. Had I really thought about my team? Was this good for them? Should I move forward with this, or hold back?

I was running out of time.

18:55

On the intercom, 'Karan? Can you come in please?'

He walked in. 'You called?'

'You're going to Chennai tomorrow!'

'Pardon me?'

'Go speak with the team there about Oriental.'

'You mean fly?'

'Drive down. Fly down. Go and get the job done.'

'But I hardly know the team there,' Karan was reluctant. Was he cracking too?

'So ... get to know them. Oh, and I need not mention that Raghu should not hear about this.'

'Boss! How am I going to manage that as well?'

'I've sent him off to Tirupur!' I smiled.

March

20

A prince never lacks legitimate reasons to break his promise

– Machiavelli

12:14 @ Home, With Dad in the Balcony

Dad and I were debating the role of faith and God in modern society. He had never been comfortable with my atheist stance, and believed that my children should not be influenced by my choices, in this matter at least.

It was getting quite intense for a Saturday morning. The afternoon sun had picked up steam. This would have ideally meant some chilled beers and hot deep-fried vegetable pakoras. But I was having to make do with strong filter coffee instead.

Make do... The story of my life!

Thankfully, I heard the BlackBerry ringing and rushed into the bedroom. It was Kumar. Hope everything had gone well.

'Ravi? Kumar.' He sounded serious.

'Yes!' I waited, fingers crossed.

'They've made 60 per cent payment into the Credit Card account. It's about the balance 40 per cent.'

'Any issues with the info I've given you?'

'Was thinking about our conversation last night. Made a few calls, but drew a blank. I then scanned the records on my PC – the data I had from the credit counselling service I was managing. The suspects were a regular feature on our collections radar. They have been operating under multiple identities, addresses and occupations. Must have scammed over ₹ 4 crore via Credit Cards and Personal Loans. The scam is much larger than even I had expected. And guess what?'

'What ...?'

'Mithilesh has been involved in these transactions directly, which is why it didn't strike me earlier. He's definitely got a role to play in this. Couldn't have gone through without him.'

What? Since when did Imperial get so shitty? More

importantly, why was I getting sucked into this muck? They could have simply fired me. Why the hell did they need to screw with my reputation?

'What's driving Mithilesh?'

'No clue. You need to figure that out.'

My mind went in a million directions. Our flashpoints were legend in Imperial. But surely that wouldn't have driven him to such lows?

'One more thing, Ravi. You sure it's Raghu who screwed you?'

A surprising question, but he did have a valid point? Did I have conclusive proof linking Raghu? Was Raghu as much a victim in this as I was? Kumar had sown that seed of doubt. I needed to think this through. But I didn't have time. To get a clean chit on Monday, this had to happen today. I didn't care, any more. I needed closure, and soon.

'Just go for it, Kumar.' I disconnected.

I stood quietly in the bedroom, eyes closed, head bowed, trying to calm my anxiety. That sinking feeling was back again! Also had to go back and continue my discussion with Dad on the change in the Indian value system and the role of religion in modern life. *Damn!* But God didn't work his ass off in Imperial. Neither could he be laid off by them!

15:30 @ Home, The Beginning of an Afternoon Siesta ...

'Hi, Karan.'

He was calling from Chennai. 'Boss? I've finished the meeting. I'm staying back overnight, will return to Bangalore in the morning.'

'Sure, where are you staying?'

'Drove to Chennai with my wife. Thought I could do with some company on the way in. Turning out to be expensive. At the Taj.'

'A second honeymoon?' I laughed.

'I'm counting on it,' Karan sounded miffed.

'How was your meeting?'

'Mixed. Don't know them too well. Had met them at the sales conferences last year. So kind of acquainted with them. It took me a while to break the ice.'

'You have issues on that?' The call with Devendra had made me restless. I was wondering if there were were any more surprises coming my way.

'I had a feeling one of them might leak it out to Raghu, but I sorted him out. He was more anxious about the hike he would get and whether his appraisal would be harmed if Raghu found out about the meeting. They're all quite nervous, but I think on board.'

I sent an SMS to Kaushal: *'Need to speak with you, sir. Can you suggest a good time? Regards, Ravi.'*

Kaushal responded: *'Let's speak tomorrow afternoon. Around 2.'*

15:54 @ In Bed, Tossing

The mobile was buzzing. I had sent an SMS to the CEO, congratulating him on his new assignment, wishing him the best.

I had built hopes on having gained his confidence over the last fortnight, and that he may consider me for a role in the new organization. I had, after all, made his new assignment possible!

'Good afternoon, sir. Good to hear from you.'

'Hi, Ravi. Thanks for your wishes,' he paused.

'Congratulations on your new assignment. We will all miss you at Imperial.'

'I'll miss Imperial too. It's been an enriching experience. I would like to think I've contributed to its growth in India,' he seemed aloof, formal.

'The organization will miss you, sir. But I'm sure you'll find the new assignment equally challenging.' With a ₹ 5 crore package, I'm sure it will be more than fulfilling.

'Yes, Ravi, I'm looking forward to the new challenge. They have big plans,' he clammed up again.

What the hell was with him? 'Sir, I'm sure you would need

to plan your resources as well with the expansion plans?' I was hoping that I had been pretty obvious in angling for a job. I actually wanted to go down on my knees. I would have definitely done it if this call was a video conference.

'They have a large team in place already, but I need to consolidate my position before we surge forward. The financial climate is quite challenging as it is. So, let's see how the canvas unfolds.'

Canvas unfolds? Man, I need a job! Couldn't he give me some job in some corner of his empire? After everything I had done for him!

I decided to get shameless, and beg. *What the hell!* 'Sir, do let me know if I can contribute in any manner to your new organization?'

A pause, much longer than usual!

'Ravi, I will make a note of that. One of the key reasons I'm joining Milsons is the strong focus they have on aspects of compliance and integrity. I would like to maintain that in everything that we do, and in the leadership team that I build.'

The jerk! I was his blue-eyed boy. I had been highlighted to the global HR team at Imperial. But for the bloody crash in Brazil, I would have been on some accelerated leadership development programme in Imperial, criss-crossing the globe, buying a yacht for my 40th birthday. And, now he was making me out to be a pariah in the world of finance!

'I wouldn't want to take up too much of your time, sir. Wish you all the very best, once again.'

'Thank you so much, Ravi. Please convey my best wishes to your family. We should meet once I've settled in Bangalore. All the best.'

'Thank you, sir.'

I made it a point to disconnect before him. That slimy son of a bitch!

20:12 @ Kumar's Residence

I downed four pegs and half a pack with Chris Rea crooning:

'And all the roads jam up with credit
And there's nothing you can do
It's all just bits of paper flying away from you
Oh, look out world, take a good look
What comes down here
You must learn this lesson fast and learn it well
This ain't no upwardly mobile freeway
Oh no, this is the road
Said this is the road
This is the road to hell ...'

'You sissy ... Why do you work? Why do you go to office every morning?'

I had wanted to celebrate. I had gotten rid of both the Credit Card fraud and Raghu Nair. And in the process I learnt that Kumar was the only one I could turn to. My goddamn existence sucked. I had found refuge in an alcoholic crook. He seemed to be the only one I could be brutally honest with.

'To earn a salary! Why else?'

'You're a sucker ... that's why! It's more than the salary. It's those fancy designations, the suits, the fancy parties ...'

'Those help. But I think it's also the power. You know, when you walk into that office each day, you see all those people around you. They salute you. They look up to you. You control their fate. Awesome, Kumar!'

'For once you're being honest! You're not as screwed as I thought.'

My interactions with Kumar had been a humbling experience. He didn't care about my designation and even less for my work. He had been there and done that. To him, we were all a bunch of ass-licking hypocrites. He was right.

'I get a feeling there's a compliment in there somewhere!'

Kumar laughed and rose to prepare a joint. The moment I had been waiting for. I was too embarrassed to ask him. The previous joint had been thoroughly relaxing and rejuvenating. I needed to get into that space again. I had a tough week ahead and an even tougher one after that, if I survived that long!

He prepared two joints this time. I took the joint like a piece of candy. I had shed my regional manager and MNC banker attitude. It was just Ravi and his joint. Nothing else mattered.

As we both lit up, Jim Morrison decided to set the tempo with '*Light my fire*'. Quite apt, I thought.

'Now tell me, Mr Banker. Have you done her recently?'

'Who, man?'

'Maithili! Who else would do you?'

'It's not like that, Kumar.'

'If you insist, man. What are your chances of keeping your ass in the game?'

I didn't want to be politically correct. 'There are enough contenders in the ring as of now … that's for sure.'

'So you're buggered, right?'

'You could say that.'

'You'll need to play this differently. They're too smart for you. Well … not in the sense that you're thinking. They don't play by the same rules that you do. So, change your game.'

'Can you be more specific?'

'You need to find their weak spots. Raghu is the guy at the bottom of the food chain. You need to work it out up to the top.'

We both paused, then Kumar muttered, 'It is better to be feared than loved … if you cannot be both!'

'Machiavelli? Not bad, dude.'

'Pick up the tempo, Ravi. Chase them down, before they run you over.'

March

	1	2	3	4	5	6
7	8	9	10	11	12	13
14	15	16	17	18	19	20
21	22	23	24	25	26	27
28	29	30	31			

Damn!

07:55 @ **Home**

Waking up late on Sunday mornings, piping hot coffee, enjoying the Sunday editorial, playing with the kids on the bed ... *Not to be!*

These days it was about restless sleep, bags under the eyes, vendettas, fury, disgust, helplessness, sense of betrayal, revenge and a million other thoughts racing through the head.

'You sleep well?'

Savitha had been fast asleep a while back. I had obviously disturbed her slumber.

'I'm sleeping like a baby ...' she smiled as she stretched.

She seemed very content with her personal and professional state. *Shouldn't she be worrying about me?*

'Come on, Sav. Rise and shine. Get up. I can't sleep!'

Savitha pushed herself up and leaned back against the head-board.

'Come on, Ravi. It's Sunday. Even your parents won't mind if we sleep in late,' she was yawning as she spoke.

'What's happening at work?'

'The project is over on the 23rd, and then I'm unemployed. Since I'm pregnant, they're sending my boss to Shanghai. That hag has to go and live on snakes and octopus for dinner. I'm loving it! They just can't fire me! Their headache! God bless babies! May we can have one at every downturn! Now can I go back to sleep?'

I was happy for her. She didn't appear to be too worried about the state of affairs in my company. Was she leaving everything in the hands of fate? Or did she actually have confidence in my ability to see it through this mess?

09:45

I was reading an article on Triton Computers in the newspaper. They were planning to expand rapidly in India in the retail market, targeting over ₹ 800 crore in sales. I decided to go for it.

'Sriram, good morning. Ravi from Bangalore.' I was banking on the element of shock.

'Good morning, Ravi. Pleasant surprise. All well?'

'Yes, Sriram. Hope I'm not disturbing you. But it is quite important.'

'Sure, tell me.'

'You read the paper today? There is an article on Triton.'

'Yes, I browsed through it. Why?'

'A big deal opportunity that has just come my way, but there's not too much time.'

'And this is linked with Triton?'

'Yes, it is. They are looking at us to issue personal loans to a large corporate in Bangalore for purchasing their laptops. Quite a large amount.'

'You must have done those kind of deals before.'

'They need 100 per cent approval. No declines. All employees should be given a loan if they want a Triton laptop.'

'But, that's impossible. Even you should know that!'

'I know, Sriram. But it's over one million USD! I wanted your opinion before they close with Oriental tomorrow.'

USD and pound sterling were magical words of reckoning for the senior management these days. And Oriental could excite even the peon at office, not that we had any.

'One million USD?! That's quite a large amount. Are you sure?' Aha! That seemed to have got his interest.

'Met the corporate as well, seems authentic. What would you suggest? Oriental is close to finalizing.' I was laying it out for him. He just needed to suggest what I had already discussed with the corporate. It had to be his idea. That was the only way for him to back it. The word 'Oriental' should have done the trick.

'I'll have to think this through, Ravi. Can't just shoot offhand.'

'Thought I should share this with you, because I believe Triton is one of our clients in the UK. Patrick may be interested in doing business with them.' I had no frigging clue if Triton was our client, but my ignorance couldn't really harm him too much.

'Actually, why don't you call Mithilesh on this one? He might be able to suggest something?' This was getting better. He knew Mithilesh didn't manage Personal Loans, but wanted him there for the free ride and credit, of course.

'Triton was telling me they had approached Mithilesh earlier, but they hadn't heard from him …'

I was expecting silence and got it, in plenty.

'Hmmm … Mithilesh must have been on leave. But bring him into the deal anyway.'

'Sure, that would be great. But I have built up a relationship and they want to close quickly …'

He had resisted, but finally relented. 'Why don't you ask the corporate to guarantee the payments from the employees?'

'But why and how would they do that, sir?'

'Oh, it's quite simple. The bank will issue personal loans to the customers where they will sign an undertaking that we are authorized to recover outstandings from their salaries, if they default. We will also have an agreement with the corporate that they will help us recover the money from their employees' salaries. We have standard contracts for things like this. We just haven't done too many of these …'

'Will the corporate go for it?'

'A long shot Ravi, but give it a try. Let me know if you need anything?' This was getting even better. He was eating out of my hands.

'Sir, one more thing. If the corporate does agree, this would mean over 2,000 applications to be processed in the next couple of days. I could do with some extra hands.'

'Sure, Ravi. I'll speak with Mithilesh. His people can give you a hand on this one and process the applications.'

'Will let you know tomorrow in case it closes. Thanks once again.'

I smiled to myself. I was a genius. But Sriram could play this either way with me. I was building a bridge with him. Now, I needed to manage Amitabh. This would definitely piss him off.

10:34 Having Breakfast

Devendra called. 'Boss!'

'Good morning, Devendra.'

'Boss, it's urgent!'

'Tell me, Devendra. What is it?'

'One of the Relationship Managers just gave me a call. They're putting in their papers tomorrow. Oriental has upped the offer and is giving them an increased joining bonus!'

'I thought you had spoken with them.'

'Yes, boss, I had, but apparently the Oriental team spoke with them again last night. I had spoken with only five. Oriental is now speaking to 21.'

'21!'

'Yes, boss. 21.'

'That will wipe out most of your good RM population! And, why didn't you know about this earlier?'

'This just happened, boss. I'm calling you immediately.'

'Well, that doesn't help much, does it? You've really not managed the situation well. I'm very disappointed. Call me in a while.' I had Revathi on my lap, and had to maintain my calm as Devendra unravelled a situation which was going to disrupt my plans on the RM movement to Oriental. But I was under the impression that Kaushal and I had an understanding. Why did he make a move on the Hyderabad team? This was twisted.

I had been planning to wait for Kaushal's call but decided to call him instead. 'Sir, Ravi ...'

'Yes, Ravi. How've you been? Thought we were going to speak later in the day?'

'Sir, something's come up and needs your attention immediately.'

'I am in the midst of something here. Can't this wait?' Kaushal's tone was brusque, standoffish.

I decided to hold my ground. 'Would prefer it if we discuss this now.'

'Okay, Ravi! What is it?' He was throwing attitude.

'Oriental has increased the offers to my team in Hyderabad?'

'But those offers were already in place when we spoke, Ravi!'

'To 21 of them?'

'I don't recollect the exact number, but why do you ask?'

'The offer was further hiked on Saturday and the RMs are putting in their papers.'

'But I haven't spoken with them, Ravi,'

Of course not! One of his cronies must be closing the deal.

'I was under the impression that we had an understanding, sir.'

'But you were going to bring them anyway, Ravi. Even if this has happened, I don't see what the harm is.'

'I would still prefer it if I could bring them in. It could impact the client transition.'

'Let me see what I can do, Ravi. But I would imagine the HR team has already rolled out the offers. We're all working very hard.'

'Can you check and get back, sir? Before we speak later in the afternoon?'

'Let me try, Ravi,' he disconnected.

Obviously, he didn't like being questioned. Was Kaushal playing me as well?

10:46 Smoking in the Balcony

The dope session with Kumar had done me good. Had cleared up the head and helped me focus on issues that really mattered. I needed to focus on ripping the heart out of anyone who came in my path!

Damn the customer, damn the business, damn the targets

and damn everyone else. I would not let them take me down. I wouldn't let any one of them walk over me or treat me like a pussy!

10:55 @ Home, My Bedroom

Devendra was clearly helpless. The RMs would switch off from tomorrow morning itself. The numbers had already been on the decline over the last couple of days. Now, they would hit rock bottom.

The outcome of the next few calls would be important. Should I speak with Amitabh or the local HR guy, or the HR head? I needed to work it to my advantage.

I called Amitabh, knowing quite well that he would just shove me into the cauldron and slit my balls in the process. But one had to go through the gates of hell.

'Boss, needed to discuss something important.'

'Tell me, Ravi.'

I could sense his exasperation. 'We have a situation in Hyderabad – 21 RMs are going to be putting in their papers tomorrow!'

Thought it would be better to give it straight to him. He remained silent for 30 seconds.

'I'm disappointed, Ravi, that the situation had to come to this. You should have handled it better. What do you propose?'

Did all managers think and speak alike? 'Amitabh, the HR team has made absolutely no efforts to retain them. None whatsoever for over three weeks now. They're getting a huge jump.'

'Don't make excuses, Ravi. This is not the best timing either. You know that!'

'But Amitabh, I have been keeping you in the loop too.'

'Keeping me in the loop is not enough. You need to do more!'

'What would you suggest, Amitabh?'

'Speak with Jaideep. See what he has to say.'

Why in frigging hell couldn't he speak with Jaideep?

I disconnected. Possibly rude, but it seemed pointless discussing the matter with him any further. Just didn't get their politics … They treated us like pawns.

Was considering calling Vinesh, even though Amitabh had told me to call Jaideep. Finally, I decided to follow the boss' orders.

'Jaideep? Good morning. Ravi here.'

'Yes, Ravi?' He was sounding wide awake for a Sunday, quite unlike him.

'This is quite important, otherwise would not have disturbed you.'

'Give me a minute, Ravi. Be right back with you.'

I could hear Jaideep wishing someone goodbye. Thought I heard an exchange of kisses as well. Or, was it my overactive imagination?

'Yes, Ravi, had a guest leaving. Tell me. What's on your mind?'

'Jaideep, are you familiar with what is going on in Hyderabad?'

'Which situation, Ravi?'

'The RMs had been approached by Oriental with very aggressive offers. Have been speaking with Vinesh on this for over three weeks. The RMs have told Devendra they will be quitting tomorrow!'

'Hmmm …'

That was all that the future Asia head of HR could do in this situation. Make strange noises! Huh!

'Jaideep, no attempt has been made to retain them. None whatsoever!'

With that, I had possibly created a solemn enemy in Vinesh. Possibly not one of my wiser moves!

'But Ravi, one must be practical. We are under tremendous pressures. Plus we can't bow down to one set of people because another bank has made them a better offer. I need to think about the impact for the rest of the country as well. You would understand that. These are policy decisions.'

'Jaideep, I hear you, but this is going to cripple Hyderabad.

HR has to intervene in situations like this. They can't clean out the whole team!'

As if I cared!

'Ravi, let me think about it. I'll also have a word with Sriram to see if he's got people to spare?'

Spare! Sriram's team was frigging idle, arranging Solitaire competitions in the office. It was going to be my numbers going down the drain. Not his. That was the agenda and the situation was playing into their hands.

'I think Vinesh should come along for the meeting in Hyderabad. I'm sure he is better equipped to manage these situations.'

The last plea.

He didn't react. Almost thought he would ignore the request.

'Let me speak with Vinesh. Connect with him later in the day. Okay, Ravi?'

'Thanks, Jaideep. Have a great day.' I hoped he would sense the sarcasm in those words.

He knew I wouldn't be in the Patrick meeting on Tuesday. I needed to be there. I needed to make an impact. I needed to be heard.

I called Devendra. 'I'm coming to Hyderabad tomorrow.'

I disconnected. Needed to pull something out of the hat on this one.

It took me a while to calm my nerves and think carefully about the situation. I was planning to move to Oriental, so why was I losing my cool? It was about sticking around till I closed my deal. I needed to close my deal with Oriental earlier than the others.

I should have closed my offer earlier, but me and my bloody conscience worked against me. Why was I taking this personally? I should have been looking out for myself. I needed something to close.

Everything was wide open right now, in a state of flux. Nothing was moving towards a closure. Was I being unrealistic in expecting the job offer with Oriental to close so quickly? Vikram had sealed his offer with Imperial in a few hours!

I logged on to my Twitter account.

Imperial Insider: Ruckus in Hyderabad ... time for biryani?

I hated this guy's guts!

12:20 @ Home

I logged into the core banking system and checked into Raghu Nair's bank account. I smiled. His balance had been wiped out. Some of his fixed deposits as well. The beauty and power of Internet banking. I loved it. I was the devil incarnate!

I sent an SMS to Raghu, asking him to call. He called instantly.

'Morning, boss, how are you?' He seemed calm, obviously unaware of the calamity that had struck his bank account. I was going to enjoy this.

'Good. How was your trip to Tirupur?'

'I think we've made some breakthroughs. Was planning to send you an update on Monday.'

'Good. You think some business is coming in this month?'

'This month might be tough boss, but next month? For sure.'

I disconnected.

Enjoyed that thoroughly. Why had I done that?

14:28

Maithili had sent several SMSs since the morning. I decided to call her.

'Hi, M!'

'Hey, Ravi ... been busy?'

'Kinda!'

'Heard you've got your hands full in Hyderabad?'

Couldn't make out if it was genuine concern or sheer sadistic pleasure that she derived when she spoke like this. There were too many shades of grey in our relationship.

'How about you?'

'Think you've got a better team than mine ... no one seems to be poaching my boys,' she laughed.

'God bless mediocre talent!'

'You could say that. You seem to be having a fair amount of action at your end.'

She seemed totally clued in on all the developments in my region. Must have heard of the Triton deal as well.

'Let's see ...'

A long deliberate pause. The conversation till now appeared to be a precursor to the subject that she had on her mind.

'Why don't you want talk about Chennai?'

'Nothing to talk about!'

'Is that all it was to you?'

She was playing mind games and I needed to keep my focus. Had to ensure I wasn't distracted by this situation, but knew that she could play a role in influencing my future at Imperial.

'Let's talk about it when we meet?'

'If that's the way you want to play it ... Ravi ...'

I was hoping she would disconnect, but she remained on line.

'Let's speak later, M!'

'Ravi ...'

'Yes ... M!'

'Things are not always what they seem ...'

16:32 @ Home

Finally, Vinesh called.

'Hi Vinesh. How's your weekend?'

'Good, Ravi. Believe you're treating me to some biryani tomorrow?' Vinesh giggled.

Couldn't tolerate giggling men.

'Why not, Vinesh? I'm sure we can make some time for that.'

'What exactly do you expect from me in Hyderabad tomorrow?'

'Retain talent, Vinesh! Simple! Retain them!'

'Easier said than done. We have discussed this before and I

think Jaideep also mentioned the same thing when he spoke with you earlier today?'

'That's why I requested your expertise,' I laughed. Vinesh didn't.

'You know my hands are tied. Why are you playing with my ratings at the end of the year? This is a dead end. You know that.'

'Thought we should swim or sink together, Vinesh!'

'Good. Then you would love to know your good pal Mithilesh is also coming in for the ride!'

I had been expecting a twist, but not so fast. 'The more the merrier. I didn't know Mithilesh had joined HR.'

'Even I didn't, Ravi? He'll possibly become my boss soon,' Vinesh chuckled.

'And how has his highness landed up on this privileged assignment?'

'Sriram, Amitabh and Jaideep have been exchanging emails on the Hyderabad issue after your call. Their joint decision,' Vinesh sighed.

'But why is Sriram in the loop on this?'

Vinesh sighed. 'When will you get this? Jaideep is buttering all sides. He keeps everyone in the loop on everything! He scratches his ass, both Sriram and Amitabh get an email on it. It's been an email duel for the last two hours. Got tired just deleting them, leave alone reading them!'

'But, what's the exchange about?'

'Sriram proposed that Hyderabad be put under some 'Emergency Action' category. Don't know where he cooked that one up from. He is making a major *tamasha* about it! He wants a senior resource stationed in Hyderabad full-time till the situation comes under control and be monitored closely by a panel of senior management.'

Shit! 'And that would include?'

'The usual suspects. Sriram, Amitabh and Jaideep, of course!'

'And what would this committee achieve?'

'Nothing much. Sriram would be able to stick his finger in and keep raking up dirt. And all the dirt needs to find a source! You and Amitabh would be the target, of course.'

'How in the hell did this get to be this big?'

'Oh, that's simple. Since Vikram is on the way out, Jaideep marked both Shinzo and Patrick on the Hyderabad email to cover his ass. So, now everyone is freaking out and is trigger happy as usual. It is Sunday after all and everyone needs something to hump!'

18:53
'Hi, Kumar.'

'Hey, Ravi, can you speak?'

'Gimme a sec …'

I was with the children in the playground. I stepped away from the play area and walked towards my residence block.

'Yes, Kumar!'

'Maithili called. Seems to have heard about Raghu's bank account getting hacked!'

'How did she find out about it?'

'I'm guessing on this one … think Mithilesh told her. But not sure.'

'But why call you?'

'Let's just say, we have a strange bond, Ravi …'

'What else?'

'She was just groping around … asking if I knew anything about it? But I managed her.'

'You think she has anything to do with this?'

A long pause.

'Can't say … but would not be surprised if she were …'

'Hmmmm …'

'And Ravi, you have a situation in Hyderabad?'

'Is my life such an open book?'

Kumar laughed. 'Nope, but I got to hear of it.'

Twitter! *Shit!*

20:36
'Hi, Karan. Anything urgent?'
 'Kind of …'
 'What happened?'
 'Raghu called … He's very hassled …'
 'And …'
 'He's planning to file a police complaint …'
 'About the hacking?'
 'Yup …'
 'He should. It's quite shocking …' I had to remain calm.
 'Any idea how this happened, boss?'

Was Karan on to me? He possibly found the sequence of events to be too suspect.

 'Nope, but let me know if you find something …'

I disconnected and clicked on the Twitter icon.

Imperial Insider: Patrick the Piper coming to town!

22:41
'We need to buy shoes for Srikanth.'

Why did the shopping list always come out on Sunday evening?

 'Sure, let's get them next weekend.'

She returned to surfing channels, disgruntled with the content spewing out of the TV set. She eventually switched the TV off and flung the remote to her side.

 'Everything okay? Should we go to the doctor?'
 'For?'
 'Coz you're expecting …?'
 'I can manage, Ravi. Don't worry!'
 'I'm sure you can, but I am concerned about your health.'
 'Are you?'

The gloves were off!

 'What's going on Sav?'

There was a long pause. She seemed to be making an effort to cool down.

'I got a call today …'
'From?'
'… Maithili …'

My head was spinning with thoughts of possible divorce and with my luck I could only hope to get the kids in the settlement!

'Why? What did she say?'
'We didn't speak for too long.'
'But what did she say?'
'A few things!'

Why couldn't she just tell me? Hated this excruciating torture!

'What, Sav?'

I realized I had raised my voice and knew it would have implications.

'Anything you would like to share with me first?'

I felt like jumping out of bed and running out of the house screaming. Did Savitha finally know about Chennai?

'Not really, Sav …'

A long pause yet again.

'I believe both of you met in Chennai?'

Maithili had lost it for sure. What did she have against me? What had I done to her that she was being so vengeful?

'… And Ravi, are you up to something that could get this family into trouble?'

'Why do you ask?'

'Well … it was the way she was talking and mentioned that people can do strange things when under pressure. You didn't tell me that your Credit Card fraud issue had been resolved?'

It had occurred to me that in the rush of things I had forgotten to mention it to her.

'It's still not resolved, Sav!'

'There are quite a few things open … Aren't they, Ravi?'

She switched on the TV again …

March

22

Of Biryani and Bastards

10:32 @ Hyderabad Airport
The flight arrived late, but Devendra was waiting. Vinesh had decided to come in by a later flight, which gave me time to catch up with Devendra. As I stepped into the car, Karan called.

'Morning, boss. Hear about Raghu?' Karan seemed excited.

'What about Raghu?'

'Heard he's been called into Mumbai to meet Sameer in Internal Audit.'

'Why?'

'Not very clear. They want to question his linkage with the four Credit Card customers. The same ones for which you were being investigated.'

At last, a sense of relief and delight!

10:55 En Route to the Hyderabad Office
Sameer called. 'Morning, Ravi.'

'Good morning, Sameer.'

'Can we speak?'

'I am in Hyderabad, but tell me, Sameer…'

'The Credit Card fraud matter is being dropped. All outstandings have been cleared. It happened over the weekend.'

'They paid the full amount?'

'Yes, the full amount. But it is very strange. Your team member made a part payment!'

'What! Who?'

'Raghu Nair, your Chennai head! He is insisting he knows nothing and that his account has been hacked! Looks too much like a coincidence that the customers and he paid up the amounts due at similar times over the weekend. Don't you think so?'

'I'm just surprised, Sameer, not sure how to respond. This has been a traumatic experience for me.'

'I can imagine, Ravi, but I was referring to Raghu's involvement …'

'I have called Raghu to Mumbai. I wanted to give you a heads up. But I was also keen to have your point of view on the matter.'

Great! Should I nail the bastard or lie low. I needed this to blow away quickly and my name cleared.

'I will speak with Raghu, but I am as curious as you are …'

Sameer didn't respond but changed tack. 'Are you sure you are not familiar with what happened? Off the record!'

Why the hell did he think I'd fall for that?

'As I mentioned, Sameer, I'm just glad this will be over with. Have you informed Amitabh?'

'Yes, I've appraised him. Will be in touch, Ravi. Have a good trip.' He still sounded tentative.

'Thanks, Sameer.'

'Ravi … One more thing. I received an email with some old personal loan account numbers and customer names. Two of them match those of the four credit cards which you had cleared.'

Now what! 'And what does that have to do with me?'

'Not sure. Just thought I'd mention it. Those loans were settled, with huge write offs!'

Hell! What was he digging into now?

'Not familiar with it. Do you want me to look into it?'

'No. Just thought I'd share that with you. Will let you know if something comes up?'

Maybe Kumar was right. There was a larger conspiracy at hand.

12:20 @ Hyderabad Office, In Devendra's Cabin

I called up Kumar.

'Thanks a ton, Kumar. Owe you, big time.'

'No worries, Ravi. Things smoother now?'

'Relatively, yes. The Internal Audit has taken the heat off. Given me a clean chit as well.'

'Sounds good. Take care and be in touch. Stay in the fight ... and don't blink.'

Kumar sounded sincere.

'Appreciate it. Cheers!'

'My pleasure.'

'Oh, and Kumar? Sameer was mentioning some personal loan account numbers ...'

Kumar cut in. 'Let it be Ravi ... This one is on me!'

He disconnected.

What was he up to now?

I called up Kaushal. 'Sir, I'm in Hyderabad. I need to speak with you ...'

'Yes, Ravi. Tell me.'

'I'm in Hyderabad, sir. Was waiting for your call yesterday ... Did you check on the offers made to my RMs here?'

'Yes I did, Ravi. My HR confirmed that they have made the offers. I don't have the specific details.'

Of course, the bastard knew!

'Kaushal, I've been thinking this through. If I do come on board ... (deliberate pause) ... I'll prefer bringing in the team myself. And, I'm sure you'll understand.' I was repeating my earlier conversation – not that he would have forgotten.

Kaushal remained silent. The message was loud and clear. 'But Ravi, these are independent transactions!'

Transactions! He was yanking my chain.

'Sir, please do not consider these as independent. You must trust me on this. It will make more business sense for you if I pull this through. Or, you may not see the benefit in Hyderabad. HR has already worked out a back-up plan.'

Sure! The back-up plan was to bring in Mithilesh's team and start screwing up the business.

Kaushal needed the Relationship Managers, and, more importantly, their clients. That's what he was paying for!

'All right Ravi. Let me speak with HR.'

'Thank you, sir. Will wait to hear from you.' Had I signed my death knell on Oriental?

'Sure, Ravi, I just thought you may like to know. I'm updating the board on the new team structure later this week, as early as Thursday or Friday. I need the confirmations before that, before we can process the paperwork. Would like to update them, so that your transition into the new role can be expedited.'

Hyderabad was turning into an auspicious city.

'Thank you, sir. I'll be in touch.'

Kaushal disconnected.

I was all charged up. I hadn't felt like this in weeks. The cards were finally turning back in my favour. Should possibly stay back in Hyderabad, retain this good stretch. I was feeling in control again.

I stepped out of Devendra's cabin and started walking towards the conference room, when I heard a voice hailing me from behind. I detested that voice.

'Good afternoon, Ravi. Welcome to Hyderabad.'

I turned to meet my nemesis. 'Hi, Mithilesh, you shifting here?'

Mithilesh smiled, 'Prefer Bangalore myself. But, thought I'd come in and support the team. Believe you're going through a crisis here?'

'Whatever gave you that idea, Mithilesh?'

'Spoke with Sriram. He suggested I come here. We need to chip in for each other in times of crisis.'

'Mithilesh, I've told you keep away from branch operations.'

'Chill, Ravi. Why are you getting so worked up?'

'I'm heading for a meeting, Mithilesh …' I turned and rushed back in the direction of the conference room, knowing I needed to be less antagonistic to that creature. He could clearly influence my future in the bank. I needed to calm down quickly.

As I approached the conference room, the BlackBerry started buzzing. It was Amitabh.

'Ravi, what's the status?'

I changed directions to Devendra's room.

'I'm just getting into a meeting with them, boss.'

'So, why does the whole office know you've got a calamity in Hyderabad?'

Amitabh must have finally logged into Twitter.

'But I've just spoken with you and Jaideep, as you had suggested.'

I could hear Amitabh huffing on the other end. He bloody well knew it was Jaideep who had escalated the discussion. He was probably in a bad position himself. Felt sorry for him, but needed to establish that I wasn't alone on this one.

'Good! You will meet Mithilesh there.'

'What's his role?'

'Management thought it best if a senior resource is stationed there till the situation is under control.'

The management! Under control! That was a hysterical illusion.

'But what is Mithilesh expected to do?'

'He'll figure that out. We will have to move some of his team in if the Relationship Managers leave. Won't have time to recruit from outside and get them on board.'

'Boss ... I can ...'

'First go and meet the RMs and update me.'

'Yes, boss.'

'And Ravi, you'll have to come in tomorrow for the meeting with Patrick. Prepare a presentation on your region and the plans for next year.' Blunt. No emotion. Nothing to it.

'Yes, boss!'

I was in! I called Karan.

'Karan, you in office?'

'Yes, boss.'

'I've got a meeting with Patrick in Mumbai tomorrow. Make a presentation with the year's performance and next year's forecasts. Figure out from the head office how many slides are needed and work backwards.'

'For tomorrow?'

'Yes and tell Radhika to book a ticket for me for tonight and a room at The President ...'

'I'll get working on it right away.'

'Speak with Triton and see if there's any progress on that account. See if you can close it. That would be a real feather in our cap for tomorrow. This one is critical. Got that?'

'Yes, boss.'

I needed a trump card. Triton could be it.

12:55

Maithili sent an SMS: *'Like to catch up for a drink in the evening :) How's Hyderabad?'*

The bitch! Yanking my chain! News here spread like wildfire. I had to swing this in Hyderabad. Else the dogs would lynch me in Mumbai.

I stepped out of the room and tracked down Devendra and took him outside the office for a smoke.

'Devendra, what's the raise that they are being offered?'

'Around an 18 per cent increment and one month's joining bonus.'

'Tell them they're getting short-changed and a better deal has been worked out. It's a matter of a few more days. They need to trust you, Devendra. Got that? So, have that chat and then call me in. Mithilesh is going to be sitting in on this and so will Vinesh. We'll have to play this carefully.'

'I'll work on it right away, boss.'

13:15 In the Conference Room

'Good afternoon, team.'

The chorus of good mornings and afternoons followed. They could never get those greetings right. It was not uncommon to hear a good afternoon when you met them for a drink in the evening!

'I believe some of you have expressed an interest in leaving Imperial and joining Oriental?'

The team was aghast at my plunging directly into the heart of the matter. There were no further greetings, just stunned silence. Even Vinesh was shocked.

Mithilesh walked in and stood at the rear. Murmurs resonated around the room.

'Well? Since you're not responding, I take it what I hear from Devendra is correct?'

Silence.

I looked towards one of the RMs to my left. 'Your name, please?'

'Satish Reddy, sir.'

'And, why do you want to leave?'

'Sir, we don't want to lose our jobs! We all have families to support. What would you do in our place?' he muttered.

Shit! I would have bailed out, man. 'You can't keep running every time you hear something. Or, if you feel there is a threat. Have you spoken with Devendra?'

They all looked at Devendra. Of course, they had spoken with him. He had offered them roles in Oriental. Of course, they didn't know I was familiar with their discussions. I was the ganglord on this one.

Devendra took the cue. 'Ravi sir and Vinesh sir have come from Bangalore to meet you. Why don't you speak up?'

Another RM rose and looked at Vinesh 'Sir, we all know there is a firing list coming out soon. What do you suggest we do?'

Vinesh remained calm. 'Firstly, a very good afternoon to you. I don't know where you've heard of this firing list. There is a performance appraisal underway like every year.'

Vinesh could be a real prick. He needed to take this bull by the horns. They would have lynched him, if I weren't around.

I stepped in. 'Vinesh, allow me …'

Vinesh seemed relieved and nodded. 'Yes, Ravi, please …'

I continued. 'You are all seasoned professionals. Not a bunch of kids, and I'm not going to treat you like kids either. You can see Mithilesh has come in from Bangalore …'

They all turned to glare at Mithilesh. The bonding was apparent. They would have throttled him, given a chance.

Mithilesh released a corny, 'Hello!'

I resumed, 'Well, you see, Mithilesh has offered that his team will step in, that is in case you leave. Now I don't want you to leave … Not like this. You need to be up for the fight. You've turned Hyderabad around for Imperial. You've fought through the downturn. Never leave a battle midway. Why do you think a bank will let go of performers? Think about it. If you think you've not done well, then that's another matter. But, if you know you've done well, why the concern?' I looked around the room.

'Team! Speak up. Any questions?' Devendra stepped in.

His discussion with the team had apparently done the trick. They were not as resolute on leaving, not for this session at least.

'Okay, guys. Devendra, Vinesh and I are going to be in the office for the rest of the day. Vinesh wants to spend some time with each one of you. Feel free to walk across and we can also discuss this on an individual basis. Okay?'

Satish got up again … 'Sir, we would like to thank you for coming to Hyderabad and speaking with us. We really appreciate the interest you've taken. If you can give us some time to think this through, we will get back to you and Devendra sir.'

'My pleasure, but decide quickly. We need to do our numbers for the month. Got that?'

'Yes, sir!' The chorus kicked in …

I was a slimeball.

Devendra walked across and whispered. 'I told them they could expect at least a 25 per cent hike …'

Damn!

14:25 In Devendra's Room with Vinesh and Devendra

Karan called.

'Boss? Good news! Triton and Axis Infomatics have agreed on the deal. They'll cover employee defaults. This is a bloody miracle. Sorry, boss, but we've never had a corporate agree to this one, ever! And the size of the deal ... great, boss!'

'Good show, Karan. Now send them the paperwork. We have to close this today, at least get an email okay from them. Got that?'

'Yes, boss.'

'That'll make one more slide on the presentation,' I smiled. It was feral. I was finally going in for the kill.

Mithilesh walked in. His over-confidence had been shattered today. He was walking around like a wounded warrior. A sight to behold!

'Hi, Mithilesh. What time is your flight to Bangalore?'

'Thinking of taking the evening flight. How about you?'

'I'm off to Mumbai in the evening. Are you coming?'

'No. I've got other engagements in Bangalore.'

Mithilesh not coming to Mumbai? Something was going down, something big. I was finding it tough to restrain my joy.

'Oh! And, Mithilesh, in case I forget ... I spoke with Sriram. We're closing a deal with Axis Infomatics and Triton for processing personal loans to their employees. He mentioned your team would chip in to process the applications. It's going to large volumes. Karan can fill you in on the details in office tomorrow.'

I was waiting for his reaction.

'But ... but Sriram didn't speak with me on this.'

'I told him I'd connect with you on this one. You can check with him if you like.'

'I'll check with him later.'

He walked out. *Checkmate!*

'Why do you take *panga* with him, Ravi? Oh and in case I forget to mention it later, you handled the situation very well

today. But do you think they won't change their minds again?'
Vinesh shook his head …

'Let's see Vinesh, let's see. Why don't you put your BlackBerry to some good use now, Vinesh?'

He smiled.

16:15 @ En Route to Hyderabad Airport

The BlackBerry was buzzing again. Vinesh had sent an update email to Jaideep and the senior management clique.

'… *Ravi & I have managed to quell the situation in Hyderabad. The RMs have been retained. Ravi's timely intervention and leadership …*'

Amitabh had already moved forward with full gusto on Vinesh's email and demolished Sriram's suggestion on the emergency crap, congratulating Jaideep and his team for their thorough support on the matter. My name had been mentioned in one of the bylines.

This round went to Amitabh! He was back on top! This would have been a moral victory for him over Sriram.

21:45 En Route to Hotel President, Mumbai

Vinesh called. 'You reached Mumbai?'

'Yup. Nice email!'

'Thought we could do with some appreciation.'

'Of course, pal. What else?'

'You're going to enjoy this. Internal Audit is now on Mithilesh's case. They have started digging into some old personal loan cases. Seems messy. Sameer is flying into Bangalore in the morning, tomorrow!'

I smiled. Kumar had been up to some mischief.

The Hyderabad knockout, the Triton deal and now this IA enquiry. Mithilesh was surely out of the race. Now on to the next challenge!

22:15 @ The President, Mumbai

I walked across to the Thai Pavilion. Dheeraj, dressed in a white linen shirt and a smart pair of khakis, had called me over for dinner. I actually wanted to eat alone, but was curious to see what he had up his sleeve.

'Hi, Dheeraj! How have you been? Sorry to have kept you waiting.'

'Good, Ravi, good. Had an IIM-A alumni dinner, but decided to skip it.'

I felt honoured. The blue-blooded gentry had decided to relinquish his martinis for a good old brew with the village folk!

The waiter came across with a mug and poured chilled beer.

'I've ordered dinner. I hope you don't mind,' Dheeraj seemed restless, like he had something he needed to get off his chest quickly.

'No, Dheeraj. Works fine for me.'

We continued with the casual chitchat till he finally broached the subject.

'Ravi, you were deliberately cornered, you know that ... right? I felt really bad when I heard about the Credit Card fraud. How I wished I could have helped! I even spoke with Sriram, but you know how it is? Once IA is on to something, there is nothing anyone can do about it.'

'Thanks, Dheeraj. But that's water under the bridge.'

We were both trying to be casual, but even the beer couldn't really break the ice.

'I think it's unfortunate the way things are playing out. Both of us ... in fact all three of us are being cornered. It's bloody unfair!'

I was too tired to guess which three he was referring to.

'Three?'

'You, Shashank and I. Maithili has been pushing for South and West. That would compromise both of us. Sriram has been backing Manoj Kohli to head North and East. The Credit Card business is in tatters and Manoj has been wanting to move out of

Mumbai for his own personal reasons. Can you imagine? Even in these times, personal preferences are being considered over achievements. Imperial has become so unprofessional!'

Another twist. Manoj Kohli, Sriram's reportee, now in the reckoning! How did the Twitter maniac miss out on this one?

Dheeraj continued, 'To make matters worse, Amitabh has given you and me a four rating this year. That means we are borderline fired under the current circumstances!'

I decided to rein in my emotions. Four? Was he out of his mind? Maithili must have been doing him really well.

'So,' I said as I sipped the beer, struggling to appear Mr Cool, 'What do you propose, Dheeraj?'

'Well, clearly, Amitabh has left us out in the dark. He doesn't keep us in the loop on anything. And look at Sriram's team. They are all well connected and up to date. Has Amitabh had even one decent conversation with you on the layoffs? We can't just be sitting down and taking this as it comes.'

'We' was an unexpected expression from Dheeraj. But then, these were unusual times …

'We have to come up with something. Any luck outside? How's the market? I'm sure you would have made headway by now. You know Kaushal quite well. Have you spoken with him?'

Bingo! The jerk actually thought I would fall for that?

'You know how Kaushal can be?! Very aloof. Have you been in touch with him, Dheeraj?'

'Let's see how it goes this month.' He smiled.

But what was Dheeraj up to? Was he also che out Oriental?

23:12 In my Room

Savitha hadn't been taking my calls. I didn't landline and wake up the kids and the pa several times, but there was no respons

I sat on the sofa beside the windo the traffic meandering down Cuffe Para

a long and demanding day tomorrow with Patrick. It struck me that I should review the presentation sent by Karan and by the time I was done, I would be at most blessed with a few hours of sleep.

The door bell rang. Room service, I guessed!

I opened the door and stood aghast.

'Hey! Won't you invite me in?'

'Hey! Maithili! ... This is quite a ...'

She pushed me away from the door and walked in. 'Lemme guess ... a surprise? Hey ... come on, Ravi ... Let's not get clichéd!'

She settled herself on the sofa and pulled out a bottle of champagne from her large tan leather bag. She looked up at me, expectantly ...

'Hey Ravi, relax! Make yourself home! Come sit next to me ...'

This wasn't a situation I was prepared for. I was drained ...

'Listen ... M ... this is not a good time ... think you should leave ...'

'And... why is that?'

'For obvious reasons, M!'

She smiled, got off the sofa and walked towards me. I realized my body was responding to her proximity. I was badly attracted to her and I hated myself for it.

I remained still as she came up and stood inches away from me, peering into my eyes.

'Ravi ... Can't you ...?'

'I'm asking you to leave!'

'You know, Ravi? Whatever feelings you and I may have for each other, we will still compete tooth and nail on professional grounds. I'm not going to back down.'

I stepped back, walked around her towards the sofa and turned around to face her. I needed the distance to clear my head. 'You know M, I don't know you any more.'

'Why do you think I set you up?' she laughed.

'Now, why would I think that?'

'I know you, Ravi. I can see it in your eyes. I am curious ... How did you clear yourself from that Credit Card mess?'

I could sense the disappointment and fury in her voice. She must have been drinking heavily, or she wasn't the one to reveal details so easily.

'I couldn't do much, M ...'

'Lucky you ... Looking forward to the next few days, Ravi ...' she winked and tottered out.

Imperial Insider: Is Sriram losing steam?

March

23

Cannon to right of them,
Cannon to left of them,
Cannon in front of them
Volley'd and thunder'd;
Storm'd at with shot and shell,
Boldly they rode and well,
Into the jaws of Death,
Into the mouth of Hell
Rode the six hundred.

– Lord Alfred Tennyson

11:20 @ Imperial Head Office, Mumbai

The meeting was being attended by all department heads and now by regional heads as well. Vikram wasn't in for the meeting. Not surprising! The schedule would stretch to 4 pm with a working lunch tossed in.

As I was heading for the boardroom, I bumped into a large white creature that blurted, 'Watch out, son!'

The 6'3" imposing frame had a ridiculously large paunch perched precariously over a black alligator-skin belt. I managed to gather my wits.

'Good morning, sir. I'm Ravi, Ravi Shastry. I manage the South Region,' I had started rattling off my curriculum vitae.

'Glad to meet you, Ravi. Aren't you the guy being hounded by the chaps in Internal Audit?'

My father would be proud. I had made the Shastry household proud. 'It's been cleared, Patrick. They were false charges!'

'Good. Also heard you quelled the situation in Hyderabad. Good show, my boy. But you need to watch out on those IA matters. We really need to be strong on compliance.'

Before I could get a word in edgeways, Jaideep whisked Patrick away to introduce him to some other hapless victims.

Amazing opening innings!

11:30

Jaideep kicked off the opening session, farting eloquent about Patrick and his vitals. Patrick, embarrassed with this sickening display of devotion and servitude, butted in to take us all out of our misery... at least that is what we all thought ...

'India is a large market of strategic interest for Imperial. But, I'll come straight to the point.

'YOU HAVE DONE BUGGER ALL!

'This bank should have been 100 times the size and 1,000 times more profitable in India. But things will now change. We'll have a new team in place. I'm going to be personally monitoring the progress in India.'

Hail Caesar! May we bend and kiss your hand! A bunch of illogical innuendoes from someone who was clearly ignorant about the regulatory environment in India. This was brash hogwash, clearly intended to shake up the team.

Both Amitabh and Sriram listened patiently, taking notes diligently, as Patrick spewed. Jaideep remained calm, exchanging smiles with anyone bold enough to take their eyes off Patrick.

Patrick continued. 'I keep hearing of the great potential here. Then all I get are some puny one million USD deals, and everyone's happy! Ridiculous! You've been unable to rein in your losses, and worse still, you still have no clue on how to resolve these losses on your Credit Card and Personal Loans!' Patrick looked at Sriram and then steered his gaze to Amitabh.

'You've got very low revenue – employee ratios, possibly the lowest within Imperial globally!' Patrick had conveniently avoided mentioning that we also had the lowest cost-employee ratios due to lower salary structures in India when compared to Europe and other economies; that we were actually generating significantly more revenue with our low-cost employee pool.

But who was going to point that out to a Patrick on the warpath?

'I keep hearing of stock market fluctuations affecting revenues. Have any of you looked at the innovations we've made in the UK market?'

Had been looked at one trillion times at least. The regulator didn't permit 99 per cent of them and the balance 1 per cent were economically unviable!

'You've got Internal Audit having to send senior regional resources to clean up the mess you've created.' He eyed me. *Shit!* Something had really ticked him off.

'You've shut down businesses when other banks are growing their loan portfolios,' he looked towards Sriram again.

'There are employees who are leaving for the competition and we sit here twiddling our thumbs!' Jaideep's turn to get the look!

'I've got a bunch of senior management professionals sitting on fat pay cheques who constantly fight with each other like a bunch of mother hens. Seriously! What kind of a madhouse are you running here?'

Madhouse?! We weren't the guys who shoved billions of dollars in some gambling racket, you bastard!

He paused for a sip of water, stood up and started walking around the table. Vikram had been quite the sophisticated gentleman in his interactions. Patrick on the other hand seemed to be Darth Vader incarnate. Could have saved George Lucas tons of money on costumes!

He continued, 'I'm going to be making changes here. I'm going to make all of you accountable. I need results, quickly. The only thing that counts from now on is what you accomplish. No more fiefdoms. You got that?'

Sure, he wanted to build his!

There were a series of nods around the table. The principal was scolding us. He might even ask us to take down our trousers and bend over so that he could whack our bottoms. Back to school!

Patrick received a call on his cell and excused himself from the room.

He left a pin-drop silence in his wake. Most of us started fidgeting with our BlackBerrys. Even if there were no emails to be checked, we kept browsing, desperately seeking content that could dilute the humiliation we had suffered moments earlier. We were better off with our spouses at home, where at least recourse was available without economic repercussions.

Patrick re-entered, 'Okay, ladies and gentlemen. Let's carry on with the agenda. Jaideep, I'm handing the floor to you.'

He assumed his seat at the head of the table and Jaideep rose, adjusted his jacket, cleared his voice and started rambling.

'Thank you, Patrick. We are all looking forward to your leadership. I'm sure the team, picked by the incumbent CEO, shall rise to your expectations as well. It has been a tough year, but as HR head I can assure you we have some of the best talent in Indian banking today. This team can steer the bank towards the vision you have.'

Maithili was holding back her giggles and Dheeraj was brave enough to excuse himself. Shashank continued scratching his balls, the unequivocal reaction to everything that happened in his sorry life.

14:15 Buffet Lunch outside the Boardroom

We had survived two hours of interrogation in the boardroom. Every number had been questioned, every analysis broken down to basics. Every assumption was thrown out of the window, every strategy castrated. No one and nothing was spared. It had been a bloodbath.

Patrick finally relented enough to break for lunch. We were asked to reassemble at *'14:30 sharp!'*

Maithili, who was in an animated discussion with Patrick while a restless Amitabh watched, smiled and came across towards me after making her excuses, her cleavage inviting, as ever.

Right there and then, I couldn't stand her.

'What a prick!' she said.

'I thought you had bestowed that honour on me, Maithili?'

'Well, you've got company!'

Dheeraj walked up, 'Patrick bludgeoned our balls in there! I guess I won't be making love for some time now!' he sniggered.

'I'm sure your wife isn't missing much, Dheeraj,' Maithili retorted.

'Better than what you've been getting, for sure,' he returned.

I butted in, 'Guys, we're up next. Chill!'

Dheeraj asked, 'You think Amitabh is still in the race? Or has the old man finally thrown in the towel?'

'I was having breakfast with Patrick when you were wrapped

in your towel, Dheeraj!' Amitabh walked up from behind and made his comment quietly.

'Hi, boss!' I smiled.

14:50 In the Boardroom

The finance team led by Suresh Ranganathan had started their presentation on profitability to an audience reeling from a heavy lunch. The South region was projected to be the worst on both revenue and profitability. They had dug the grave, shoved me into it and also poured the dirt back on. If I left it alone, Patrick would just lay the tombstone and piss on my grave when I walked up for my presentation.

I decided to make my presence felt and set the stage for my turn.

'Suresh, I would need to know how costs have been allocated to each region. Especially the head office costs and the other add-ons not associated with the branches.'

By others, I was referring to the costs of the Credit Card operations.

Suresh glared at me. He was obviously following instructions and didn't appear keen on getting into the details. Amitabh released a hesitant smile as Sriram decided to excuse himself from the room. Jaideep started fidgeting with his BlackBerry again.

Patrick finally decided to add fuel to the fire. 'Yes, Suresh, I'm curious. How have costs been allocated?'

Suresh stuttered, 'Sir, they have been allocated on the basis of revenues of each of the regions and a host of other factors ...'

'So, whose revenues are the highest? And where are the Credit Card costs shown in this statement? And what OTHER factors?'

'S ... s ... sir, the West has the highest revenues, followed by the South, North and East.'

'Now show me the costs and revenues of the head office separately and the regions separately,' Patrick cut in. 'And,

I need to see how the head office costs have been allocated to each region.'

'But sir, it is complicated. I can take this up with you separately …'

Patrick was not to be put off in the least.

'We should do this now. Use the whiteboard, start jotting down the numbers.'

Suresh glared at me again. But I wasn't going to go down without a fight. This round went to me. I was thrilled with myself.

The whiteboard was soon covered with a cacophony of numbers and formulas. It soon emerged that Dheeraj had managed to include a significant portion of his costs into the head office costs, which in turn were distributed to the other three regions. This obviously gave a fillip to his profitability! The Credit Card sales team costs for some strange reason had been allocated on the basis of the size of the Personal Loan portfolios, which was the largest in my region. The double whammy had done me in.

Patrick smiled as the complete picture emerged. It was feral and made all of us squirm in our seats. But I still had a chance. Each zone and the head office had chipped in for my demise. But I was still there. Just you watch, you bastards!

Suresh finally returned to his chair. But the glares didn't subside. He was pissed off that he had been forced to undertake the workings again. Amitabh and Sriram remained silent throughout. They had both obviously played key roles in approving this approach.

I owed Mayur big time.

The sessions continued and we moved on to presentations by the regions. Maithili and Dheeraj had completed their presentations. They had both been given 20 minutes, cut down from the earlier 30, to accommodate for my last minute inclusion. Patrick had taken apart Dheeraj on the first slide and Maithili couldn't make it past the second. I looked towards Amitabh, pleading for a re-schedule. He just smiled and messaged.

'You don't get away so easy :)'

As Dheeraj sat, Amitabh signalled to me to start. I sipped some water and walked across to the laptop on which all the presentations had been loaded. I had already spotted 14 issues on which Patrick could take me apart. I searched for my presentation on the folder and clicked. As the presentation opened, I clicked on the slide show button ... 'Good afternoon. I will share with you the performance review for the South and the plans for next year.'

The audience looked at me blankly and Jaideep raised his eyebrows. I turned and noticed the slides weren't getting projected on the screen. Shit!

Patrick got up in a huff and walked out screaming, 'Can't you guys at least get the damn projector to work? How are you to get a bank running?'

Murphy had struck.

The technicians soon resolved the issue, a loose connection. Patrick walked back, but remained standing.

The opening slide was finally on. Patrick asked, in a mellow tone, 'Ravi, let's forget the fancy presentation. Tell me what should the bank do to expand profitably in your region? I would like your views ...'

Amitabh looked towards me, eyes pleading. *'Please say something sensible ... 'coz you're on your own on this one.'*

I gathered my thoughts. The Triton deal had not impressed him as much as it had earlier on the golf course. Or, it may have been a tactic to shake up the audience? Large revenues, however, seemed to be the focus more than profitability. For all you knew, he wanted to increase the market share quickly to enhance the valuation for the business to be sold off.

'Sir, I agree with Jaideep.'

Patrick butted in. 'Call me Patrick. Let's get rid of this "Sir" business, shall we?'

Yes, Your Highness! An ideal platform to make an impression, but a window of two to three minutes at most. I needed to go for the kill.

'Patrick, as I was mentioning, we have good resources. We need to enrich their skill sets. The Indian consumer is evolving.'

Patrick started to fidget again. *I was losing him.*

'We need to come out with tailor-made products for key customer segments.'

'Such as?'

'For example, the deal I had mentioned with Triton earlier. Though it is a starting point at one million dollars,' *The words 'starting point' resulted in a nod from Patrick.* I was finally on the right path. '... we need to turn it into 5 million USD and then 10 million USD and so on!'

Patrick seemed intrigued, 'And how would you do that?'

'Well, as in corporate banking, we need resources specializing in different customer segments, corporates, traders, medium-sized enterprises and so on. Then we need entry products that make lower profits but have a high impact on the corporate. The Triton deal works with a good profit margin, but even higher impact.

'In the case of the Triton deal, along with Sriram's team, we are planning to set up camps to open bank accounts and sell Investment products. Can we also tie up with a company that can assist employees in filing their Income Tax returns? Again high impact!'

Might just pull it off with this bullshit ... it was probably new shit for him, but timing and packaging always made the difference. The faces around the table began yawning or frowning. Shashank continued scratching his balls.

'But why haven't you done all this earlier?'

'We have done some or even all of these, but, if we are able to collectively draw in all our experience and firm up a strategy for each segment, we might be able to pull off bigger and better things.'

Hadn't thought Patrick would hear me out for this long.

'You've got some good ideas. How quickly can you execute them?'

Dude, if you leave me with a job, I could tell you.

I looked at Amitabh and Sriram. They both nodded. This was the first positive sign from Patrick since the session had begun.

'I'm sure we can come out with a blueprint for your review in the next four weeks.'

'Four weeks! The whole world can change in four weeks. That's your problem ... the lot of you. You think brilliantly but execute poorly. You're all great in these boardrooms but a bunch of prancing toddlers out there.' Patrick had taken off again.

I had my one minute of fame. Now I could stand on the table and piss on the screen for all he cared. He wouldn't notice me.

The Tommy gun was out again. Everyone was in the line of fire. The attendant walking in with the bottled water was sarcastically offered the position of chief operating officer, to which his response was *'Kai zaala?* (what happened?), much to Patrick's chagrin.

16:30 In Amitabh's Cabin

Patrick wound down at 16:15, leaving in a huff.

Everyone had been slaughtered. There had been no discrimination. There had been a decorum that had always been maintained in the past. But Patrick had changed the rules. These were new days, new principles. And a new principal!

Maithili, Dheeraj, Shashank and I were in Amitabh's cabin.

Shashank, not looking his cheerful self, was first off the block, 'Boss, what's with the list?' He was scratching his balls again.

'What about it, Shashank? You know it is a reality!'

Shashank's ball scratching increased. 'I know, boss. But how many people are going to be impacted? I need to share something with my team.'

'It's not been finalized. The laggards will find it tough to hold on. We need to tighten our belts and work harder.'

Dheeraj, frustrated with the bureaucratic mumbo-jumbo, blurted, 'Boss, I think what we are all keen to understand is how this new zonal structure is going to pan out? What will happen to the others?'

'You'll be the first to know,' Amitabh closed the subject.

There were no discussions on business performance, sales targets, number deficits or business projections, nothing related to, or pertinent to, sales and profits. March would have typically been a high-pressure month for all of us as we attempted to close the year on a high. Now, everyone was trying to save their arses, including Amitabh.

It then struck me. Amitabh hadn't backed me in my presentation to Patrick. He had helped out both Maithili and Dheeraj, but just sat through mine. No words, no reactions. He left me in the cold. What had I done wrong? I hated his guts.

17:15 Having a Smoke Outside the Head Office

I noticed Jaideep smoking round the corner and walked across.

'Hi, Jaideep. I didn't know you smoked!'

'I don't!' he smiled.

'Interesting day?' I wanted to start a conversation.

'Yup. One of the more entertaining ones in some time. This must have been fun for you too.'

'Had its moments,' I chuckled.

'So, what time's your flight?'

'I need to book. Have asked the office to put me in the last flight out. I had something on my mind Jaideep ...'

'Tell me.'

'Was thinking through what Patrick mentioned. Do you think we need to have a team for strategy? If he is looking for that kind of heady growth, it would make sense.'

Jaideep cut in, 'I don't think Patrick would be going in for theory stuff like that. He wants to see action, and quickly!'

It had been a long shot. My ship was still sinking!

18:15 @ Geoffreys, The Pub, Marine Plaza

Dheeraj decided to play host and took us out for a round of drinks before we left for our respective locations.

Maithili and Dheeraj clung to scotch on the rocks. Shashank and I retained our rustic passion for rum and coke.

Shashank glanced at his watch. 'Dheeraj, I've an 8:30 to catch? What time would we have to leave here?'

'Ideally, 15 minutes back,' Dheeraj and Maithili exchanged high fives.

'What are both of you up to?' Shashank sensed something amiss.

'On a serious note, if we leave now you could make it in time. But, we have other plans!' Dheeraj grinned.

My flight was at 9. 'Dheeraj…'

'Ravi … Shashank … Maithili and I have some news for you. You've been booked on morning flights,' Dheeraj smirked.

Shashank shouted, 'What?!'

'You didn't think I'd let you leave Mumbai with just a couple of drinks, did you?' Dheeraj smiled.

20:14

'Hi, Sav.'

Savitha had finally taken my call.

'Hi, Ravi, boarded your flight?'

Ouch … this was going to be tough.

'Well, got delayed …'

She shot back, furious, 'No Ravi, you've been drinking, heavily! Do you think you're the only one stressed? You know my condition and you still want to stay back and party with your friends!'

'Sav … believe me, it's not like that …'

'Well, one thing's for sure. I'm not going to talk about this till your damn list is out! And then, we're going to have a long, hard chat on all that's been going on!'

She disconnected.

23:35 The Blue Station, Central Mumbai

Prohibition and laws have historically been one of the greatest stimulants for crossing the line.

Speeding, breaking three red lights, driving under the influence of alcohol, urinating in public places and now a dance bar! We had covered it all in one wild night of frenzy.

Jackets off, cufflinks flung, sleeves folded and our inhibitions shed. We figured this was it.

'Dheeraj! I thought these joints had been shut down ages ago!'

He smiled and shouted into my ear, 'They have!'

A slew of young girls were dancing on an elevated platform in the centre of the room, lit to a dim red glow. The dance bar was segregated into three floors. The girls on the lower floor either didn't look that good or were novices. The girls on the third floor, in contrast, included a mix of seasoned dancers, including college students from '*good*' families and could give most models a run for their money! We settled down on the ground floor, not sure if they accepted credit cards! Or perhaps, not wanting our families to see the name '*Blue Station*' on our credit card statements. The waiters were serving drinks and garlands of hundred-rupee notes. The DJ was sticking to Hindi remix concoctions as industrialists, bankers, brokers, students and hookers sat next to each other, rubbing shoulders in this voyeuristic space.

Shashank joined the ladies on stage, attempting his interpretation of dancing. We were in splits. The attendants pushed him back on the sofa gently.

'Okay, guys, that's it. Getting too crowded. Let's get out of here.' Dheeraj was screaming to make himself heard.

We settled the bill, tipped the waiter and Shashank left him a piece of advice, 'Never join an MNC bank!' The waiter obviously didn't comprehend but was delighted with the tip he had just received.

We hobbled out. Dheeraj struggled to find the car and Maithili staggered along. I tapped her on her back and she cleared her throat. Shashank was taking the support of a street lamp to get his bearings, as Dheeraj tried to open a car and kicked its tyres when he realized it wasn't his.

'Guys? Let's take a snap.' I guessed this might be the last time we would be meeting as a group, with this bank at least.

I got one of the bouncers to take a snap of the four of us with our backs facing the neon sign screaming 'Blue Station' in flashing neon. I thanked the bouncer, checked the photograph on the camera. It had come out well, under the circumstances and the seamy background.

Shashank decided to scream on top of his lungs, 'I need to pee. Can someone undo my zip?'

There was a fair amount of traffic on the road, but fortunately the pavements were sparsely populated. Taking Shashank's state into consideration, we figured he would be safer within the confines of a conventional washroom.

I let Maithili rest against the wall and asked Dheeraj to stand guard. I took Shashank by the arm and led him back into the bar. The bouncers suggested we go to the first floor to relieve ourselves as one of the guests had made a mess in the bathroom on the ground floor.

I took Shashank to the toilet and urged him to relieve himself in the urinal and wash his face. I came out and lit up a cigarette. There were no 'No Smoking' restrictions here, possibly one of the USPs of this establishment!

As Shashank stepped out with water dripping from his hair and face, I held his arm again and walked towards the stairs. As we walked across the floor, I caught a glimpse of two men dressed in smart black suits, red ties and garlands, attempting to balance beer bottles on their heads with one arm and holding nubile nymphets by their waist with their other arm, as they danced alongside the platform in the centre of the room.

The suit closer to me turned and dropped the beer bottle on his head on the floor, shattering it. The other suit looked up at me as well. But the delighted look soon dissipated.

I rushed Shashank down the stairs and hurried out of the bar. Dheeraj had fortunately found his car and parked outside the entrance waiting for us. I popped Shashank into the backseat and got in from the other side.

As Dheeraj started the car and sped away, my horror was replaced by a smile.

I loved banking! I clicked on the Twitter icon.

Imperial Insider: Heads to roll ...

March

	1	2	3	4	5	6
7	8	9	10	11	12	13
14	15	16	17	18	19	20
21	22	23	**24**	25	26	27
28	29	30	31			

Twists and Turns ...

04:15 The Coffee Shop, ITC Grand Maratha, Near Mumbai Airport

Dheeraj and Shashank had dozed off on their chairs. Maithili was sipping black coffee. I decided chilled water was the need of the hour. We had traversed three watering holes, one restaurant and were seated in the fifth and possibly the last destination before we finally made it to the airport.

Maithili had downed over eight rounds of scotch, and I was running slightly ahead with 10 rounds of rum interspersed with beer. Dheeraj had oscillated effortlessly between scotch and margaritas whereas Shashank started with rum, and then moved to scotch, perhaps to acquire some finesse.

This has been a wild night by any standard. We were just four people hanging out. Different backgrounds, varied personality types and conflicting motives, drawn by the need to bond and break free…

My eyes were struggling to remain open, but Maithili seemed wide awake. She must be made of sterner stuff. She looked as immaculate and sharp as she had 10 hours earlier. The wild evening hadn't ruffled her at all.

'Maithili, feel like a walk? Will drop dead if I sit here any longer.'

She nodded. We started walking towards the hotel lobby entrance. We were both booked on 6 am flights, anyway.

'I'm sure you would have heard from Akash by now!'

I smiled. This was Maithili's way of pushing. 'Just as surely as you!'

She reciprocated the smile. 'So … Ravi … how's Savitha doing?'

'You've been in touch with her … you should know, M!'

The duel of words was on.

'And the kids?'

I wanted to pin her against the granite lobby wall and punch her. This banter sickened me. Why was she was messing with my life?

'Did you sleep with Amitabh?' I asked abruptly.

Clearly taken aback, she responded, 'What do you think?'

'That's not an answer!'

'Do I owe you one?'

'You seem to be involved in some rather sticky stuff ...'

She halted and turned to face me. 'I don't have to respond to any of your crap, Ravi. Is that clear?'

Had I finally managed to crack her façade? I decided to plough further. 'You said once, never mix business and pleasure.'

'I did?'

'Well, don't do anything you may regret tomorrow!'

'With you or in general?

'I can't comment on the latter, M!'

'Funny, Ravi. Life brings us to strange crossroads.' Maithili was now peering into my eyes.

I couldn't make out if it was passion, ambition, vendetta or all of it – but it was an attractive and heady concoction.

'And, what kind of crossroads are we at now, M?'

She smiled again and resumed walking. 'Let's cut the crap, Ravi. I'm gunning for the zonal head position. I have ambitions, and so do you. It's there for the taking. I'm not backing off 'coz it's you!'

'I'm flattered by your gracious confession!'

'Cut the sarcastic bull, Ravi. And you have no right to judge me. Both of us know what's on your mind. It is for you to resolve. If your infidelity is causing you sleepless nights, you should have thought about it before we slept together in Chennai! Now ... get your head out of your ass and shove that ego of yours up it or better still down some drain in Bangalore. Don't think I'm going to let you walk all over me, just because I slept with you and because we have history. You may hear several things about me, and I've heard tons about you ... Don't take that moral high ground with me either. The entire office is talking about how conveniently the Credit Card fraud matter was resolved overnight! And those KYC documents for those accounts? It's a small world, Ravi. It wasn't Kumar who covered your ass on that one!'

'What do you mean?'

'You think Sameer didn't see through that shabby stunt you tried to pull off? He owed me one and I banked it for you, Mr Wise Guy!'

'But ...'

'Now you want to know how he owes me?'

'Yes!'

'Well ... Kumar may have a story on that one ...'

Was this a confession? Had Maithili handed over Kumar to Internal Audit? But why was she sharing this with me? Did she realize I couldn't harm her with this information?

But did she have a hand in the Credit Card fraud?

She continued. 'I can read you like an open book. Now your sick mind thinks I had something to do with the Credit Card matter too, right?'

I did not take her bait.

'Let me put you out of your misery. I didn't, Ravi!'

'Why didn't you tell me this earlier?'

'There are some things better understood!' she smiled sadly.

She was trembling now.

'You all right, M?'

'Go to hell, Ravi!'

09:23 En Route from Bangalore Airport to the Office

'Hi Ravi!'

I had been hesitating to call her.

'Hi Sav, reached office?'

'Yup.'

'Do you plan to come home tonight?'

'Sav ... Don't say that ...'

'Thought you may like to know …'

'What?'

'Srikanth fell yesterday. He's sprained his ankle!'

'What? Why didn't you tell me?'

'Thought you'd be stressed at work, didn't want to add to it!'

'But …'.

She had disconnected.

11:44 @ Office

Karan walked into my cabin.

'So, boss! What news from the head office? Lots of fireworks, I hear?'

He always had the latest. 'Some, but nothing to get excited about.'

'Any update on the reorganization or the firing list, boss?'

'Nothing we didn't already know. It's going to be a wait-and-watch right now. It's only a matter of another week.'

It hurt when it sank in that we had less than a week for all this to unfold. I was in the same position as three weeks ago, if not worse.

'Where's Raghu?'

'He left in the evening yesterday … and so did Sameer.'

'Boss, I spoke with the team in Chennai. Raghu is all shaken up about what happened to his account. He has been insisting that his account had been hacked. Internal Audit is really coming down hard on him. His team is also shaken up. All game for joining Oriental.'

'That's good. You're sure about this?'

'Yes boss. 100 per cent!'

12:18 @ Office, In My Cabin

I called up Kaushal. 'Can we speak?'

'Yes, Ravi. Tell me.'

'We need to firm up the details and next steps on moving the teams.'

'I was about to call you as well, Ravi. I hope the Hyderabad situation is under control.'

'It got messy. But I hope we have a clearer understanding now?'

'Of course, Ravi. It's going to cost us much more now!'

He wouldn't let go of anything. 'I'm sure it's for the better, sir!'

'By when can you come on board?'

Tomorrow! He hadn't been taking my hints, so I decided to be direct.

'I thought we should work out my numbers as well.'

'Of course, Ravi. I have a senior management meeting on Friday. So, I might be a bit tied up, but will get the HR team to connect with you and close it.'

'Thanks, Kaushal. Look forward to hearing from you.'

'Bye Ravi, and hang in there!'

Why did he say *'hang in there'*? Was there something Kaushal already knew?

I looked at the calendar. The list would be out next Monday or Tuesday latest. It was unlikely they would leave it till Wednesday. Just another two days to go this week. It was too close for comfort. I didn't want to be in no man's land if my neck was indeed on the line.

14:21

'Hi, Akash. How've you been?' I was hoping for some update on the Singapore Development Bank.

'Good, Ravi. What's happening at your end? Heard that your big daddy was in town. Ripped you guys up!'

'There were some fireworks, Akash, but that's how he is!'

'Is it his nature to rip apart the potential CEOs as well? What kind of hellhole do you guys work in?' Akash laughed.

My sentiments exactly! 'Some are like that, Akash. News at your end?'

'I have a call lined up with the Singapore HR team for later in the day.'

My heart started beating heavily again. 'I'm in Bangalore the next couple of days. Do let me know in case you hear something.'

'Sure, Ravi. The moment I hear. Take care.' He disconnected.

I needed to know one way or the other. I had a sinking feeling and the hangover didn't help matters either.

15:42

Vinesh stood smiling outside my door. 'You look a mess!'

An apparent observation delivered bluntly!

'What's with you today? Won the lottery?' I retorted.

Vinesh's smile could either mean good or bad news.

'No such luck. But you're in luck,' he ambled in, pulled the chair and plonked himself on it.

The suspense was killing me. I wished he would hurry up.

'Luck and me? The two haven't met for some time now... But try me, Vinesh?'

'Your friend in Kolkata has put in his papers!'

'What? Shashank?'

'Yup! He called Amitabh and submitted his resignation.'

'But I was with him last night. He didn't mention anything.'

'Rumour is he's joining Milsons. Vikram seems to have picked him.'

'Good for him. I'm surprised.'

'At least one less for you, right?'

I didn't respond to that.

Vinesh continued, 'He was out of the running. Think he has made a smart move. It's not as if Milsons is a great move. They hardly have any business in the East. Unless they're planning to expand ... We're planning to prune aggressively in the East anyway. He would have been out in the cold.'

This was the first time Vinesh had given any indication of the cutback plans. But a fair amount of headcount reduction in the East would mean a lesser cut in other regions. *Shit!* We were getting vicious in our thinking and just didn't care about anything any more. It was all about protecting one's ass …

17:02

'Can we speak?'

It was Radhika at the door.

'Sure! Come on in and close the door behind you.'

Radhika remained standing near the desk. I looked up, curious.

'Sir, I'm putting in my papers …'

'What! Why?'

'I would like to leave by the end of the month. I've really thought this through. It's been a very tough decision. Have spoken with my husband too. We both think this is the right step.'

'May I ask, where are you going?'

'I've been told not to disclose the name. But I will tell you. I'm joining Oriental as a Relationship Manager.'

The bastards were still poaching. My boss-to-be had just picked up my assistant, from right under my nose! Frigging slime ball!

'That's wonderful. Congratulations! I'm very happy for you. RM is a good break!'

'Well, I will be in the Relationship Management team. Not a manager position, but at least it'll put me on the path to where I want to be.'

I was taken aback, but had to be happy for her. She deserved it. 'Wish you all the best, Radhika. You do know I mean it, right?'

'I know you do. Wish you the best of luck as well, Ravi. I can't thank you enough for everything you've done,' her eyes were moistening.

'Take the rest of the day off, Radhika. Even I'm headed home. Have had a long night.'

17:12

I was waiting for the car outside the building, when I noticed Vinesh returning after a smoke.

'Hi, Ravi. Leaving early?'

'Yes. Needed to get some rest. I'm available on the cell if you need anything?'

'We have an eventful week coming up. FYI, Mr Patel has arrived in India. He will be taking over from Amitabh from today itself.'

'What?'

'Yup, Patrick dropped in an email to Jaideep, asking him to make arrangements for Patel's cabin.'

'But what happens to Amitabh?'

'Anybody's guess, Ravi!'

Amitabh was surely out of the race now. Or, was he? This could be an aggressive succession plan by Patrick and the senior brass.

Nothing was making any sense any more!

Imperial Insider: Catch 'em young! New kid at the helm of Imperial!

18:43 @ Home

Savitha opened the door and forced a smile.

'How's Srikanth?'

She hadn't been taking my calls through the day. It had been exasperating. I wished we would just fight and get it all out and move on. But with my parents at home, it had been getting quite a challenge trying to find a way to vent our emotions.

'He's better ... it wasn't a sprain.'

I walked to the children's room and hugged Srikanth as he hobbled towards me and jumped at me. I hugged him tight. Revathi was soon behind him. She, too, jumped into the fray and decided to claim her share of hugs.

The family sat on the floor, as Srikanth recounted his tale of bravery and proudly showed off his new scars.

I noticed Savitha sitting quietly as she cuddled Revathi and pampered her.

Srikanth insisted he had to go show off his 'battle scars' to his friends and Revathi followed as they left the house screaming, making a ruckus.

Savitha and I remained seated on the floor. I decided to break the ice.

'Sav, it was a tough day with Patrick yesterday!'
'I'm sure …'
'You can't believe the muck flying around at the head office!'
She closed her eyes, rested her head against the wall and rubbed her forehead.

'Got a headache?'
'Not feeling well, Ravi.'
'Want to go to the doctor?'
'Let's go over the weekend … not in the mood today.'
'Okay.'
'Ravi …'
'Yes?'
'Just don't do anything that could harm your reputation. A job you can always get again, not your reputation. Just take it slow.'
'Sure, Sav…'
I reached out and hugged her, relieved.

21:58

We had finished dinner and Dad had asked me to accompany him on a walk. I was feeling drained from the previous night's escapades, but didn't have the heart to deny him some company.

We were about to step out when Savitha called out from the bedroom.

'Ravi? Shekhar on the line!'
Dad suggested that I join him later.
'Hey, Ravi! How've you been?'
'Can't complain too much!'

'Believe Patrick blew the India office to smithereens!' Shekhar laughed.

'Yup, lock, stock and barrel!' I laughed.

'And, Mr Patel getting into the action?'

'Yup!'

'He's received a briefing from Patrick and has some game plan in place. He may actually get more reinforcements from the UK to help him with his assignment.'

'But we're in the midst of a headcount reduction.'

'Come on, Ravi, that doesn't apply to the top.'

'So, who else is he getting and whom are they going to replace?'

'Early days yet, Ravi ... will let you know for sure as I find out. Also thought you would know your colleagues are meeting Patel tomorrow.'

'Who?'

'Heard Maithili and that guy who heads the West?'

'Dheeraj?'

'Yup ... must be him.'

'And how did you find out about this?'

'As luck would have it, Patel and I are on some Global Business Excellence council. So I have access to his PA in London!'

'Any other fireworks?'

'Not for today, bro! Take care ...'

Imperial Insider: More heads to roll tomorrow.

22: 36

I decided to speak with Mayur and catch up on head office gossip.

'How've you been, Mayur?'

'Just peachy keen! Making presentations yet again, some Asia-level IT contingent is coming to Mumbai tomorrow. Need to babysit them throughout the day.'

'Sounds exciting!' I laughed.

'Tell me about it. By the way, you must be relieved?'

'Why?'

'Haven't you heard?'
'What?'
'Your old man, Amitabh, is calling it a day tomorrow!'
'Must be a rumour …'
'Nope … certain.'
'So, a clear road for Sriram?'
'Don't bet on that. Patrick may still have something up his sleeve! Catch you later, buddy!'

Damn! Sriram definitely didn't augur well for me.

March

25

Of Quests and Questions

06:32

Savitha had been up since 5 am.

'Hi Sav! What happened?'

'Feeling a bit queasy… and a stomach ache too.'

'You've been complaining of pain for some days now. Let's go to the doctor, okay?'

'Chill, Ravi… it'll be fine… these things are normal during pregnancy. Don't worry about it.'

'Sure?'

'Yes, my dear husband.'

'How're things otherwise?'

'I don't know… but I do know you've been drinking more than you should be.'

'I know, Sav. Sorry…'

'You've also been extremely distracted. Hardly paying any attention to the children either!'

'Sav, gimme some time … there's quite a bit happening.'

'You also seem to be hiding something …'

11:02 @ Office

I missed the morning review with the Bangalore team. I felt ridiculous going through the motions. No one else was. It had been ages since Amitabh had followed up on sales performance.

As I stepped into my cabin, I noticed a Mumbai number. It wasn't Amitabh or Jaideep.

'Good morning, Ravi here.'

'Good morning, Ravi. Keshav Patel.'

This was unexpected. There hadn't been any call from Amitabh on the subject. We hadn't spoken after what Vinesh had told me the previous evening. Neither had there been any formal email.

'Welcome to India. A pleasure speaking with you, sir.'

'Thanks, Ravi. Is this a good time? I wanted to speak with you for about 10 minutes. I know I haven't scheduled this with you, but …'

'That's quite all right. If you'll give me 10 minutes, I could call you back?'

'Great. Call me back on this landline number. I'll await your call.'

I stepped into my cabin and called Amitabh. 'Boss, needed to speak with you.'

'I'm busy right now. I'm with Patel. Call me back later.'

Shit! The first hint Amitabh had possibly thrown at me.

I looked around for Radhika, but couldn't find her. Her PC was switched off. I closed the door and called Dheeraj.

'Chief, what's happening there? Just got a call from Patel.'

'I'm not too clear. I came into office and found that he had been parked here for over one hour. Kept digging in and digging in. The bastard talks sweet but takes potshots at just about everything. Not the best way to start, isn't it?' Dheeraj was obviously pissed.

'Not sounding too good?'

'Good? Ravi, he was all over me. He is taking apart everything. Crazy man … absolutely crazy!'

'Cool down, Dheeraj. I'm getting into a call with him.'

'All the best, man. Trust me. You'll need it!'

Was he setting me up?

The BlackBerry vibrated again. *Shit!* Patel …

'Ravi? I was waiting for your call.'

I checked the time. Eleven minutes since we had spoken …

'I was just about to call you.'

'Sure, Ravi … Thought we could take this time to get acquainted. As you may know, I've never worked in India before and will be looking forward to your inputs as I get into the role.'

There was no mention of taking over from Amitabh or when

he would be formally assuming the new role. None of the usual ice-breakers ... He was going to be a tough nut to crack.

'I'll be glad to assist. How would you like to get started?'

'I've been seeing some of your numbers. You've had a mixed year, haven't you?'

'It's been looking up over the last two quarters.'

'But you're way behind, Ravi. You will be ending the year with a huge shortfall.'

'It has been a tough year across India. But you will notice we've really picked up momentum.'

Patel cut in again, 'I've also noticed you've registered huge losses in the Personal Loans portfolio.'

'That was a portfolio we received when the business moved into us last year. We hadn't ...'

He cut again, 'But Ravi, we are all senior professionals. It's been over one year now. We can't keep blaming others for our mess. We have to take ownership.'

'But ...'

'Please allow me to finish. As I was saying, you've had charge of this portfolio for over a year and you haven't been able to cut down losses. What have you done to reduce delinquencies?'

This felt like an inquisition, only I was already deemed guilty.

'We've been working closely with the Collections team. The situation has improved considerably. We have been faring better than the competition in the South.'

'Ravi, that is clearly not enough. It's been pulling your profitability down.' *I could hear him flip through some pages.* 'Hmm ... I see that you've been distracted this month. Must have affected your business. But I'm glad that's behind you!'

The bastard was referring to the Credit Card fraud. 'We've done better than last month, and we've still got a few more days to go.'

'Yes, of course. Please convey my congratulations to your team.'

The questioning and cross-questioning continued. He came

out with guns blazing on every front. He had done his homework. This wasn't an introductory session. This was an ambush to show who was boss!

12:18
Vinesh lit up outside the office and looked at me.
'So, you and Patel hit it off really well, I hear?'
He had ceased to surprise me. 'Like two long-lost buddies!'
Vinesh laughed. He seemed very relaxed.
'Jaideep would love to hear that!'
Jaideep? 'What's that angle?'
'Let's just say, it's rumoured he and Patel are known to be close.'
'What?! But ...'
'Come on, Ravi! You thought everyone was joking when they said *"he swings both ways"*!'
'Great! I'm happy for the blessed couple.'
'They're not serious, you know!' Vinesh giggled.

14:26
'Hey Maithili! How's Mumbai?'
'Good. You seem to have some kind of GPS on me!' she laughed.
Could make out from her tone that I had fuelled her curiosity.
'We have a strange bond connecting us, M!'
'Really? That's a line I haven't heard in a while.'
'That's a fairly quick trip back to Mumbai.'
'Had some stuff to do here.'
'Enjoy your meetings. Catch you later!' I disconnected and dialled Mayur.
'Hi Ravi ... In the middle of something ... Call you later?'
'Will only take a minute.'
'Yes, Ravi, what's the rush? Some good news you want to share with me?'
'No such luck, but do let me know if you've got something for me?'

'Actually, it's funny you should be calling me now!'
'Why's that?'
'Well, I told you this Asian contingent is here, right?'
'Yup!'
'Well, they're looking at some business guys to offer our consulting services to other banks and financial services firms in the region. We've developed a fair amount of IT expertise that may be of value to other organizations. You think that may be of interest to you?'

It would make for an interesting opportunity. My mind started to race across the millions of possibilities and then I realized Mayur was possibly making polite conversation.

'Sounds interesting. Let me know when it crystallizes?'
'Sure Ravi. Now tell me, what can I do for you?'
'How are you keeping your Asian contingent engaged in the evening?'
'Was hoping to pack them off to some strip club, but don't think that would look too good on their visit reports!' Mayur laughed.
'Don't you think it would be great if they were to meet Mr Patel for dinner?'

Mayur sniggered. 'What's your angle?'
'No angle ... just thought about it ... and called you ...'
'You owe me one, Ravi!'
'I owe you nothing!' I laughed and disconnected.

I hadn't noticed, but Radhika had walked into the room and had been overhearing my conversation with Mayur.
'What was that?'
'Just looking after our neighbours from the Far East!' I winked at her.

15:04

An apparently jovial Mayur called back. 'Hey Ravi, what's up?'
'Not too bad, Mayur. You?'

'Frigging awesome. I've had my dose of laughter therapy for the year today!'

'What happened?'

'Apparently Sriram and Patrick have had a lovers' tiff again!'

'Don't tell me they're having an affair?'

Mayur laughed again.

'What? No Ravi, they're not having an affair! Their love – hate relationship is asexual, as of now!'

'What happened?'

'I believe one of Sriram's currency option tips to Patrick turned sour. Patrick lost a big packet in the markets and is not thrilled with him right now.'

'So Amitabh is back in the race?'

'He was always in the race, Ravi. It just got better for him!'

'So, Amitabh is not putting in his papers?'

'Not just yet!'

The pendulum was swinging wildly, again!

'What else is happening at the head office tonight?'

'I'll be meeting Patel along with the contingent for dinner tonight. Apparently, he had to cancel some other pressing engagements for this dinner. I don't know what that other engagement was though.'

'So, how did you swing it?'

'Can't reveal all my secrets, Ravi. But let's just say... my charm works and I couldn't deny the only request my reclusive friend from Bangalore has asked of me!'

Mayur disconnected.

I noticed I had a wide smile across the breadth of my face.

19:14

'Hey Maithili ...'

'You've been remembering me quite a bit today. All okay?'

'I'm missing you, I guess!'

'You're such a poor liar, Ravi!'

'You're sounding disturbed. All well, M?'

'At the airport. Boarding a plane. Taking the 7:30 back to Delhi!'

'Thought you were staying back tonight ...'

'Yes, but dinner plans changed ...'

'Have a good flight, M!'

I disconnected. Radhika had walked in again and I couldn't understand the beaming smile.

'The second time today. What have you been up to?'

'Let's just say, I didn't allow Mr Patel the privilege of meeting my colleague from Delhi over dinner!'

'You're such a bastard!'

'Hey Radhika, just the rules of engagement, my dear.'

'Good night. Sometimes, I'm just glad I'm getting away from all this madness!'

'But it's there everywhere, Radhika. Everywhere!'

20: 36

I had been trying to get across to Kaushal throughout the day. Thought I would give it one more shot. I hadn't heard from the HR team at Oriental yet.

The mobile rang. Kaushal picked up and said, 'Hi, who's this?'

I was surprised he hadn't saved my number on his mobile.

'Ravi, boss.'

'Oh! Hi, Ravi. How're you doing? All well?'

'A casual call ... we hadn't connected in a while.'

'Let me guess ... the HR guys didn't connect with you ... right?'

'Yup.'

'Take it easy Ravi. I'll get them on it first thing in the morning! Gotta rush now. Speak with you later!'

20:43

Amitabh seemed to be back in the saddle. But I clearly wasn't in.

Both Akash and Kaushal had gone silent. Maithili seemed to be in. She had Amitabh by his balls and Sriram tied in. Shashank's exit was of academic interest. I had managed to steer her away from Patel, but that wouldn't last too long for sure.

Mithilesh had been taken care of, for the moment at least. Sameer was relishing it. He needed a big kill for his job and rating.

With Patel coming in, Dheeraj, Manoj Kohli and I seemed to be vying for the only available slot. I didn't have anything to throw at either of them. If Amitabh made it, Manoj was out. But that still left Dheeraj in play ... a very strong player at that.

The helplessness set in again. I felt like one more joint, but decided to hold back. The pressure was killing me!

I logged into my Facebook account. I wanted to escape to another world for a few minutes. As I scrolled through the updates, I noticed that I had been connected with Dheeraj so I clicked on his icon and started scrolling down his updates and connections. I needed to get to know the enemy better.

There had to be some chinks in his frigging IIM-A armour.

I was about to shut the browser, when I noticed his latest update. He was in Bangalore? What was he doing in Bangalore? That too at a time when Patel was in the head office, taking charge. He was up to something, for sure! It was too small a coincidence for him to be in Bangalore. I had a hunch and decided to follow up on it.

I called Ravindra from Milsons. 'Hey bugger, where are you?'

'Hey dopey, how did you remember me at this hour?'

'Tell me, does the name Dheeraj from Imperial ring a bell?'

A long pause. 'How did you find out about that?'

'Find out what?'

'Why did you call me, Ravi?'

'Coz ... hang on ... wait a minute ... is Dheeraj being poached by Vikram?'

A long muted silence on the other end. It was a confirmation.

'We should catch up for a beer some time soon, Ravi. Take care, buddy! Cheers!'

I kept holding the mobile though it had been disconnected

on the other end. I had been shortchanged. Vikram had opted for Dheeraj even though I was the one that had opened the door for him. The slime ball couldn't even consider me for an opening there.

But then, this would mean one less person to compete with. This could be good news for sure.

Now it was a three-horse race between Maithili, Manoj and myself. And there were two zones to compete for!

There was a silver lining after all.

Imperial Insider: Patel getting some of his lieutenants from UK. Fish and chips is back in vogue at Imperial!

Who was Patel bringing in now? And, more importantly, for what?

Damn, couldn't I get one night of decent sleep?

March

	1	2	3	4	5	6
7	8	9	10	11	12	13
14	15	16	17	18	19	20
21	22	23	24	25	**26**	27
28	29	30	31			

Adios Amigos!

11:17 @ Office

Dheeraj had been trying to reach me. I had seen several missed calls in the morning, and wondered why.

'Hi, Dheeraj. What's up?'

'Just wanted to give you a heads up, Ravi.'

'On?'

'I'm putting in my papers, Ravi. Had enough of this crap.'

'What happened?'

Ravindra was right. Dheeraj was joining Vikram at Milsons.

'Let's just say, it has been simmering for a while. My discussion with Patel was the final nail. I don't need to take this kind of shit any more. And not from some wet-behind-the-ears punk. Just wanted to tell you about it. I know we really haven't bonded that much, but I think we had a good time when all of you were in Mumbai this week. Have fun and wish you all the best, Ravi.'

'But where are you going?'

'Got another offer. Had been thinking about it. Decided to go for it. Nothing left here. This place is a junkyard!'

'Best of luck, Dheeraj. Do well, man!'

'Thanks, Ravi. But I did want to ask you one thing.'

'Sure …'

'Why are you hanging around, man? I'm not in the game now, so you can trust me on this. The chips are really down. If you think my leaving can help you, you'd be surprised. See if you can use it to your advantage …'

'You look after yourself, Dheeraj!'

The coast was clear! But Dheeraj's words disturbed me. The restlessness returned. I needed to press my advantage. The discussion with Patel had not gone well … he was definitely gunning for me.

12:23
Kumar called. *Were the police raising new demands on the hacking? Or was there some other twist in the tale?*

'Hi, Ravi ... got a minute?'

'Sure ... tell me ...'

'More of your colleagues jumping ship?'

I was relieved that it wasn't about the account hacking, but dreaded what he had in store for me.

'You've heard about Dheeraj?'

'Yup, the word is out.'

'Where's he off to?'

'Heard he is joining Kaushal at Oriental.'

'What?'

'Yup, met Kaushal yesterday in Bangalore.'

'Kaushal was in Bangalore yesterday?'

'Yup, that's what I heard.'

'You met him?'

'Yes, I had reached out to Kaushal to see if he had something ...'

Both Vikram and Kaushal had steamrollered me?

'So, any luck with Kaushal?'

'You know how it is Ravi ... *"will get back to you"*, *"it's year-end ..."*, *"you're too senior"* ... the usual!'

'Hang in there, Kumar!'

The upside was that Dheeraj would be leaving for sure. The downside was I possibly wasn't *'market ready'* as yet! It sucked.

I wanted to call up Kaushal and yell at him, but realized it wouldn't serve any purpose. I needed to vent my anger, but maintained my calm.

14:10
Manoj Kohli called – the heir apparent to Sriram's throne, in case the man did become CEO, which was looking quite bleak right now. Or, maybe the next zonal head for North and East. *Shit!* There were too many permutations.

'Hi, Manoj. How are you doing?'

'Good, Ravi. You've heard about Dheeraj, right?'

'Yes. Just heard …'

'But I heard even you're putting in your papers, Ravi. Is it true?'

The classic technique of throwing doubt. Speculate or better still, trigger rumours … till they become reality. The greater the frequency and amplitude, the more real they become.

I was about to say 'I wish' but then thought otherwise.

'Not that I've heard of, Manoj!'

Manoj laughed. 'You know how it is out here, Ravi … Every 10 minutes one hears of someone resigning. So many changes …'

'What else?'

'Patel is bringing in another kid to head sales strategy!'

Then what would Patel do?

'Who?'

'Don't know, but heard it could be someone from Singapore!'

'Would have worked with Patel or Patrick in the past?'

'Quite possible, Ravi. Got to go for a meeting. Let's speak later?'

'Sure, Manoj. Cheers!'

Imperial Insider: East down, West down… and now South!

Mithilesh sent an SMS: 'Will be sorry to see you go!'

Damn!

15:18

Maithili called.

'Hi, Ravi, you've been keeping this from me all this time? So SDB finally made you the offer?'

There was resentment in her voice.

'Let's see, M!'

She laughed. She knew I hadn't put in my papers and was having a field day at my expense.

'Feels good to be out of this place?'

'Absolutely!' I laughed and disconnected.

The restlessness …

16:12

SMS from Akash: *'Positive from SDB. Working on offer letter! Maybe through by tomorrow. Cheers Akash'*

The sun was shining again.

18:34

I had been doodling the whole afternoon. Akash's SMS had bolstered my plummeting confidence, but this bit about Dheeraj … his departure should have been good for me, but if it were to Oriental, my defence would be considerably weakened.

Kumar called, 'Hey, Ravi, you're not going to like this.'

'What? Let me guess?'

'Yup, Dheeraj is joining Oriental for sure, but … only Kaushal and the HR head seem to know of it. I spoke to a senior guy in HR there and even he doesn't seem to know.'

'So, he could be joining in another position?'

'Possible Ravi … possible.'

The ship was sinking again. I had to bank on Amitabh making it through. With Sriram, I would be history. I just had the Singapore Development Bank offer to bank on for now!

19:23

Karan rushed into the room and shut the door behind him.

'Sir!'

'What happened?'

'Tension in the ranks. The word is out that Dheeraj is joining Oriental and the team is getting restless. They haven't heard of any offers or anything concrete from Oriental either! Any word from Kaushal sir?'

I had been expecting this but wasn't prepared with a response.

'Yes … in touch with him. Don't worry… keep them calm. Why should they be worrying about Dheeraj joining Oriental?'

'They think he's coming in to head South and would bring in his own team. Is he?'

I had no clue and had reached a dead-end on finding out about his role at Oriental.

'Tell them to take it easy and that applies to you as well. You can't appear to be rattled. Ask them to be calm.'

'Boss ... you do know they've finalized the list, right?'

'Just focus on your numbers, Karan. You're very distracted!'

Karan realized I wasn't in the 'gossip' mode and left.

20:14

'Hey, Ravi, still at work?'

'Don't ever accuse me of working? I am guilty of coming into office, but nothing else!' I winked at him.

Vinesh laughed and seated himself. 'I love your sense of humour!'

'Thanks, Vinesh. It's an honour to hear that from you.'

'Stop pulling my leg, Ravi. What's going on with you? Heard that you've put in your papers! You didn't even care to inform me!' He laughed again.

'What to do, Vinesh? Been so busy clearing my desk, didn't get the time to reach out to my HR guru!'

Vinesh got up. He was looking restless. He walked around the table, towards the window behind my chair.

'Ravi, you'll need to work with me on the list. I've got a draft in place, but would need your inputs.'

'The only thing, Vinesh, is I don't know if I have a job or not myself!'

'That's the strange irony of the situation, Ravi... but at least see what you can do for your team?'

'Should I check with Amitabh on this?'

Vinesh shook his head vigorously. 'Amitabh knows. Jaideep has briefed him!'

This was bizarre!

'By the way Vinesh, you got the team appraisals, right?'

He smiled and didn't respond.

20:34

Amitabh had been caught up with Patel in a multitude of reviews and discussions. Had tried reaching him several times during the day, but to no avail. He finally returned my call.

'Hi, boss!'

'Hi, Ravi, you were trying to reach me?'

It was a mellowed and exhausted Amitabh on the other end.

'Yes, needed to discuss this headcount reduction plan …'

'Had asked Vinesh to connect with you and take your inputs! Will have to call you later, Ravi. Need to step into one more meeting.'

A cold response lacking any emotion. Or maybe it was helplessness.

22:32

I was savouring a glass of scotch on the rocks. The kids had thankfully, gone off to sleep and my parents had gone to watch a movie at a friends' place and decided to stay over.

Savitha was reluctantly sipping a glass of juice, ashamed that she was yearning for a drink herself. She had been looking restless when I had returned home. We hadn't spoken much and the pregnant silence was bearing heavily on both of us.

'You worried about the list?'

'Yes Sav … it's natural.'

'So, how many are you losing.'

'The final numbers are not out yet, but will be meeting Vinesh tomorrow on that one.'

'Why tomorrow? It's a Saturday.'

'Too sensitive to be done in office and too much happening there anyway. Need to do this when I'm calm.'

'You were supposed to take me to the doctor tomorrow.'

She sounded crestfallen.

'Can come back and still take you, Sav.'

Silence for a few more minutes. I sipped the scotch.

'Ravi, what's your gut feel? Something going to work out for you?'

'I don't know Sav ... working on quite a few things ... something should come out of it.'

I clicked on the Twitter icon:

Imperial Anonymous: Chopping board coming out on Black Sunday. The final casualty list to be finalized!

23:44

Shekhar called.

'Hey bro, enjoying your Friday drink?'

'Sipping yes ... enjoying? Not sure!'

'Buckle up, Ravi. Got something for you.'

I was beginning to detest his calls, the twists and turns they inevitably presented.

'Now what, buddy? It can't really get any more interesting than it already is? Or, can it?'

Shekhar laughed, 'Hate doing this to you, but you have to hear this.'

I took a deep breath and sighed, 'Shoot!'

'Both Sriram and Amitabh may be under threat!'

'What! How?'

'Well ... that Internal Audit investigation on Sriram is getting murky on all his trading transactions and that whole Maithili incident with Amitabh, which has been hushed up, is like a skeleton in the closet. Plus Amitabh isn't really the darling boy in Singapore! So, they may actually be hiring someone altogether new!'

Was this good or bad for me? The scotch was finally kicking in when I didn't need it. I wasn't thinking too clearly.

Shekhar continued, 'Patel is getting in another guy to head sales strategy from Singapore and may also be giving this guy additional responsibility of managing one of the zones!'

'I heard about the strategy bit ... but not on this doubling up as a zonal head as well. Who is this guy anyway?'

'Parthiv Shah. Has worked quite a bit in India and South Asia. Joined Imperial last year. They're shutting down his retail loans business in Singapore, so they're thinking of getting him into India!'

'But why would they want to risk it by getting in new people to head sales and at a zonal head position?'

'May not be too bad an idea, actually. A breath of fresh air I guess, but this along with getting in a new country head ... well ... that I'm not too sure about.'

'Whom are they looking at for country head as an alternative?'

'Couple of options right now. Patrick is scrounging across the globe, but he may not be in too much of a rush on this right now.'

'So you're essentially telling me the competition just got crazier for the zonal head position?'

Shekhar laughed.

'I think I just screwed your Friday night, bro!'

March

	1	2	3	4	5	6
7	8	9	10	11	12	13
14	15	16	17	18	19	20
21	22	23	24	25	26	**27**
28	29	30	31			

With or Without You ...

05:42 Tossing in Bed Again

I had been up the whole night. The SMS from Akash had raised my hopes. Just couldn't sleep.

Where was Dheeraj headed? Would Kaushal have screwed me that badly? He didn't seem to be that kind of a guy. Should have closed my offer letter. I had delayed it much too long.

10:52

I tried calling Kaushal again. SMS, email, voice mail, chat. This might have sounded desperate to him, but I needed to get in touch.

All attempts failed!

11:36

Vinesh called me across to a Barista for coffee.

'So Vinesh, what's happening at the head office?'

'What isn't? They should have a ticker on our screens with updates. Even our Twitter friend seems to be finding it tough keeping up with everything going on there these days. You've seen the latest one?'

Vinesh handed over his mobile.

Imperial Insider: Is Jaideep Mehrotra being asked to leave?

I laughed aloud and Vinesh joined in. It took us a few seconds to settle ourselves again.

'We're both sailing in ships where the captains may bail out any moment.'

'But what's the issue with Jaideep? I thought he was heading for an Asia posting?'

'No clue, Ravi. It's getting chaotic. The only thing I know is that I spoke with my boss an hour back and he still seemed to be at the helm. So let's get going with this list?'

I had fired quite a few people in my career, but hacking the team apart en masse was a first. It was a sickening feeling.

'How do you plan to go about this?'

'Well ... I've got the list with me ... let's review each person individually and then drop them into two buckets!'

'You're kidding me, right? These are people with families that we are talking about!'

'Let's just do this, Ravi!'

I looked at him and realized he, too, wasn't particularly enjoying this task.

'Where are the ratings I had sent?'

'They're here, but we'll need to make two workings!'

'Two? Why?'

'Quite simple Ravi ... if Sriram makes it, then most of his boys will move to the right of the bell curve and if it's your old man, then his boys. As simple as that!'

The HR bell curve – it's a graph depicting the normal distribution of people sorted by virtue of their ratings with a large rounded peak tapering away at each end. Employees with higher ratings would fall to the right of the curve and those with lower ratings fell to the left. Average performers would land in the centre.

The fight was to fall on the right of the bell curve, which was reserved for exceptional performers. The ones to the far right however were typically reserved for those who were very well connected and had made a significant impression on their bosses. Ratings usually determined increments, bonuses and promotions. It was even more vital for those seeking an international career, which in the current context seemed like an unviable pipe-dream!

'So, in effect the ratings I've given you can land up in the wastepaper basket!'

'If you were to put it as bluntly ... yes!'

Vinesh pulled out his laptop and opened the Excel file with the names arranged by branch, city and region. He had ensured I could see only the personnel of my region.

'But what's the number we are looking to drop?'

'Was wondering when you would come to that. Let's work on 30 per cent for now … see how it goes?'

'Thirty per cent!' I shrieked.

'Yes, Ravi … I thought you knew! Patrick had rolled out a memo after your senior management meeting in Mumbai. He's targeting a 30 to 35 per cent headcount reduction!'

'But I didn't hear of this! I need to check with Amitabh!'

'He is aware of it! He can't do much about it and neither can Sriram. It's a diktat!'

We started reviewing each name. I was familiar with most, but I couldn't place a face against several. It was easier when there wasn't a face associated with the name. It got tougher when there was.

There were conversations, interactions, jokes, experiences and even arguments. There were families attached with each. Unfortunately, I had met most families as well at the Christmas party held earlier last year. It didn't help as images of babies, wives and mothers zipped past me as I looked at each name.

'Vinesh, don't tell me all the regions are cutting down by 30 per cent? That's not possible!'

'They are at this stage. Will see how it goes later on!'

The mobile rang. It was Maithili. I stepped out and took her call.

'Hi, M!'

'Ravi, very quickly. How many have they asked you to cut?'

'You tell me first!'

She paused and reluctantly revealed, 'About 25 per cent. Now tell me how much with you?'

HR had been playing games in this as well, and knowing Maithili, she may be bluffing on the 25 per cent as well.

'M, don't bullshit me. Tell me how much?'

She paused and then replied, 'No BS on this, Ravi. It is 25 per cent! I'm not moving beyond 20 per cent. I've spoken with Shashank and Dheeraj as well. They are with me on this one, are you?'

'Yup!'

She disconnected.

I called up Amitabh.

'Boss, I am with Vinesh. Now they're talking about 30 per cent layoffs?'

'Was speaking with Dheeraj a few minutes back. Don't go beyond 20 per cent. You got that? Don't give in!'

Finally operating as a team! It had taken a massive shakeout and a firing list for us to do so. The irony amused me!

I called up Kaushal, but it went to voicemail. I needed to know. Was Oriental going to make an offer for me and the team? Or was Kaushal backing off? I could manage the list and at least save the jobs of the people I wasn't taking along! I hated the desperation of the situation.

I noticed a missed call from Savitha but decided to call her back in a while. I walked back in and starting from the first name again, I decided I would have to be ruthless about this, but smart too. I decided to highlight some of the team members I was planning to take along to Oriental, so that I could protect some of the others who would be left behind.

'Are you sure, Ravi? You're highlighting some of the better guys in your team?'

I wasn't. I could potentially be jeopardizing their careers!

'Vinesh, by when do you need to give this list to Jaideep?'

'Jaideep, Sriram and Amitabh will be reviewing this at noon tomorrow! But I need to work on it tonight.'

'Tomorrow is a Sunday!'

'Then they shall drink blood on Sunday, Ravi!'

I continued highlighting the names. Vinesh was perplexed with the shortlist that I was proposing.

'Ravi … I'm asking again! What are you doing? Is there something that I should know about?'

It was a gamble I was taking, not only with my life but with many of my top sales team members as well. I didn't respond but continued working on the shortlist.

The mobile rang. I placed it on silent mode.

13:49

It had taken us over three coffees and two hours of bickering to arrive at the first draft. I wasn't comfortable. It still seemed outlandish. I was suggesting knocking off a good portion of the top performers. Sriram and Amitabh would surely see through it, but that was the only way I could save some of the others left behind. An added bonus was that I was making way for some of Sriram's team to move in, which suited Vinesh nicely.

I just wasn't comfortable with the gamble. 'Vinesh … I need more time … why don't you email this to me? I need to take Savitha to the doctor and am already running late …'

'I can't email this, Ravi. Too confidential.'

'Cut the crap, Vinesh … I just need to leave right now.'

'I understand, but if you've got any changes you would like to make, buzz me!'

'But how can I remember all those names?'

'You and I know which ones you would like to reconsider!'

Was I giving away too much? Had he read my mind? Did I just prove his suspicion about the exodus to Oriental I had been planning?

I had felt like I was falling.

'Okay, Vinesh! Have it your way,' I rose and left without goodbyes.

14:06 In an Autorickshaw … Heading Home

'Ravi, where are you?'

'In an auto, coming back home, Dad.'

'How long will you take?' he was sounding tense.

'What happened? You're getting me worried!'

'It's Savitha. She wasn't feeling well. We brought her to the nursing home. Where have you been?'

'Be there in 20 minutes. Hang in there.'

Shit, why had I put my phone on silent? The auto screeched to a halt outside Shanti Nursing Home. I opened the door and rushed to the second floor. Dad was at the door. As I looked up at him from the staircase, he shook his head.

'Dad! What happened?'

'Not good, Ravi. It's Savitha. She lost the baby.'

Did I get what I had wished for? Savitha must have been a mess ... everything was heading downhill again!

I stood still on the staircase clinging to the railing for support. A wave of guilt consumed me. I should have been in time for the doctor's, been there with her, taken care of her ...

17:28 @ The Nursing Home

Karan called.

'Hi boss, got a minute?'

'Not a good time, Karan. Can't this wait till Monday?'

'A minute, boss?' He was insistent.

'What, Karan?'

'Hearing rumours about Oriental ...'

'Be quick. What about Oriental?'

'Heard that Kaushal sir is under stress there!'

The doctor was on his rounds and approaching Savitha's bed.

'Karan, will have to speak with you later.' I disconnected.

19:16

Savitha was still sleeping. The doctor had indicated we could take her home. I was standing at the reception waiting for the nursing home staff to present the final bills.

I clicked on the Twitter icon.

Imperial Insider: The first draft is out. Keep your fingers crossed!

By force of habit, I quickly checked the emails on the BlackBerry. There was an email from Amitabh. I read it carefully and discovered Vinesh had already sent the first draft to him as well as Sriram. He was concerned with my choice of employees on the list.

I called up Vinesh. 'I thought you would be sending the list tomorrow morning?'

'Didn't have a choice. Jaideep called and insisted I send it across right away ... I couldn't hold back, Ravi!'

'Damn!' I muttered to myself.

I tried reaching Kaushal, but it kept going into voicemail.

Damn again!

20:43 @ Home

Savitha was resting. We had spoken briefly and she had insisted that she just wanted to be left alone. The mood was sombre at home and my parents were very anxious. They finally made a call to her parents in Singapore and shared the tragedy.

The mobile rang. It was Vinesh.

'Hi Vinesh, not a good time ... anything urgent?'

'Hey, Ravi, you didn't respond to Amitabh? He's been trying to reach you.'

'Can't right now, Vinesh. Tell him I'll connect tomorrow!' I disconnected.

For a change I got the feeling I had got my priorities right, but had I screwed my team? Where the hell was Kaushal?

March

28 29 30 31

When the going gets tough ... the tough get screwed!

04:34 @ Home

Sleep was not meant to be this weekend. I felt responsible for the aborted pregnancy. I must have contributed to her stress, what with everything at work. It just wasn't worth it! I was better than this. This situation that I was going through could not define me. I needed to figure out what was important to me, and what truly mattered!

Surely, I could make a livelihood even if I lost my job. Savitha, too, could chip in. We could start something together. We were a smart couple. I had a few contacts. Scrounging a living should not be too difficult. Was I making this whole situation out to be darker than it was?

What was really disturbing me? The fact that I would be out of a job and the social stigma associated with it? Or that I would be letting down my family? Or that Maithili would possibly beat me in this race? I just couldn't bear the thought? Was it that I was being denied what I thought I deserved?

Had I crossed the line? Had I steered off course? Had I made a mistake in cornering Raghu Nair? Should I not have presented those fraudulent KYC documents?

Damn!

And why the hell did I sleep with Maithili?

09:53

Savitha was on tranquillizers. She had slept well, but woke early. She seemed to be in good spirits or maybe the shock had yet to set in. It was difficult to interpret the situation.

'Morning, Sav!'

'Don't look so worried. It doesn't suit you,' she closed her eyes.

'How're you feeling?'

'How do you think? I'm feeling pathetic. I just gifted my boss the last chance of being employed. I'm back on the road!'

'Sav, listen to yourself. Calm down. You've just gone through …'

'I know what I've gone through. I don't have time to cry over spilt milk. I need to move on and so should you!'

I was getting worried. We needed to get away from this madness.

10:23

I just could not get through to Savitha. She remained in a foul mood and finally my parents suggested I step out and get some fresh air.

I had switched off my BlackBerry the previous night and decided to switch it on and see what chaos had transpired overnight.

Missed calls from Shekhar, Vinesh, Maithili and Amitabh. I had started dreading calls from Shekhar. The mails were downloading when Maithili called.

'Hi, Maithili!'

'Hi, Ravi, good time?'

'Not really, but tell me …'

'Have you finalized your list?'

'Yes, yesterday itself!'

'How many?'

'Stuck to 20 per cent, though Vinesh wasn't too thrilled.'

'Same here! Jaideep is fretting … he's having a huge spat with Amitabh and Sriram!'

'Are they still having their meeting today?'

'Think so, heard they are now meeting around 4 at the office …'

'Okay. Will speak later, M.'

'Ravi, quick one. Has Raghu filed a police complaint against you?'

'For what?'

'I don't know ... heard it's something to do with his Internet banking hacking ...'

'But what would I have to do with that?'

'Don't know, just heard ... see ya!'

11:22 @ Home

Vinesh called.

'Mr Shastry, trust you've cooled down?'

'Yes, Vinesh.'

'Good. It is decision time. I wanted you to take the call.'

The bastard wanted blood on my hands.

'You enjoying this, Vinesh? We discussed many things. So, what do you want my decision on?'

'Who are you letting go? Devendra from Hyderabad or Karan from Bangalore? Mithilesh has to place his Bangalore ASM. He is willing to accept either location. He has been flexible, you know.'

It had been a decision that had been pending when I left Vinesh yesterday. I hadn't given it any thought and wasn't in the frame of mind to do so. I wasn't able to think clearly, but I had to respond to him.

Vinesh continued, 'You will realize some day, Ravi, that decisions are vital. This might just prove to be good for you.'

'Take Karan out!' Shit. I hated saying that.

'You sure?'

'You've already taken 14 of my RMs and are replacing them with Mithilesh's team. So why do you need my concurrence?'

'How many times do I need to tell you, Ravi? I need to set a balance with both teams. Jaideep and I need to manage Sriram and Amitabh. Even Sriram is letting go of several people.'

'Go for it, Vinesh. But in case I forgot to mention, this makes me sick!'

'I know the feeling, Ravi. Bye for now.'

I was hedging my bets. If Sriram did make it as CEO, then at least I had a chance with the proposed plan I had initiated.

If Amitabh made it through, I was going to be in a deep pile of shit. I realized I hadn't really hedged my position. I had made an emphatic declaration in support of Sriram. I wasn't sitting on the fence any more. It was a point of no return from here.

I had also sacrificed Karan. I needed Oriental to come through for him and the other RMs I had planned to take along.

Even if it didn't, Karan would easily have got something outside. Devendra was on a weaker wicket. He needed me to look out for him. I had done the right thing! I was going with the flow. I just wasn't sure where it was heading.

12:13

Amitabh called.

'Hi, boss.'

'Where have you been, Ravi? You're not responding!'

'Been caught up in a family situation, boss.'

'What happened?'

'It's okay, boss.'

'You don't sound okay and your list doesn't look okay either!'

I didn't respond.

'You there, Ravi?'

'Yes, boss.'

'Why did you give in to Vinesh? I didn't ask you to take Sriram's team in full flow and knock off our better guys! What are you doing? Didn't you feel it necessary to even discuss it with me?'

'I got stuck in a family emergency ...'

'That didn't stop you from taking some brutal calls. You've compromised my position! Now, revisit that list and send me an updated one in the next 30 minutes!'

He disconnected. I had been cornered.

I called Mayur to see if he had any update on the Sriram–Amitabh race!

'Hi, Mayur, got a minute?'

'Just heading out with the family ... but tell me ...'

'What's happening at the top?'

'The jury is still out, but it still seems to be a close race. Amitabh's business has performed better than Sriram's. But Sriram is clearly more suave and connected. It's anyone's guess right now!'

'I need your gut feel on something ...'

'Shoot!'

'Who would you put your money on?'

Mayur laughed. 'Don't have too much money, but would still bet my Rolex on Sriram!'

'Thanks Mayur, enjoy your Sunday!'

12:24

Shekhar called.

'Hey, just spoke with Savitha. Sorry man! It's tragic. How're you?'

'Not sure.'

'Take it easy ... I know it's not easy. Try and de-stress ... you guys need to stick together through this.'

'Thanks, Shekhar!'

'A quick one! I know this is not the right time, but thought you should know ...'

'Sure ... tell me.'

'Just heard from a friend in Singapore that Sriram may be heading to a posting in Singapore.'

'What?'

'They're looking at some Asia-level strategic group formation, and he is a top contender to head that one!'

'You sure?'

'One can't be sure about anything these days, Ravi. Just giving it to you as I hear it!'

'There was also talk of someone from that region being considered for the top spot!'

'Looks unlikely for now, but that's my sense at least!'

'By when are they going to finalize the structure?'

323

'Would have to be before they announce the new organization structure for sure, else it wouldn't make sense. Hang in there, bro! Catch you later!'

Hang on to what?

Amitabh would be expecting the revised list. I still hadn't heard from Kaushal.

I called him. Voicemail again. I called up Kumar.

'Have you spoken with Kaushal after his Bangalore visit?'

'Nope, why do you ask?'

'Generally …'

'Come off it, Ravi, were you looking at an option with him?'

I had given it away …

'Will call you back, Kumar!' I disconnected.

Had Kaushal left me out in the cold?

12:42

I called up Vinesh.

'We need to make some changes!'

'Kind of late for that!'

'I'll speak with Jaideep if I have to. You need my signoff. You know that!'

'Tell me. I'll incorporate the changes!'

'No, Vinesh, Amitabh has emailed the document to me. I'll send it across to you!'

'In that case, you've got 10 minutes! After that, I'm going to send whatever I've got!'

How was I going to play this? There were people's livelihoods at stake here. Each and every cell represented a family. I had interviewed several myself and brought them on board. I had placed some of the top performers on the firing line, hoping to take them to Oriental. I had also taken in some of Sriram's team to manage both ends.

Which way would the pendulum swing?

There were over 38 regional managers that I had planned to take across to Oriental; I had placed 12 in the firing line.

With the Oriental offer nowhere in sight, it didn't seem like a feasible option. Had I been foolish in even thinking of it earlier?

I was running against time and had to submit the revised list in the next few minutes. If only I could at least speak with Kaushal! I would have taken his word. Should I remove them from the firing list and not make way for Sriram's team?

I felt like tossing a coin, but that would have meant leaving it to chance and not taking the onus for my actions. An easier choice for sure, but one my conscience didn't permit. I kept scrolling up and down the listing, hoping to find some clue in the names and numbers. There wasn't any. I had to take the call now.

I reinstated the 12 RMs and replaced them with some of the non-performing ones, also ensuring that I had retained some of Sriram's team, but Karan had to be out as I had already committed that to Vinesh earlier.

I finished the Excel list and emailed it to Vinesh with a cc to Amitabh, ensuring there was no change en route.

I couldn't be a martyr. Some of my team members would lose their jobs for sure. I couldn't save them all.

14:53

Mom and Dad had taken the kids to the movies and the amusement park. The tranquillity allowed Savitha and me to calm down and spend some time with each other. I had already spent a few hours lying down beside her as she slept.

I had switched off the BlackBerry. It had been ages since we had any such quiet moments.

I had gone through a severe panic attack in the first half hour as I looked at the switched off BlackBerry. Did it reflect the state of my impending life? Would I miss out on some significant events that would require to me to get into the fight again? Would I miss an important update that could potentially influence my way out of this mess? That damned instrument had become my

325

lifeline. I kept looking at the dead screen. Was it a portent of things to come?

Is this what being unemployed meant?

Savitha noticed me tossing around in bed and grabbed my hand.

'Missing your BlackBerry?' she smiled. A beautiful, effortless smile.

'Not any more, Sav. Not any more! How're you doing?'

'Not sure. I think at some level I possibly didn't want this baby. I know it doesn't make sense, but I think my body figured that out. I'm sad, though. Not making too much sense, am I?' she snuggled closer.

I stroked her hair. 'Sav, why don't you quit your job?'

'No discussion, Ravi. They can fire me. But, I'm not quitting. What's happening with you?' she seemed uncertain.

'Sav, there's something I need to share with you. I know this is not a good time, but ...'

'Go on, Ravi ...'

'I've done some things which I'm not very proud of over the last few days ...'

'Like?'

I needed to get it out of my system. It was ripping me apart whenever I saw the kids. I knew this was not the right time for Savitha, but I couldn't keep it inside any longer. 'Forgery, hacking ...'

'I think I've got the hang of it. I don't think I want to know. It's better for both of us that way!'

'But isn't this idiotic? We lie, cheat, deceive, threaten and whatever else, and then ...'

Savitha got up and sat in front of me. 'Ravi! You're thinking too much about it. Remember, you are not what you do at work. So, just hang in there!'

She wasn't getting it! Or maybe, I wasn't getting it! I should have been comforting her. And what was I up to? Or maybe, she already had a clue about Maithili?

18:10

Dad would often say, 'When the going gets tough, the tough get going ...'

If they weren't going to find a role for me, I would need to find one for myself, even if it meant I had to create it. It had to be something that was important to the new CEO and possibly Patel as well. But the key would lie in understanding what the new CEO wanted? What would be the flavour of the month and the quarter? What excited them? What pissed them off?

I opened a spreadsheet and made two columns under the headings – Sriram and Amitabh. Then I started jotting down everything that came to my mind about these crazy bastards. It took me well over two hours to get into the ryhthm. I reviewed my years at Imperial in a flashback, the screw-ups, the strategic victories, the bureaucratic tussles, the ego hassles, the debris from personal conflicts, rumours and pride ... pretty much everything.

It was shocking to believe that after all these years I still didn't have anyone backing me!

But, did anyone? It was all a transient flow of chaos. No one could be relied upon! No one could be trusted! No one!

Self-pity engulfed me for over an hour, till I managed to extricate myself. No one cared! So I needed to care. Not the smartest breakthroughs of all times, but an obvious one nevertheless.

And then it started to flow. The thoughts, ideas, strategies, numbers. I had managed to displace the muck, games and politics that had besieged all of us. I was focusing on the business and the role I could play given a free hand, which in itself was a paradox.

It felt ridiculous, almost insane. Midway, the document looked theoretical and towards the end it looked almost fantastical. It hadn't been made to cover my ass, or lick my boss's ass or his boss's ass. It hadn't been made to impress shareholders or my colleagues. It hadn't been made to influence the HR team. It hadn't been drafted to conjure up some fancy numbers that would allow the finance guys to get erectile saturation while making Excels with unheard of profit statements.

But who was going to read this? That too, now! Plus, I would need to at least meet them in person to convince them about what I had in mind? They weren't going to go through a faceless PowerPoint presentation, get a hard one and say, 'Hey, Ravi! Come on board!'

It had taken me well over five hours to gather my thoughts and articulate it on a presentation. I was going to email it ... but to whom? Amitabh or Sriram or both? Or maybe Patrick?

23:17

Savitha and I had both skipped dinner.

I switched on the BlackBerry again. There was an overload of messages, emails and missed calls.

I noticed one from Kaushal.

Damn!

It was too late to call now. Good, maybe there had been some traction. Maybe this document I had prepared wouldn't see the light of day after all. Oriental would offer a fresh start!

A few messages from Karan. Possibly trying to find out the status of the offers from Oriental. He had been banking on it as much as I had. I had taken him out of the equation at Imperial. On Wednesday, he would realize he didn't have a job at the bank.

I had pulled down the one resource that had fought hard for me. He had stretched himself and covered up for the shortfall in the other regions as well. He had backed me throughout. This was the low point in my life. How was I to face him in the office tomorrow?

March

	1	2	3	4	5	6
7	8	9	10	11	12	13
14	15	16	17	18	19	20
21	22	23	24	25	26	27
28	**29**	30	31			

Attitude is more important than resources ...

06:14 @ Home
I sipped the tea and browsed through the section on Banking and Finance. On the bottom corner was a headline about Oriental.

'Kaushal Sinha submits resignation.'

Kaushal Sinha, the Head of Branch Banking at Oriental, resigned on Saturday following a board meeting on Friday. Oriental declined to comment. Sources within Oriental indicated Mr Sinha's lacklustre performance had come in for criticism, triggering his resignation.'

Shit! This was worse than ground zero. I had been exposed to the whole team. I had let them down. I had screwed myself. Had I been relying on this? This couldn't be happening. Not now. Not after everything I had gone through! Wonder what happened to Dheeraj?

08:12
An SMS from Maithili, 'Is Karan on the list?'

Had Vinesh leaked the list or had she got it from Sriram?

I called Vinesh.

'Hi, Ravi ...'

'Has the list been discussed in Mumbai?'

'Yup, at a session yesterday!'

'Who else has access to the list?'

'For South, only you and I apart from the three usual suspects!' Vinesh laughed.

'Are you sure?'

'Why?'

'I think there's a leak.'

'Not possible, Ravi.'

There would be mayhem in the office if it had leaked.

'I need to change the list!'

'You want to add some more?'

'You kidding me? I need to change some names.'

'You'll need to check with Amitabh.'

I disconnected. I needed to save the team I was planning to shift to Oriental, but needed to do it without raising alarm bells.

08:23

'Hi, boss …'

'Good morning, Ravi!'

'How did the meeting go yesterday?'

'I was quite surprised with some of your choices!'

'Has the list been finalized?'

'Not yet … will have to be completed today though. We're still trying to figure out how many from each region … East might take a larger hit than other regions … let's see …'

'And the zonal structure?'

Amitabh laughed. 'I was wondering when you would ask? I can't say right now, Ravi …'

He seemed to be quite warm, even talkative. Maybe there was something good brewing for me?

'Boss, if you have some views on the list … then let's change some … We haven't had the time to discuss it in detail. It kind of happened in a hurry!'

'I know, Ravi … you know how Jaideep is. He waits for everything till the last moment. I had told him we definitely needed to take the team's views, as you guys would have a much better understanding of the ground realities, but why don't you send me the changes? Let me see what I can do?'

'Sure, boss …'

'But Ravi, we will have to accommodate more of Sriram's team members with us …'

It was powerful statement from Amitabh. Were the wheels of power shifting in another direction or had some compromise formula been brokered by Jaideep?

'What did you have in mind?'

'I'm sending you some names ... have a look and get back to me.'

He disconnected.

A further twist in the tale?

08:28

I was reviewing the names sent by Amitabh. It wasn't *'some'* ... it was a frigging army! A royal sweep. They wanted to replace half my team with Sriram's! What the hell? Had he already taken the call? Or did he seriously want an opinion? Did he even care?

Savitha walked in. 'Ravi ... was speaking with my boss. I need to discuss something with you ...'

'Sav, can't this wait ...?'

No reaction, neither any words exchanged. She left quietly, but I realized she would be livid. I followed her into the kitchen.

'Sav ...?'

'I don't want to talk about it now!'

'What's your plan for the day?'

'Going to office, Ravi.' She left the kitchen.

She was in one of those zones. I wouldn't be able to get across to her. I just needed to give her some space.

I walked back to the room and realized I needed to figure out what was brewing in the other regions. I sent messages to Maithili, Dheeraj and Shashank.

09:23 En Route to Office

I had set up a bridge number for the four of us to join in on a conference call.

'Hi, guys!'

Dheeraj spoke, 'Hi, Ravi, how've you been?'

'Cooking and getting cooked!' I laughed.

'Okay! What's happening with this list? It's quite bizarre!' Maithili was sounding restless. Unlike her.

There was hesitation in all our voices. For some reason,

Amitabh had managed to ensure there wasn't much camaraderie between the four of us. We weren't sure how much could be discussed and shared with each other. I was hoping Shashank would open up as he had put in his papers.

'Shashank! Heard there's a bloodbath in the East?'

'Bloodbath? Ravi ... It's genocide. HR has just taken out a Tommy gun and randomly selected people. They're possibly firing over 35 per cent of the staff here.'

There should have been a sigh of relief amongst the three of us, but we all remained steadfastly mute. East had a lower headcount, but a higher percentage impact there would lessen the pain in other regions.

Now I had to figure out if they were being asked to take in Sriram's people.

'What's happening to the Personal Loan and Credit Card teams?'

Silence for several seconds. I hadn't expected Maithili to respond, but she did. 'Getting shoved down my throat, Ravi!'

Was she bluffing?

The call lasted barely a few minutes and then all of us started getting calls from Amitabh and the HR team. It was obvious there was significant pressure to take on Sriram's team across the board!

10:44 @ Office

My palms were sweating again. Akash had messaged that he would be calling me at 10:30. I wasn't able to focus on the list, and was distracted. Why hadn't he called yet?

He finally called about 15 minutes late. The longest 15 minutes of my life under the circumstances.

After the pleasantries, I plunged straight in, 'So ... Akash, any update on our discussions?'

'I spoke with them earlier. Apparently there's a reorganization at SDB. So Chang is moving to another assignment in the bank.'

'So?' I was just too exasperated to hide my emotions.

'So ... Ravi ... we'll have to wait till the new management settles in. You know how these things can be!'

'I know, Akash. I know!'

Shit! I was livid. I hated these sophisticated bastards who kept raising false hopes. Damn him!

11:02

'Vinesh, we need to speak.'

'Come on in, Ravi.'

'Why are you shoving Sriram's cronies down my throat?'

'I'm not doing anything, Ravi. All this is coming from up there. I just follow what my boss tells me to do. You should know, Ravi ...'

'Quit the bullshit, Vinesh! What's happening out there?'

Vinesh got up, closed the door and walked back to his seat.

'Jaideep is calling for a truce. This list and the reorganization has created havoc. Patel has no idea how to go about it and he doesn't know anyone out here. But he can be very objective ... important in situations like this. There are more Personal Loan and Credit Card guys here than in any other region. Jaideep has worked this out as a settlement between Amitabh and Sriram. But Amitabh too has had his pound of flesh!'

'What's Amitabh's game?'

'I don't know, but he was up against some shit and wanted to protect some turf or people. Even I'm not clear, but Amitabh has given his handshake on this one!'

I had been cornered. I could at most save some top performers. The poor performers would definitely need to be axed with some of them being replaced by Sriram's cronies.

I got up to leave.

'And Ravi ... one more thing ... change the list, but you can't change your position on Karan!'

'Why?'

'Let's speak later, Ravi?'

What had I done? I just had to save Karan!

12:23 Back in My Cabin

Radhika on the intercom, 'Mr Amitabh on line.'

'Yes, thanks.' Amitabh calling on the intercom? Checked the BlackBerry. It was working and I had already sent him the revised list.

'Ravi?' Amitabh sounded tense.

'Yes, sir. Good afternoon.'

'Got some bad news.'

Shit. This was death by telephone.

'Sir, am I on speaker phone?'

'No, Ravi, but I'm with Sameer from Internal Audit. They've decided to terminate Raghu Nair with immediate effect!' Amitabh paused.

'Terminate?' *The best news so far.* Misery for one, hysteria for the other.

'Yes, Ravi. He will be relieved in the next hour. The security and HR have already been briefed. Now, either you can inform him or I can ask HR. It is a sensitive matter, but I'll leave it to you.'

'This is quite a shock, sir.' *That slimy asshole deserved this earlier, sir.*

'I know, Ravi. You'll need to speak with the team there and ask them to hold the fort till a replacement is found.'

'Yes, sir. I'll speak with Raghu.'

'All right, Ravi. I'm getting into another meeting. Will have to speak with you later. Sameer and Jaideep will be sending you an email with the formal communication and reason for termination.'

He hung up.

12:52

'Raghu?'

'Yes, Ravi.'

The tone had changed. It wasn't sir or boss any longer.

'I'm sorry it had to go this way, Raghu.'

'It happens, Ravi. It happens.'

'I just got off the line with Amitabh. You would know what this call is about, Raghu?'

'Yes, Ravi. How long do I have?'

'Would suggest you leave soon. The team can assist you with your personal items.'

I was feeling sad. He did have a family to support and his name would be tarnished after this. Banking would be ruled out as an option forever.

'Sure. I'll leave the room keys.'

I cut in, 'You'll have to leave the room and its contents with the security team. The local HR team will be meeting you after this call. Your email account will also have been suspended, Raghu.'

I could hear Raghu tapping the keys on his keyboard. He was composed. Didn't he get it? Had he understood what had hit him?

'Yes, Ravi.'

I had to understand what had driven him to this.

'Raghu, why?' I had thought anger and resentment would be overflowing at this moment. But even I remained indifferent. I couldn't figure it out – was just too tired and sick of it all.

'Why? I didn't get you, Ravi.'

Was he resisting or playing me? Had he understood the impact this was going to have on his life? Or was he in a state of shock?

'Why did you do what you did, Raghu? Clear enough?'

'You didn't leave me any choice, Ravi. You and your freak MBA degrees keep coming into these senior positions. We, on the other hand, start off from the cashier levels, move up the ranks and then just wait here. There's a bloody divide, Ravi, and you know it. I'm no MBA, so I'm doomed. All my good work means nothing. All that people like you can do is mock me in large groups and keep making fun of me. Just because I'm from a small town and don't have a fancy American accent, doesn't make me inferior, Ravi. I was in banking, working my ass off when you were probably smoking pot in your undies. Seriously, Ravi ... you don't get it ... do you?'

'Raghu, what I do get is that you've lost the plot?! You're on some hopeless self-pity trip and need to get a reality check. You don't need to look far, Raghu. Look at Amitabh. He doesn't have a 'fancy' MBA degree, but see how he's risen? And Raghu, I respect him ... not because he's my boss ... but 'coz he's a good banking professional!'

'Just listen to yourself, Ravi. That's always the problem with people like you. You can never think about how it is for people like me.'

'People like you, Raghu, are a sorry ass bunch. You crossed the line. Many lines, Raghu! You can't rationalize your actions. You were bloody wrong and you know that!?'

I had begun to lose my cool. But I needed him to spill his guts out.

'Don't judge me, Ravi. You have no right. You think I was in on this alone? Well, some of your creed were involved in this too!'

'Creed! What creed? Who?'

'It can't be proved, Ravi. So why drop names? Let's just say it's people you trust ...'

'And your motive?'

'Simple. VP-level position in the head office.'

'What position?'

'This kicked off before this re-organization came out.'

'So, why did you continue with it?'

'The ball was already in play. We couldn't roll it back,' Raghu cackled.

Had he gone senile?

'So ... who was in this with you?'

'The apple of your eye, Ravi! The apple of your eye ...'

Karan?

'And, why him? Why didn't you tell me earlier?'

'He was played. Poor guy. The head office told him he'd be the new regional head in the South. But Brazil changed everything.'

'Who in the head office, Raghu?'

'Why should I tell you, Ravi?'

'I don't know, Raghu. But you've got nothing more to lose, I guess! And you are possibly the only one losing out right now.'

'A good argument. Let's say, someone close to Sriram. You've really been upsetting his boy in Bangalore. You were getting to be quite a pain.'

He could have been referring to Manoj or Mithilesh. But who else?

'So what happened with this *"apple of my eye"*?'

'Expendable. Rules changed. The game became different. We were both expendable … and so are you.'

He disconnected.

Why would they resort to framing me in a case of fraud? It was uncalled for! They could have just fired me!

15:18

Vinesh stood outside the door. He was beginning to look like the harbinger of doom. The image actually made me smile.

'So, what have you come up with now, Lord Yama?'

'You flatter me, Ravi. I am but the messenger, my dear friend.'

'Out with it!'

'It's Sriram!'

'Is he out?' I was hoping … I was praying … I would break a hundred and one coconuts at the temple. *God damn it*! I would crack my head open a hundred and one times.

'Ouch! You jumped the gun,' Vinesh laughed, walking into the room.

'You're kidding me?'

Vinesh pulled back the chair and settled down. 'Patrick just announced it. Sriram is the new CEO of Imperial India. In fact they've made him the CEO for South Asia!'

'South Asia?! What the heck does that mean?'

'I believe that includes Pakistan, Bangladesh, Sri Lanka.'

'I know what South Asia means Vinesh, but we don't have any business there.'

'I know. Sriram thought it would sound better.'

'And what about Amitabh? What happens to him? Thought he was riding a high!'

'He just put in his papers. Possibly riding too high for his own good. Was trying to get some Asia-level position as a back-up. Pissed Patrick off. Couldn't stand the sight of Amitabh getting too powerful.'

'What?! But I just spoke with him about Raghu Nair. Is it official? I thought Sriram was trying for an Asia Strategy head position?'

It still wasn't sinking in. It was confirmed. I was out of a job. I had a slight chance if it had been Amitabh. With Sriram and his cartel, I would be in exile at best… or out at worst!

'I know. He spoke with Patrick after the announcement. Patrick had hinted a position for him in Singapore, but Amitabh didn't want to loiter around,' Vinesh picked up the paperweight on my table and started fidgeting with it.

'So, Vinesh, this is it!'

'Gawd is great, Ravi. Gawd is great!' Vinesh remained smiling.

Imperial Insider: Gordon Gekko in a lungi at the helm!

17:28

Patrick had sent out an email to the India staff, announcing Sriram's appointment. Sriram would have been busy with the senior management lining up to pay obeisance to the new monarch.

I hesitated for several minutes and then finally asked Radhika to set up a call with Sriram via his secretary. At times like this the secretary routes were more effective. It wasn't just about getting through to the boss. The boss needed to be spoken with at the right time, depending on the purpose. This was going to be one of those times, when one needed a few quiet moments, without anyone else in his room or any meetings for at least 10 minutes after the call. The conversation needed to be spot on. The tone, choice of words, the balance in talk time between both parties and of course, the last line. Always of greatest relevance.

Sriram could be a sweet-talker when inclined. This was his day. He was now the CEO.

I jotted down the lines and re-drafted them. This felt ridiculous. I felt like some frigging elocution competition in school.

Radhika came in, smiling, obviously amused by my attempts at drafting lines. 'Should take another 10 minutes, Ravi. Spoke with his secretary. You will have a clear five minutes max, so make it quick!'

'Will it be announced or unannounced?'

Announced would mean Sriram would have given his consent. Unannounced would be when secretaries undertook a guerilla ambush on their bosses!

'I'm guessing unannounced. She kinda asked me to wish you luck!'

Radhika stood there looking at my dreary frame, bending over the table. I was looking a mess and feeling like one too!

'Ravi, when's the last time you got a good night's sleep?'

I looked up at her, 'Can't remember, Radhika. I look that bad?'

'You look like a woman on a bad hair day.'

'Thanks! You really made my day.'

'Ravi, I'm sorry about what happened. I just got off the phone with Savitha. You should have taken the day off. At least today!'

Savitha and I had barely exchanged words in the morning. Wasn't even sure if she had gone to work. I wasn't being fair to her …

'Thanks, Radhika. But I needed to get some things sorted out.'

'There will always be stuff here, Ravi.' She left the room on that disapproving note.

17:44

Radhika connected me to Sriram.

'Good evening, sir, and heartiest congratulations.'

'Thank you, Ravi. Thank you so much.'

'Looking forward to working with you, sir.' I was lying through my teeth, and it must have been obvious. Should have taken drama as an option in school.

Sriram remained silent.

I needed to get this going. 'Do let me know if there is anything you may need from me, sir.'

I was overdoing this 'sir' nonsense.

'Sure Ravi. All the best! Let's speak later ... okay?'

'Sure, I understand ...'

He disconnected. A thorough washout. The whole script had gone for a toss. Hadn't budgeted for that painful silence. This must surely be the end of the road.

Imperial Insider: Has Amitabh been shown the door?

18:32

'Hi, boss!' *Amitabh!*

'Hi, Ravi, how're you? That Raghu incident was quite sad!'

'Extremely. Didn't think stuff like that could happen.'

'He was planning a police complaint against you.'

'For what?'

'Hacking into his account, apparently. Can you believe that?'

'It's crazy. Heard something about you as well?'

'Yes, Ravi. I've decided to call it a day!'

'What are you planning?'

'Have a few options ... but for starters was thinking of picking up golf!'

We both laughed.

'Any update on the restructuring and the list?'

'They're working out options. Now Sriram and Patel will take the final call.'

I thought he may just open up as he had put in his papers, but that didn't appear to be the case. The conversation meandered to golf, family life and the ruthless pressures of corporate life, but he kept his cards close to his chest.

The agony and suspense would continue.

20:32 @ Home
'Sav …'
'Don't feel like talking, Ravi.'
'We need to …'
'What, Ravi?'
'Stuff is not going as I had planned. We seriously need to weigh and evaluate our options.'
'I'm working on some options myself as well …'
'Such as?'
'Not now, Ravi! Just very tired. I need to think this through.'

22:43
'Hi, Maithili!'
'Quite late?'
'It's okay. Tell me …'
'I think Manoj Kohli got one of the spots …'
'And … Dheeraj? Is he back in the race?'
'Yes.'
That would mean Dheeraj, Maithili and I were chasing the other zonal head spot.
'Interesting …'
'Gets even more interesting. Patrick is looking at that Indian guy from Singapore as well for one of the other zonal head spots …'
'You are kidding!'
'Not kidding, Ravi. We are both screwed!'
Had even Maithili's charm and luck run out?

March

	1	2	3	4	5	6
7	8	9	10	11	12	13
14	15	16	17	18	19	20
21	22	23	24	25	26	27
28	29	**30**	31			

Opportunities multiply as they are seized ...

– Sun Tzu

06:34 @ Home
'Hi Mayur …'

'Hey, Ravi, didn't think you would be sleeping!' Mayur laughed.

'All set for tomorrow?'

'It's all happening here, Ravi!'

'What are today's headlines?'

'Patel in full flow. Manoj is getting one of the zonal head slots!'

'Yup, I heard. But which one?' It didn't feel good to know that was confirmed.

'Not quite clear right now, but there are going to be some other changes at the head office as well with some of the top brass.'

'Who's kicking the bucket?'

Mayur laughed again. 'The word is that they will be merging Legal and Compliance, so one of them will be heading out for sure. And there are strong rumours of Maithili coming into the head office as well!'

'As what?'

'Not clear, but could be the other zonal head post!'

'What about Dheeraj?'

'Everyone knows he had ventured out and burnt his fingers with Kaushal.'

'Heard he was talking to Vikram for Milsons as well!'

'Yup, so did I. But I think it's still early days for Vikram to be hiring. You may have heard about Mithilesh?'

'What about him?'

'Being sent off to Singapore, on some special assignment that they cooked up.'

'But he was under some Internal Audit investigation!'

'You know how these things work. It was getting too hot for him here, so they are packing him off till it cools down!'

'How about you?'

'Let's see, working on something.'

09:08 In the Kitchen

'Have you gone bloody mad? Totally out of your mind? What the hell did you think you were doing?'

I threw the vase on the floor. It shattered with a satisfying crash, the pieces strewn across the kitchen floor. I was livid. My head was bursting. I wanted to pull my hair, wanted to pull hers as well – do some serious body injury. What had she done? The abortion had made her senile.

She started screaming, 'Don't you dare raise your voice at me! You have no right, you selfish pig! You bloody hypocrite! All that you can think of is yourself. None of us matter. It's always about you. The rest of us are servants who should be at your beck and call. You're no different from the others. Just another MCP! It's always about you, isn't it?'

She threw the glass of piping hot coffee at me. It missed me by a whisker and I traced its trajectory till it banged against the wall behind me and made quite a splash.

'Have you gone mad? Do you want to kill me, you crazy woman?'

'I don't need to, you bastard. You'll do it to yourself. You …'

'Shut up! Not another word. I can't take another word from you. Do you have any idea what I'm going through, Sav. Any bloody idea?

'There you go again. See? Exactly what I was saying!'

'Shut up, Sav. Just shut up. You can't manage your office. You can't manage this house. You can't manage the kids. You can't manage anything. You just can't take crazy decisions which impact all of us unilaterally. What were you thinking? Oh! I'm sorry. "Thinking …" Not a term you've possibly heard!'

She flung the plate at me this time. I ducked, ran at her and gripped her upper arms tightly. She tried to shake me off, but I held firm. She couldn't free herself.

'How could you take a posting in Shanghai, Sav? How? You just can't pack up and leave. It's just not done.'

'I was sick with everything, Ravi. Just sick of it. Sick of you, your job, this house, my job, my boss ... everything. I don't care any more. Just need to get away from it all ... run away ...'

'So ... you take a call to go off to Shanghai?'

'What do we do if you lose your job as well? Or if your damn bank sends you to Vietnam? Wouldn't you go? Why is it different if I take a posting? Is it because I'm a woman? Typical Indian male mentality.'

'You're talking nonsense, Savitha! Listen to yourself. You're just not making any sense.'

We kept glaring at each other. The kids were standing nervously by the kitchen door. Behind them, looking on very disapprovingly were my parents. She broke down. I tried to reach out and hug her, but she sank to the floor in a flood of tears.

12:12 @ Office

'How're you holding in there, partner?'

'Not too bad, Kumar, not too bad. Screwed, actually! But you've already heard that several times in the last few days, haven't you?'

Kumar laughed.

'Tell me, Kumar ... How does it feel to be at home?'

'Don't be cute, Ravi. You want to know how it feels to be fired and unemployed?'

'I guess so!' *I was vulnerable, but had to hear it. I needed to be prepared.*

'You know, it's the helplessness that drives you insane. You know, everyone starts looking at you funny. It's as if none of your past ever mattered. Right now, in their eyes, you are useless!'

'I'm sorry, Kumar. Didn't want to put you through that again. It can't be all that bad!'

'No worries. I had actually called about something else. I've got something that may be of interest to you.'

'What's that?'

'The letter of incorporation of that company that I had mentioned. The one that provides "counselling services". It's better than I had expected. It's not only Maithili's uncle. Even Maithili is a shareholder. A direct link. It proves beyond doubt that she is linked in this. Sriram is still clean, of course. He's kept an arm's length on this. The smart ass that he is.'

'And where did you find this document ... and now?'

'Long story, but your friend Mithilesh has pissed off a few more people. One of them slipped this in last night. He didn't want to go public with this. Had too much at stake.'

I had got what I wanted. This would incriminate Maithili beyond doubt. I still had time. The announcements hadn't been made yet. But how would Sriram take this if it came in from me?

My heart started racing again. I could nail that bitch. I could give it back to her. She had played me. Manipulated me. My turn now!

I needed to share this with the compliance guys. At least they would maintain anonymity. The bank couldn't turn a blind eye to this. It was too lethal.

13:06 @ Office

I called Maithili. Just to check on her and chat about Amitabh.

'Hi, Ravi. Did you hear?'

'What?'

'Your friend Mayur has hit big time! He's been given additional responsibility for operations in addition to IT!'

'Good for him. Should call him.'

'I just tried, Ravi ... but not getting through. Can you imagine? He has no clue about Operations.'

She didn't mention anything about her role. I heard some noise in the background and could hear departure announcements. It sounded like Delhi Airport.

'Where are you, Maithli?'

'Catch you later Ravi ... Gotta rush!'

The bloodbath had started. She was going to Mumbai! What the heck was she going to do there? Something was happening. I needed to act fast.

'Radhika!' I yelled. 'Get me onto the first flight to Mumbai. Pronto! I'm on my way to the airport. Ask the driver to get the car.'

I needed to meet the big boys in person, to look them in the eye when they fired me. It wasn't going to happen over an email. After all, the other slot for ZSM was still open.

Karan walked in. 'Boss! I'm hearing stuff. What's going on? You're axing me? After everything I've done for you. *Jesus!* Is it true?'

'I don't know what you've heard. But even I've heard quite a bit, Karan. I really need to rush now!'

Karan remained standing. He wasn't requesting a discussion. He was demanding one.

'Ravi, this is serious,' Karan lowered his voice this time.

I could have punched him, but decided it wasn't worth it.

'I'm equally serious, Karan. Get out!'

As I stepped out, Vinesh walked across. 'Going somewhere?'

'Possibly. Why, Vinesh?'

'Just checking ...'

'Your list out?'

'About to send the final draft. Jaideep and Sriram are discussing it in the evening. And then they get into a call with Patrick.'

'What about Patel? Not in the picture?'

'Of course, he is! He is down with a stomach flu. They just can't seem to get him out of the toilet since morning,' Vinesh laughed.

He obviously didn't like Patel, but didn't know why.

'Vinesh, you need to let me know this and it's very important. Who's slotted for the zonal head positions? I need to know!'

Vinesh remained silent. He looked at me, the laptop and then around the office.

'What the hell! Not that anyone can do much. Could be Maithili and Dheeraj!'

'Dheeraj? But ... but ... he had wanted to leave the company!'

'In fact, they're possibly sweetening his offer and keeping him back. Might even get a promotion to the next grade!'

That would mean Manoj would be getting Sriram's position.

'What?'

'Jaideep is with Dheeraj right now, ironing out the details.'

They preferred getting Dheeraj back rather than considering me?

Vinesh smiled. 'I know what you're thinking, Ravi. But it's much simpler. Amitabh recommended Maithili and Dheeraj. Patrick happened to mention it to Sriram. And knowing Sriram, he wants to please Patrick on every possible count. He knows you've extended the olive branch, but his ego is still hurt. You know how he can be? And, he wants his boys below Patel, to keep him in check.'

'Maithili is Sriram's boy?'

'In a figurative sense. She is probably everyone's boy!' he winked.

I felt like slapping him, implying that Maithili was a slut!

Vinesh continued, 'You don't like what you hear, Ravi?'

'Doesn't matter, Vinesh, does it?'

'It should, Ravi. Maithili has been called in for a meeting to Mumbai today, before they formalize the appointment.'

'So, it's not sealed yet? What're they going to discuss with Maithili?'

Vinesh winked. 'It's not closed till it's closed, Ravi!'

'But Vinesh, why are they calling her to the head office?'

'She's got something up her sleeve for sure ...'

'Vinesh, set up a meeting with Jaideep tonight and even Sriram if possible. Swing it, Vinesh ... somehow ...'

'Tough, Ravi. Even if I do manage it, what time would you be able to meet him? You need to reach south Bombay. You won't be able to before eight. That too if you're lucky!'

'I'm on my way to the airport even as we speak. Give me a call on the way. I'll know better about my arrival time in a short while.'

'I can't promise anything, Ravi. What should I say is the agenda?'

'Cook up something and find out what Maithili is going to be doing.'

I walked back towards Radhika's desk. 'Check which flight Maithili is taking for Mumbai and text me.'

'Okay. But Ravi, I wanted to leave early today. Need to ...'

I cut in, 'Not today Radhika! Not today. Once I'm back!'

'Are you coming back?' Radhika winked.

'Damn you,' I smiled at her.

God bless her! She had made me smile.

Imperial Insider: It's not EQ any more at Imperial ... It's SQ (Servility Quotient) that will save your ass!

14:12 En Route to Bangalore Airport

The BlackBerry buzzed. A message from Devesh (the Compliance Head), but there was no subject line.

I opened the email and was aghast as I read the brief text: *'Adios Ravi. Cheers ... and all the best!'*

Radhika called. 'Spoke with Maithili's office. She missed her flight. She's scheduled on the 3:30!'

'What time is mine?'

'Depends on what time you reach. How far away are you?'

'The driver is like Schumacher right now. If I survive, in another 25 minutes.'

'If you make it by 2:30, you might make it for the 3:00 pm!'

14:24 Still En Route

Radhika called back, 'Ravi, meeting with Sriram at 6:30.'

'How did you manage that?'

'Maithili was running late, so he had a slot free. This would be unannounced, Ravi!'

It would be near impossible reaching south Bombay by 6:30, but I had to give it a shot.

'But, how the hell am I going to reach south Bombay by 6:30?'

'Can't help you on that, Ravi. I really had to sweet talk Sriram's secretary. She's already throwing attitude now that she's the CEO's secretary. I told her you could fix up a good discount at the spa at Orange County!'

'Make sure she gets a dozen Swedish massages!' I disconnected.

I knew I needed to reach before Maithli. I was desperate, sweating profusely again. I called Vikram, the only decent chance I seemed to have. 'Sir? Good afternoon!'

'Hi, Ravi. Good to hear from you.'

Would find out bloody soon. 'Nice of you to take this call, sir.'

'How many times have I told you Ravi, please call me Vikram.'

You asked for it, you sucker! 'Thanks, Vikram. There are quite a few changes being announced …'

I recounted the recent organization announcements.

'Let me see what I can do. But can't assure you. You know how it is. I am boarding a flight to Delhi. Let's connect after I land there?'

'Thanks, Vikram.'

Bastard was going to leave my ass facing the wind again!

14:54 Boarding the Aircraft

As I walked in through the aero-bridge, I called Savitha.

'Hi Sav, something urgent. I'm rushing to Mumbai.'

'What for?'

'Boarding the aircraft. Will let you know once I reach Mumbai.'

'Have you lost your mind?'

Savitha disconnected.

Hardly surprising. The morning episode hadn't worn off yet. Was she really going off to Shanghai?

18:32 Outside Sriram's Cabin

Sriram's secretary looked at my crumpled suit and wavy hair in an unsurprisingly disapproving manner. Must have looked like a desperate water-filter salesman.

'Ravi ... you're late!'

Okay! No good evening. How are you doing? She used to call me 'Sir'. Now that she was the CEO's secretary, it was different. She held the gates to the palace!

'Came in straight from the airport. Slightly delayed!'

'Hmmm ... it's going to be tough now, Ravi! May not happen at all ...'

Wanted to tell the bitch there wasn't going to be any tomorrow if I didn't get to meet Sriram.

'But we had a meeting scheduled for half an hour?' I remained firm. I had little to lose and everything to gain from here.

'Hmmm ... he's on a call. Might take long. I'll let you know in case he's free.'

If only I could shove her *'Hmmm'* up her ass!

Sriram would have changed his mind surely. These were blocking tactics. I needed to gatecrash. Hadn't heard from Vikram either.

As I walked towards the restroom, I noticed Dheeraj's cabin. His red carpet return was troubling me.

I called up Vinesh, 'Hi, Vinesh.'

'Hi, Ravi. Guess you reached Mumbai?'

'Yup. In the head office as we speak. Tell me, what does Dheeraj have up his sleeve?'

'Was wondering why you hadn't asked me earlier.'

'I'm asking you now, Vinesh.'

'Vikram put in a word for him while leaving. The same alumnus!'

Frigging great! After all these years, where you did your MBA still counted!

'And why is Sriram being so benevolent?'

'You don't want to burn your bridges, Ravi. He did have a decent rapport with him ... unlike your boss!' Vinesh giggled.

Couldn't understand how grown men could giggle, but he could ...

'But why did he leave in the first place?'

'Dheeraj wanted the National Sales Head role, but with Patel coming in, that wasn't happening ...'

'So, why's he back now?'

'They must be working out some sweet deal. Plus with Kaushal leaving Oriental, he would have been on a sticky wicket there.'

'Great!'

'Ravi, a quick update ... Sriram and Jaideep are at loggerheads right now on the firing list. Sriram has been trying for a complete sweep for his boys, but Jaideep is resisting. They're at each others' throats now!'

'Just curious, Vinesh ... let's say, hypothetically of course, if I had access to some incriminating documents, against a senior resource. And let's just say that she's deep into this major shit ...'

'I would say you're playing with fire. You may want to check if this senior lady has an uncle in NY who heads Compliance. And you may want to further check who in hell wants to hold a can of worms on a day that the firing list is being finalized. Do you think, hypothetically of course, anyone is going to have the balls to look at that document, leave alone doing something with it?'

'But why do they want to meet her? It would be sealed right?'

'Yes. But I heard Maithili kinda insisted on the meeting with Patel and Sriram to make sure there were no slip-ups. There's some baggage with that sexual harassment case as well. She may just pull that out of the bag if cornered. The top brass don't want any scandals right now. There's too much happening.'

So, Maithili had brought out the heavy artillery on this one. Not that she needed it. Her little venture with Sriram would have sealed it.

I could send this into the open Internet and see what came out of it. Even if it didn't help me, it would shake the establishment. The top brass would come down like a pack of cards. I had their fate in my hands. It felt good. But there was no certainty that it could help my position. Could it possibly backfire?

Imperial Insider: Why is Jaideep trying to exceed his target? Someone tell him it's people and not sales numbers here!

18:58

I finally relieved myself and scrubbed my face clean. My eyes were tired and so was the rest of the body. I needed to make it through this day somehow.

As I walked back to Sriram's den, I noticed Jaideep walking out. He glanced at me. He wasn't his usual cheerful self.

'Hi, Ravi. Good to see you, Vinesh told me you were coming. Here to see Sriram?'

'Yes, Jaideep. Think he's tied up right now?'

'Yes, we are all tied up with the deadline for tomorrow. You know how it can be?'

Of course, genocide can be tiring. Trigger-happy fingers needed a massage surely!

The BlackBerry buzzed.

'Damn! One of those blasted Tweets again!'

He turned the screen in my direction and asked me to read it.

Imperial Insider: The List Coming Out in India tomorrow! Pack your bags and cartons! New bunch of jokers at the helm.

'Has the list really been finalized?'

'We're getting there. Re-organization and restructuring is creating some chaos. Let's see how it goes. We have to wrap this up by 8 pm,' he was smiling again.

'I needed a few minutes of your time, Jaideep.'

'Would love to Ravi, but not today. On your next trip, perhaps?'

19:12 Still Waiting Outside Sriram's Cabin

The calm in the waiting area had helped. Needed to arrange

and piece together the events and variables. I had one trump card. It was secure in my jacket pocket.

I got an SMS from Savitha. *'Take care. All the best.'*

It gave me some hope, even though I knew she hadn't given up on the fight. But then, neither had I.

I called up Shekhar. I didn't know where he was or what time it would be. I was desperate.

'Shekhar, how're you?'

'Ravi, I should be asking you. What's happening out there?'

'In the trenches, but not looking too good. Back against a wall. Got less than an hour, Shekhar. Any ideas?'

'Would love to help, Ravi, but there's another list hitting us tomorrow! Everyone is shitting bricks.'

'Thanks, Shekhar, but had to ask ...'

I was exasperated. Everything was caving in around me. My palms started perspiring. I was losing it again.

19:36 Still Outside Sriram's Cabin

It had been over an hour, felt like 12. I was just sitting there helplessly, twiddling my thumbs, praying for my fate to turn around.

My hands were shaking again as had been happening too often in the last couple of days, when I heard a familiar voice and turned around.

'Hi, Ravi, thought I'd see you here.'

Maithili was beaming. Dressed in a smart, well-tailored grey suit, pink blouse and white pearls around the neck, she looked stunning. Even Sriram would get a hard-on when he saw her. I was no match. I should have bloody thrown in the towel and left for the airport right there and then.

'Hi, Maithili!'

She was about to sit down when Sriram's secretary called her, 'Maithili, the boss is ready to see you now!'

The bitch! I subjected the secretary to one of my nasty looks. She deflected it smartly with a smirk.

I could hear hearty laughs and giggles emanating from the room. This was going sparklingly well for them, which didn't bode well for me. I loitered around the waiting room. The chatter continued for over 15 minutes, when I noticed Patel walking towards me.

'Hi, Ravi. Good to meet you in person!'

'Thank you. I hope you've settled in Mumbai well?'

'Getting there. The stomach has been playing with me the last couple of days. The apartment is going to take some getting used to. Would love to chat but need to step in with Sriram. Great meeting you.'

He did the ceremonial, meaningless handshake and left.

The laughs and guffaws resonated even more. I sat down again and noticed the clock. It was moving fast towards 7:30. I had less than 30 minutes. This was the end.

I felt the paper in my jacket pocket. It was still there. I just couldn't do this to her. I was such a sucker, but I wasn't going to stoop to her level. I was frigging suicidal. I smiled at myself. My choice had sealed my fate. I closed my eyes and took deep breaths.

'I didn't need this shit,' I thought to myself.

I fiddled with my BlackBerry again. I didn't feel like reading any more messages, so started scanning the photographs. Looking at family snaps always cheered me up.

As I scanned through the recent photographs, I noticed one snap of particular interest. It had been sent to me by Shashank.

I called up Vinesh, 'Vinesh, I'm forwarding you a picture. You may want to check it out.'

'Sure, but let me warn you. I have very high standards …' He giggled again.

'You may want to forward it to Jaideep. He'll understand.'

19:48 Sriram's Cabin

Maithili and Patel left Sriram's cabin. Both avoided eye contact and walked out immersed in an intense discussion.

Jaideep walked in, nodded at me as he opened Sriram's door

and shut it behind him. He emerged within a couple of minutes and hurried out, no glances exchanged.

I was finally called into the emperor's room. Sriram's disposition had changed. He was looking at his emails, pensive. He acknowledged my entry with a nod. We exchanged inconsequential pleasantries.

'So, Ravi ... tell me, what's on your mind?'

What's on my mind?! Your frigging neck in my hands and your balls under my shoes. I could have been diplomatic and beaten around the bush, or could take him head on. I had a few minutes with him.

'You would have finalized the organization structure?'

He was taken aback by the candour and didn't respond for several seconds. 'It's being worked upon as we speak, Ravi.'

It felt belittling to have a conversation to protect my job. Wasn't my contribution sufficient to secure my position? Hadn't I delivered on my several assignments at Imperial? Why did I need to beg? Or maybe, I really wasn't as good as the others and needed to be honest with myself. It had been a tough year for the rest of the team as well. But I had pulled through in the final quarter – I was going to exceed and even meet the stretched targets. They couldn't overlook that?

'You would have heard, I've done the stretched targets for the month. I've made up for the other regions.'

Numbers always spoke for themselves. Did I need to resort to deceit and blackmail for my slot in this damn bank? Did I really need to screw Maithili? How would I be different from her if I did hand over that paper to Sriram?

'Yes ... I was seeing the numbers earlier today ...'

He couldn't say 'good show' or 'great work' to a guy he was most possibly planning to fire. The hesitation in his body language and voice revealed it all. I was going down.

I was thinking of sharing the ideas I had written down a few nights earlier to turn the organization around and create new business opportunities, when it finally became clear. They didn't care!

Had I become too cynical? I could see it in his eyes. He had my blood on his hands! I instinctively drew out the paper from my pocket and held it with both my hands. In a fit of rage, I wanted to fling it at him and tell him how I would take him and his bunch of cronies down.

His mobile rang. His wife. He spoke with her briefly and promised to call her back shortly.

'I've got a good team, Sriram. They can deliver under pressure, and you can see from the numbers ... they have ... once again!'

Long pauses were getting excruciating. He finally relented. 'I know, Ravi ...'

His secretary walked in with a file and placed it on the table. This would be the cue. Had I flown into Mumbai for these few moments? Would this eye contact and brief conversation be enough to save my job? I was at a loss for words. I replaced the paper in my pocket and got up.

'Thanks for your time, Sriram. Wish you all the very best.'

'Thanks for dropping in, Ravi. All the best!'

He stood up, we shook hands. His mobile rang again. I turned and walked out.

I clicked on the Twitter icon.

Imperial Insider: The list is out!

I called Savitha. 'Hey Sav.'

'Hi Ravi, what happened? Radhika told me you were meeting Sriram.'

'It's over, Sav... I've done my best ... Let's move on ...'

'Don't worry, Ravi. I don't want to add pressure, but I turned down Shanghai!'

We were going to be two unemployed professionals on 1st April! Appropriate, given that it was Fool's Day!

'Take care, Sav ... Catch you later ...'

I walked across to the lift and pressed the down button. I didn't have a return ticket. Wasn't even sure if I would reach the airport in time for the red eye. Most of the office personnel had left. It wore a deserted look. This was the metaphorical end of the road.

I looked at my watch. It read 7:58. Two minutes from Armageddon.

'Hi, handsome! Leaving already?'

'Hi, Maithili. Cheerful as ever. Had a good day?'

She smiled. *Shit, I hated it when she smiled.*

'All right ...' she continued smiling.

We became silent. I reached into my jacket pocket, took out the paper and handed it to her.

She opened it, smiled, read it a couple of times, folded it and placed it in her handbag.

As we stepped out of the lift, Maithili broke the silence, 'Got time for a drink?'

I smiled back. 'Sure ... and in case I forget ... Congratulations for the zonal head position.'

'Oh, that! Let's see. Tomorrow is still very far, you know! By the way, did you share this paper with anyone?'

'I almost did, M!'

'Why didn't you?'

'I don't know ...'

'I don't get you, Ravi ...'

'You never did ... See you around, M!'

'Hey ... what's the hurry? It's not as if you have a job to rush to?' she winked.

I looked at Maithili and laughed. 'What do you have in mind?'

'You're not going to make it for the last flight now ... so ... champagne?'

'What are we celebrating?'

'The pleasures of uncertainty!'

Sent an SMS: *'Sav ... too late for return flight. Will fly in tomorrow.'*

Imperial Insider: Naukri.com offering discounts for premium packages to Imperial employees J.

March

	1	2	3	4	5	6
7	8	9	10	11	12	13
14	15	16	17	18	19	20
21	22	23	24	25	26	27
28	29	30	**31**			

The future's uncertain and the end is always near ...

– Jim Morrison

10:35 En Route from Bangalore Airport to the Office
I had originally planned to go home from the airport, but as I sat in the cab, I gave the driver the office address.

'Hi, Sav …'

'Hi, Ravi … how're you holding up?'

'Not sure … how're the kids?'

'All right.'

'Am heading straight into office.'

'Okay, Ravi …'

'Where are you?'

'Reached office some time back … packing my stuff. They have said I can take an extra month or so for compassionate grounds, what with the baby and all that, but I don't want to wait…'

Silence for several seconds.

'Got any spare cartons?' I laughed… then wasn't sure if this was the time for humour.

'Yup! Will send them over to your office, you slime ball!' She laughed and disconnected.

11:12 @ Office
I could hear the Gayatri mantra playing in the background. There were an unusual number of foreheads smeared with ash and tikkas. Horizontal stripes, vertical bands, large spots, red on white, orange on red on white, red specks on the neck. They were all over. Freshly broken coconut shells could be seen strewn at the entrance to the branch and the office.

Monitors and laptops had not been switched on. The staff just sat there looking blankly at the screens. Some of the Relationship Managers were assembled in the conference rooms, trying to determine their next step.

Radhika was clearing her desk as I walked in.

'Good morning.'

'Morning, Radhika! Do you have any spare cartons for me?'

She smiled.

I walked into the room, I didn't switch on the laptop, but unfortunately, couldn't switch off the BlackBerry. Still addicted to it – could be my last day with it for quite some time.

11:43

'Hi, Kumar'

'Hi, Ravi. What happened? Didn't hear from you yesterday.'

'Yup. Took the morning flight from Mumbai.'

'What happened? Did that paper help?'

'Yes. It did …'

'And?'

'I found myself!'

'Don't follow, Ravi?'

'I'll talk to you later,' I hung up.

The BlackBerry beeped. It was from Maithili. *'Hang in there kiddo!'*

12:00

Radhika walked in. 'Sir, the new sales organization chart is out. You may like to see the email.'

I looked at her. She didn't look positive. Must have been as expected.

I opened the email. It was as I had heard.

Subject : New Organization Announcement

We are pleased to share with you the senior sales organization structure. To optimize business impact and increase profitability, the regions are getting merged into zones.

Effective April 1, the new sales organization would be as follows:

National Head, Assets: Manoj Kohli
National Sales Head: Keshav Patel
Zonal Head, North & East: Maithili Rao
Zonal Head, West & South: Dheeraj Kapoor
The new zonal headquarter locations would be Delhi and Mumbai.

We wish them all the very best in their new assignments.

Regards,

Sriram Iyengar
Jaideep Mehrotra

I read the email four times over, unable to close it. I kept staring at it.

So, how would it work out? Would I also receive an email? Or would they at least be polite enough to call? I was a regional head after all. But, did that matter?

I finally pulled myself up from the chair as Mithilesh walked in.

'Hi, Ravi? We'll miss you here.'

I decided it wasn't worth responding to.

'So, what will you do now?' He settled himself on the sofa.

'Gardening?' I replied. 'Congratulations on Singapore!'

We both laughed. Don't recollect laughing with him about anything. Ever. Now that this shit was over, he looked like any other human. I didn't believe I was saying this to myself – Mithilesh and human in the same sentence ...

'Let's see, Ravi ...'

We shook hands. He was a crook, but he had played it smarter. It didn't matter in the end. We were all crooks.

Radhika walked in with cartons.

'Three enough?'

Imperial Insider: The king has his harem in place!

11:20

A spate of announcements continued.

I had lost over 17 per cent of my team. East was the worst hit with an over 40 per cent headcount reduction. Maithili had managed to rein in her count to below 10 per cent, and I heard that West was similar to mine. The exact numbers in the head office were still unclear.

Karan was out, replaced by a chap from the Credit Cards sales team. Devendra was in. Chennai was handed over to some novice who had never handled branch banking, apparently related to Mithilesh.

I had lost several RMs from my original Bangalore team, conveniently replaced by able-bodied members of the Credit Cards team. I lost count of the casualty list in Hyderabad and Chennai, but it would have exceeded 40 for sure.

The regional operations head, Sridhar Reddy, who had helped me with the KYC forms was out.

Sameer Prabhu, the Internal Audit head, had been relieved with immediate effect, no rationale provided. His replacement was not announced. It was being rumoured that his investigation on Mithilesh had ruffled senior feathers. Poor chap!

It had been confirmed that Jaideep was moving on to become the Asia HR head. He had achieved an over 26 per cent headcount reduction.

I heard a knock and looked up ... Vinesh Menon at the door again.

'Started packing, Ravi?'

'Am sure you're busy packing for Mumbai yourself?'

He walked in and quietly seated himself. He looked outside the window and heaved a sigh of relief.

'So ... what plans, Ravi?'

'Was thinking of checking out the cashew business!' I winked at him.

Vinesh laughed. 'There is something you need to know, Ravi. Amitabh backed you till the very end. In fact, you would have got the West, if Dheeraj hadn't pulled some serious weight from New York. He had some really big guys batting for him from there!'

'It doesn't matter any more, Vinesh.'

'Aren't you curious?'

I smiled.

'Go on …'

'You would have been reporting directly to Maithili … only Patel came into the picture and then it got very messy for Sriram, having to decide between you and Maithili.'

'The choice was obvious, I'm sure …'

'Not really, Ravi. Her numbers were really weak and even Patel was kind of backing you!'

'That's a surprise!'

'You know, Ravi, I'm just glad this is over.'

'And I thought you enjoyed the ride?'

'Need a new one, Ravi.'

'So, when are you leaving for Mumbai, Vinesh?'

Vinesh just continued looking outside. Then in a low, flat voice, 'Not going to Mumbai, Ravi. The chap in the North got the role.'

'He must have been sleeping with that slut, Jaideep!'

Vinesh broke into loud laughter and clapped his hands ferociously. Tears ran down his eyes.

'I'm sorry to hear that!' I continued.

'Ravi … all these days that we've been talking, have you realized you didn't ask me even once about how I was doing?'

He was right. I had always assumed he would be fine. Had this affected him? I hadn't seen any email on the HR organization chart.

'What's happening with you?'

'I'm off, Ravi.'

'Where to?'

Damn! Had he been asked to leave as well?

He got up from the sofa and started walking out. As he neared the door, he turned around, 'Always wanted to check out the cashew business!'

He smiled again.

Imperial Insider: If you think … you're out!

11:46

An SMS from Maithili: '*Mayur quit!*'

I walked across to Vinesh's room.

'What is this about Mayur?'

Vinesh smiled. 'You're not going to believe this!'

'Out with it …!'

'Mayur is the Twitter guy!'

'Not possible!' I was shocked.

'How did this come out?'

'You read the last tweet?'

'Yup.'

'Well, I think he got cocky … he was writing that when he was in a meeting with Sriram …'

'He got caught in the act?'

'Something like that … think he had left his mobile on the table and Sriram glanced at it.'

12:35

Karan walked into the room and threw the sales report on the table.

We had achieved our target for the month.

'Why, boss? After everything I did?'

I didn't respond. We just looked at each other. He left.

The BlackBerry was buzzing again. I switched it off. I started clearing the table and packing the contents into the cartons.

Radhika walked in. 'Think you should check your email. I've taken a print out.'

She was smiling.

Subject: New Organization Announcement

We are pleased to announce the appointment of Mr Ravi Shastry as the Head, Strategy and New Market Development. This is a new position. He will report into me directly. Ravi will work with me in formulating strategy and in setting up operations in Sri Lanka and Bangladesh.

He will be assisted by Mithilesh Sinha, who moves in as Vice-President, New Projects.

We wish Ravi and Mithilesh all the best in their new assignments.

Regards,

Sriram Iyengar
Jaideep Mehrotra

I read it three times. Radhika remained standing, but was beaming from ear to ear. She had tears in her eyes, but obviously happy ones. I looked up at her and asked, 'But why didn't they call me?'

'Sriram's secretory was trying to reach you, but your mobile was switched off. She sent me an SMS moments back. And then, this came ...'

I went blank again. Then called Savitha.

'Hi, Sav.'

'Hi, Ravi ... what's up?'

'Got something.'

'What? ... Wow! ... What ... then, why are you sounding so low?'

'No ... not low ... it's just happened ...'

'What has?'

'Just got an email. Given me something in Mumbai ...'

'Hey ... wow ... thats awesome ... what?'

''Head of Strategy ...'

'Sounds good! ... but ... why aren't you excited?'

I paused and reflected on the situation. She was right. I had an option. I wasn't going to be on the road. So ... why was I feeling low?

'Can't explain it ... but are you okay about moving to Mumbai?'

She laughed. 'Do we have a choice?'

It was always about making choices. Did this role excite me? Is this what I wanted to do? Or ... was it time to move on? It wasn't making any sense. How did I get this role? And then, I had let down my team. I couldn't save their jobs. How could I take some plum posting which would appear to be a step up as they scavenged for jobs?

They hadn't even discussed it with me. Was this a parking spot? Or did the role have significance in the new dispensation? Had I made an impact on Sriram in my brief meeting?

'Hey Sav ... we need to think through this carefully ... will speak with you later?'

'Ravi ... I don't know what's running through your mind but we are together in this ... you got that?'

'Thanks, Sav ... Catch you later.'

13:23

Congratulatory messages had been flowing in. SMS, email, personnel walking in and shaking hands. Some reflected delight, some remorse, but most were indifferent.

Sriram had called me. A brief call. He congratulated me and wished me all the best for the new assignment. He spoke of the various challenges and how he and Patrick had high hopes from me, but were confident that I could deliver. It didn't sound genuine. He seemed to be going through the motions.

Amitabh called, 'Congratulations, Ravi ...'

I had gone numb. Anger, despair, hysteria, relief – all together. I hated his guts, but admired his tenacity. He had been a fighter. I respected him for it. But just couldn't understand him.

We remained silent, our thoughts doing the talking.

'Ravi …'
'Hmmm …'
'You're better than this!'

13:44

I walked to Vinesh's room.

'Did you know about this?'

'Kinda …'

'And you didn't even mention it to me?'

'It was very dynamic!'

'But I don't understand. Where did this position come from? It hadn't been mentioned before?'

'Coz … it didn't exist!'

'What?'

'It came up late last night!'

'What triggered it?'

'Maybe you have a godfather after all?'

'And I thought Mithilesh was heading to Singapore!'

'He will … not right away … they needed to park him somewhere! And, keep a leash on you!'

'So … mine is also a parking slot … right?'

'Quite obvious … but no harm in being an optimist! Think of it this way … you now report directly to the country head! It's a step up!'

14:35

'Hi, Mayur …'

'Hey, Ravi … good to hear from you. Though I'm sure you'll want to kick my butt!'

I did! 'Heard you're leaving?'

'Yup … they can't stand my sense of humour!' Mayur laughed!

'What plans?'

'Hey Ravi … forget about that. Congratulations on your new assignment!'

'You don't mean it ... do you?'

He seemed unusually calm. It troubled me.

'Hey ... you have a job! Chill, man ... don't take life so seriously!'

'Any more stock tips, Mayur?'

Mayur laughed again. 'I'll tweet it, Ravi! Catch you later ... and stay in touch!'

'You too, Mayur ... hang in there!'

16:29

I had spent over an hour taking calls from RMs, some of the better ones who to their utter horror had found their names on the firing list. It was senseless and I had little reason to comfort them with. It was my lowest moment. I had betrayed them all!

At least that's how I felt!

I looked at Revathi's and Srikanth's photograph on my desk.

17:24

Maithili called.

'Hi, Ravi ... Congratulations!'

'Thanks, M! Same to you.'

'Come off it, Ravi. This is a sham. Both of us know. I was managing the North anyway. There's nothing left in the East!'

'It's important to have something, right?'

Maithili laughed. 'Illusion versus reality. One should never lose sight!'

I smiled.

'I hate you, M!'

17:43

I started typing ...

Dear Sriram,

At the outset, I would like to thank you for the confidence that you and Patrick have reposed in me. It is a challenging assignment that you have offered me.

I, however, regret to inform you that I will not be taking up the new assignment and herewith tender my resignation with immediate effect.

Regards,

Ravi Shastry
Regional Manager, South India

I read the email three times over and was about to press send, when Vinesh walked in.

'Ravi, I forgot to ask. What was the photograph you had sent me?'

I smiled. 'Why do you ask?'

'Curious,' Vinesh smiled back.

'A snap of Maithili, Dheeraj, Shashank and me outside a bar in Mumbai.'

'Why did you ask me forward it to Jaideep?'

'Have you heard of the Blue Station, Vinesh?'

'Don't be rude, Ravi. Of course, I have. But, why did you ask me to send it to Jaideep? I'm still not clear.'

I glanced the email I had just typed, and ...

'Now, Vinesh, hypothetically speaking of course ... it is possible that I ... we may have seen the current CEO and HR head of an MNC bank in there ...' I looked straight into his eyes.

Vinesh's expression had changed to disgust and then moved to mischievous delight. 'Hypothetically speaking right, Ravi?'

'Of course, Vinesh.'

'Did you have any more pictures?'

I didn't. 'Maybe ...'

'All the best, Ravi. Keep in touch!'

'You too, Vinesh. Do send me some cashews!'

Vinesh giggled, 'Did I mention, Ravi? I didn't forward that

snap to Jaideep after all. My damn MMS wasn't working. I hope it wasn't important?'

'It doesn't matter, Vinesh. I've crossed that bridge.'

'Ravi, before I leave, just thought you should know something …'

'What?'

'Maithili called in a favour for you!'

'What?'

'Yup … I don't know what you did … but she rolled out all the dice for you, Ravi … I just don't get the two of you!'

I smiled and looked at the email.

My finger was still on the send key.

Damn!